LANKYBOX

EPIC ADVENTURE!

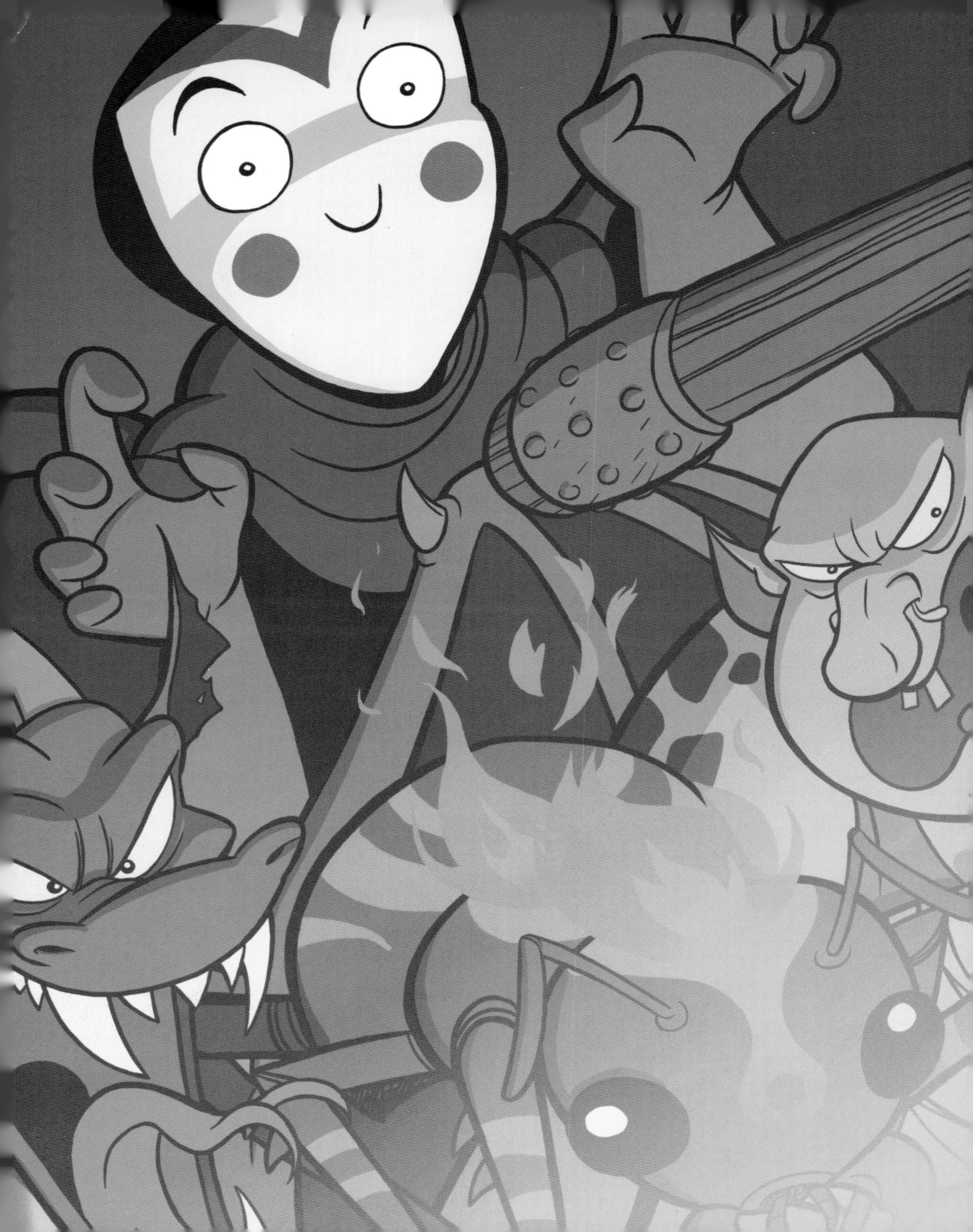

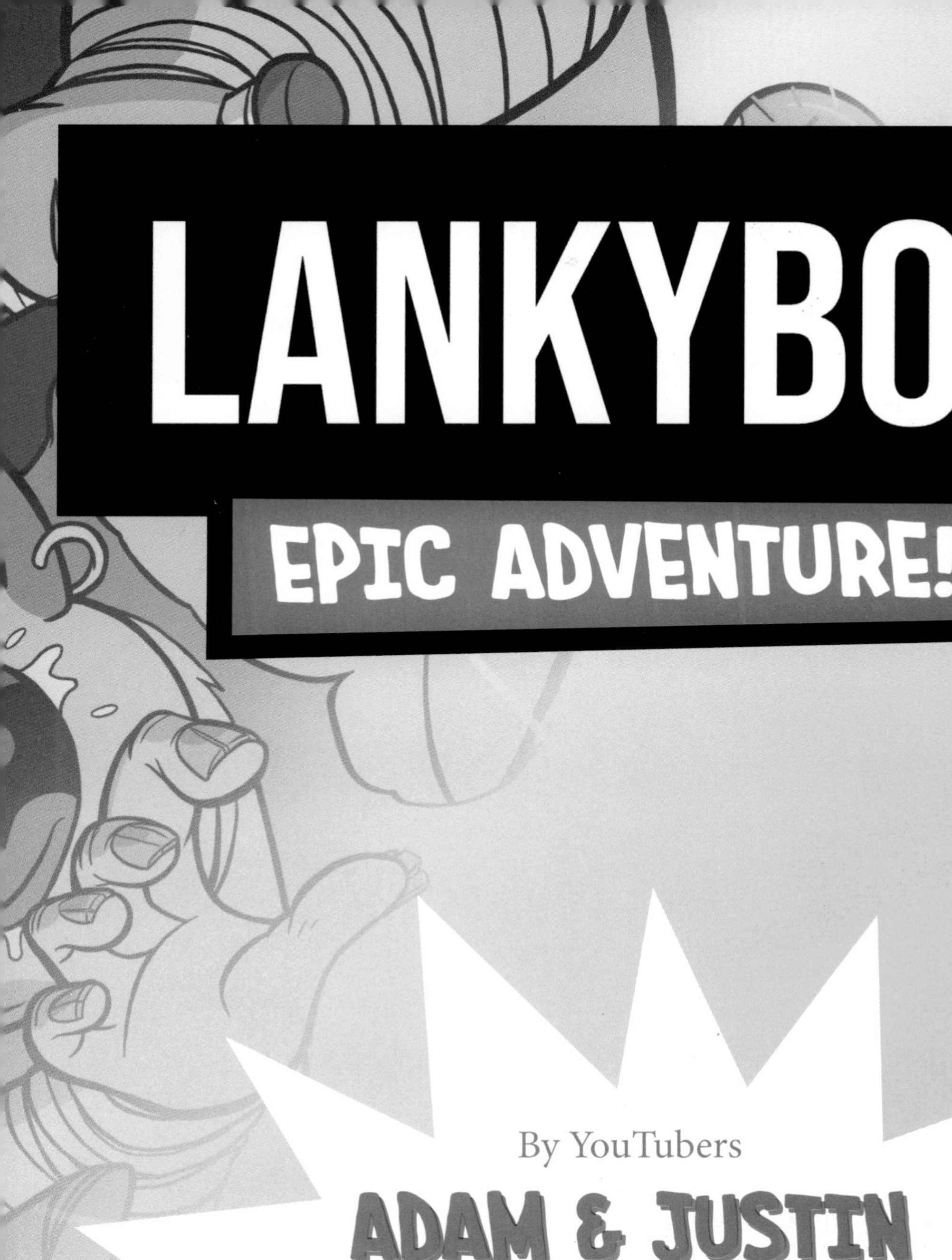

LANKYBOX

EPIC ADVENTURE!

By YouTubers

ADAM & JUSTIN OF LANKYBOX

Illustrated by Alex Lopez

HARPER alley

An Imprint of HarperCollins*Publishers*

HarperAlley is an imprint of
HarperCollins Publishers.

LankyBox: Epic Adventure!
Copyright © 2023 by LankyBox LLC
All rights reserved. Printed in Canada.
No part of this book may be used or reproduced in any manner
whatsoever without written permission except in the case of
brief quotations embodied in critical articles and reviews.
For information address HarperCollins Children's Books, a division
of HarperCollins Publishers, 195 Broadway, New York, NY 10007.
www.harperalley.com

Library of Congress Control Number: 2023930373
ISBN 978-0-06-322995-2 (hardcover) — ISBN 978-0-06-334458-7 (special edition)

Typography by Joe Merkel
23 24 25 26 27 PC/TC 10 9 8 7 6 5 4 3 2 1
First Edition

ANKYBOX

EPIC ADVENTURE!

LANKYBOX CHARACTERS

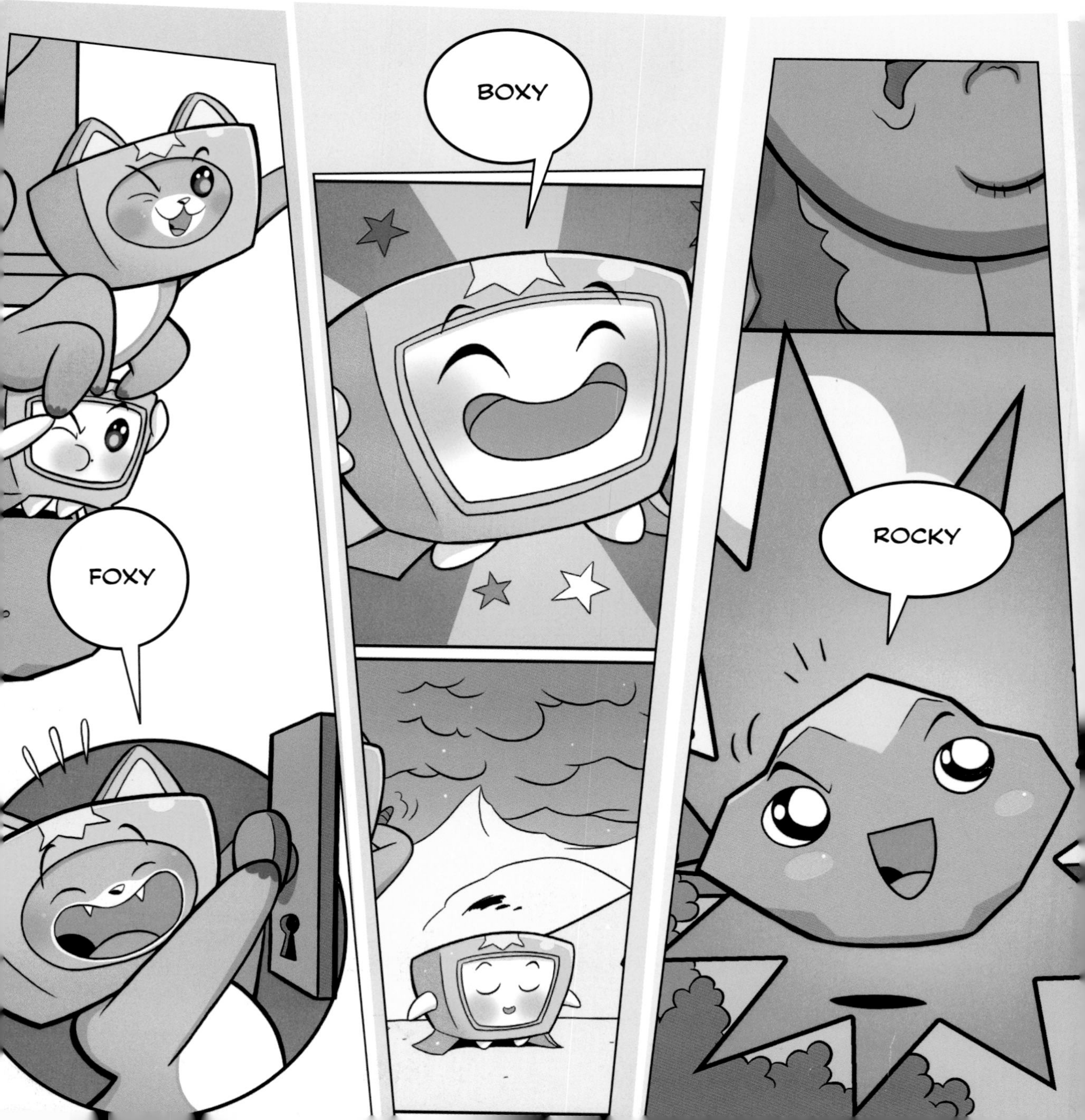
FOXY
BOXY
ROCKY

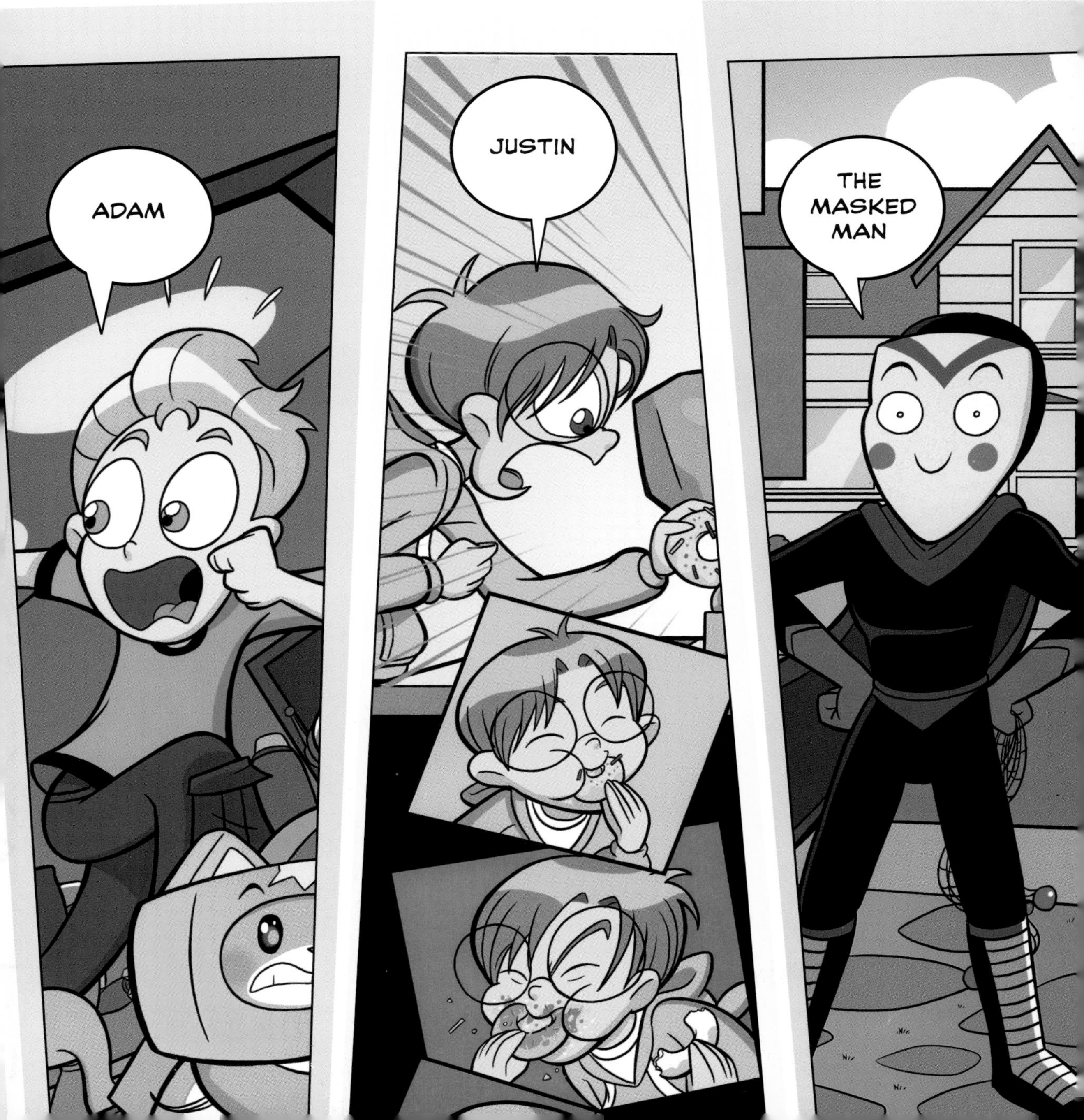
ADAM
JUSTIN
THE
MASKED
MAN

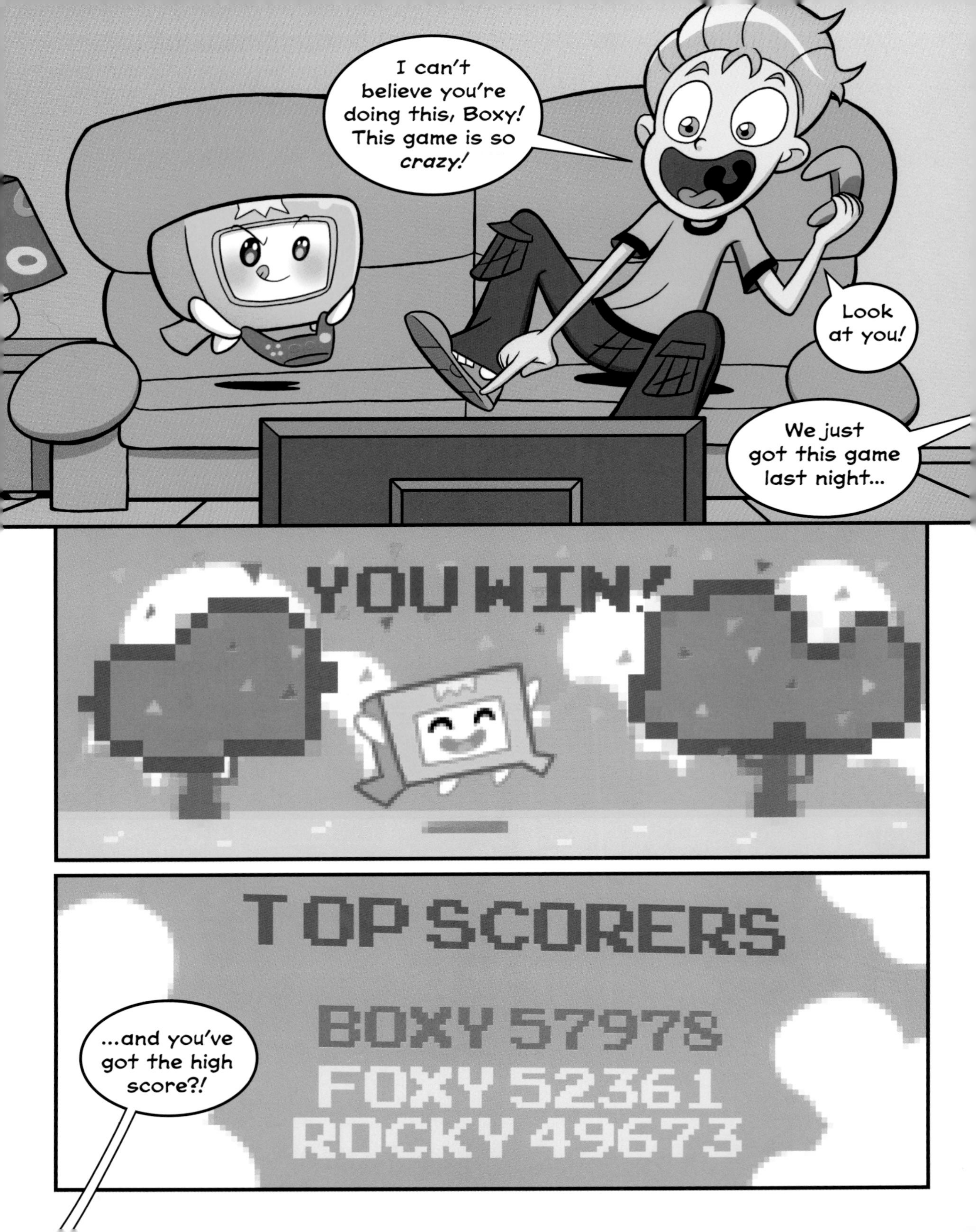
I can't believe you're doing this, Boxy! This game is so *crazy!*
Look at you!
We just got this game last night...
YOU WIN!
TOP SCORERS
BOXY 57978
FOXY 52361
ROCKY 49673
...and you've got the high score?!

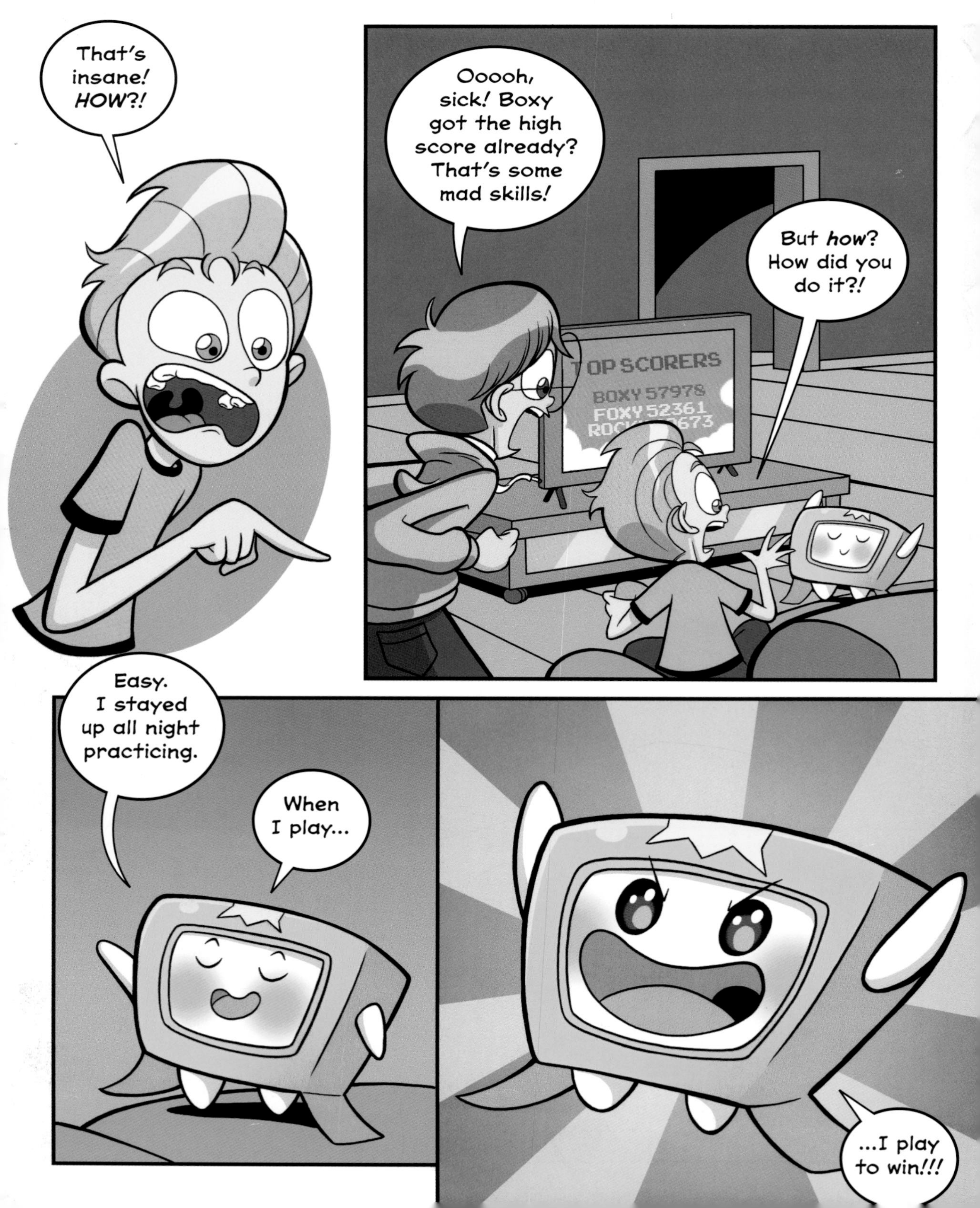
That's insane! HOW?!
Ooooh, sick! Boxy got the high score already? That's some mad skills!
TOP SCORERS
BOXY 57978
FOXY 52361
But how? How did you do it?!
Easy. I stayed up all night practicing.
When I play...
...I play to win!!!

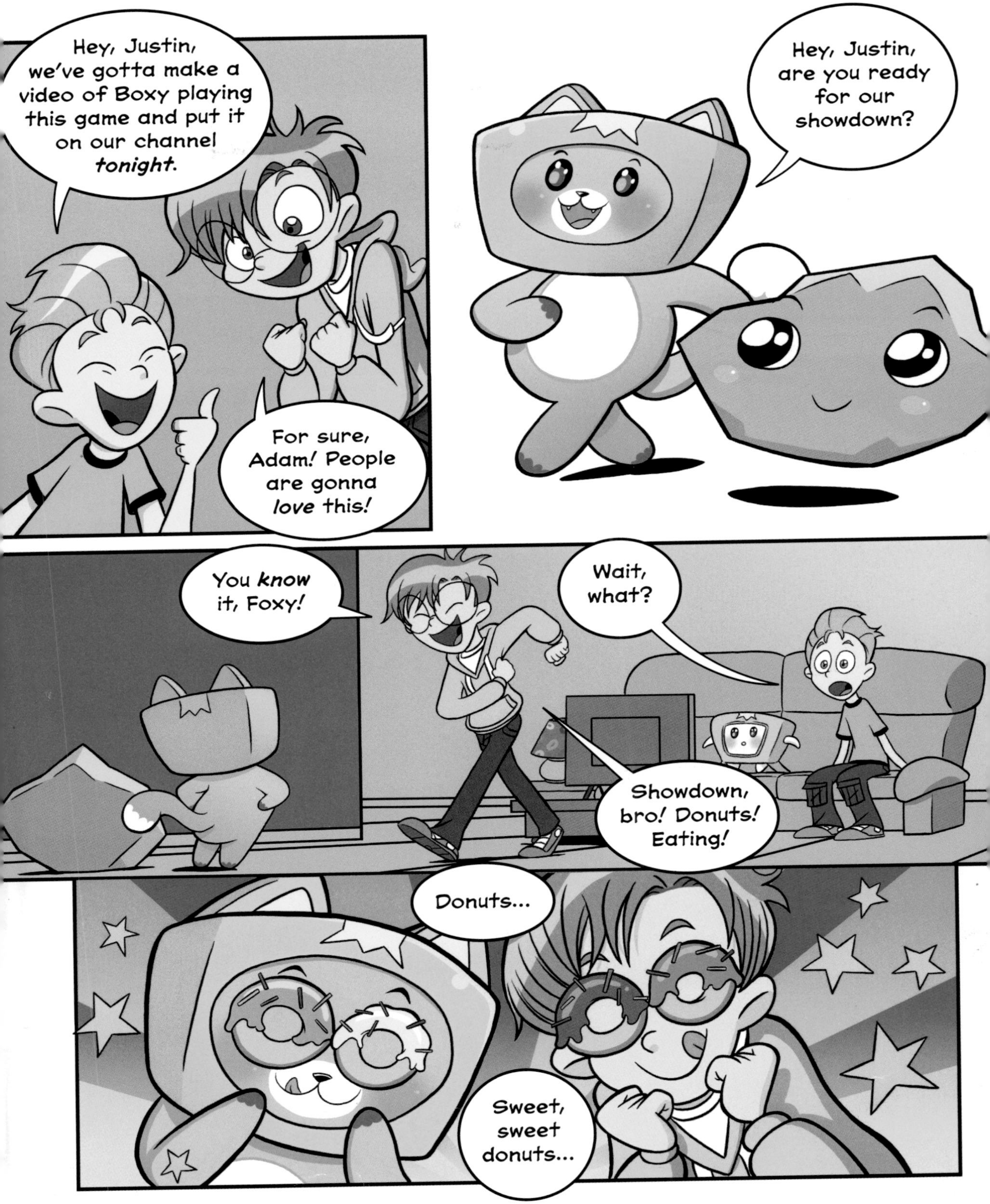

Hey, Justin, we've gotta make a video of Boxy playing this game and put it on our channel *tonight*.
For sure, Adam! People are gonna *love* this!
Hey, Justin, are you ready for our showdown?
You *know* it, Foxy!
Wait, what?
Showdown, bro! Donuts! Eating!
Donuts...
Sweet, sweet donuts...

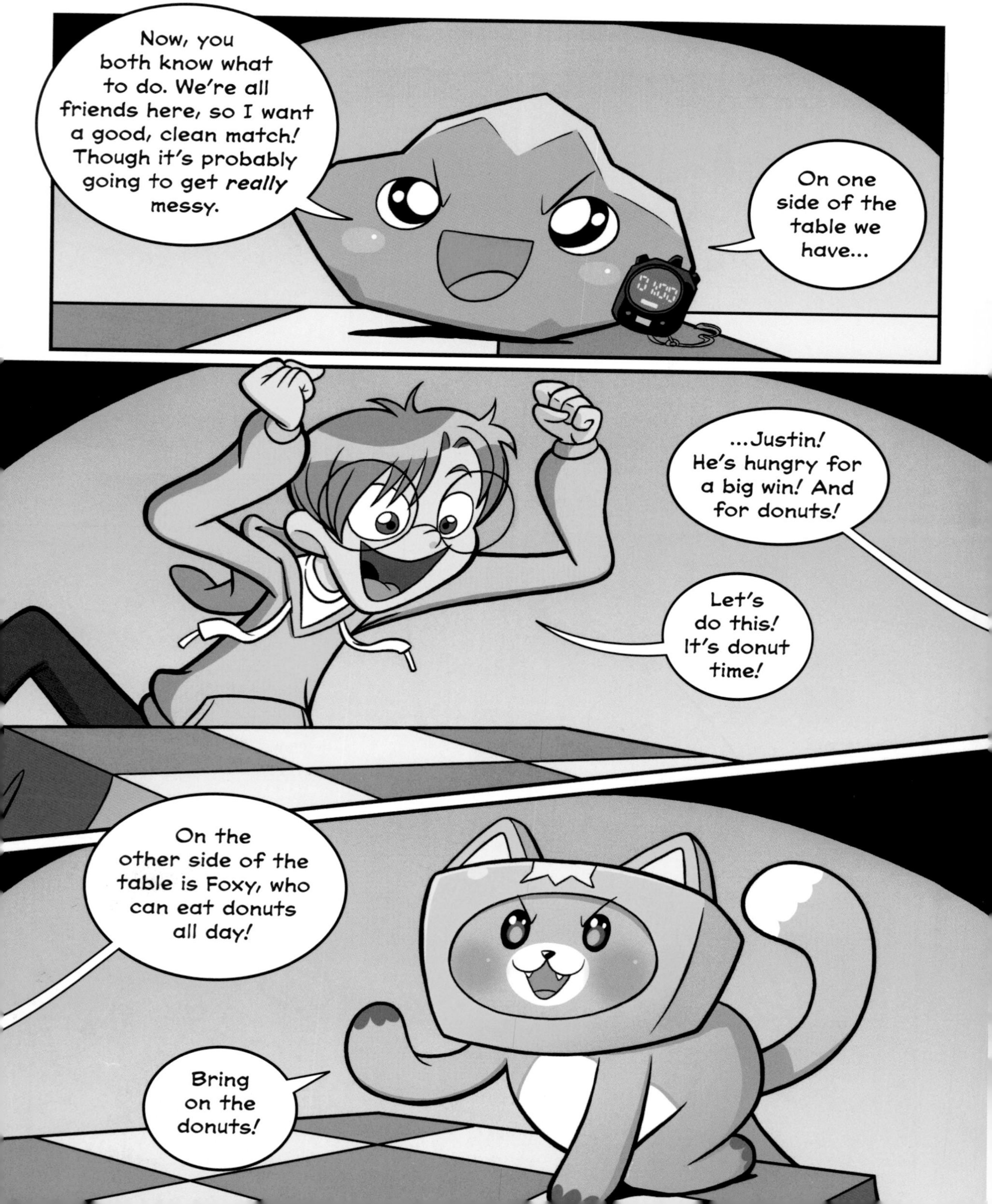
Now, you both know what to do. We're all friends here, so I want a good, clean match! Though it's probably going to get *really* messy.
On one side of the table we have...
...Justin! He's hungry for a big win! And for donuts!
Let's do this! It's donut time!
On the other side of the table is Foxy, who can eat donuts all day!
Bring on the donuts!

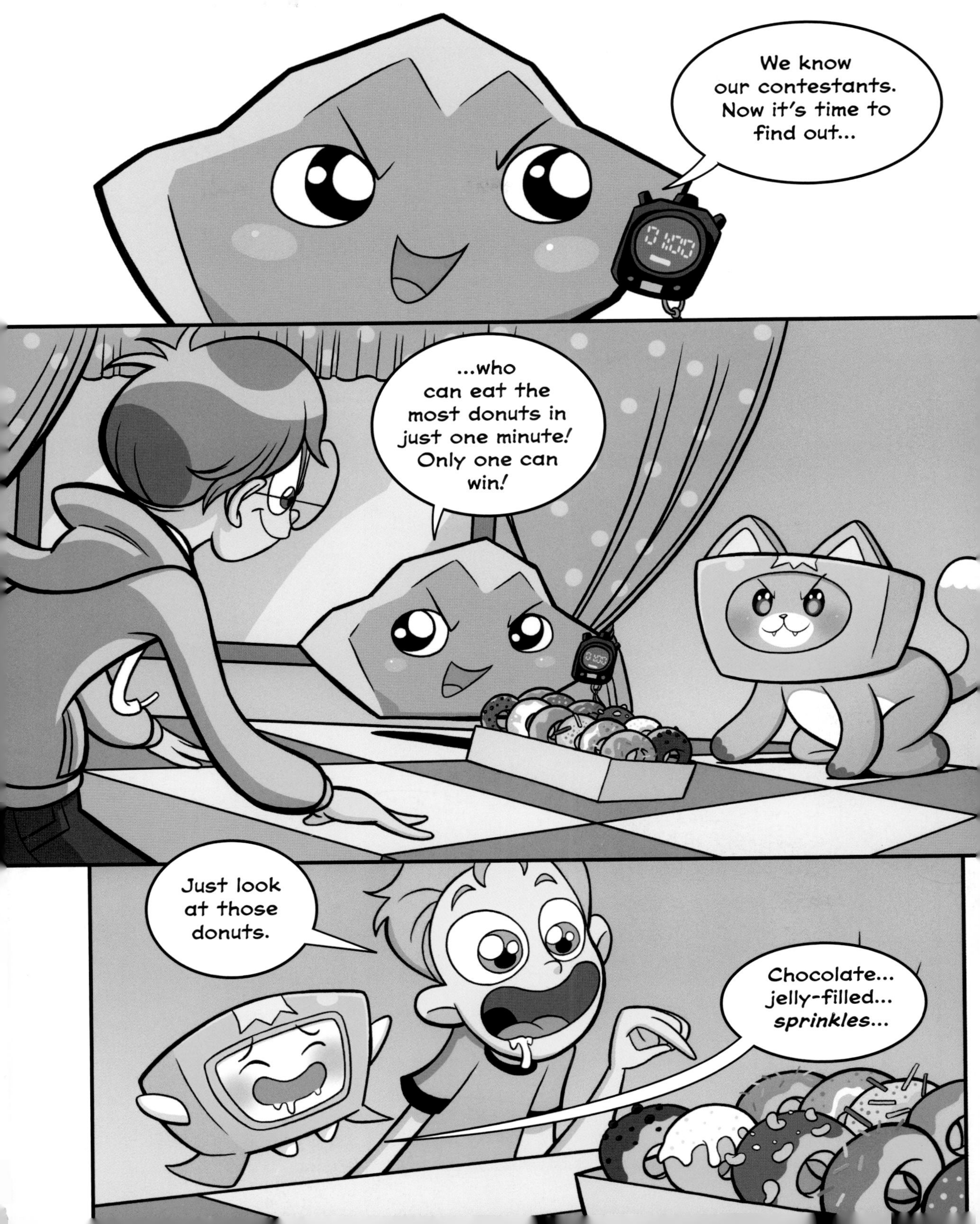
We know our contestants. Now it's time to find out...
...who can eat the most donuts in just one minute! Only one can win!
Just look at those donuts.
Chocolate... jelly-filled... *sprinkles*...

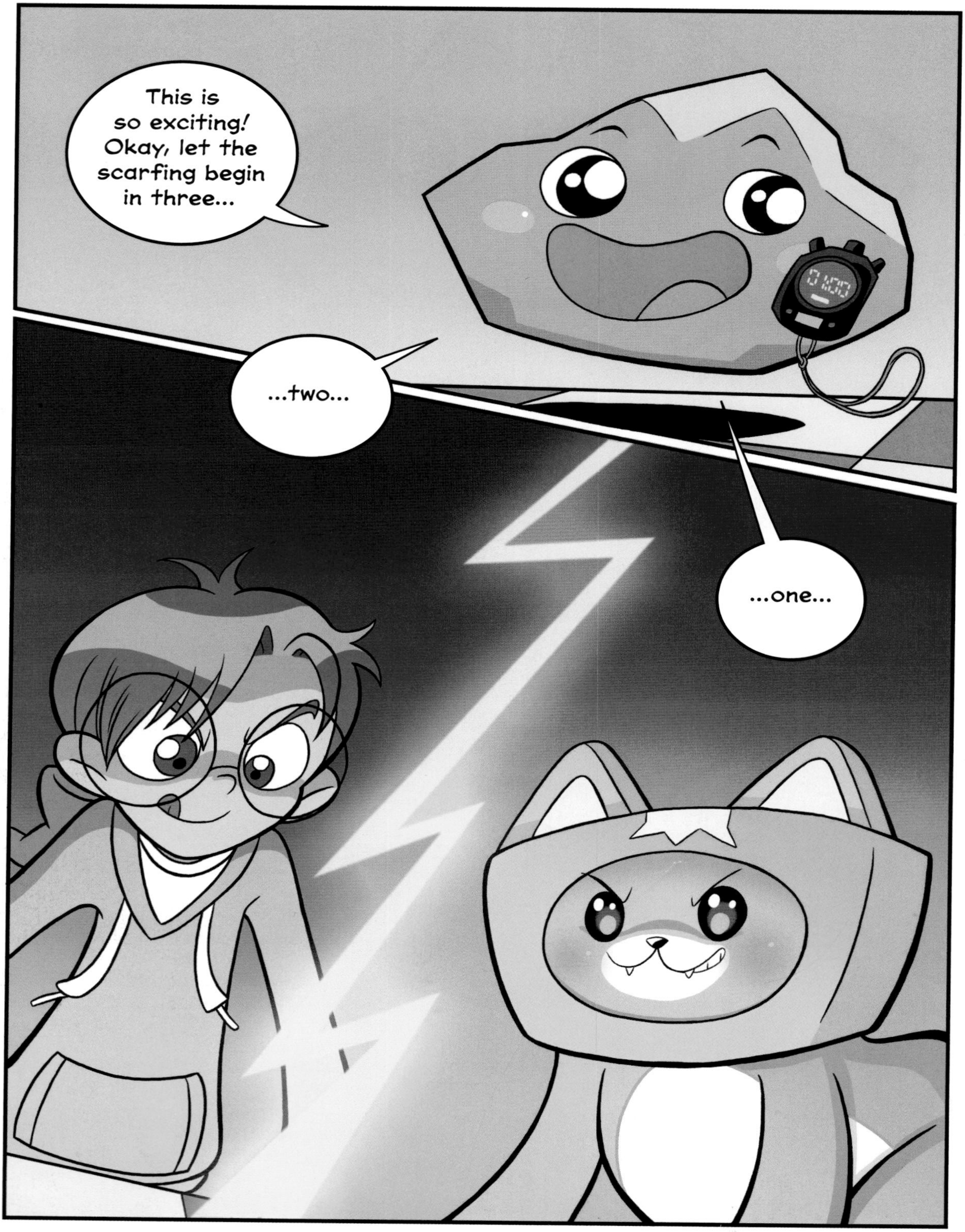
This is so exciting! Okay, let the scarfing begin in three...
...two...
...one...

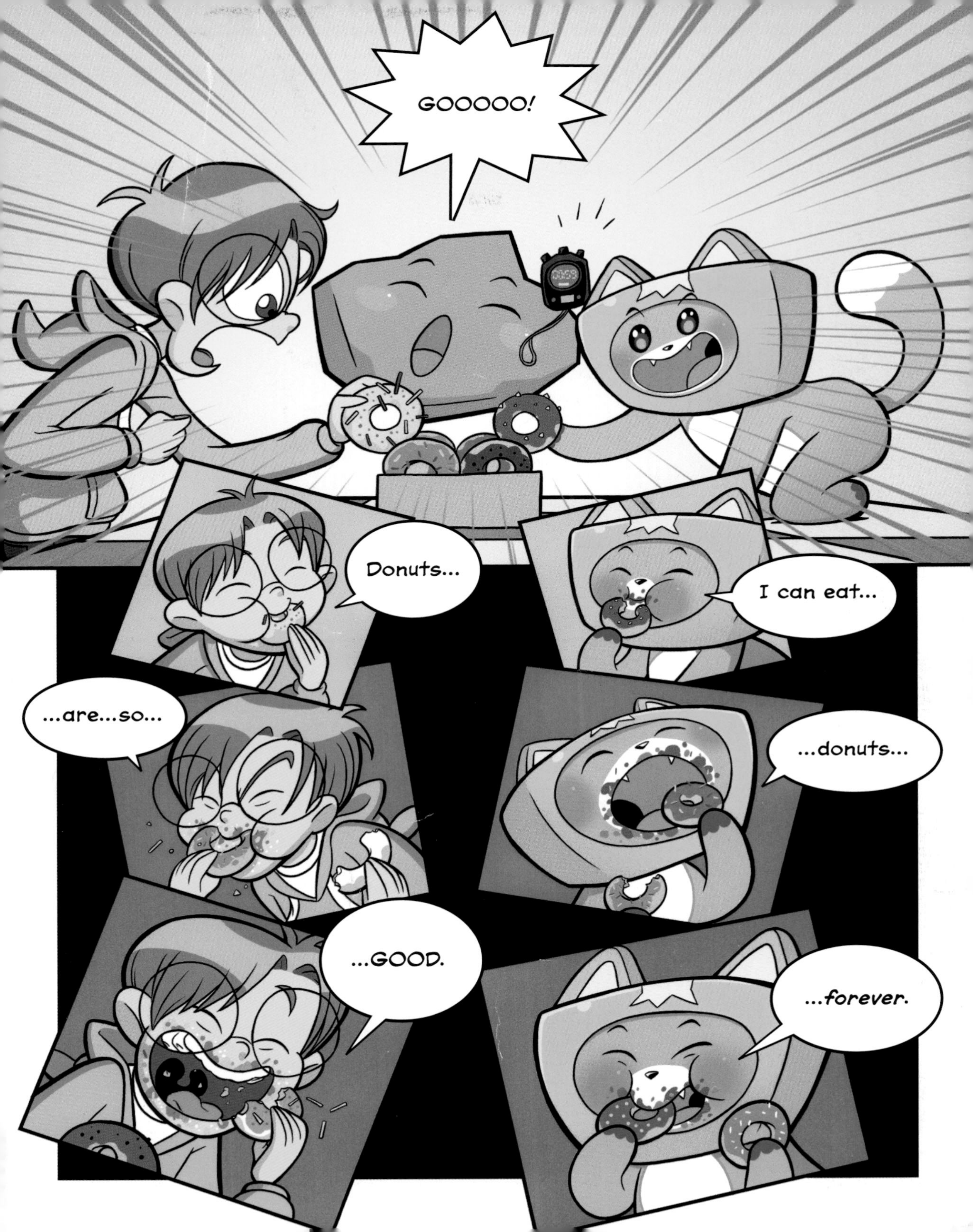
GOOOOO!
Donuts...
I can eat...
...are...so...
...donuts...
...GOOD.
...forever.

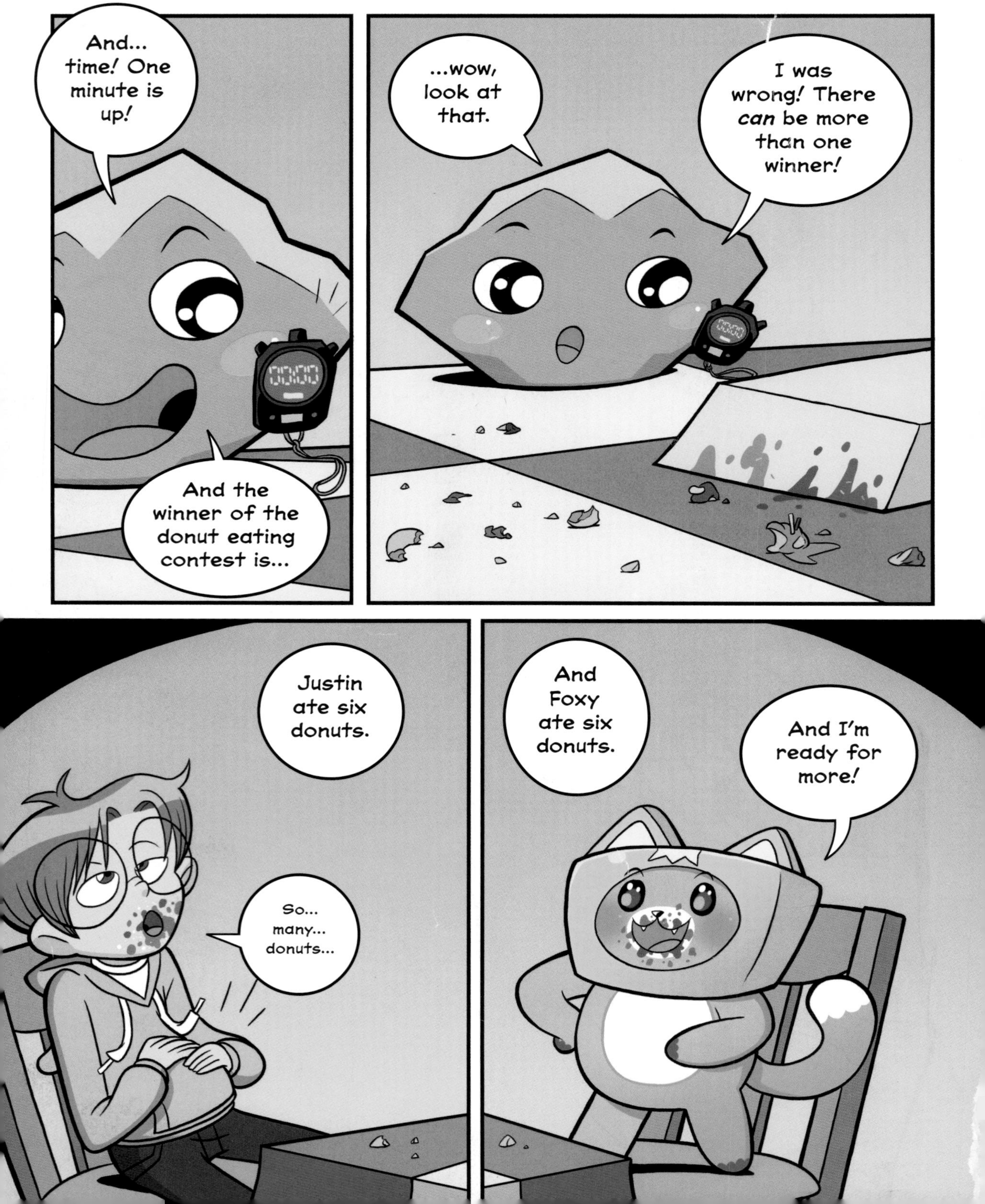
And... time! One minute is up!
And the winner of the donut eating contest is...
...wow, look at that.
I was wrong! There *can* be more than one winner!
Justin ate six donuts.
So... many... donuts...
And Foxy ate six donuts.
And I'm ready for more!

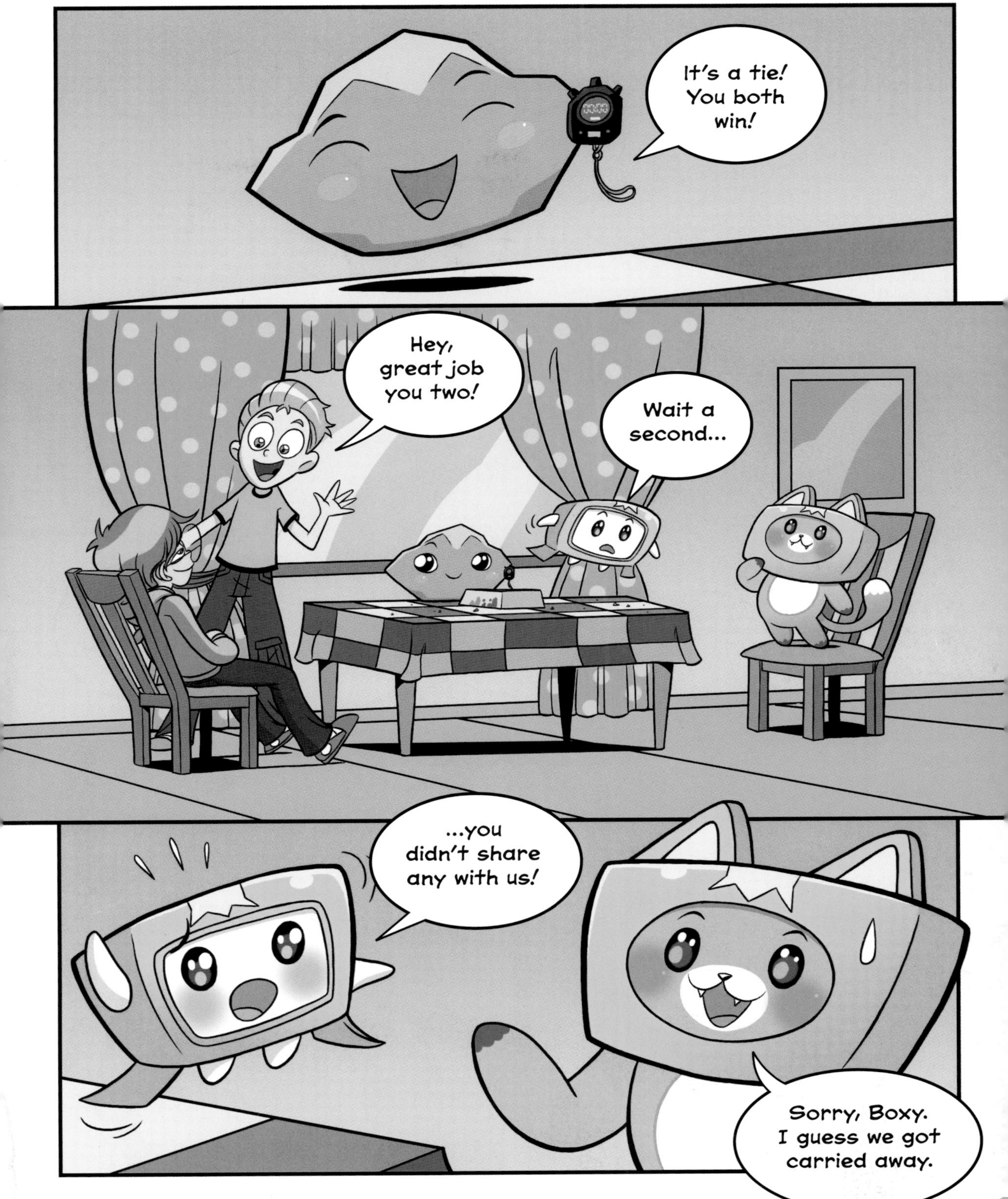
It's a tie! You both win!
Hey, great job you two!
Wait a second...
...you didn't share any with us!
Sorry, Boxy. I guess we got carried away.

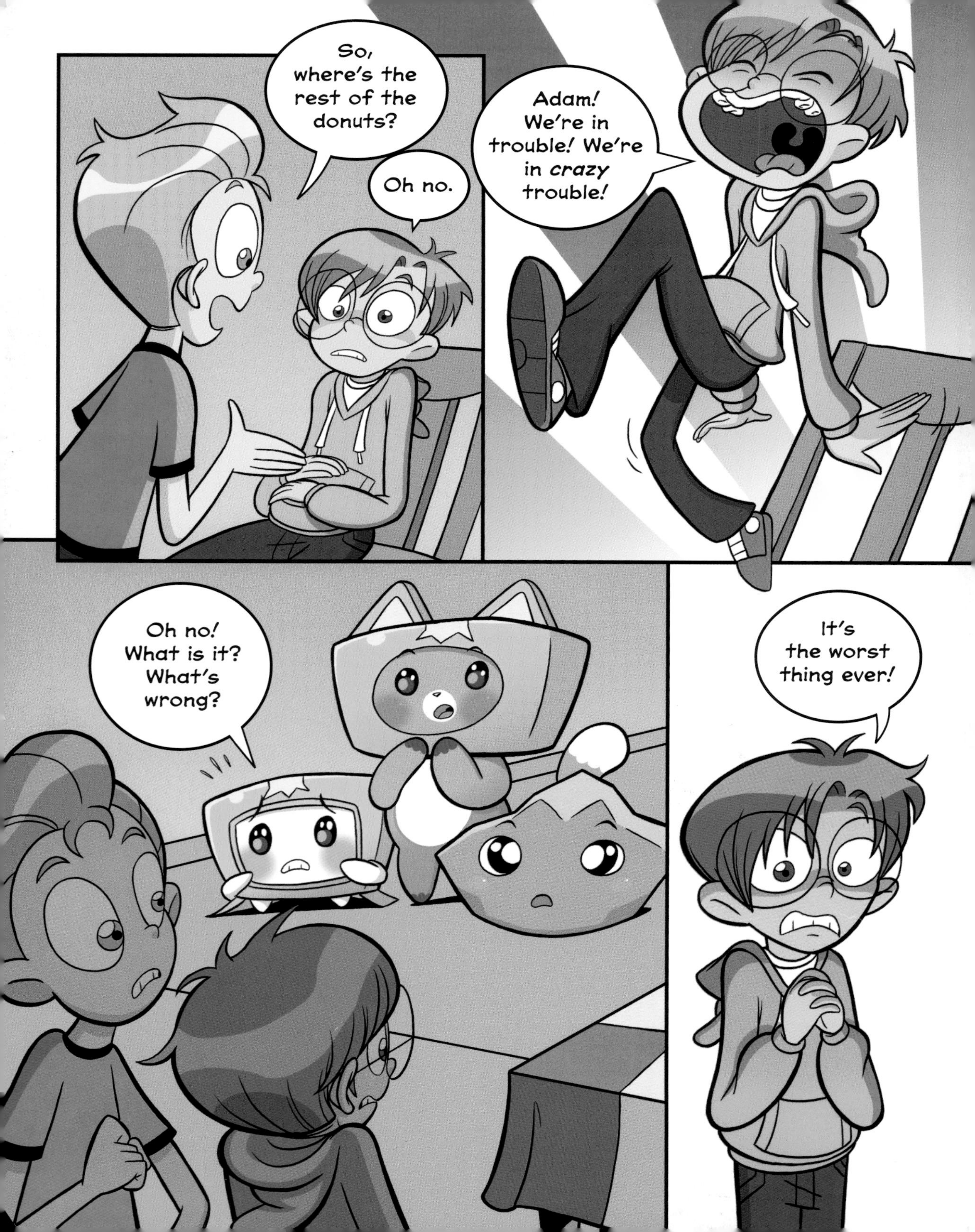
So, where's the rest of the donuts?
Oh no.
Adam! We're in trouble! We're in *crazy* trouble!
Oh no! What is it? What's wrong?
It's the worst thing ever!

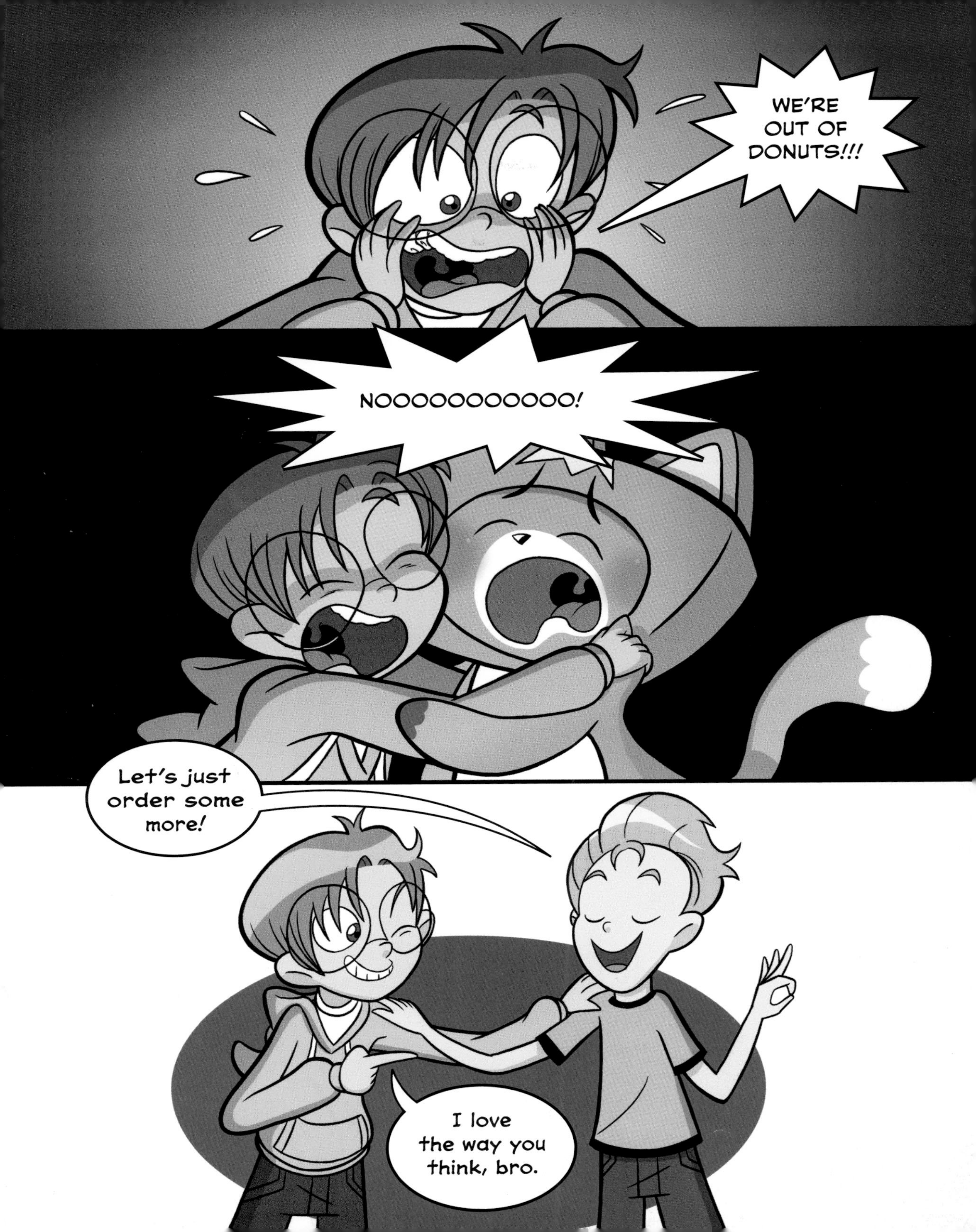
WE'RE OUT OF DONUTS!!!
NOOOOOOOOOOO!
Let's just order some more!
I love the way you think, bro.

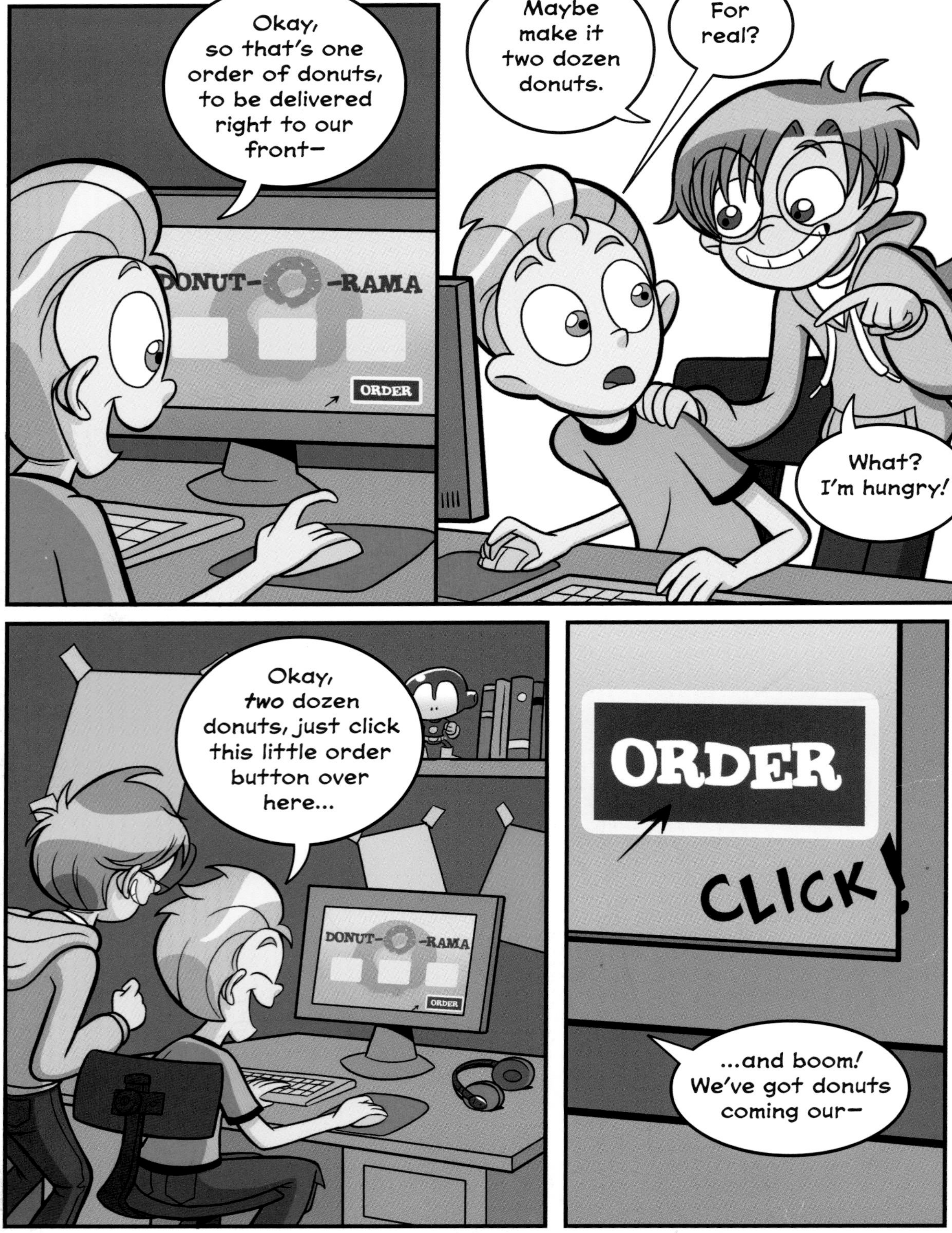
Okay, so that's one order of donuts, to be delivered right to our front—
DONUT- -RAMA
ORDER
Maybe make it two dozen donuts.
For real?
What? I'm hungry!
Okay, *two* dozen donuts, just click this little order button over here...
DONUT- -RAMA
ORDER
ORDER
CLICK!
...and boom! We've got donuts coming our—

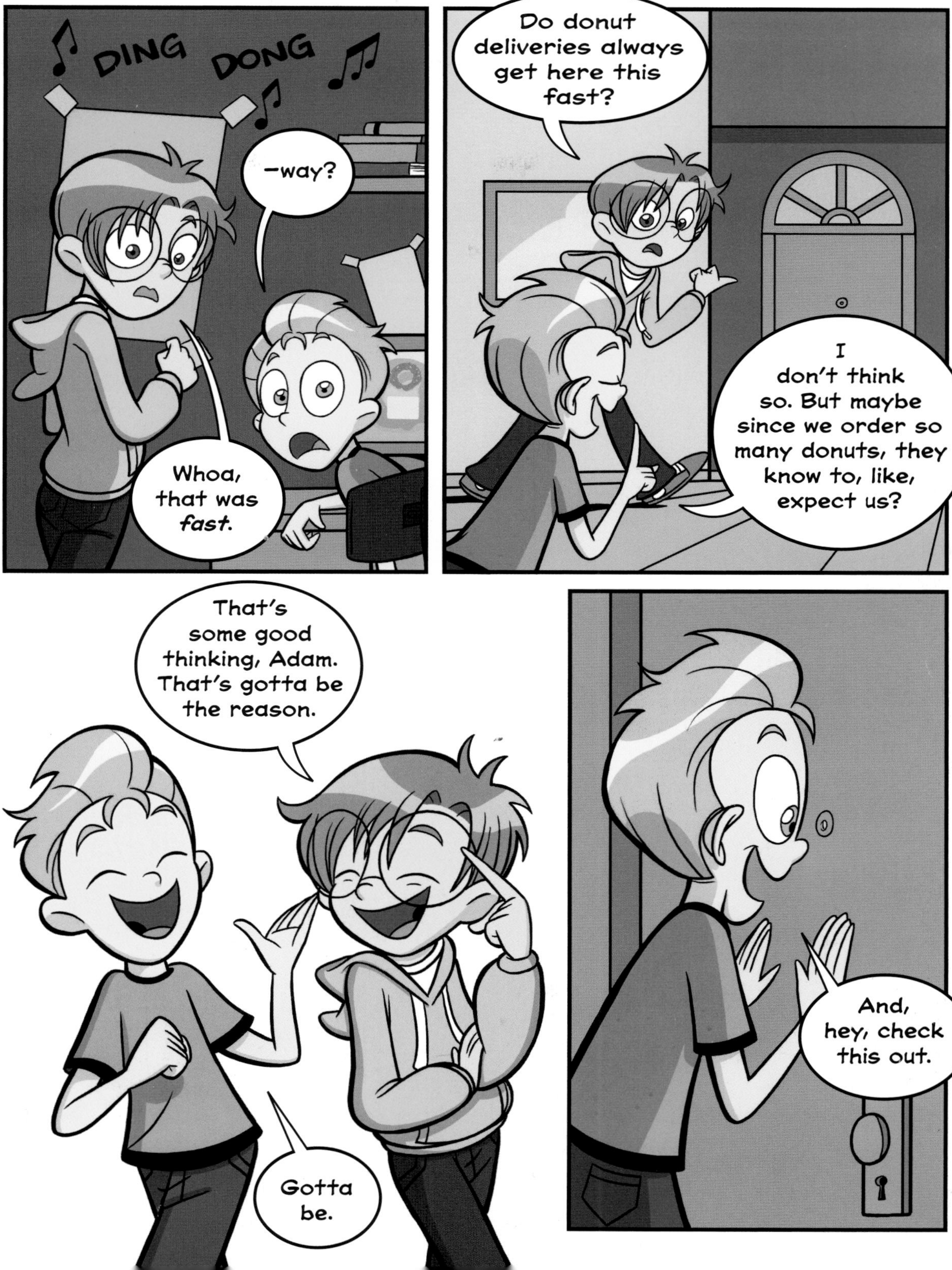
DING DONG
Whoa, that was *fast*.
—way?
Do donut deliveries always get here this fast?
I don't think so. But maybe since we order so many donuts, they know to, like, expect us?
That's some good thinking, Adam. That's gotta be the reason.
Gotta be.
And, hey, check this out.

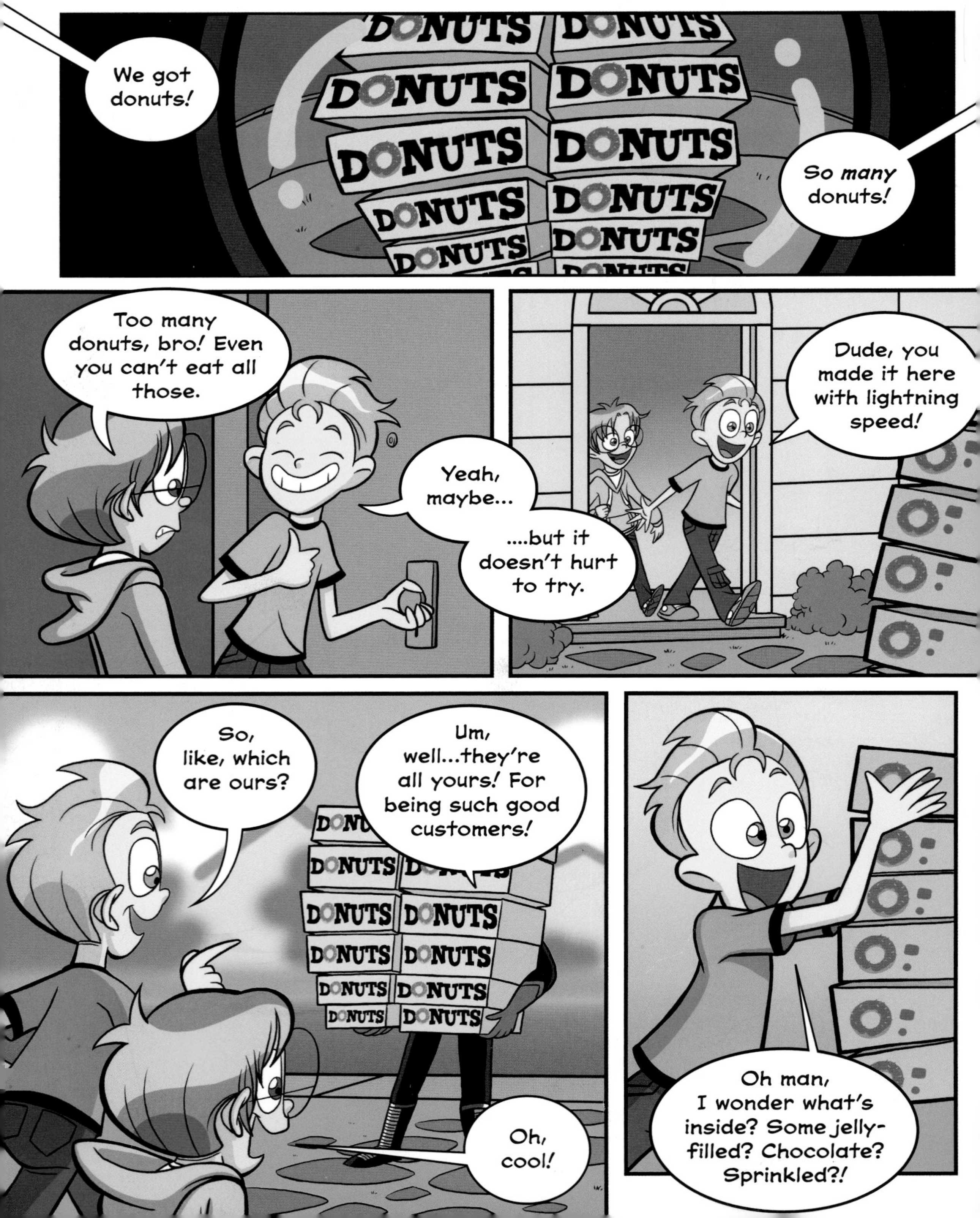
DONUTS
We got donuts!
So *many* donuts!
Too many donuts, bro! Even you can't eat all those.
Yeah, maybe...
....but it doesn't hurt to try.
Dude, you made it here with lightning speed!
So, like, which are ours?
Um, well...they're all yours! For being such good customers!
Oh, cool!
Oh man, I wonder what's inside? Some jelly-filled? Chocolate? Sprinkled?!

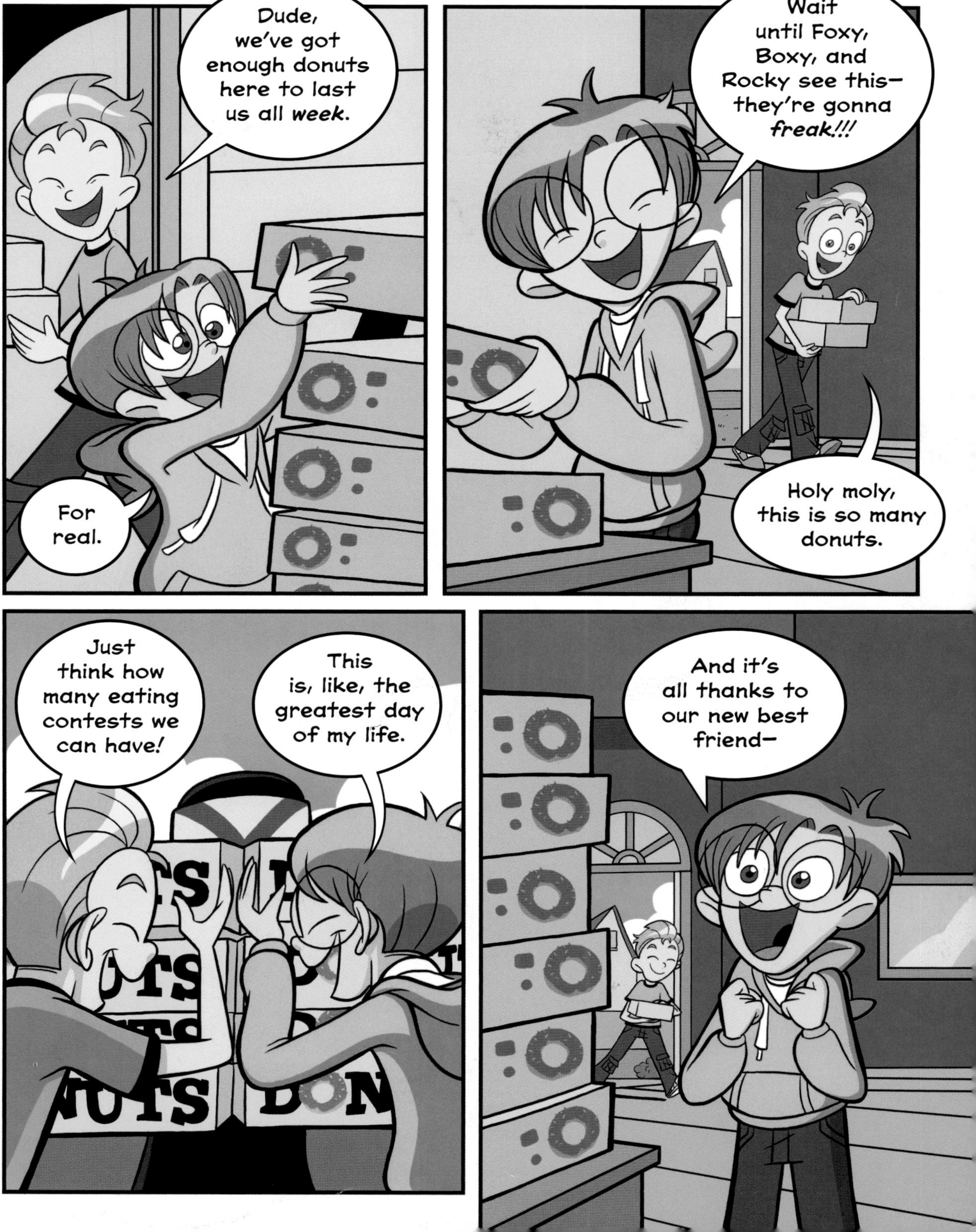
Dude, we've got enough donuts here to last us all *week*.
For real.
Wait until Foxy, Boxy, and Rocky see this—they're gonna *freak!!!*
Holy moly, this is so many donuts.
Just think how many eating contests we can have!
This is, like, the greatest day of my life.
And it's all thanks to our new best friend—

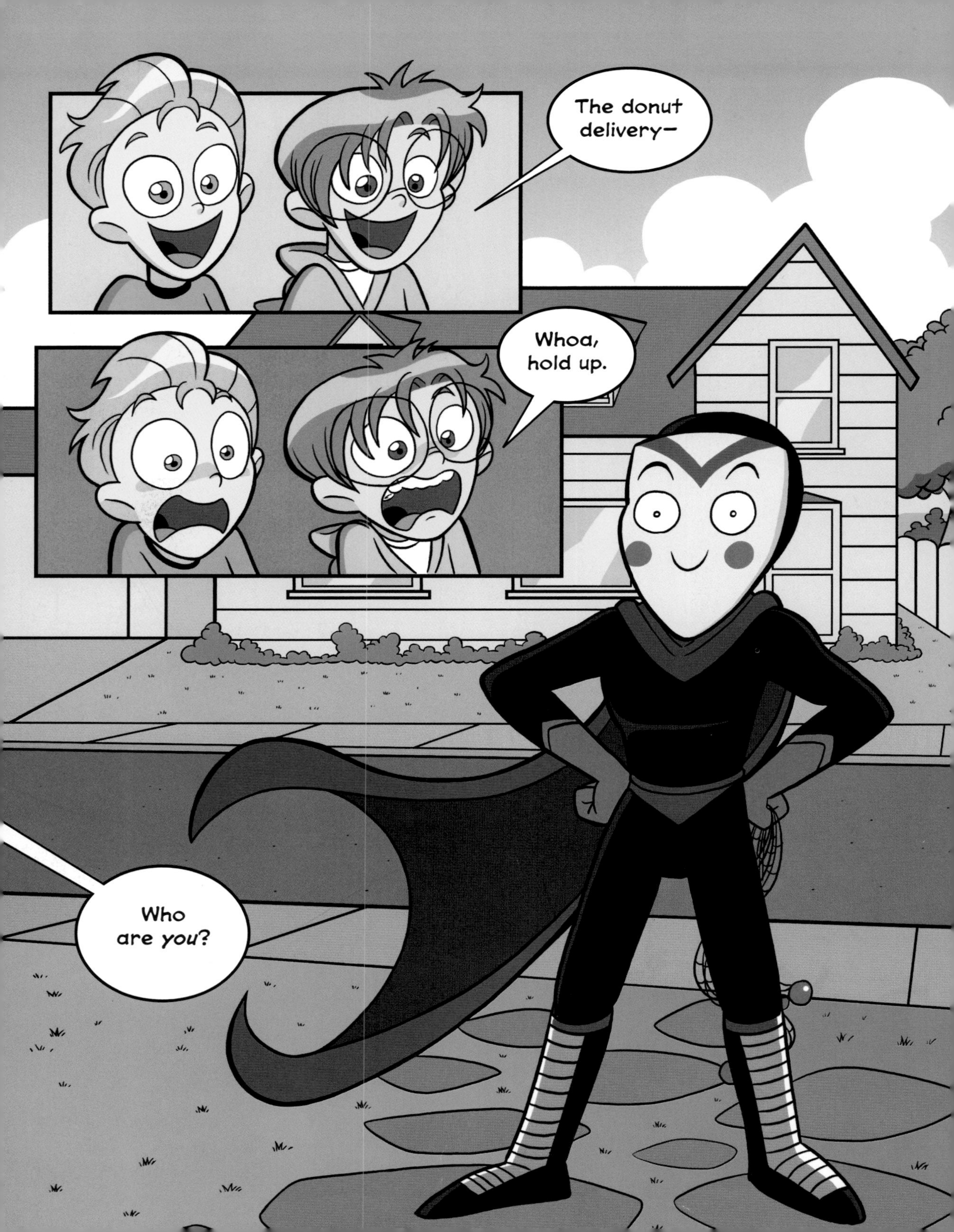
The donut delivery—
Whoa, hold up.
Who are *you*?

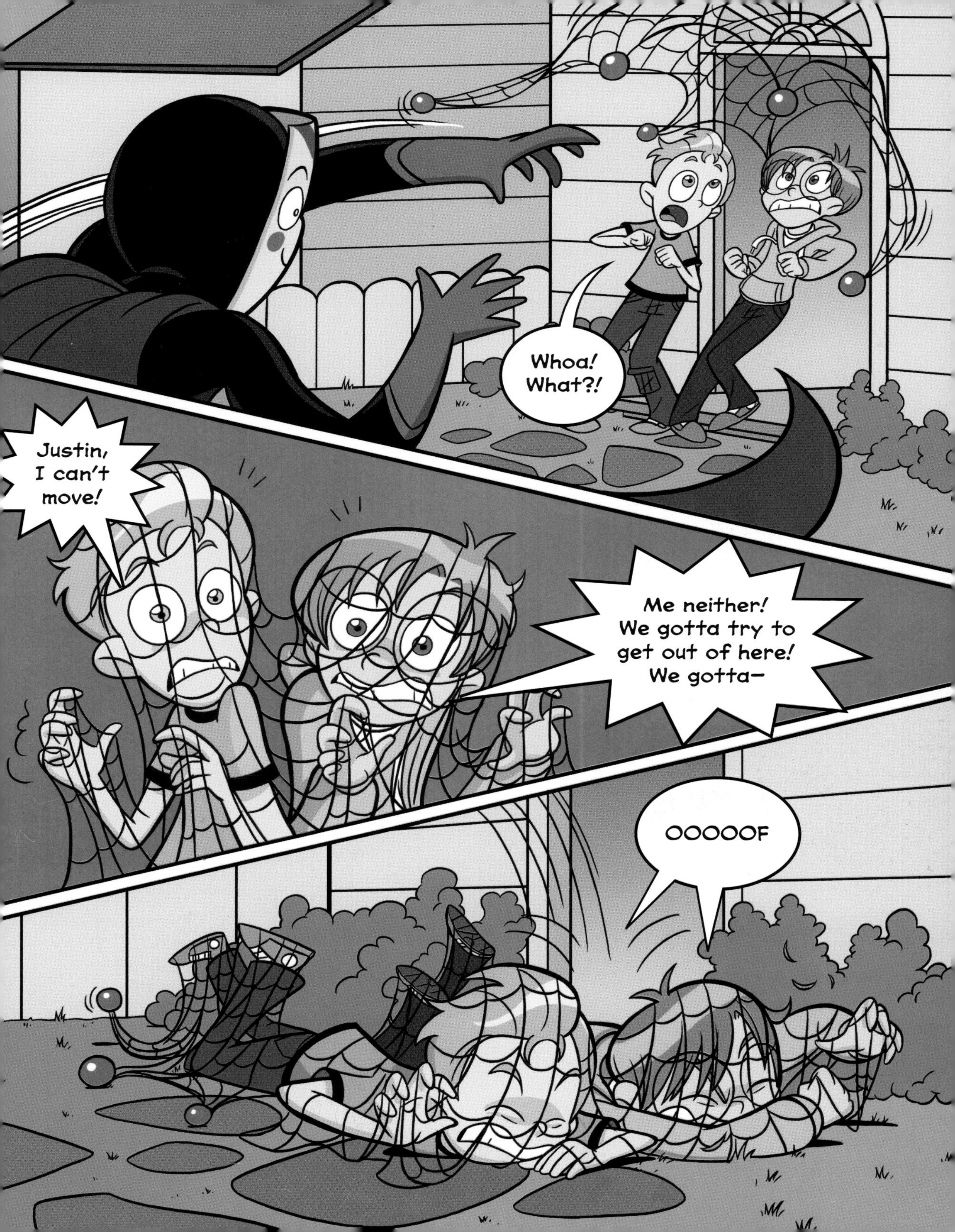
Whoa! What?!
Justin, I can't move!
Me neither! We gotta try to get out of here! We gotta–
OOOOOF

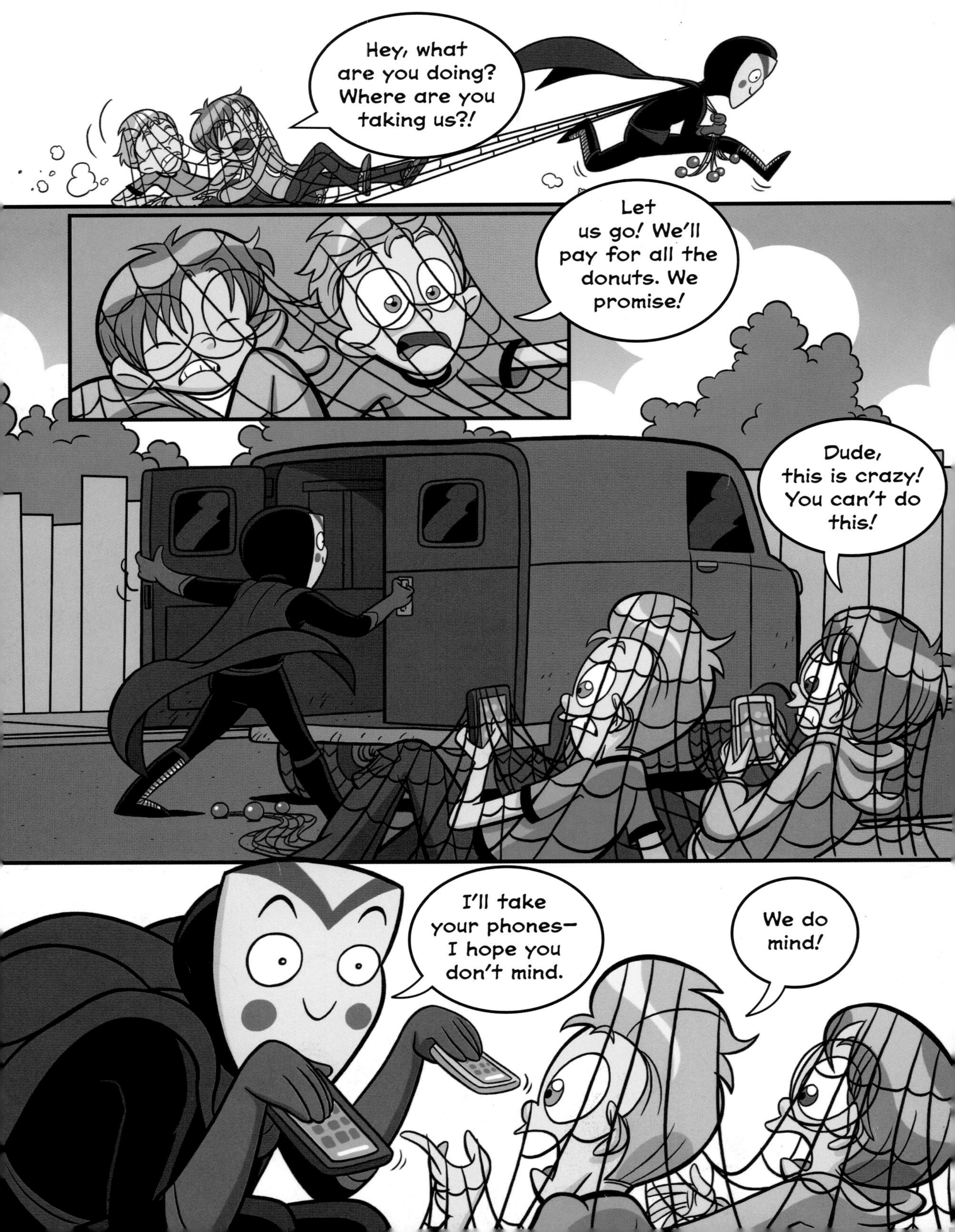

Hey, what are you doing? Where are you taking us?!
Let us go! We'll pay for all the donuts. We promise!
Dude, this is crazy! You can't do this!
I'll take your phones— I hope you don't mind.
We do mind!

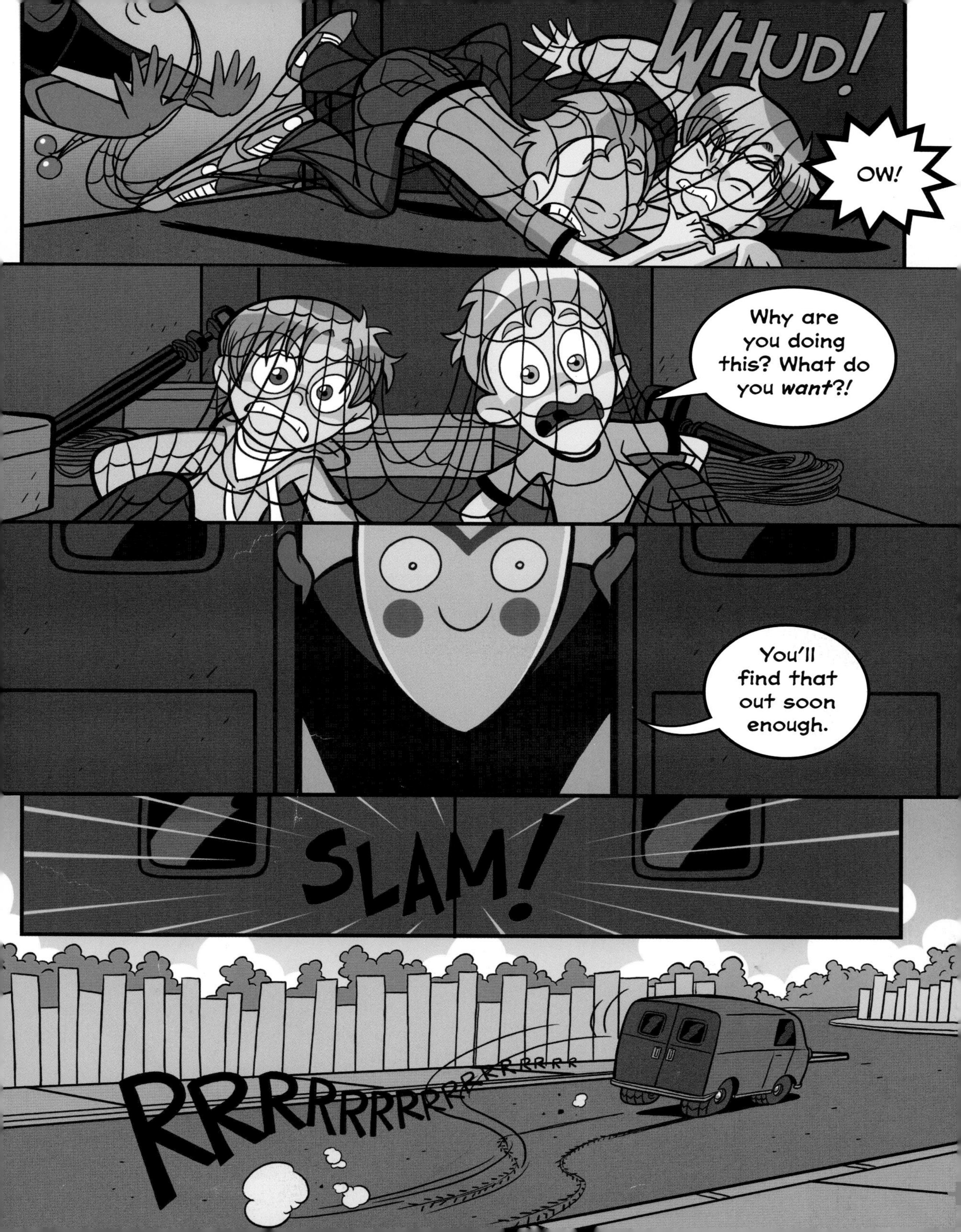
WHUD!
OW!
Why are you doing this? What do you *want*?!
You'll find that out soon enough.
SLAM!
RRRRRRRRRRRRRRRRRRR

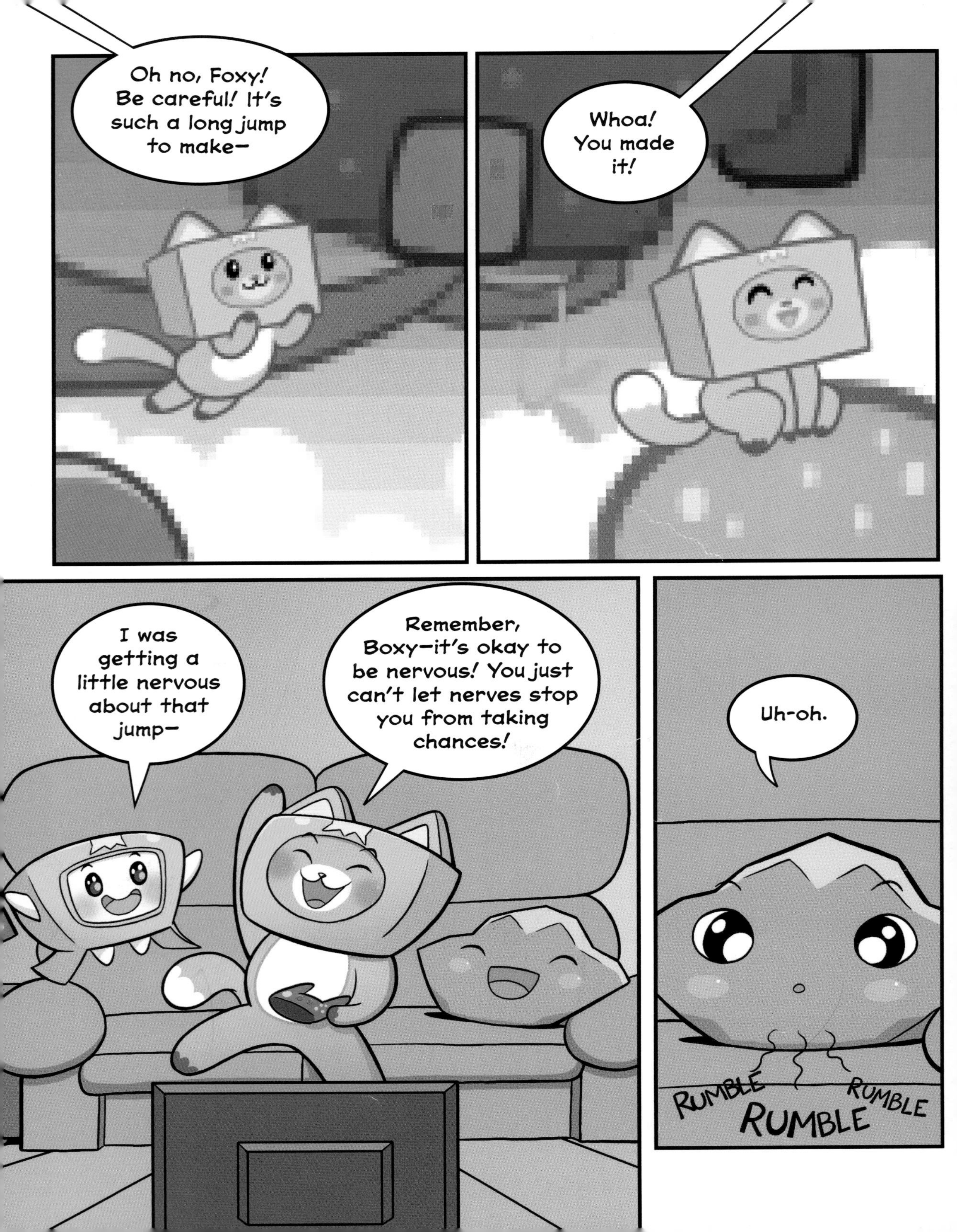
Oh no, Foxy! Be careful! It's such a long jump to make—
Whoa! You made it!
I was getting a little nervous about that jump—
Remember, Boxy—it's okay to be nervous! You just can't let nerves stop you from taking chances!
Uh-oh.
RUMBLE
RUMBLE
RUMBLE

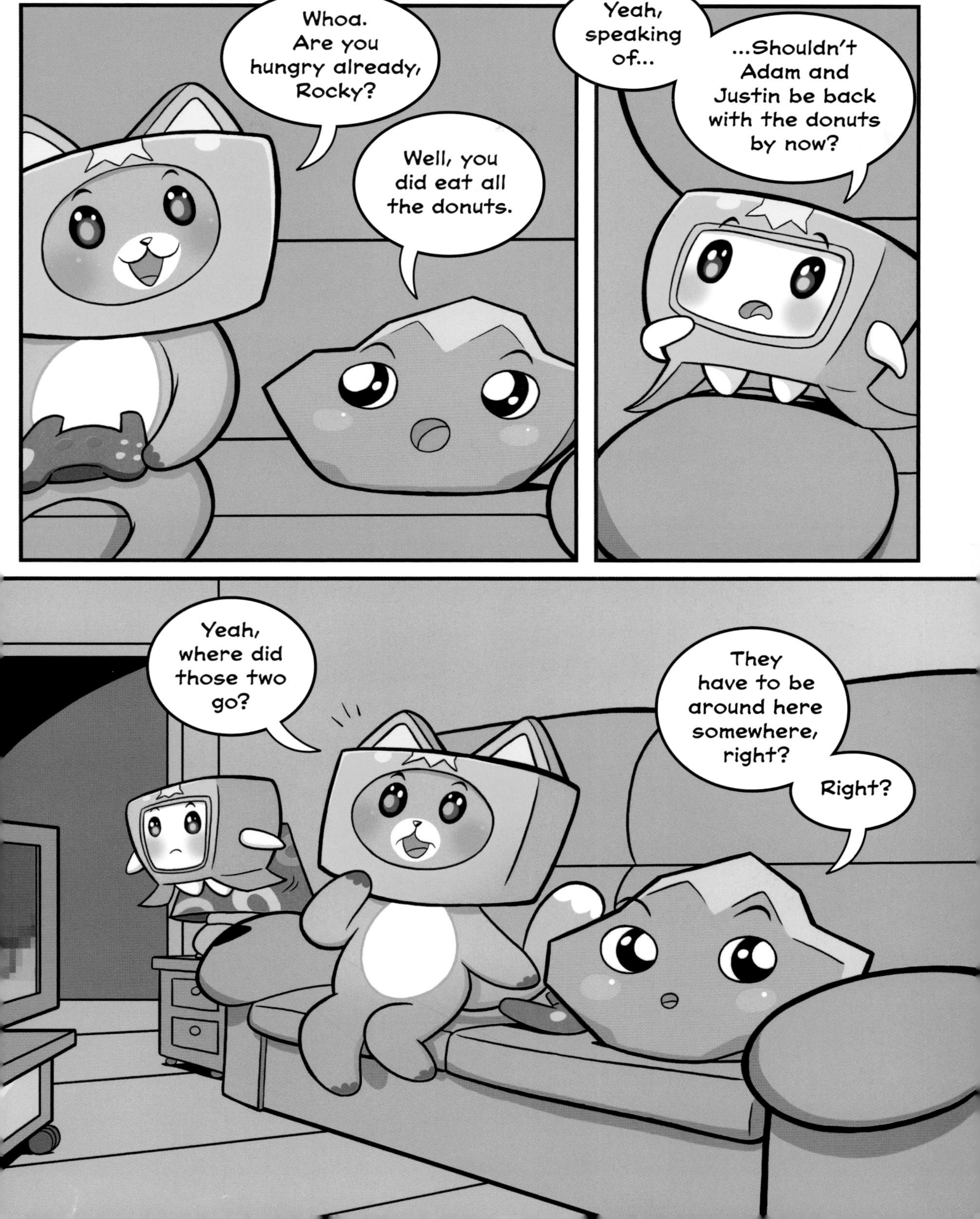
Whoa. Are you hungry already, Rocky?
Well, you did eat all the donuts.
Yeah, speaking of...
...Shouldn't Adam and Justin be back with the donuts by now?
Yeah, where did those two go?
They have to be around here somewhere, right?
Right?

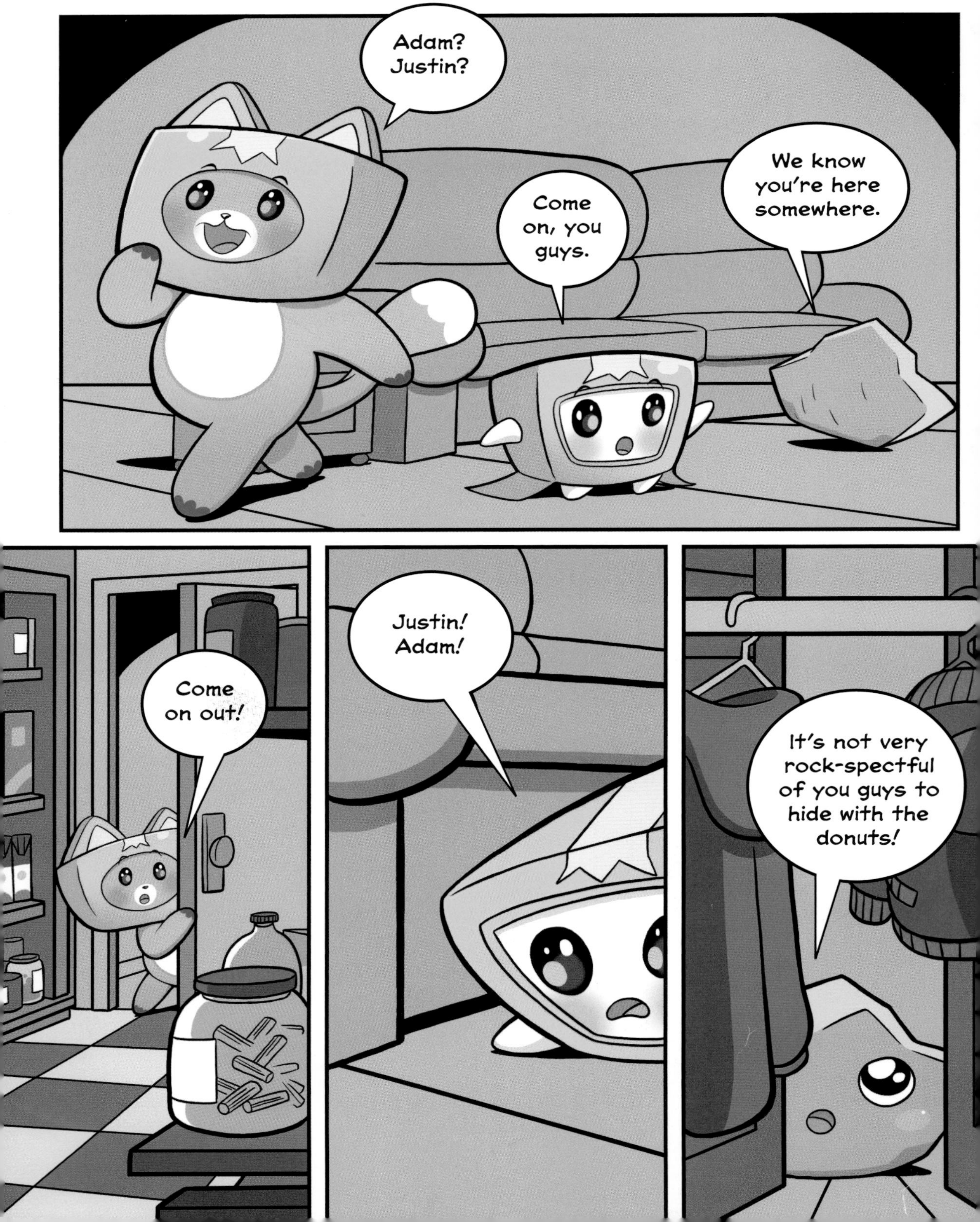
Adam? Justin?
Come on, you guys.
We know you're here somewhere.
Come on out!
Justin! Adam!
It's not very rock-spectful of you guys to hide with the donuts!

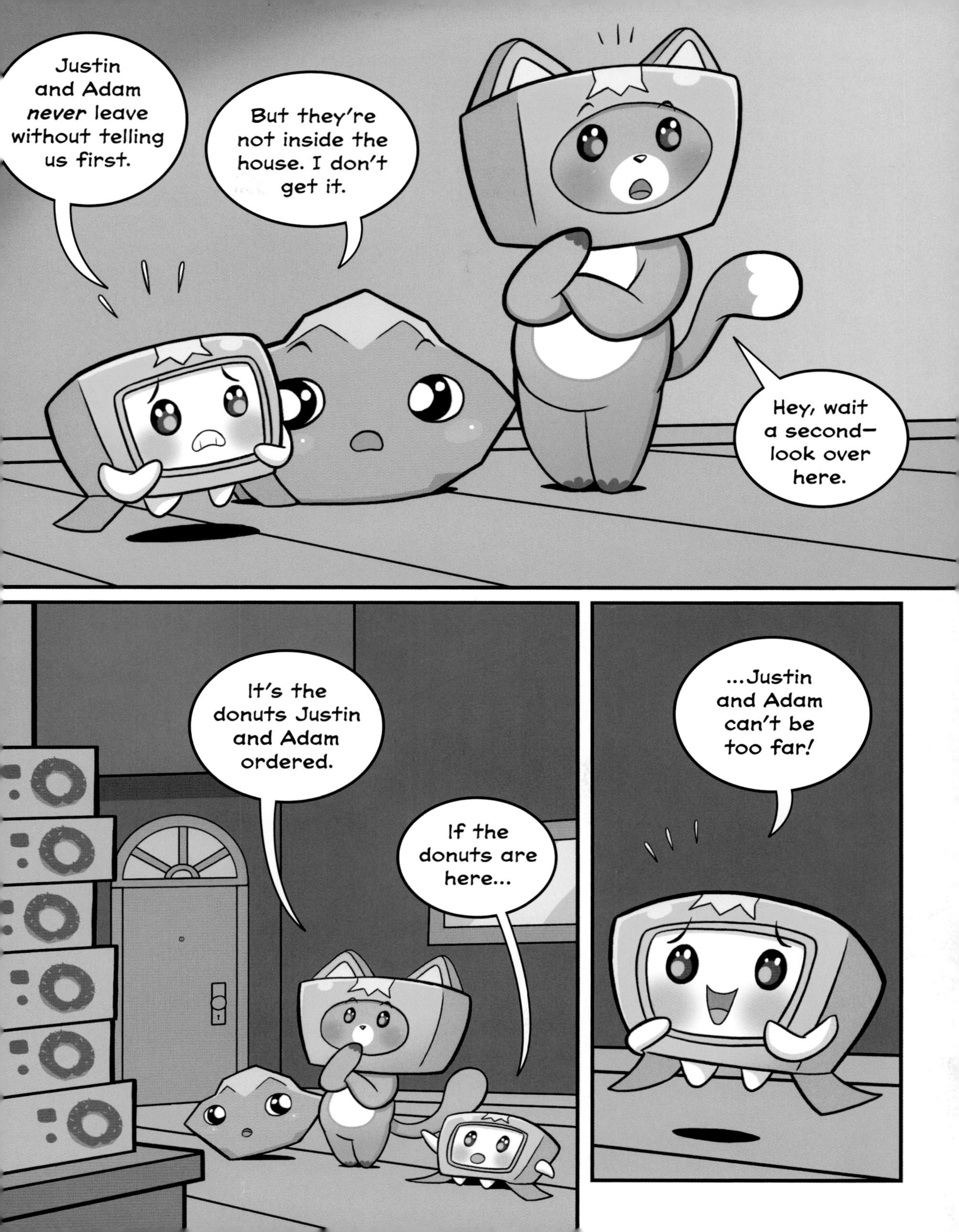

Justin and Adam *never* leave without telling us first.
But they're not inside the house. I don't get it.
Hey, wait a second—look over here.
It's the donuts Justin and Adam ordered.
If the donuts are here...
...Justin and Adam can't be too far!

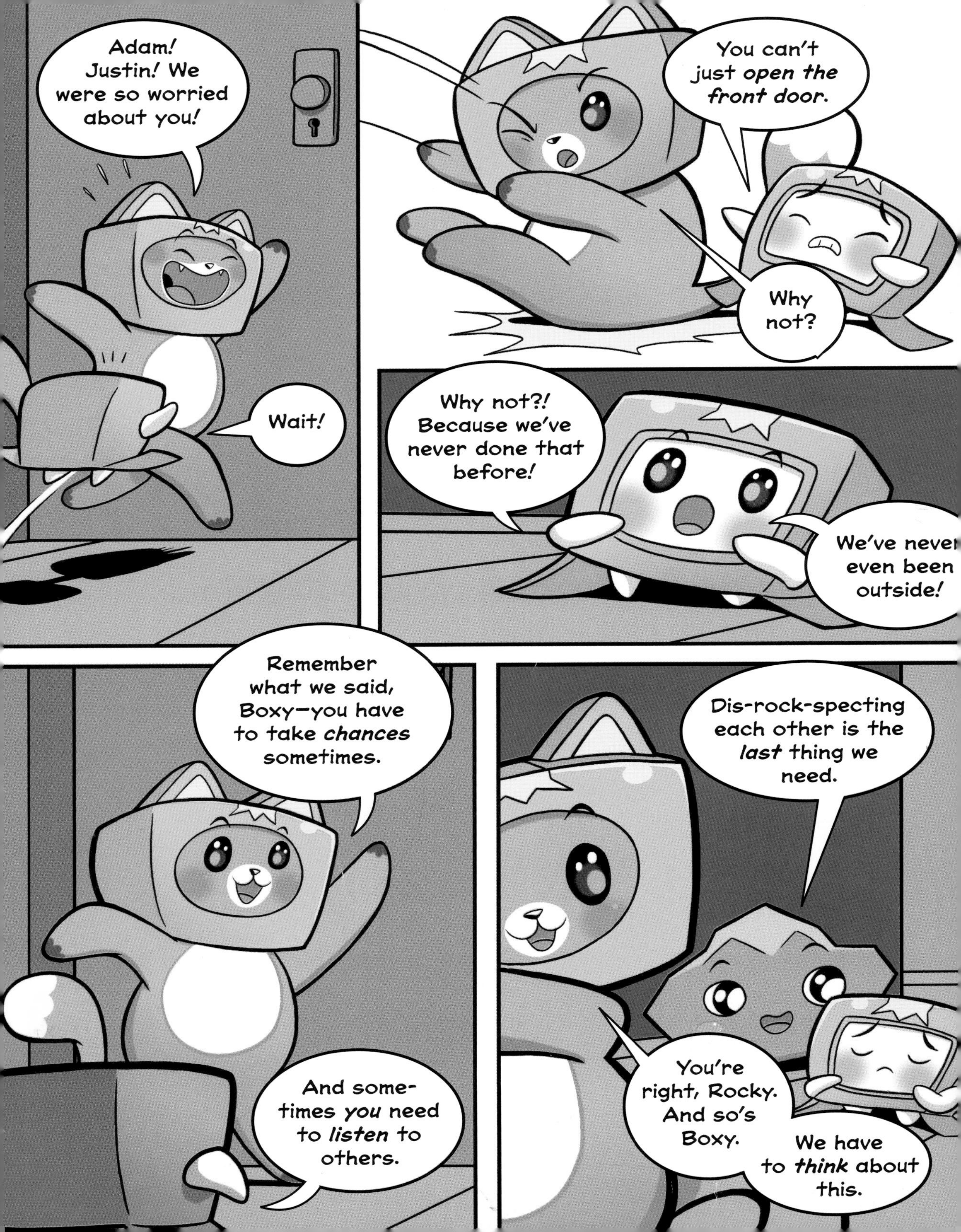
Adam! Justin! We were so worried about you!
Wait!
You can't just *open the front door*.
Why not?
Why not?! Because we've never done that before!
We've never even been outside!
Remember what we said, Boxy—you have to take *chances* sometimes.
And some-times *you* need to *listen* to others.
Dis-rock-specting each other is the *last* thing we need.
You're right, Rocky. And so's Boxy.
We have to *think* about this.

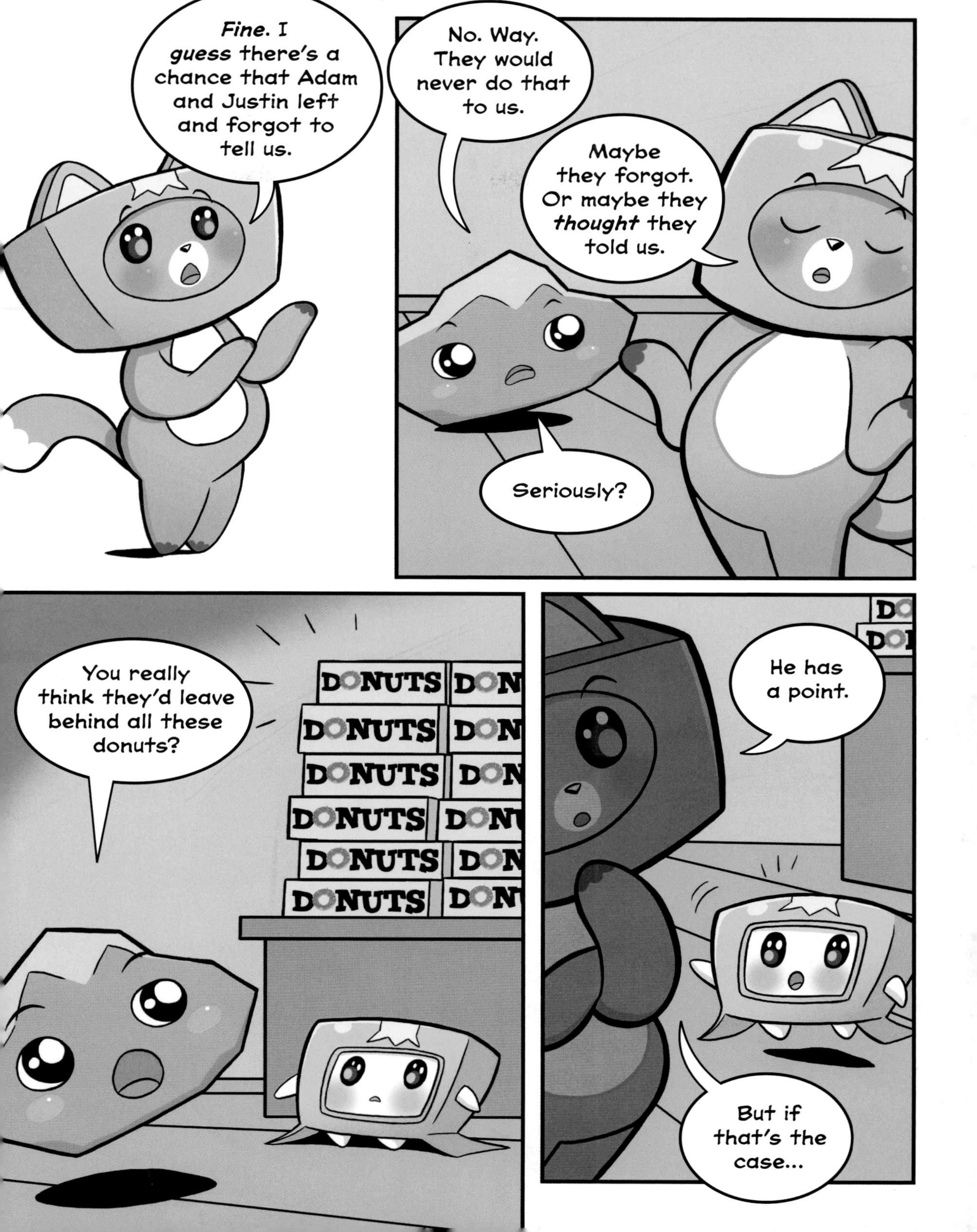
Fine. I *guess* there's a chance that Adam and Justin left and forgot to tell us.
No. Way. They would never do that to us.
Maybe they forgot. Or maybe they *thought* they told us.
Seriously?
You really think they'd leave behind all these donuts?
DONUTS
He has a point.
But if that's the case...

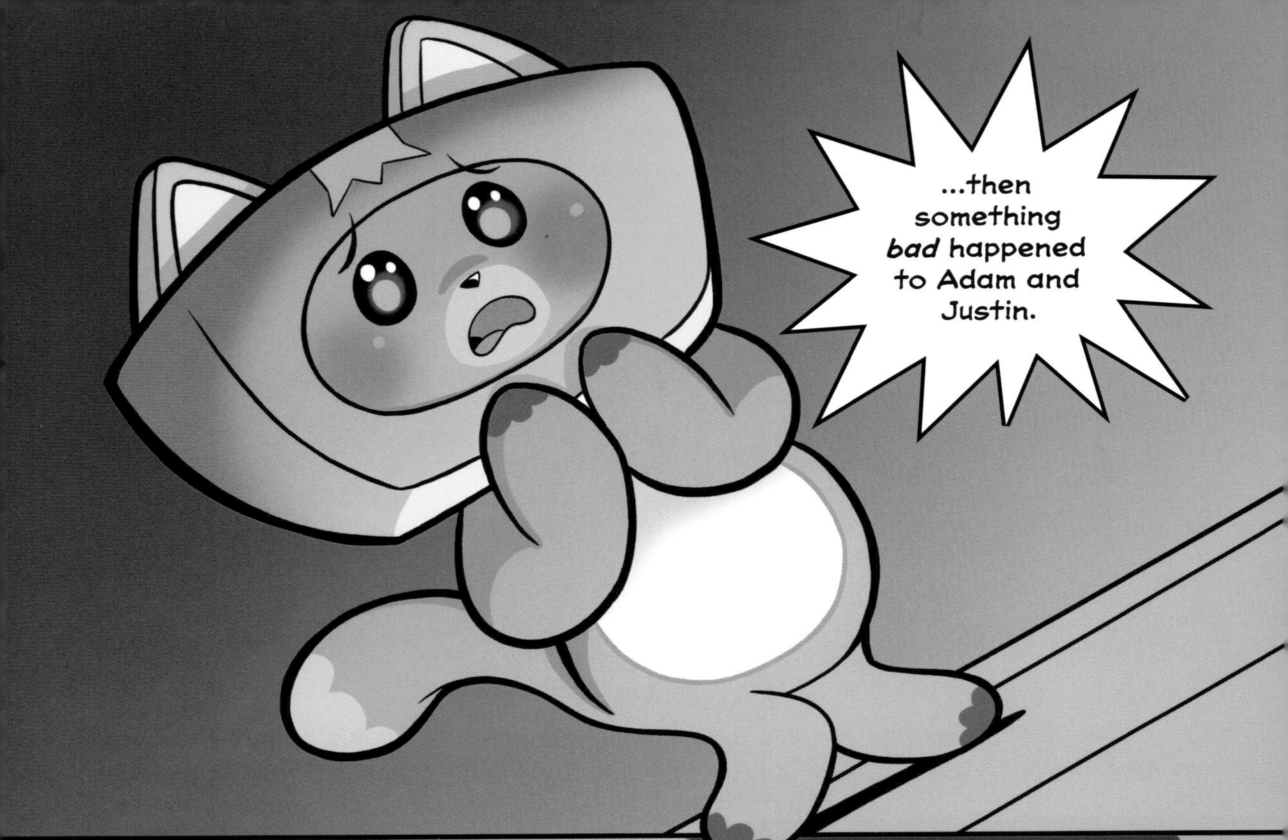
...then something *bad* happened to Adam and Justin.

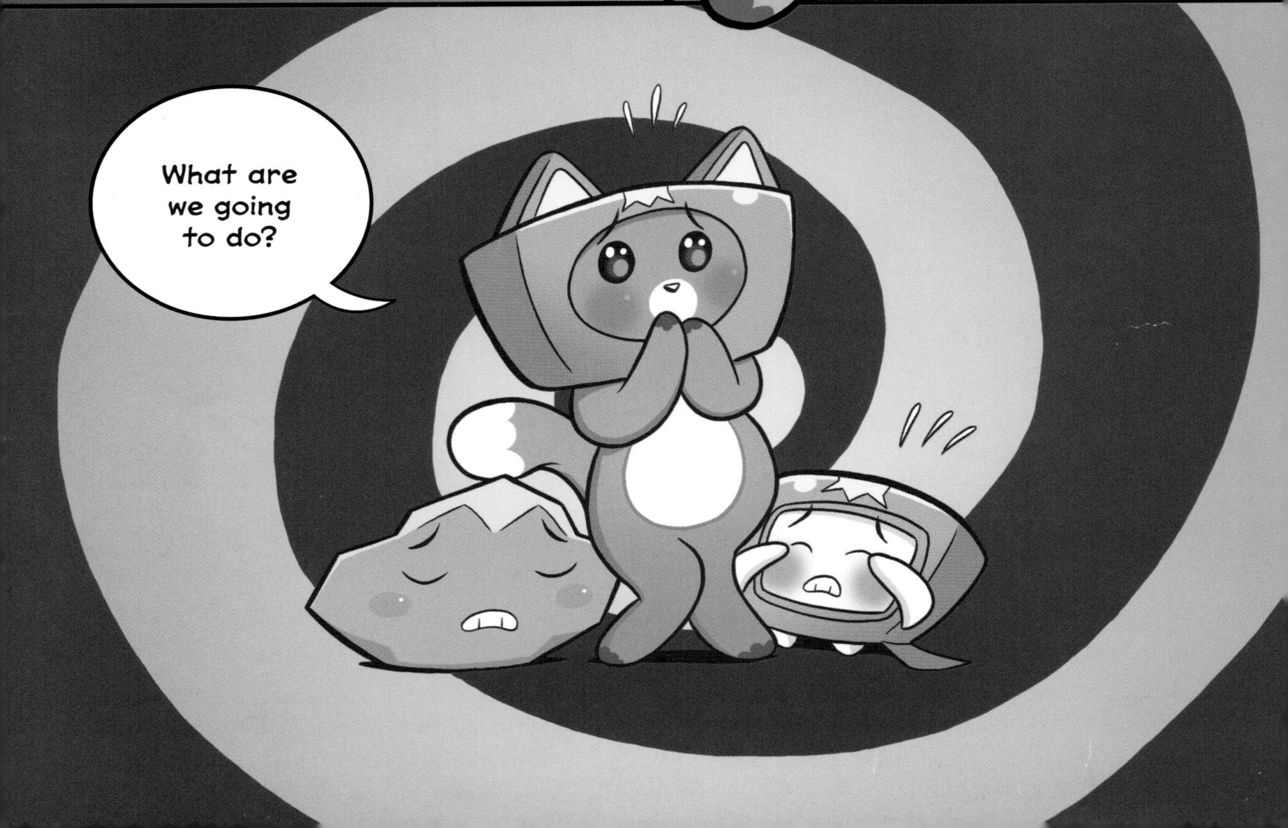
What are we going to do?

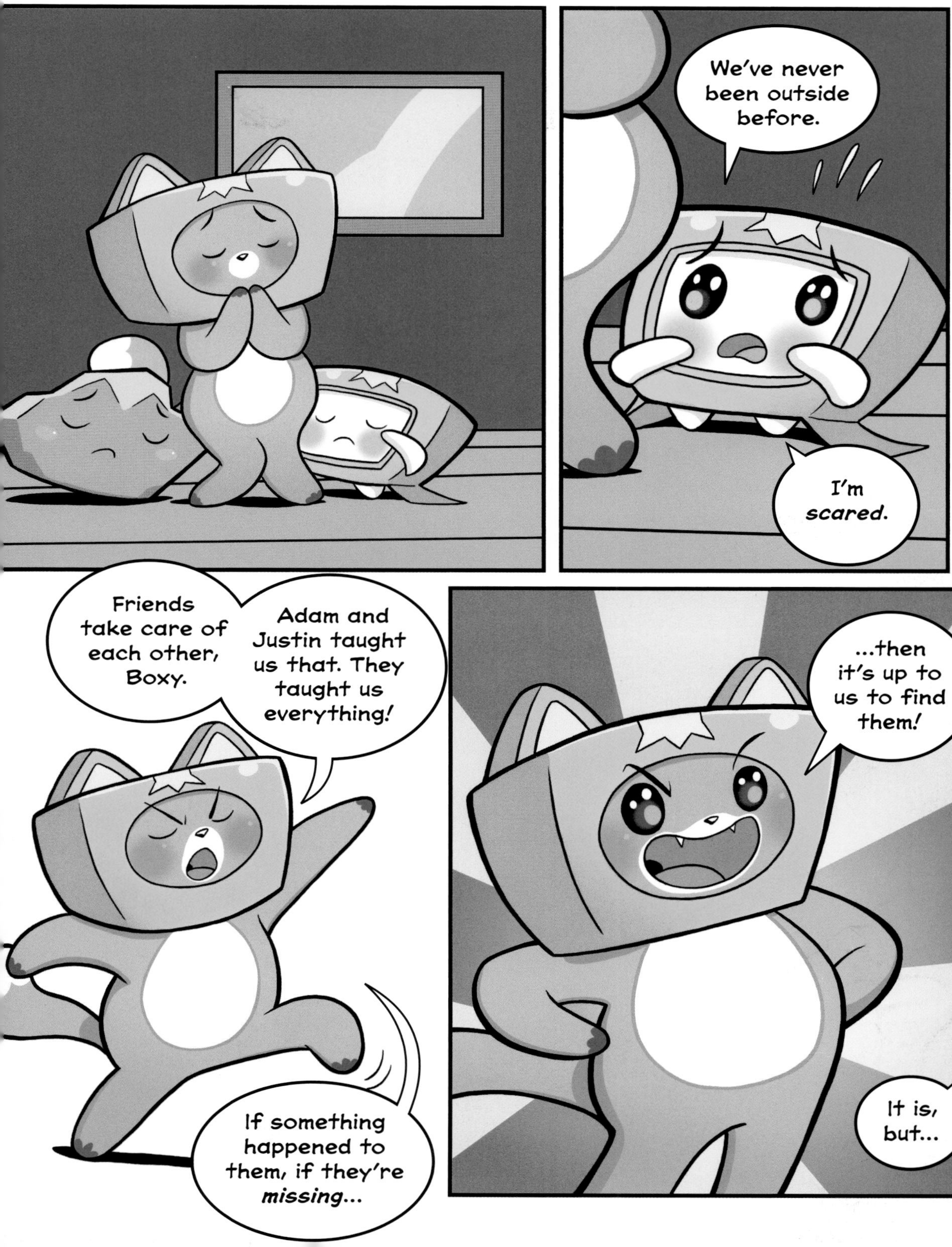
We've never been outside before.
I'm *scared*.
Friends take care of each other, Boxy.
Adam and Justin taught us that. They taught us everything!
If something happened to them, if they're *missing*...
It is, but...
...then it's up to us to find them!

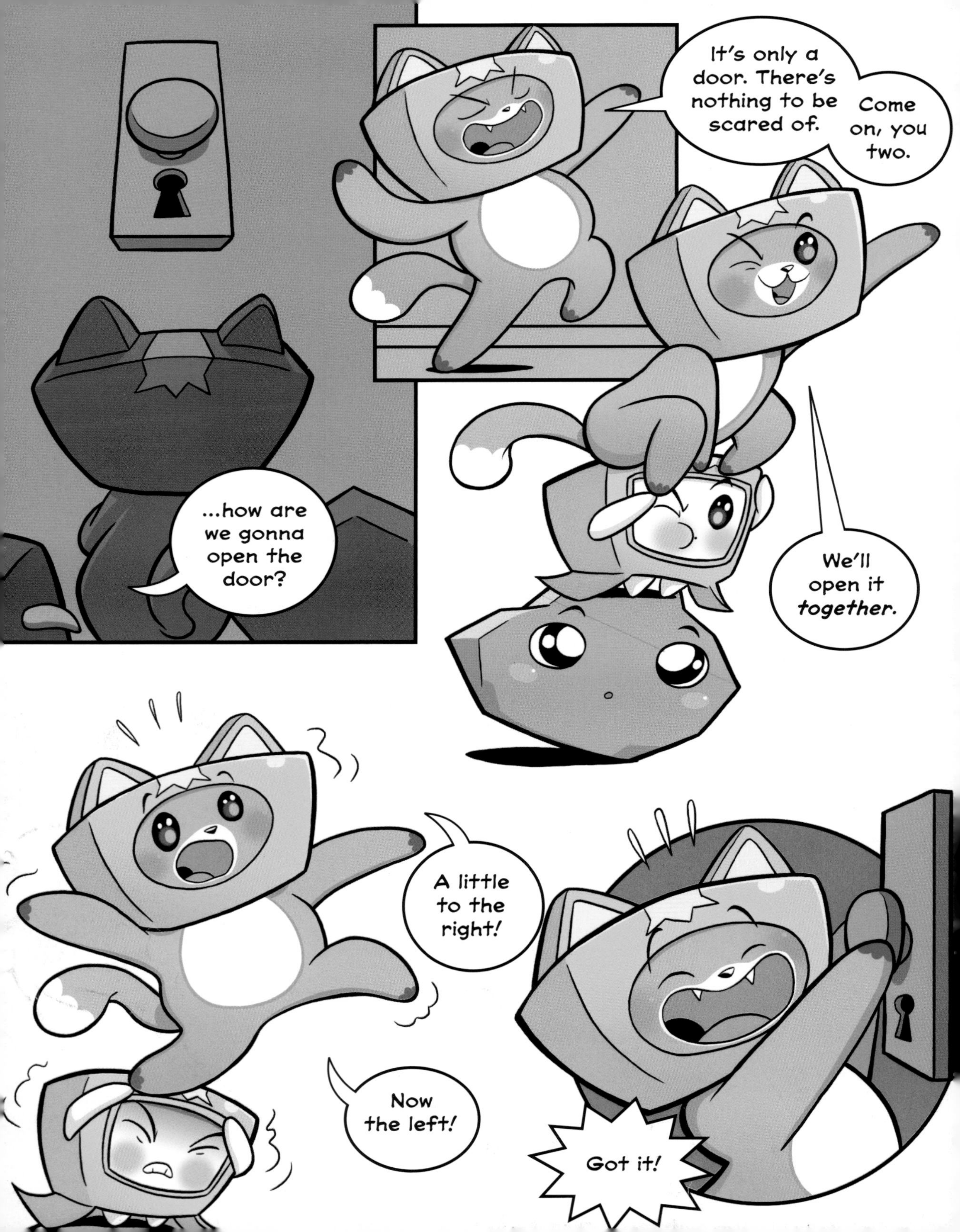

...how are we gonna open the door?
It's only a door. There's nothing to be scared of.
Come on, you two.
We'll open it *together*.
A little to the right!
Now the left!
Got it!

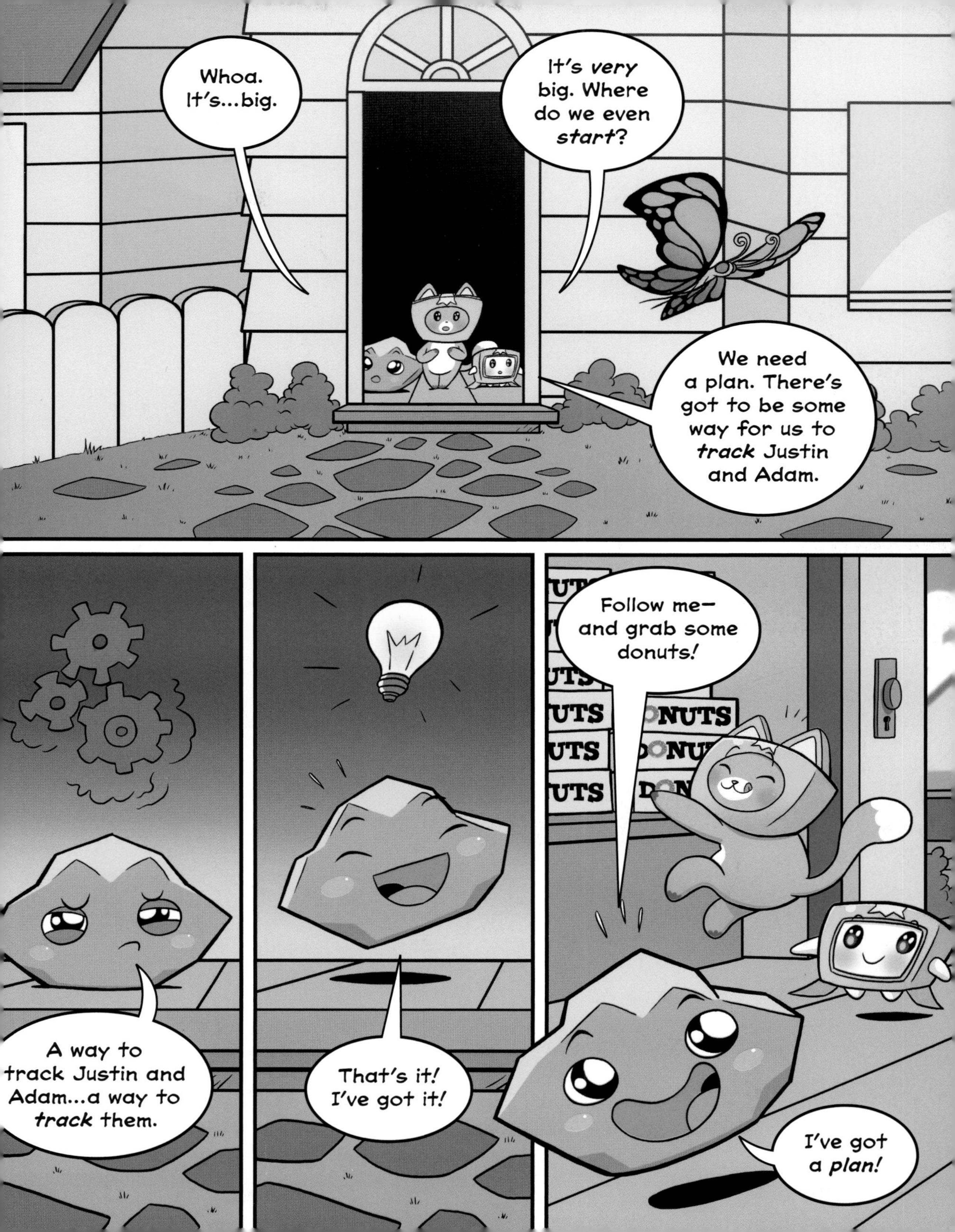
Whoa. It's...big.
It's *very* big. Where do we even *start*?
We need a plan. There's got to be some way for us to ***track*** Justin and Adam.
A way to track Justin and Adam...a way to ***track*** them.
That's it! I've got it!
Follow me—and grab some donuts!
I've got a ***plan!***

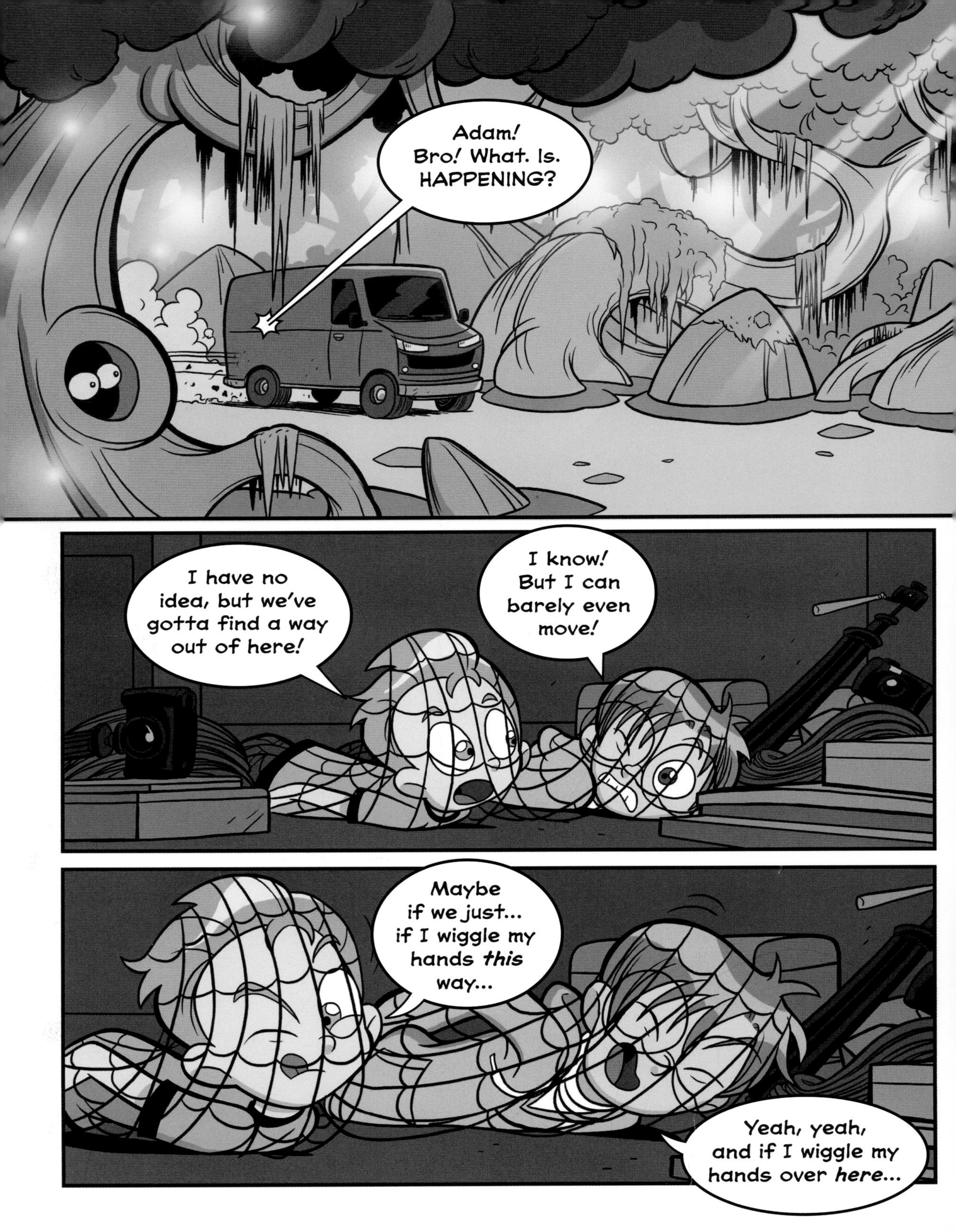
Adam! Bro! What. Is. HAPPENING?
I have no idea, but we've gotta find a way out of here!
I know! But I can barely even move!
Maybe if we just... if I wiggle my hands *this* way...
Yeah, yeah, and if I wiggle my hands over *here*...

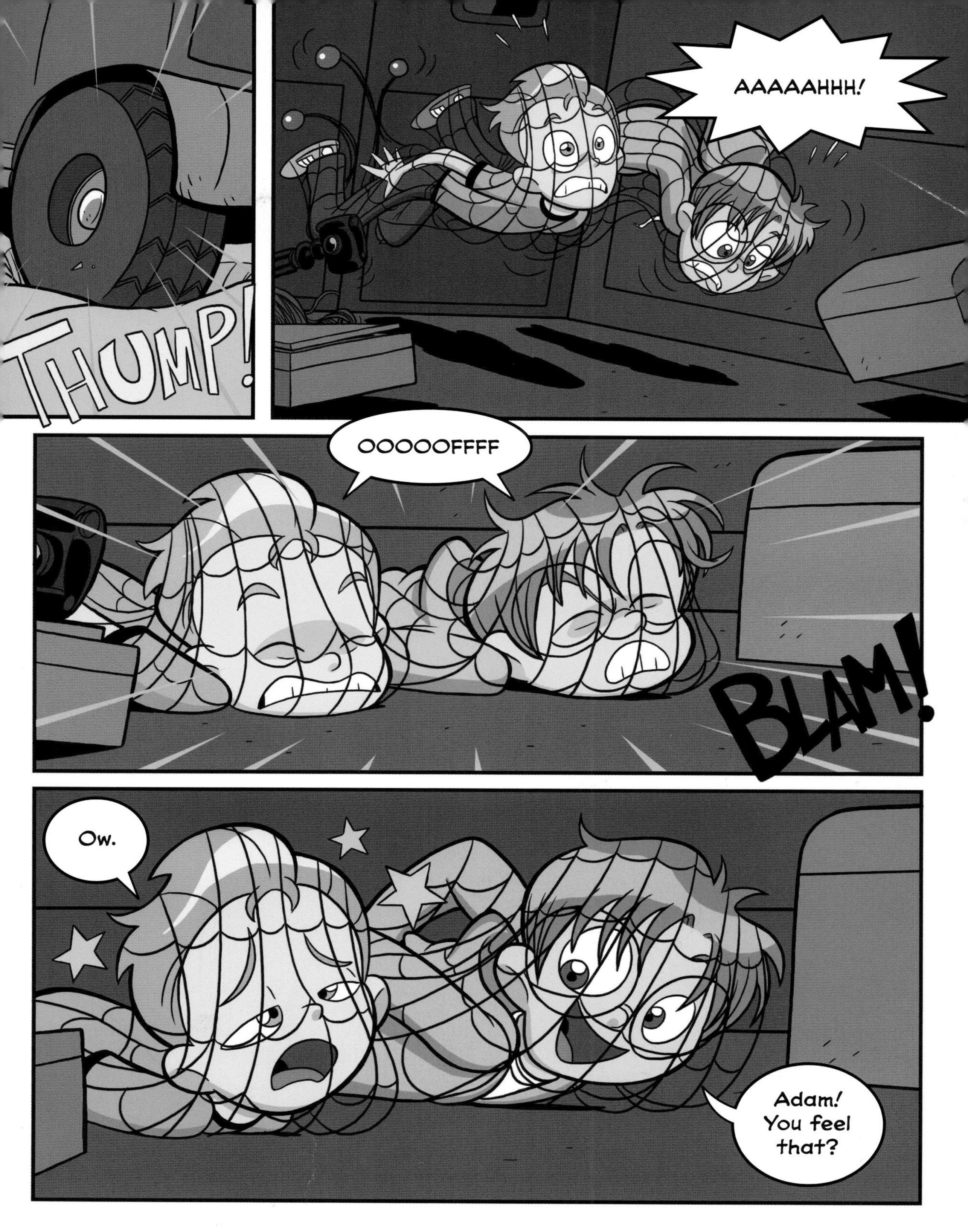
THUMP!
AAAAAHHH!
OOOOOFFFF
BLAM!
Ow.
Adam! You feel that?

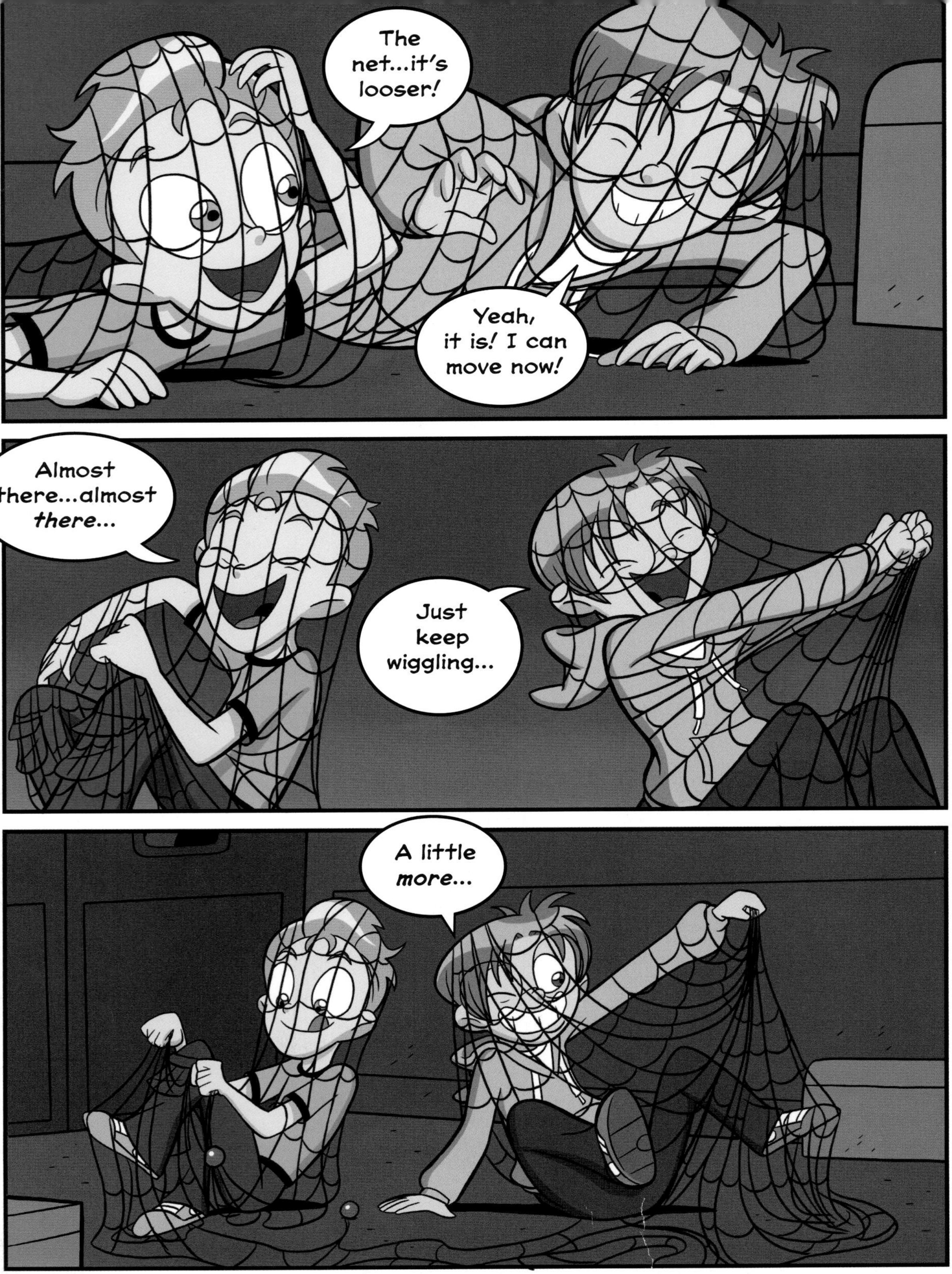
The net...it's looser!
Yeah, it is! I can move now!
Almost there...almost *there*...
Just keep wiggling...
A little *more*...

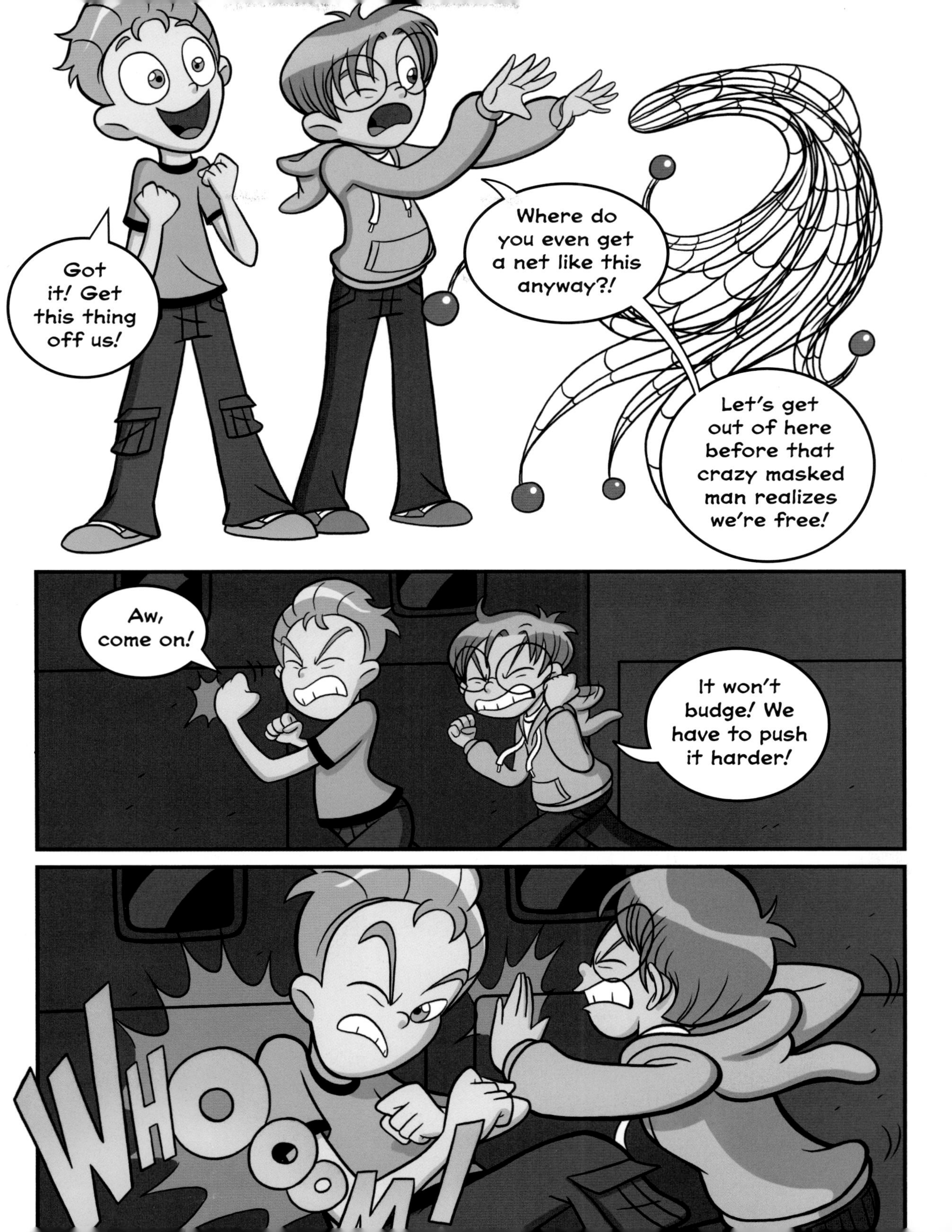
Got it! Get this thing off us!
Where do you even get a net like this anyway?!
Let's get out of here before that crazy masked man realizes we're free!
Aw, come on!
It won't budge! We have to push it harder!
WHOOOOM!

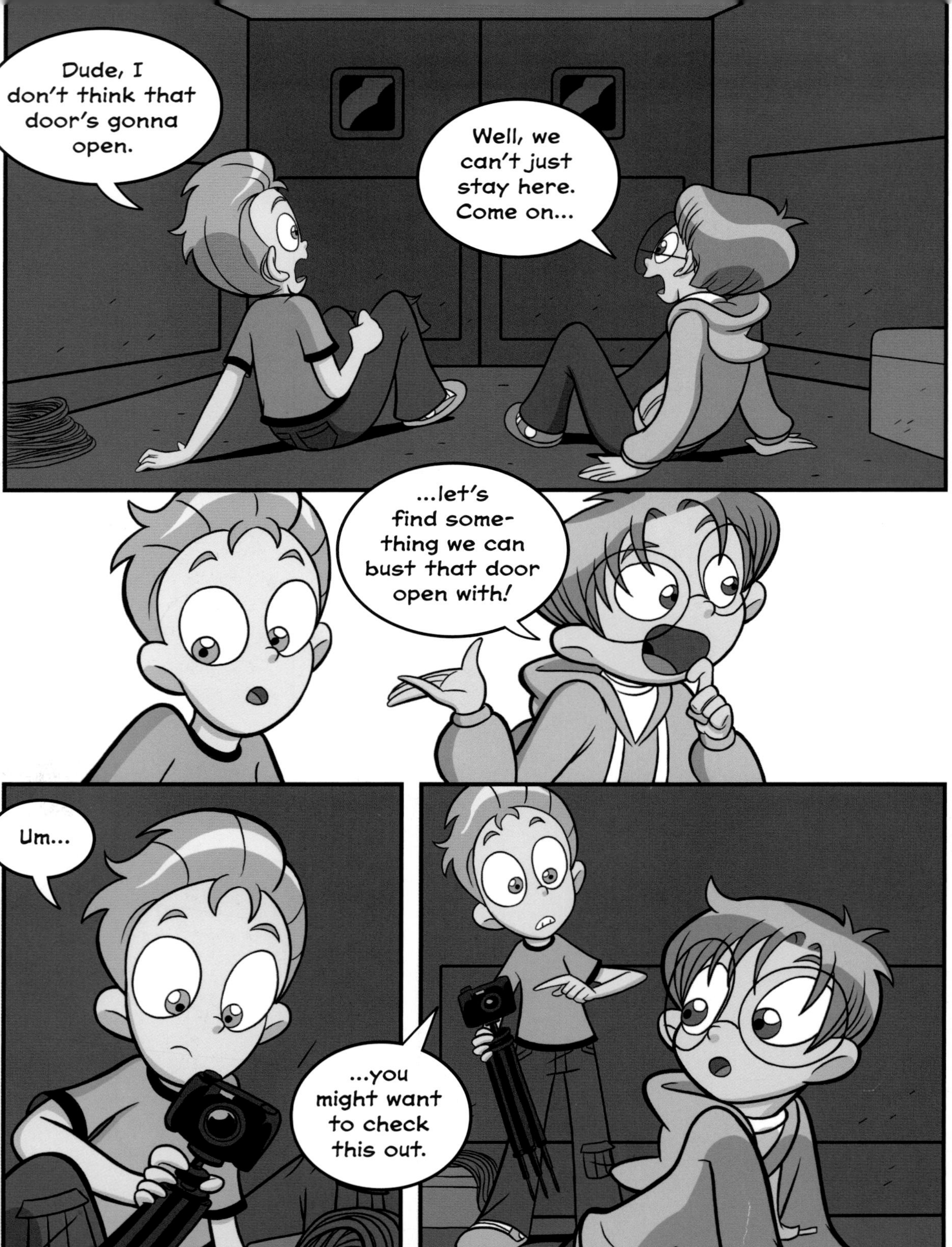
Dude, I don't think that door's gonna open.
Well, we can't just stay here. Come on...
...let's find some-thing we can bust that door open with!
Um...
...you might want to check this out.

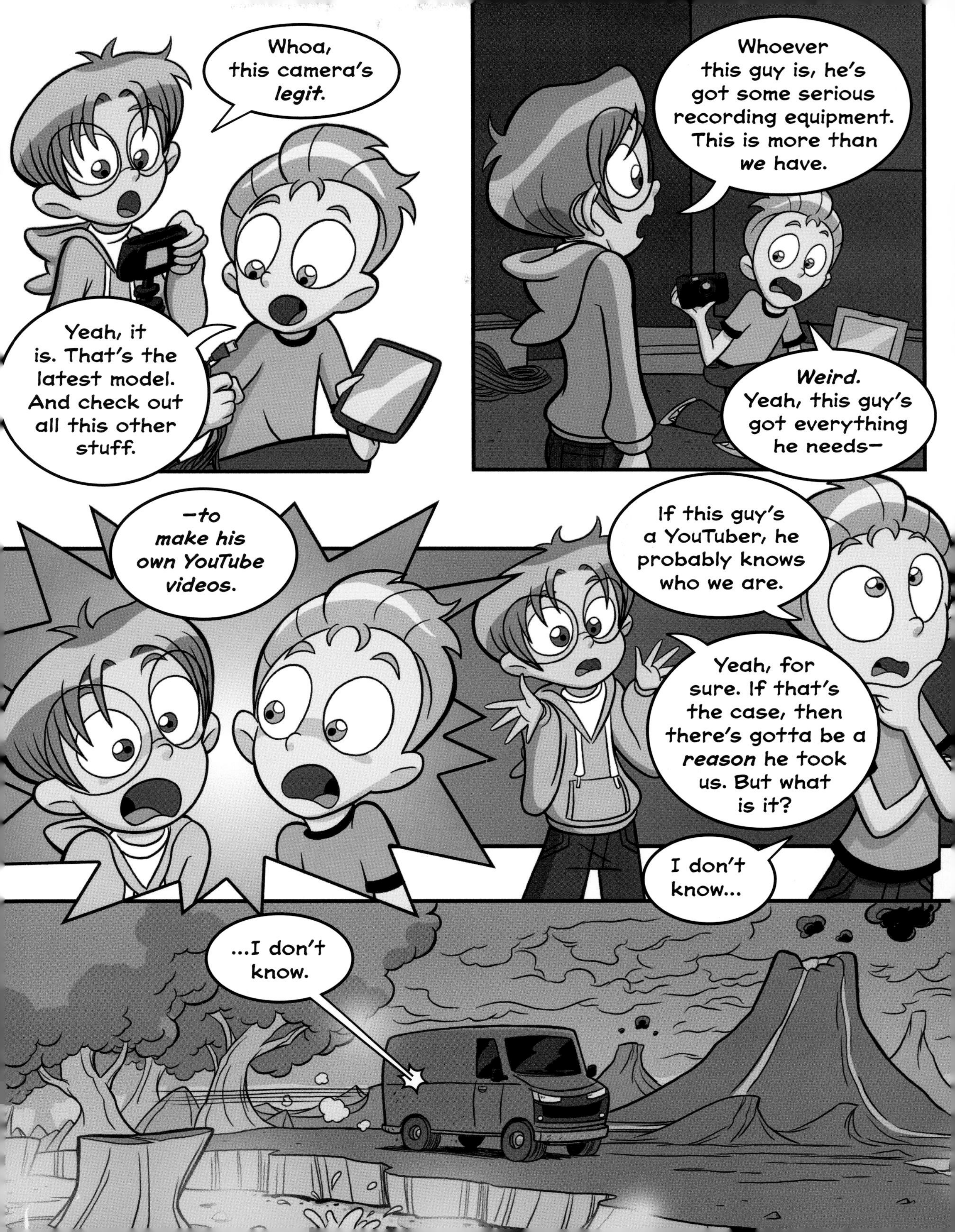
Whoa, this camera's *legit*.
Yeah, it is. That's the latest model. And check out all this other stuff.
Whoever this guy is, he's got some serious recording equipment. This is more than *we* have.
Weird. Yeah, this guy's got everything he needs—
—to *make his own YouTube videos.*
If this guy's a YouTuber, he probably knows who we are.
Yeah, for sure. If that's the case, then there's gotta be a *reason* he took us. But what is it?
I don't know...
...I don't know.

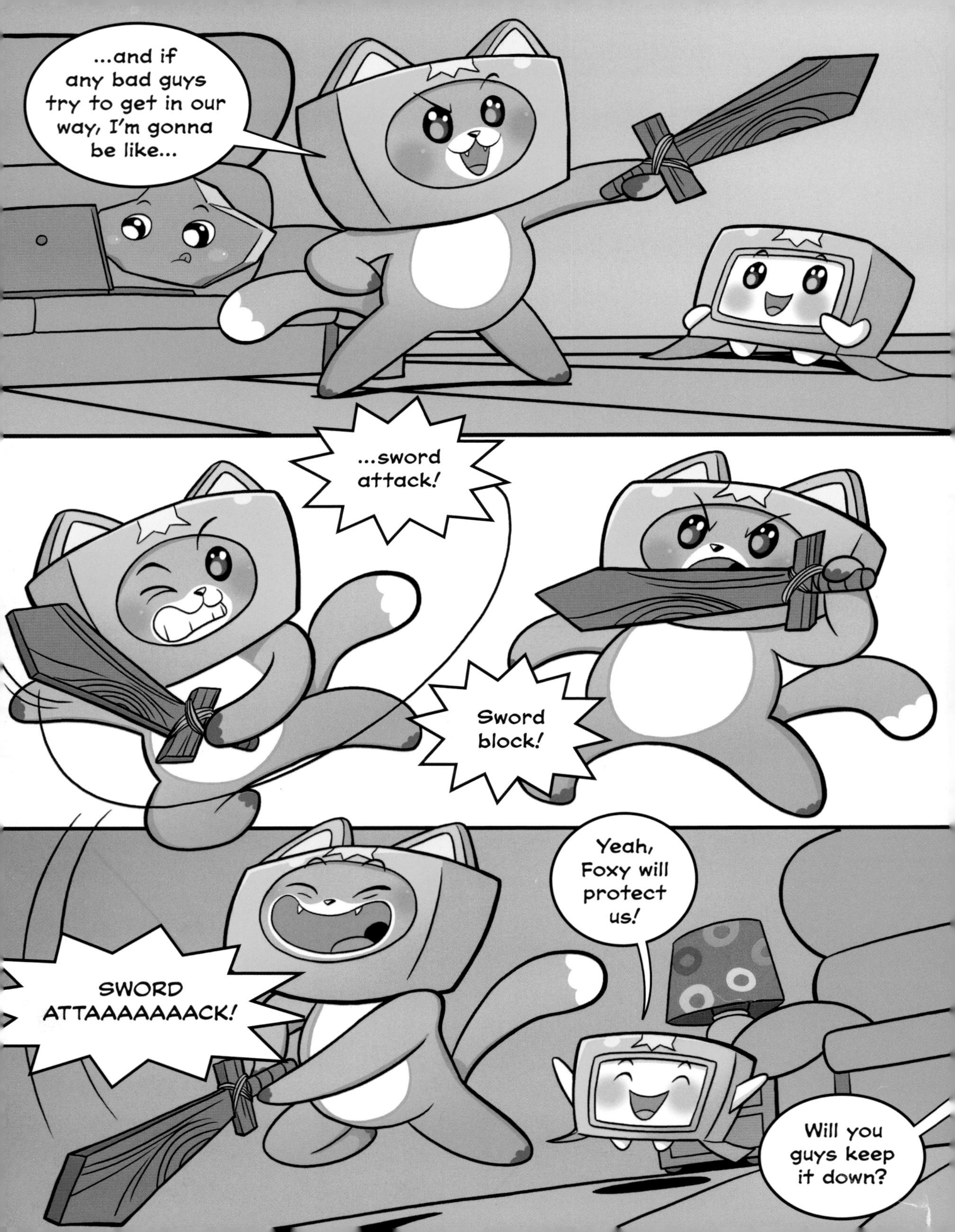
...and if any bad guys try to get in our way, I'm gonna be like...
...sword attack!
Sword block!
SWORD ATTAAAAAAACK!
Yeah, Foxy will protect us!
Will you guys keep it down?

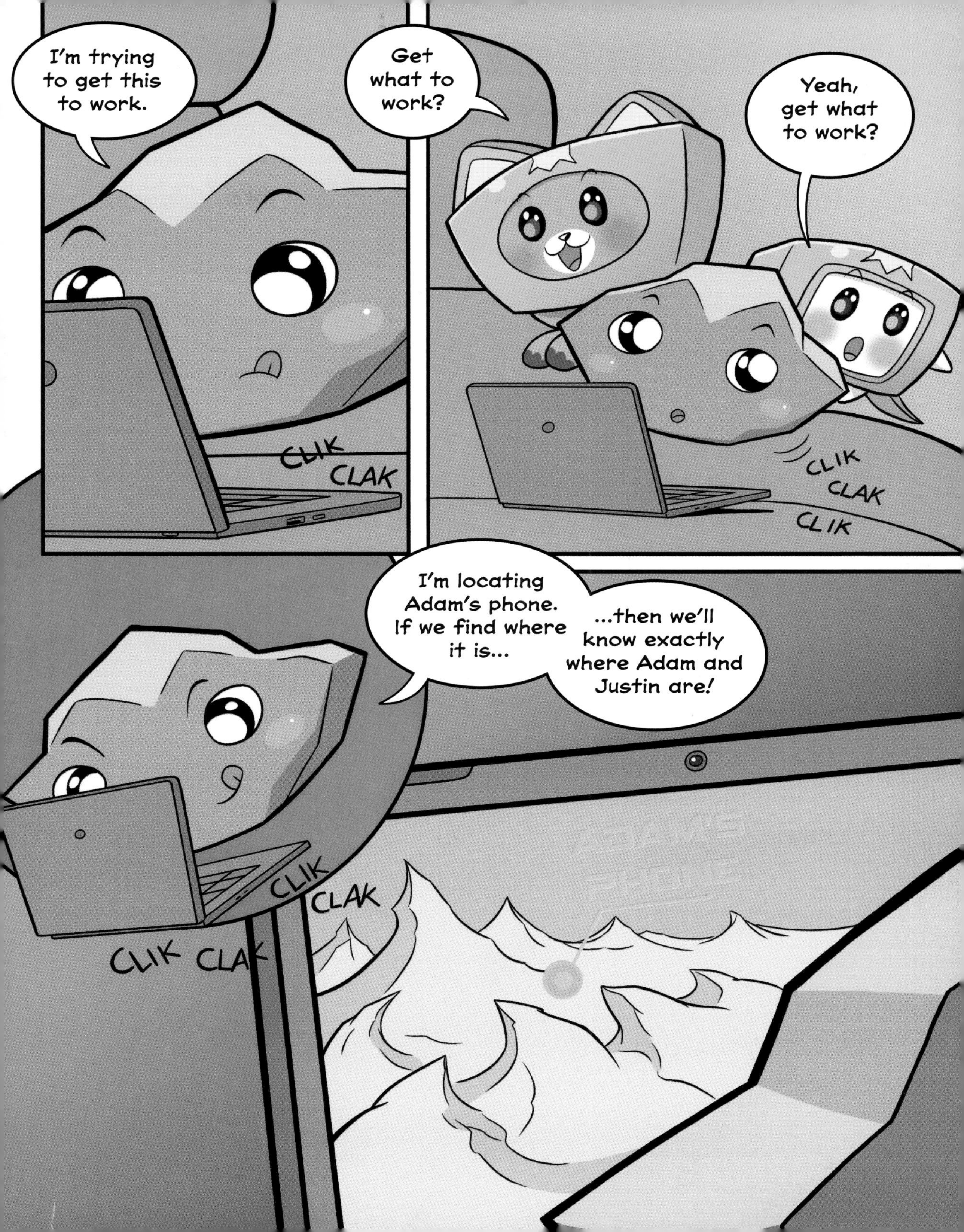
I'm trying to get this to work.
CLIK
CLAK
Get what to work?
Yeah, get what to work?
CLIK
CLAK
CLIK
I'm locating Adam's phone. If we find where it is...
...then we'll know exactly where Adam and Justin are!
CLIK
CLAK
CLIK CLAK
ADAM'S PHONE

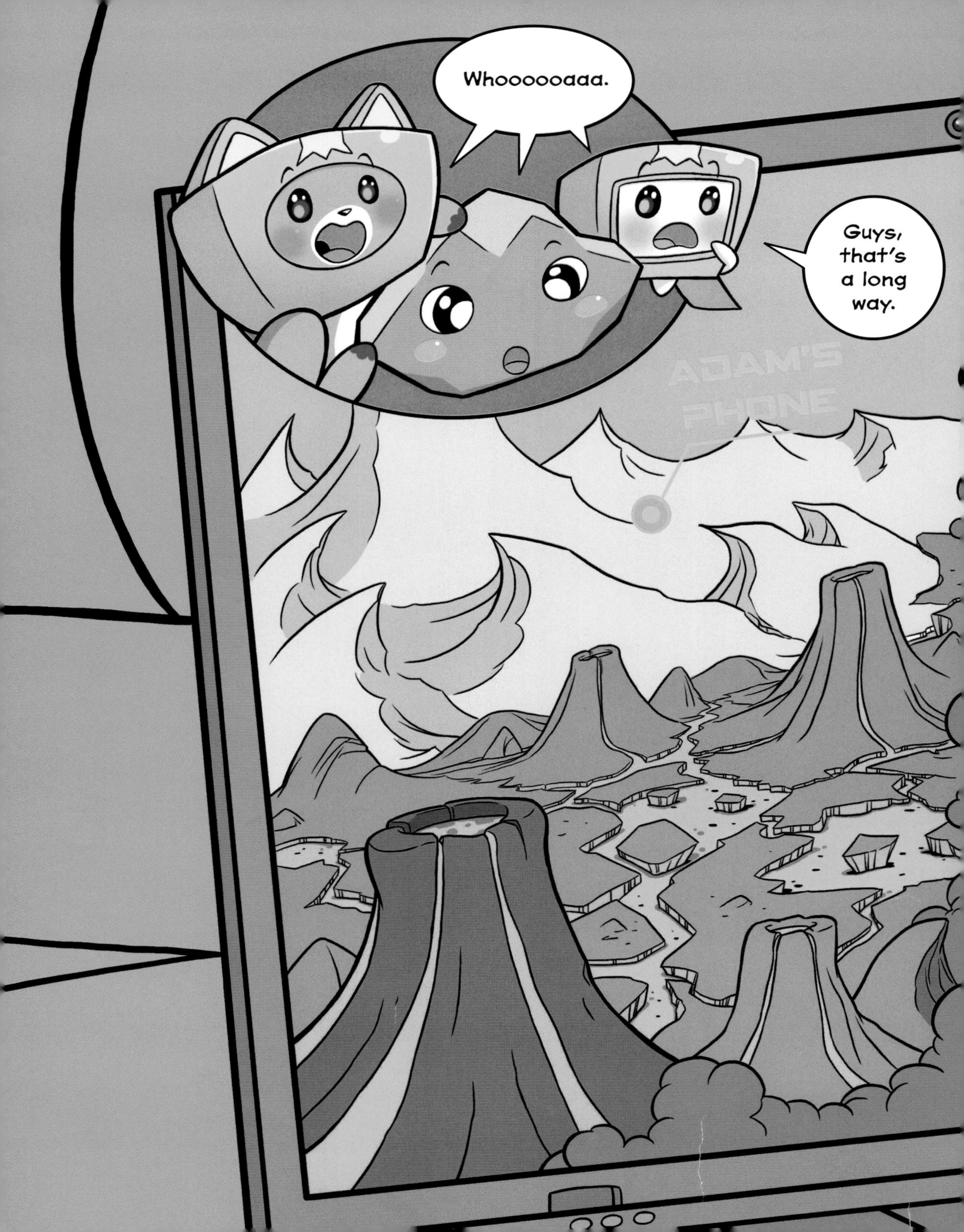
Whoooooaaa.
Guys, that's a long way.
ADAM'S PHONE

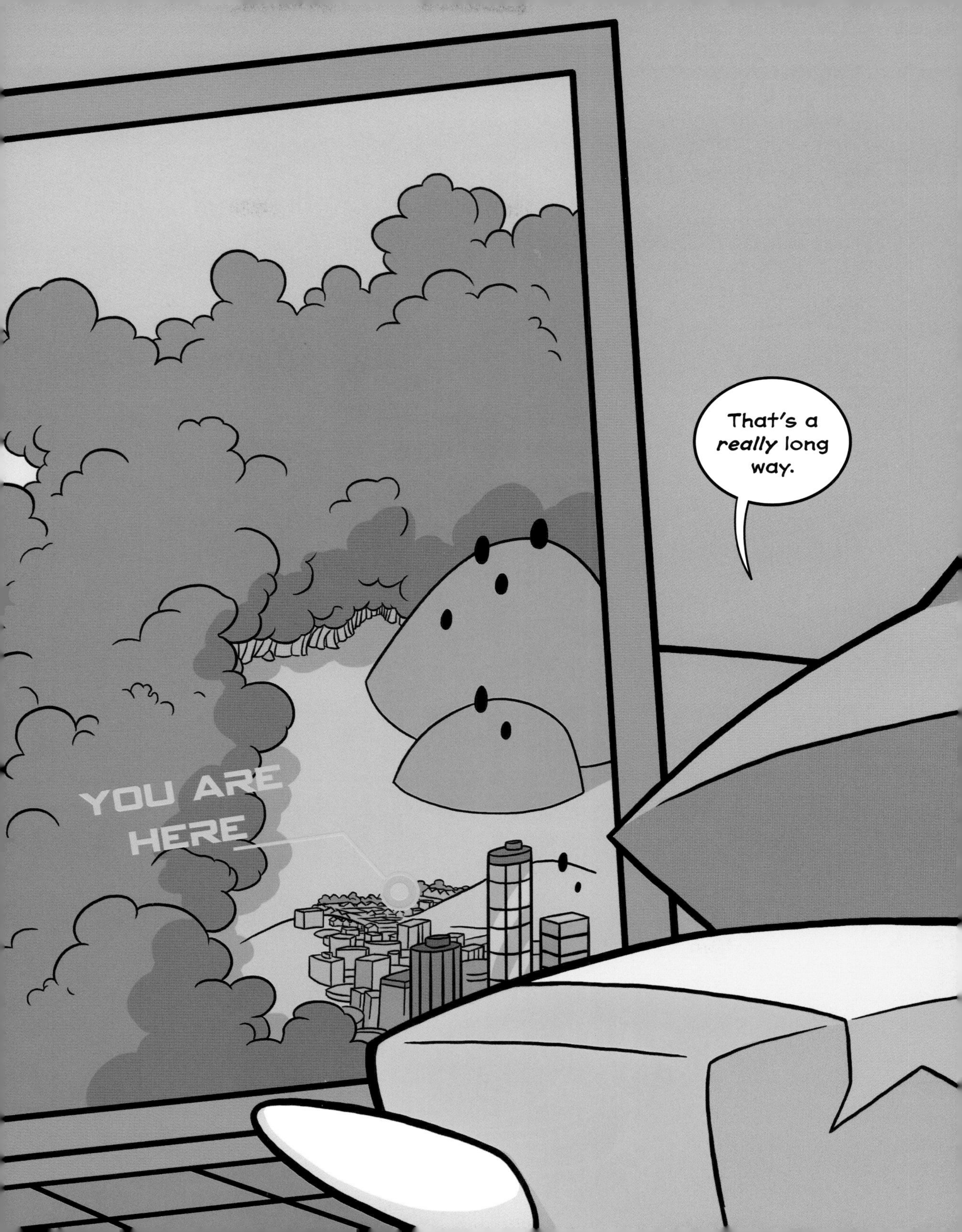
YOU ARE HERE
That's a *really* long way.

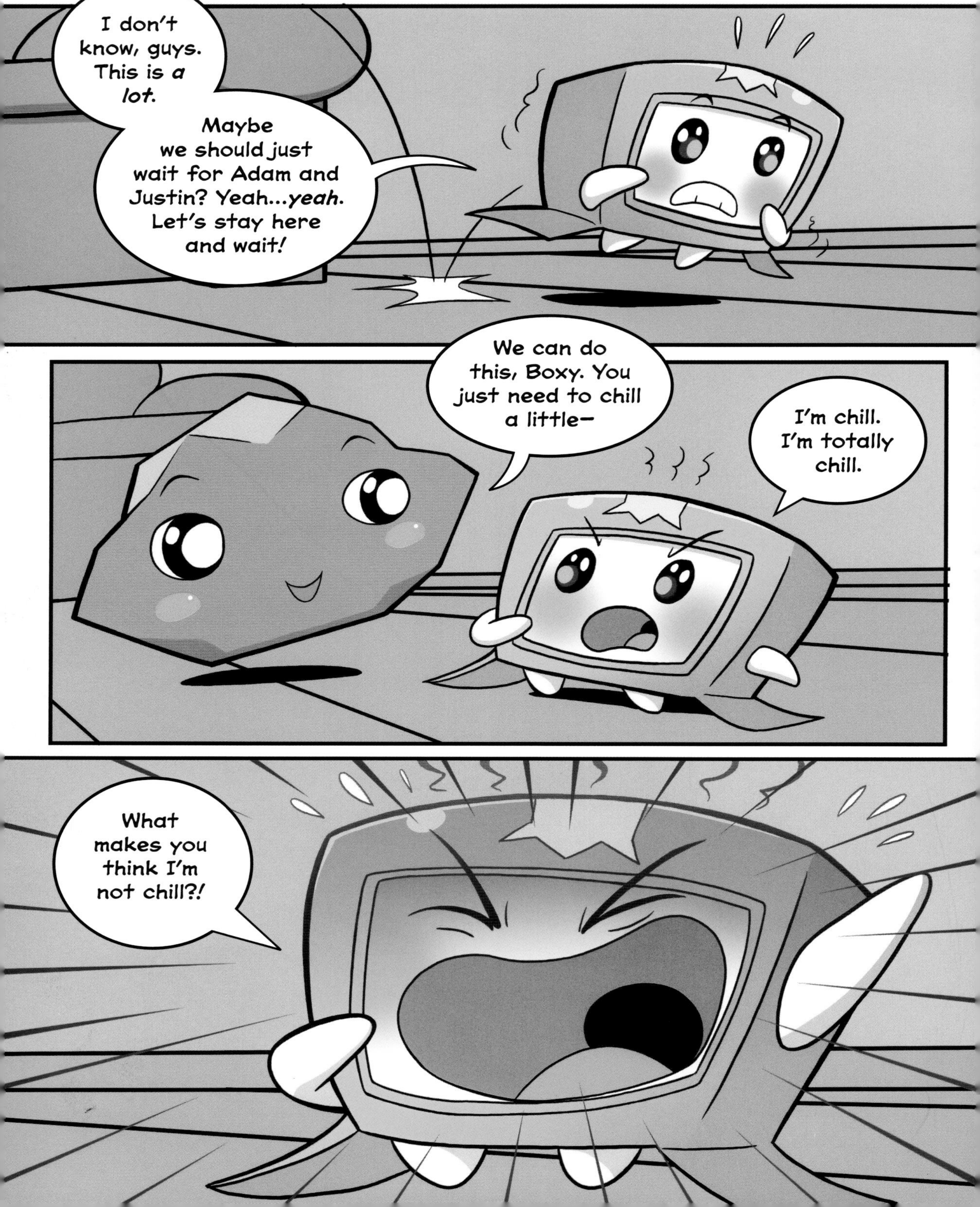
I don't know, guys. This is *a* *lot*.
Maybe we should just wait for Adam and Justin? Yeah...*yeah*. Let's stay here and wait!
We can do this, Boxy. You just need to chill a little—
I'm chill. I'm totally chill.
What makes you think I'm not chill?!

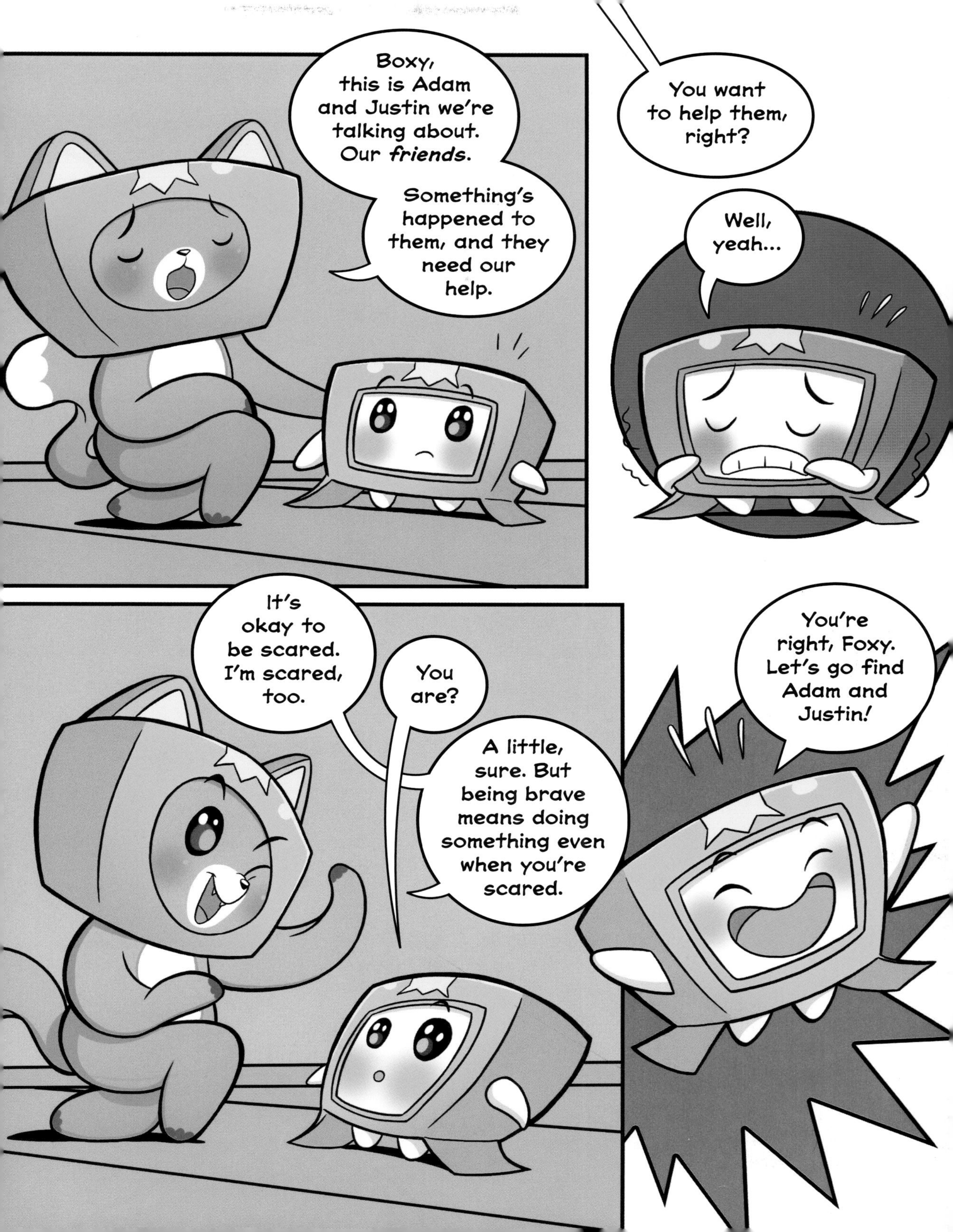
Boxy, this is Adam and Justin we're talking about. Our *friends*.
Something's happened to them, and they need our help.
You want to help them, right?
Well, yeah...
It's okay to be scared. I'm scared, too.
You are?
A little, sure. But being brave means doing something even when you're scared.
You're right, Foxy. Let's go find Adam and Justin!

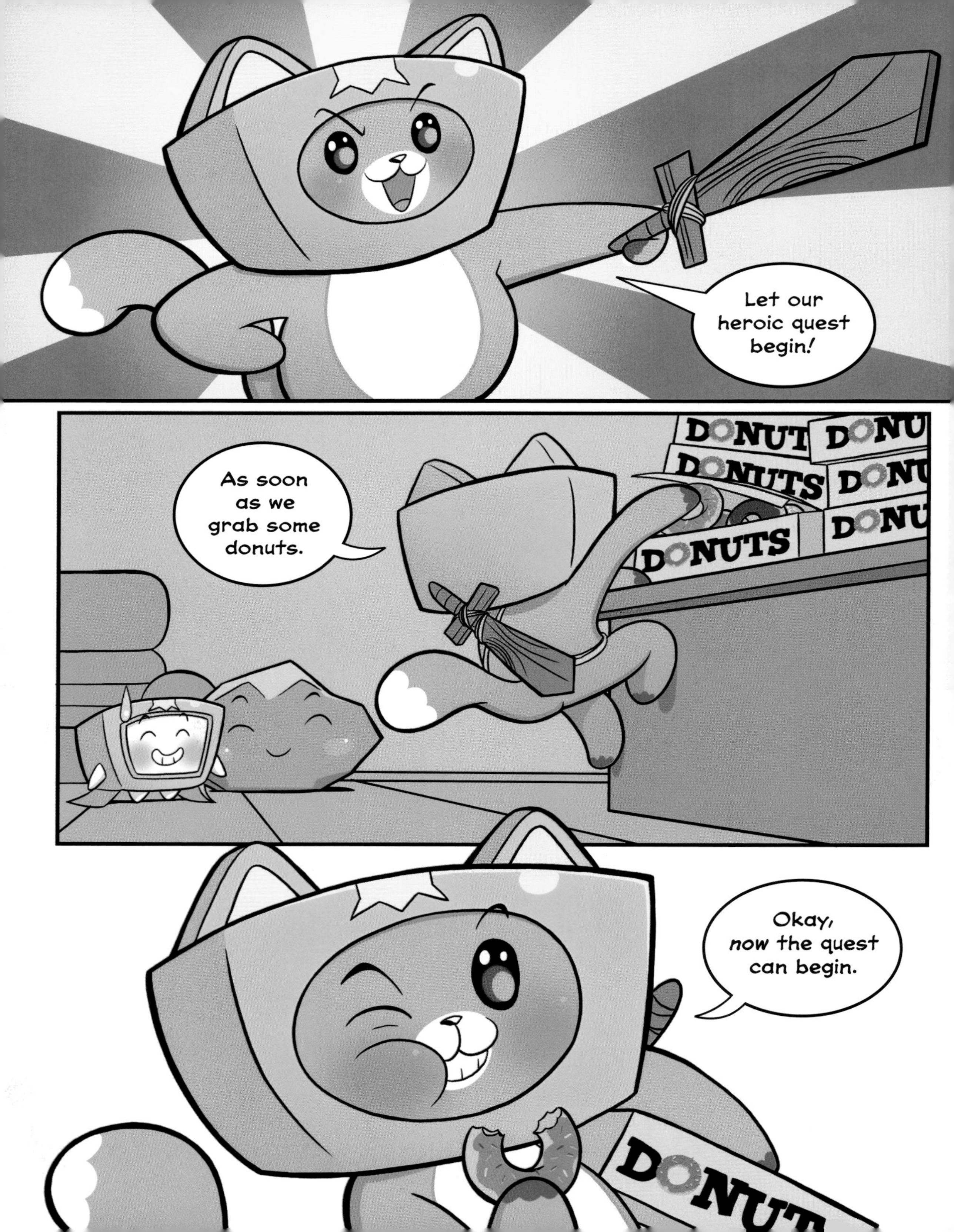
Let our heroic quest begin!
As soon as we grab some donuts.
DONUT
DONUTS
Okay, *now* the quest can begin.

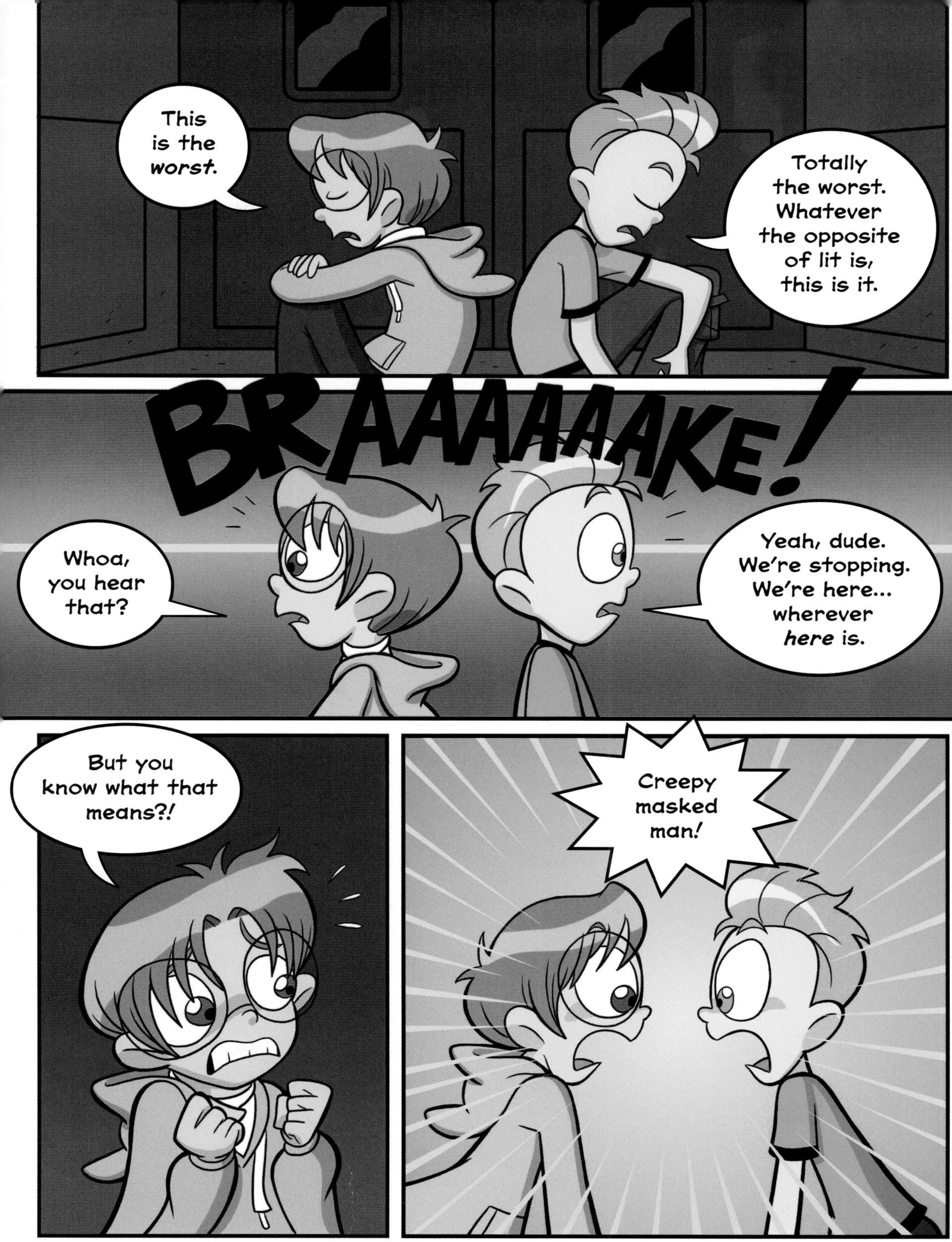
This is the *worst.*
Totally the worst. Whatever the opposite of lit is, this is it.
BRAAAAAAKE!
Whoa, you hear that?
Yeah, dude. We're stopping. We're here... wherever *here* is.
But you know what that means?!
Creepy masked man!

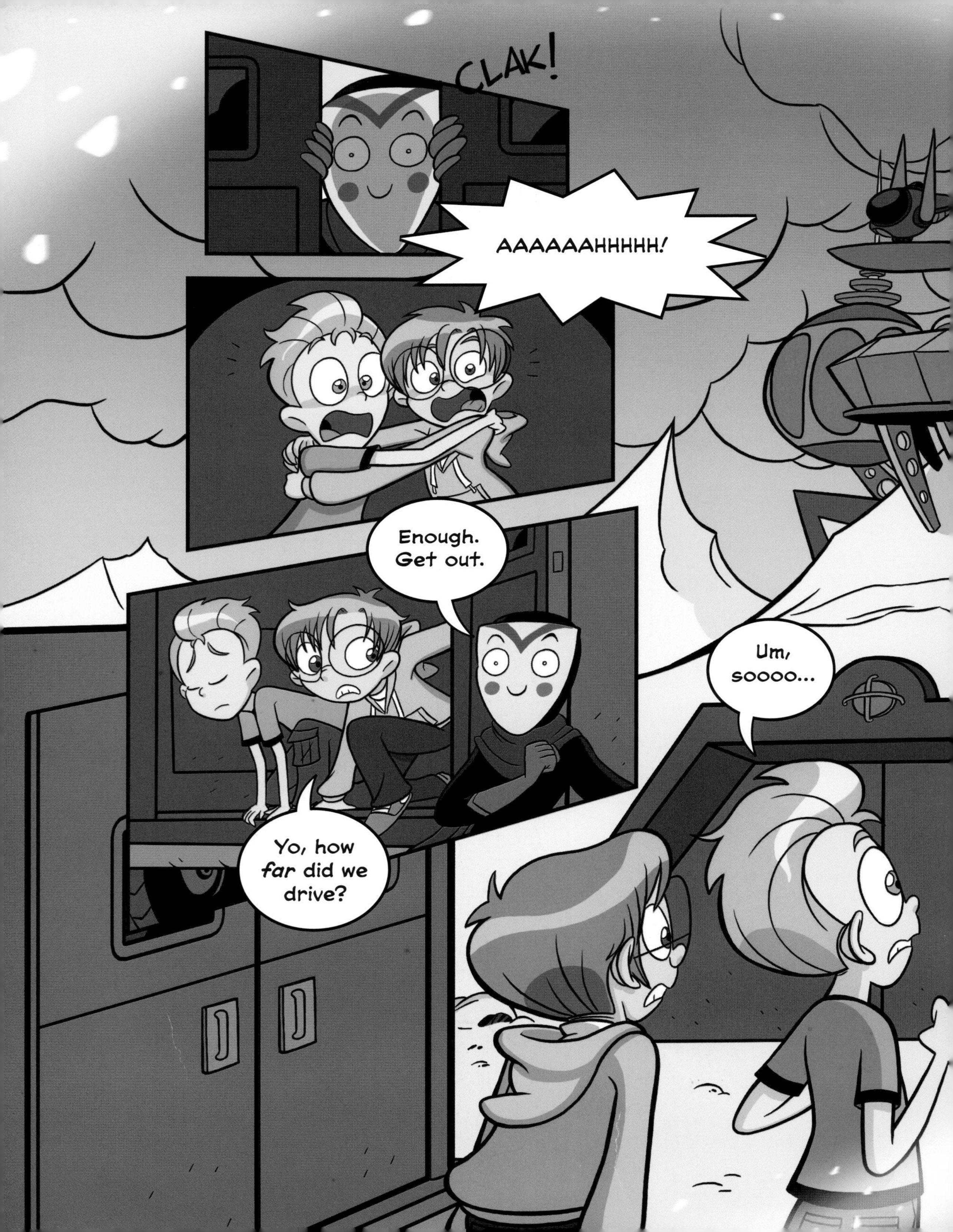
CLAK!
AAAAAAHHHHH!
Enough. Get out.
Yo, how *far* did we drive?
Um, soooo...

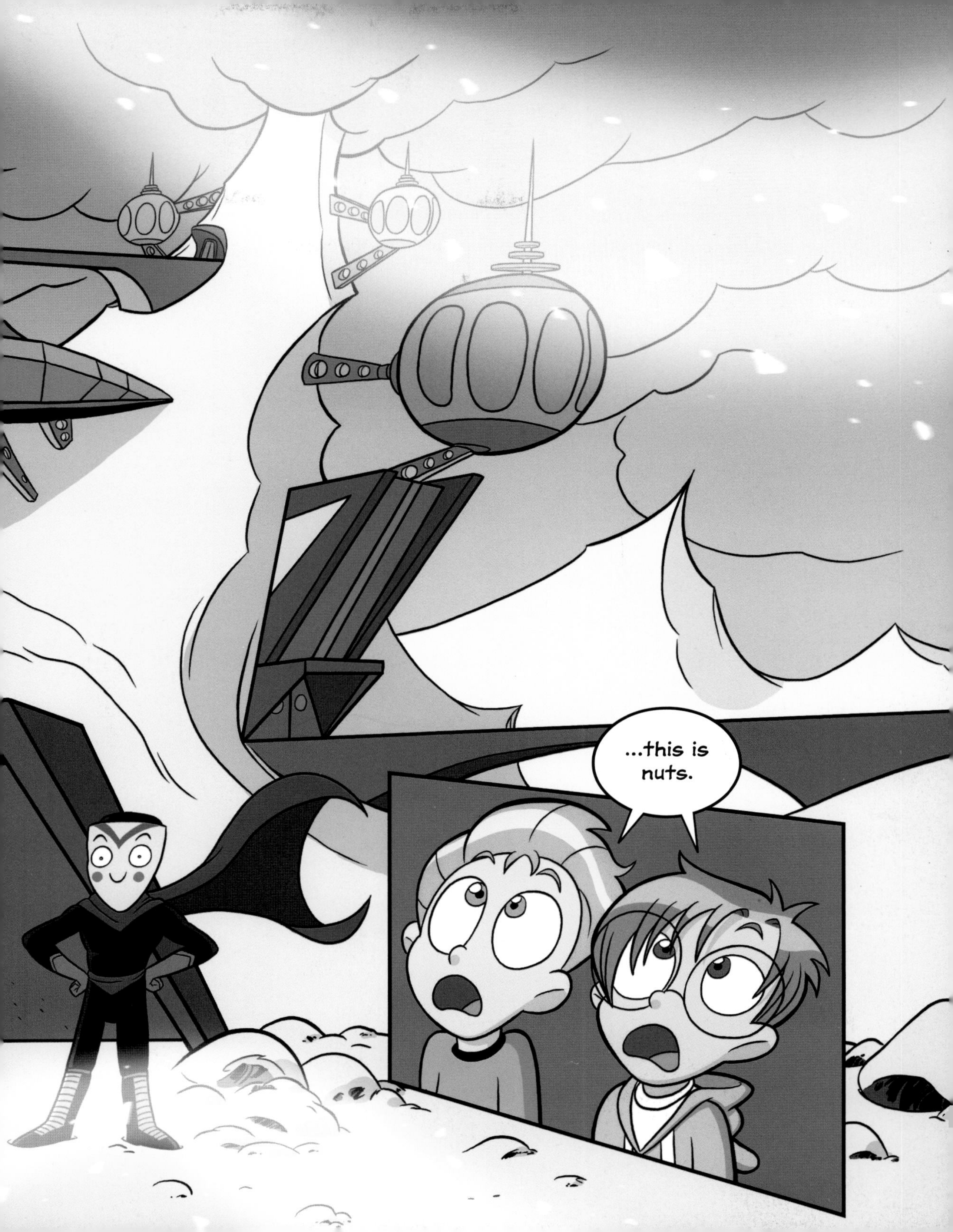
...this is
nuts.

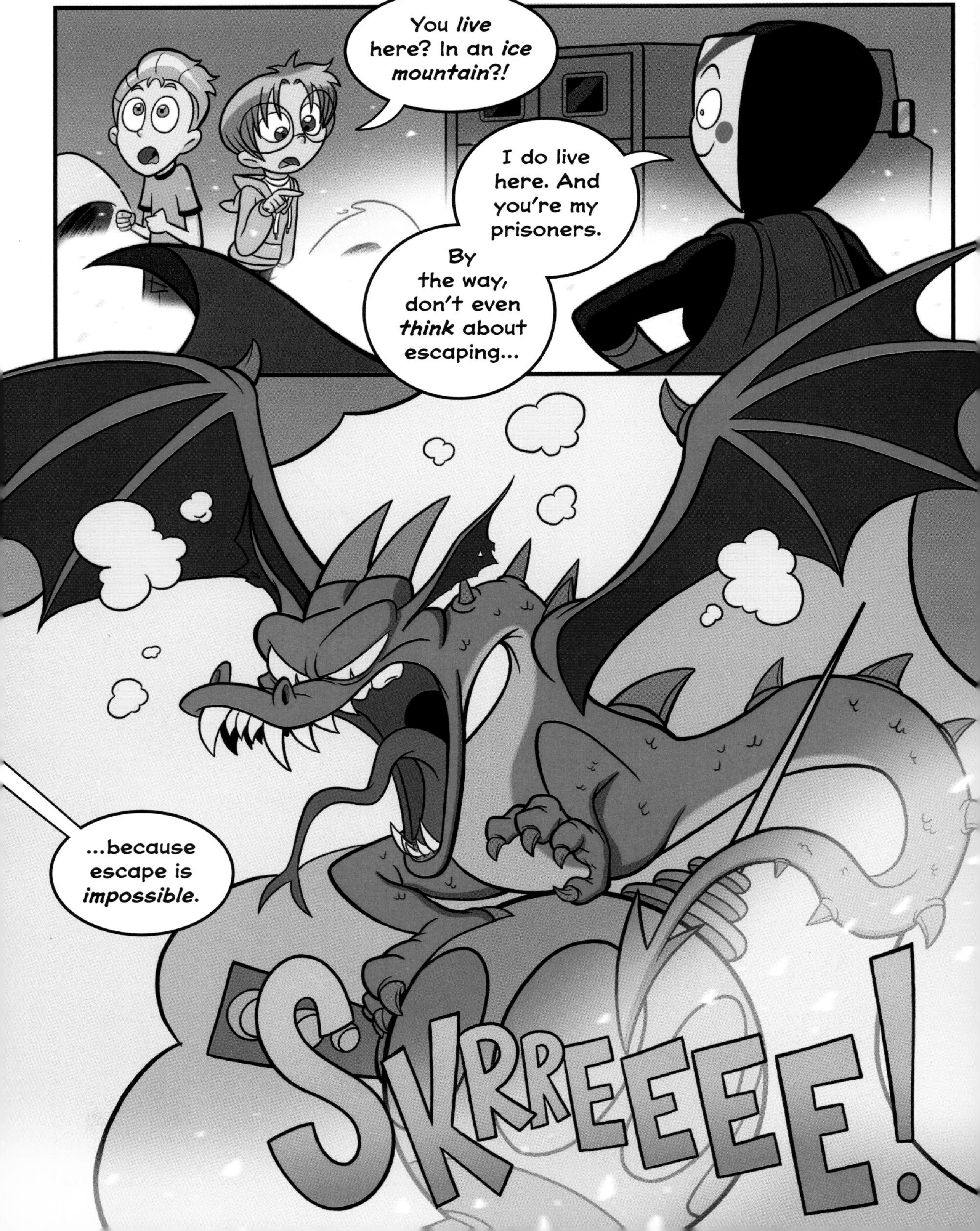
You *live* here? In an *ice mountain*?!
I do live here. And you're my prisoners.
By the way, don't even *think* about escaping...
...because escape is *impossible*.
SKRREEEEE!

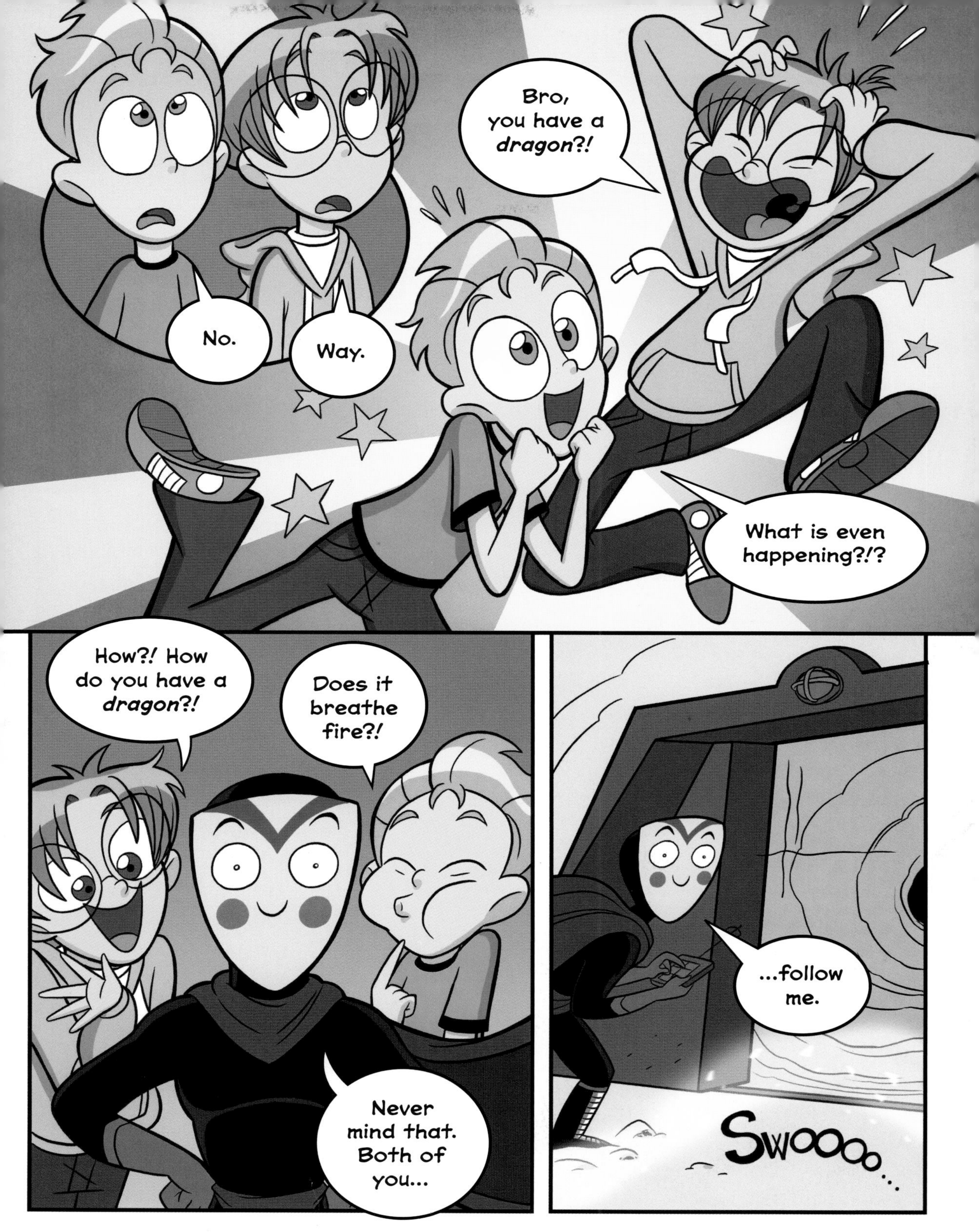
No.
Way.
Bro, you have a *dragon*?!
What is even happening?!?
How?! How do you have a *dragon*?!
Does it breathe fire?!
Never mind that. Both of you...
...follow me.
SWOOOOO...

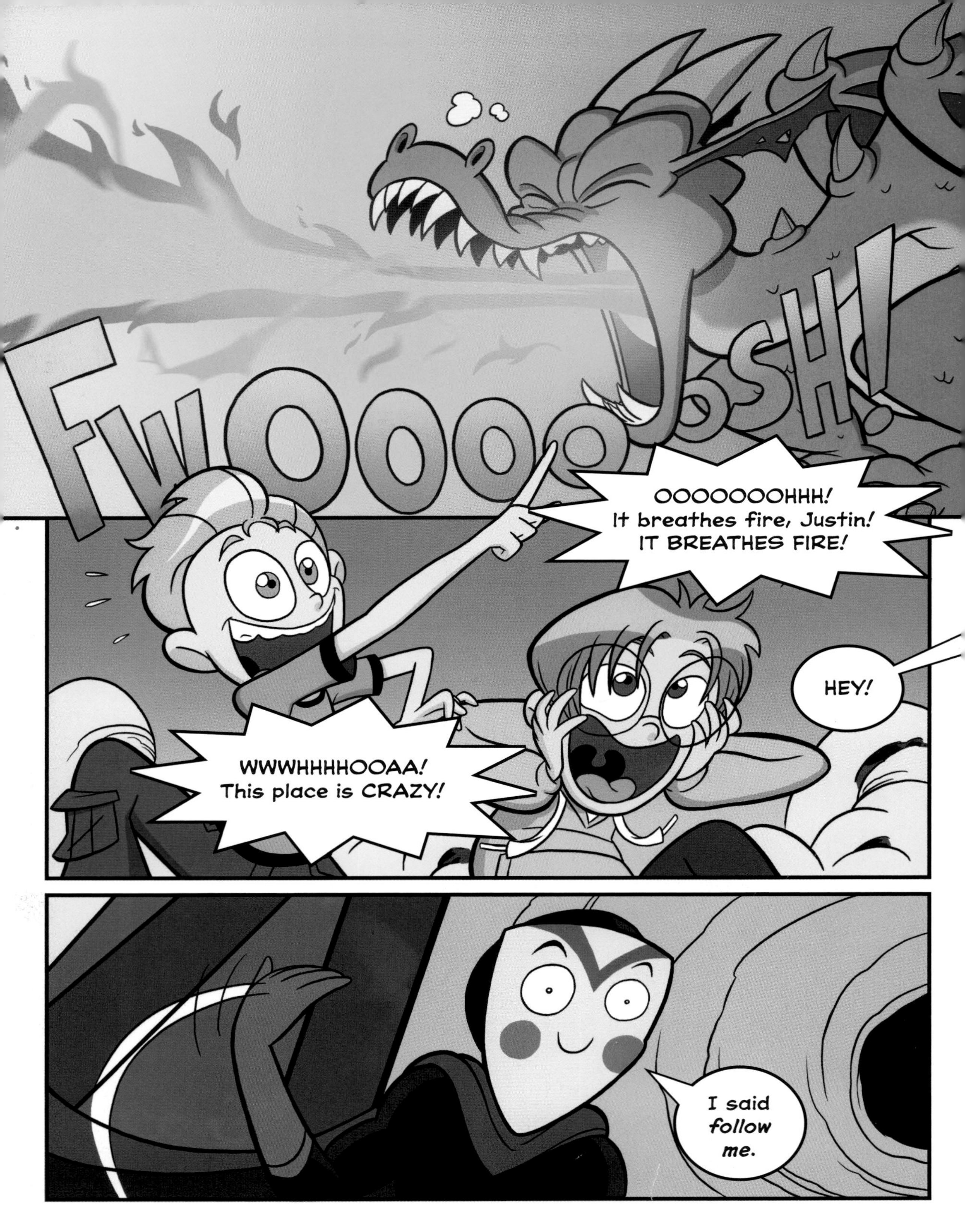
FWOOOOOOSH!
OOOOOOOOHHH! It breathes fire, Justin! IT BREATHES FIRE!
HEY!
WWWHHHHOOAA! This place is CRAZY!
I said follow me.

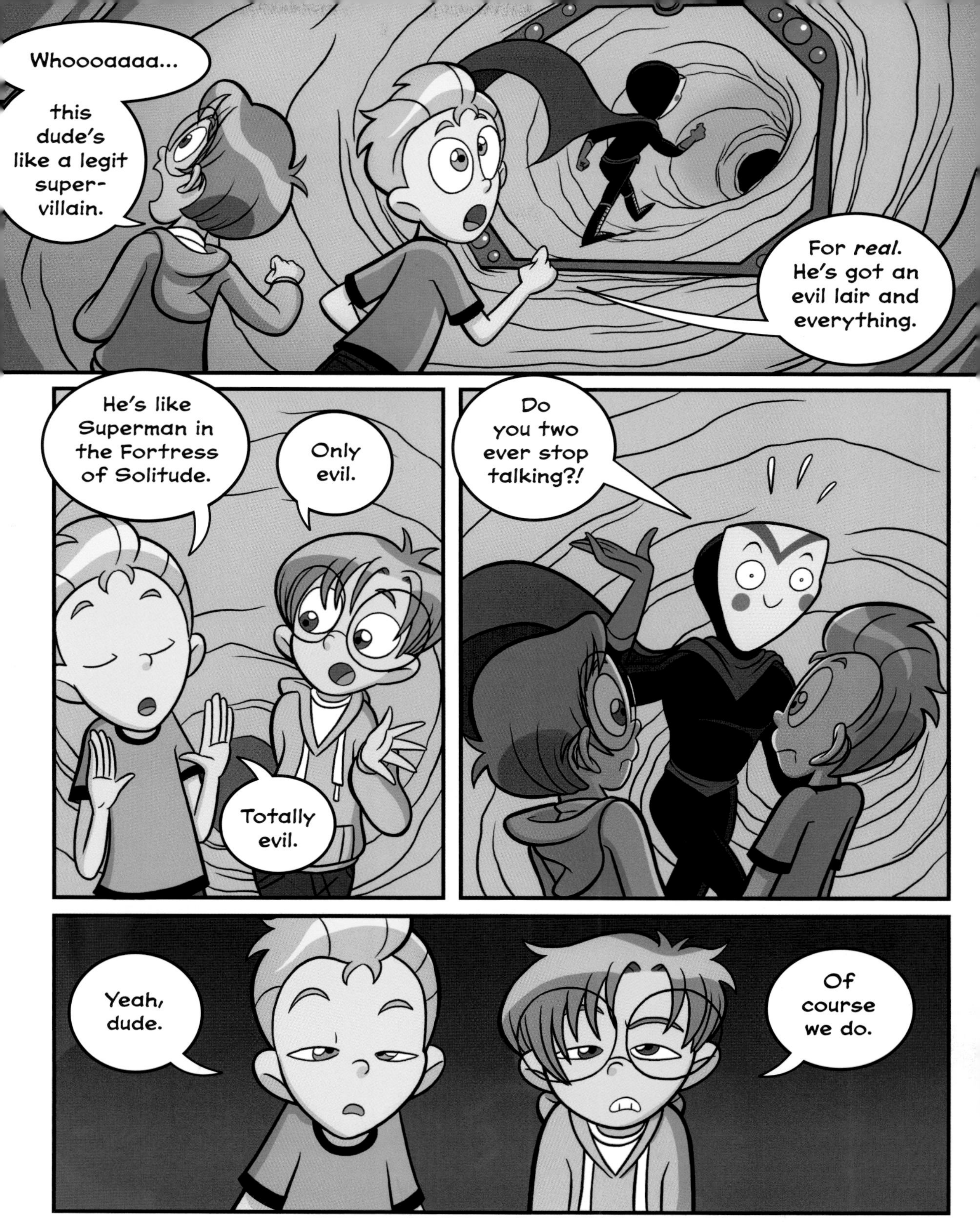
Whooooaaa...
this dude's like a legit super-villain.
For *real*. He's got an evil lair and everything.
He's like Superman in the Fortress of Solitude.
Only evil.
Totally evil.
Do you two ever stop talking?!
Yeah, dude.
Of course we do.

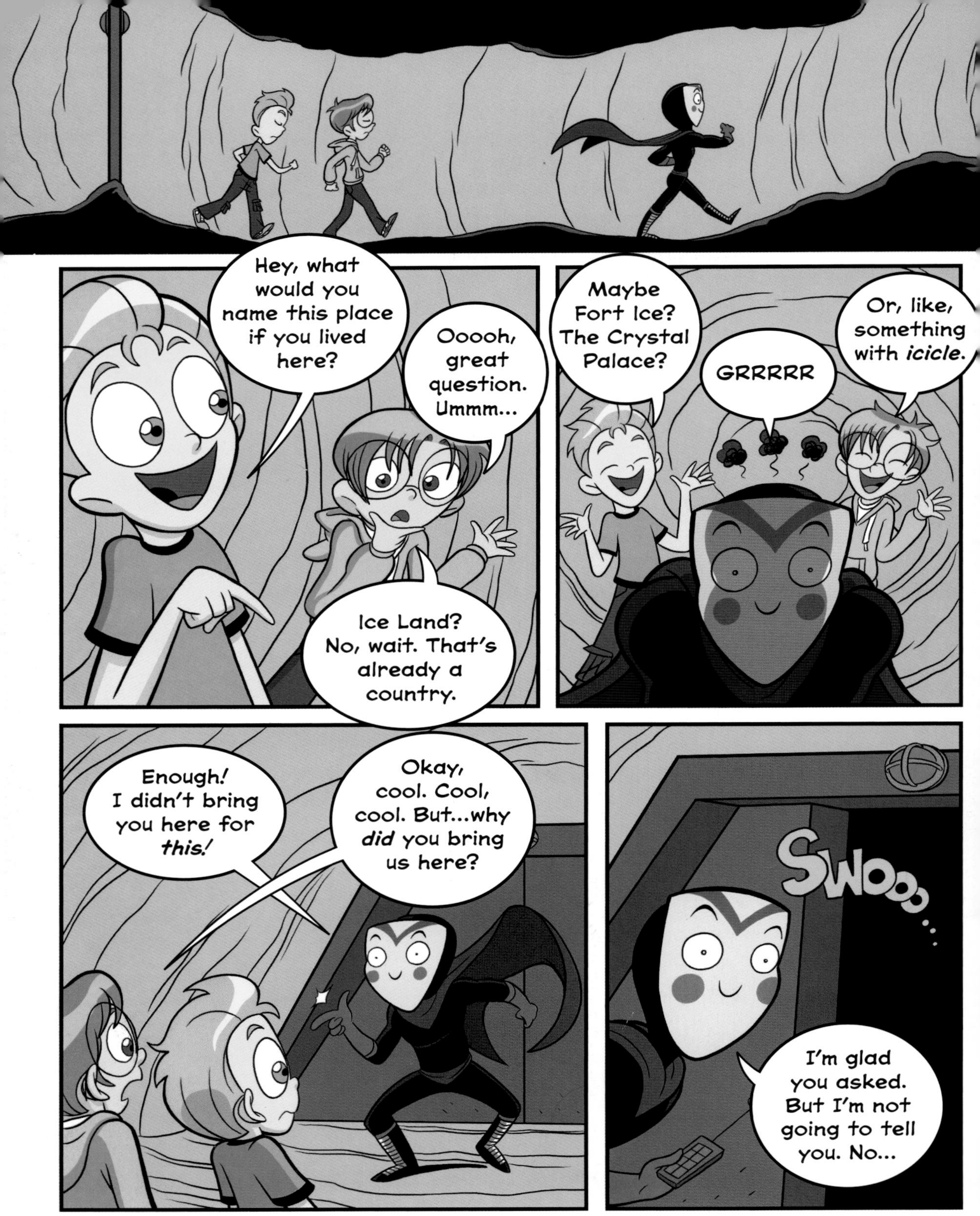
Hey, what would you name this place if you lived here?
Ooooh, great question. Ummm...
Ice Land? No, wait. That's already a country.
Maybe Fort Ice? The Crystal Palace?
GRRRRR
Or, like, something with *icicle*.
Enough! I didn't bring you here for *this!*
Okay, cool. Cool, cool. But...why *did* you bring us here?
SWOOO...
I'm glad you asked. But I'm not going to tell you. No...

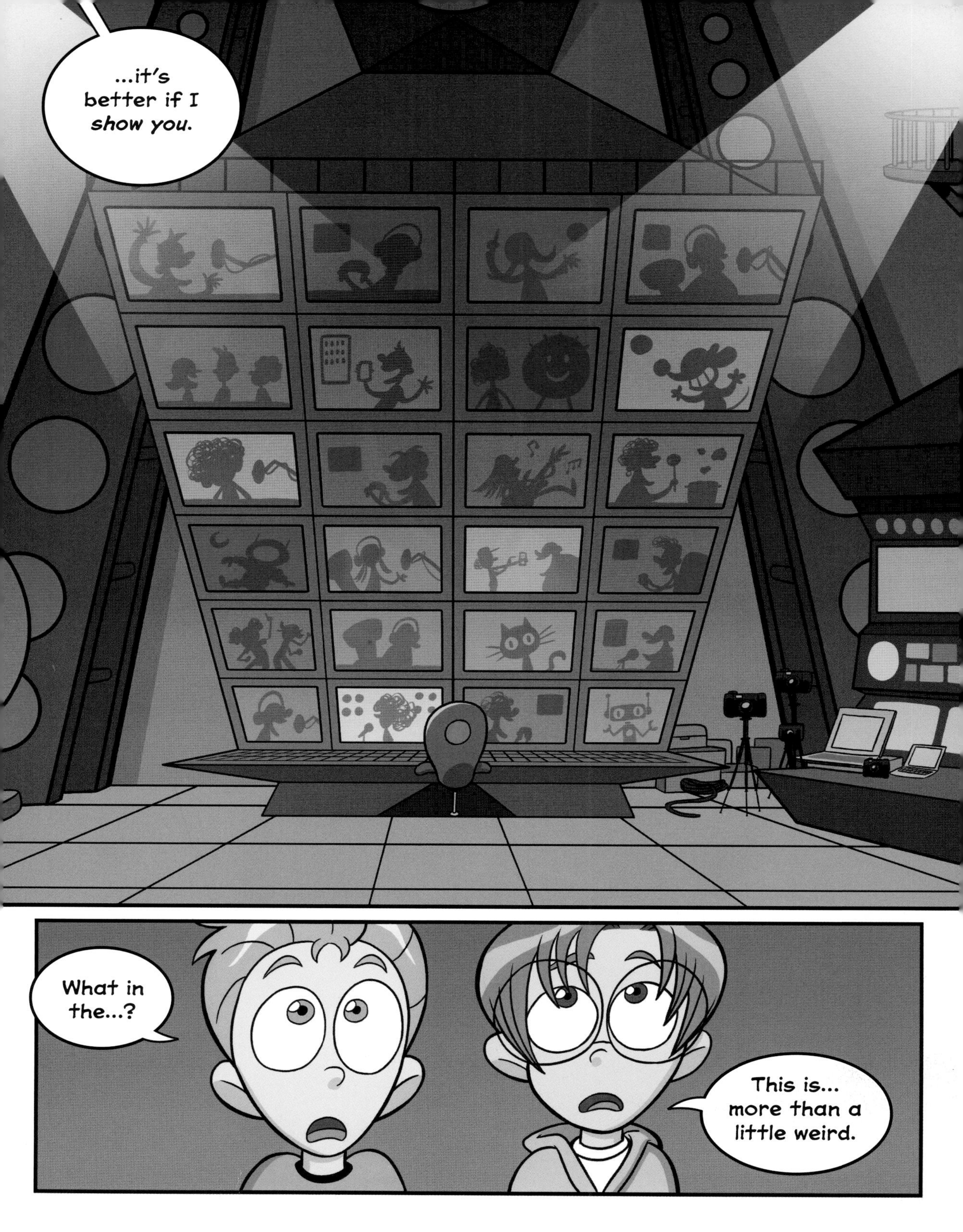
...it's better if I *show you.*
What in the...?
This is... more than a little weird.

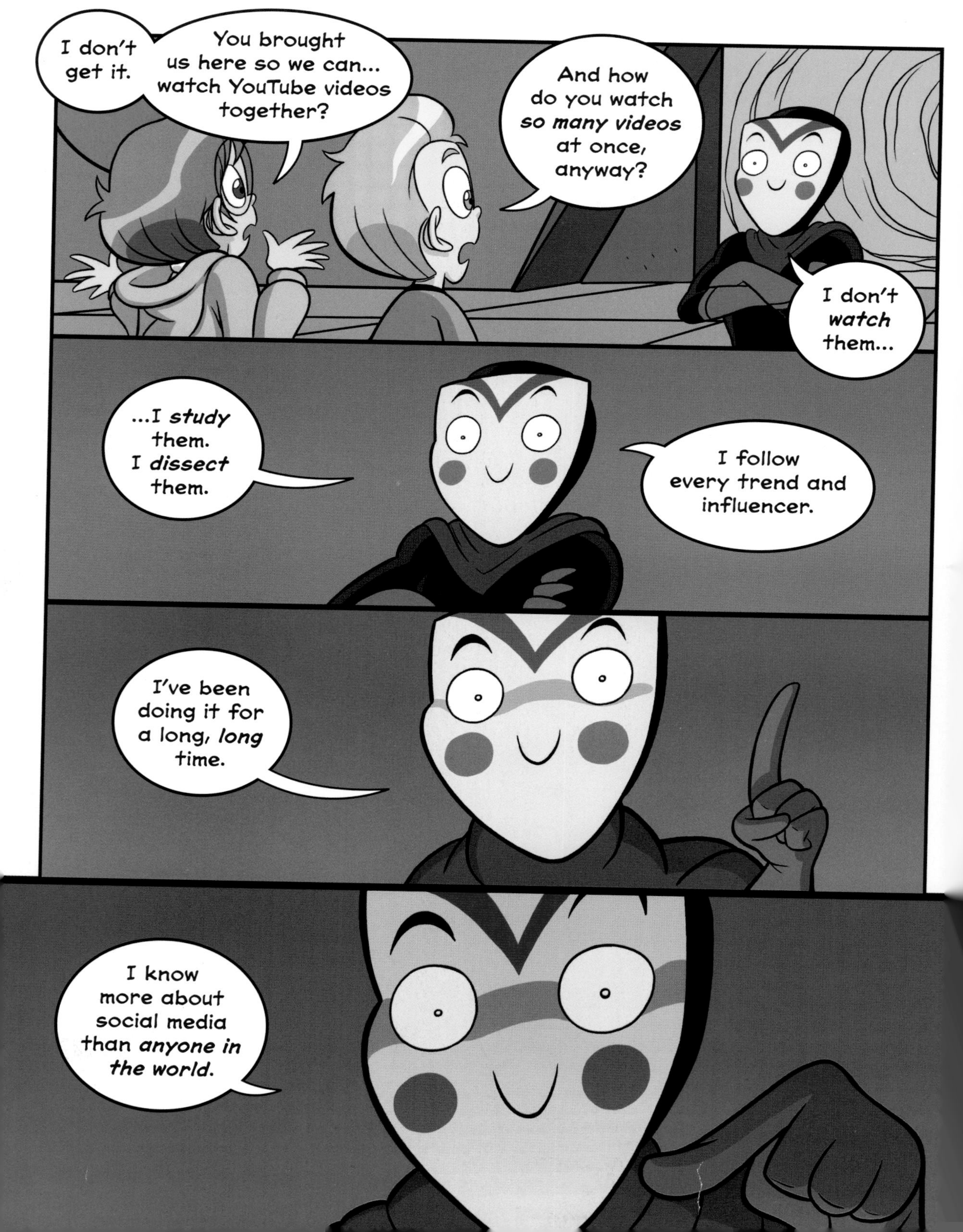
I don't get it.
You brought us here so we can... watch YouTube videos together?
And how do you watch *so many videos* at once, anyway?
I don't *watch* them...
...I *study* them. I *dissect* them.
I follow every trend and influencer.
I've been doing it for a long, *long* time.
I know more about social media than *anyone in the world*.

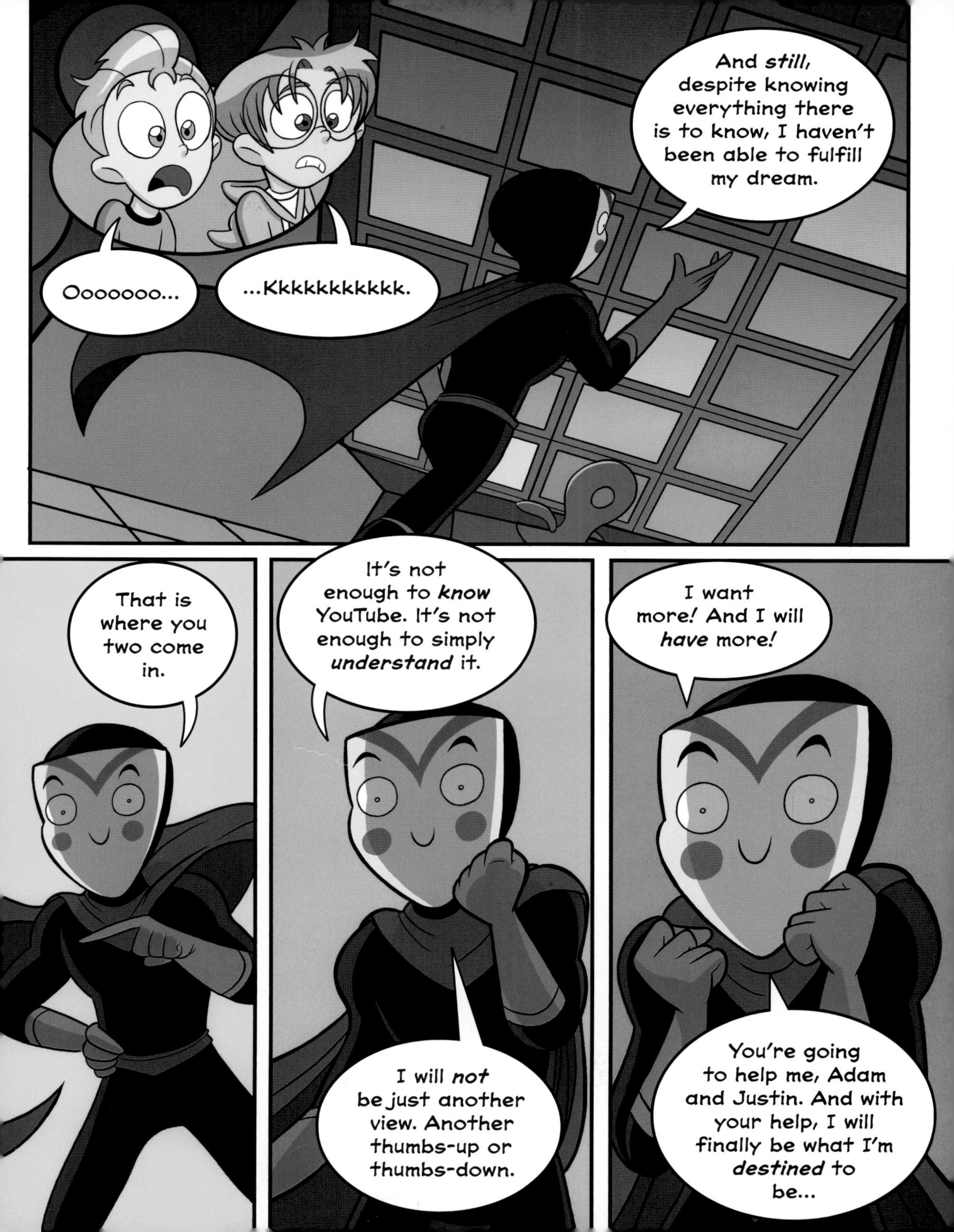
And *still*, despite knowing everything there is to know, I haven't been able to fulfill my dream.
Ooooooo...
...Kkkkkkkkkk.
That is where you two come in.
It's not enough to *know* YouTube. It's not enough to simply *understand* it.
I will *not* be just another view. Another thumbs-up or thumbs-down.
I want more! And I will *have* more!
You're going to help me, Adam and Justin. And with your help, I will finally be what I'm *destined* to be...

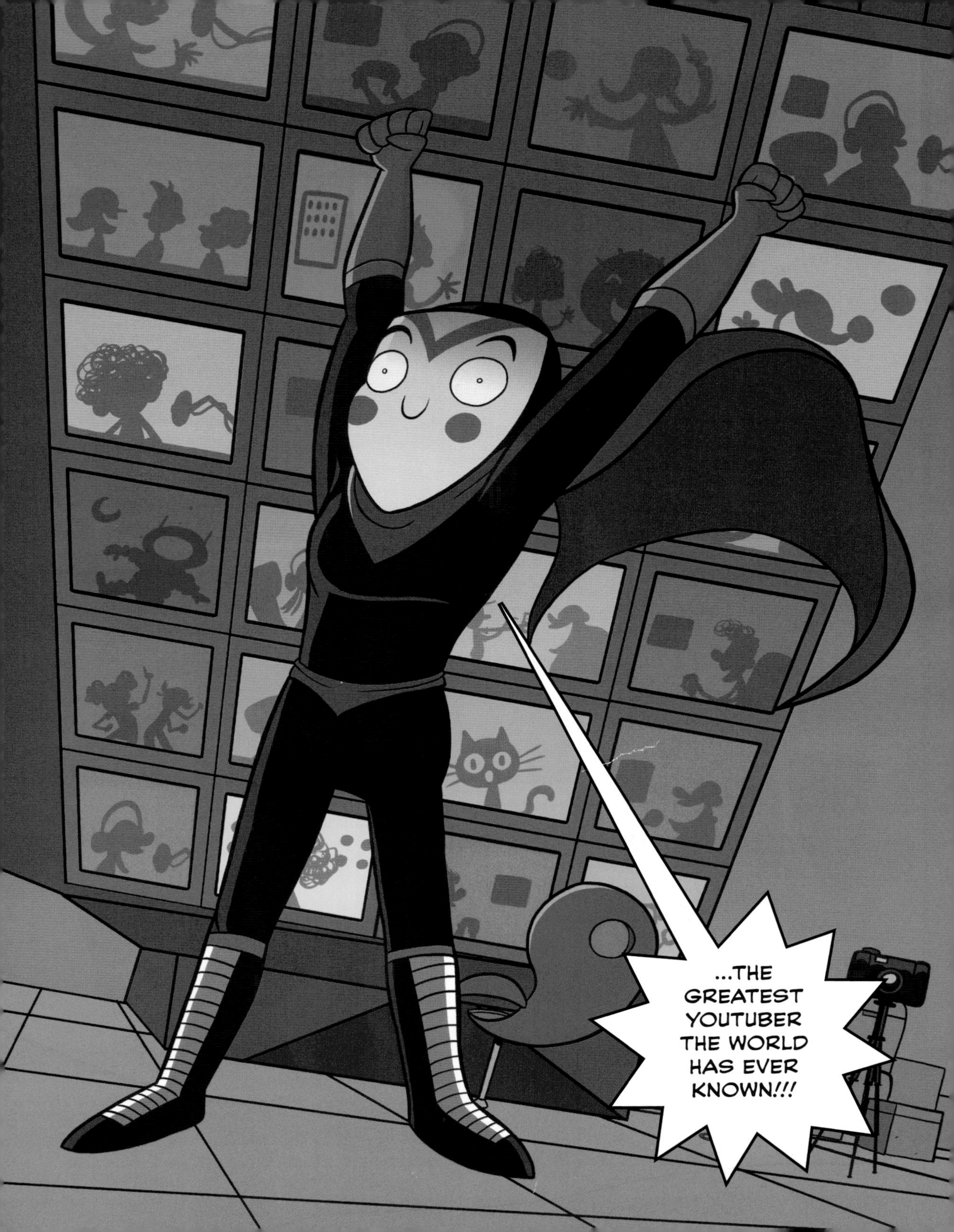
...THE GREATEST YOUTUBER THE WORLD HAS EVER KNOWN!!!

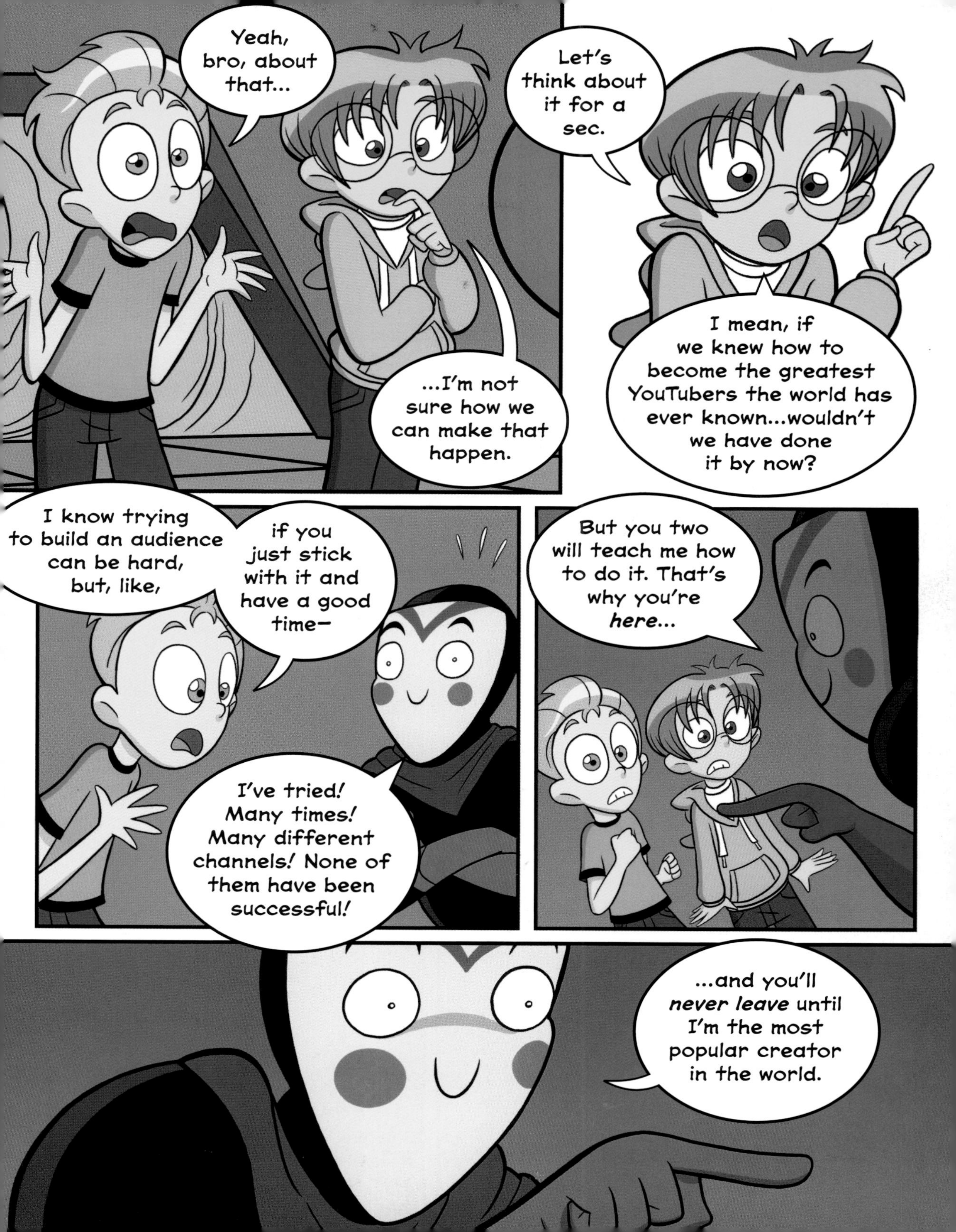
Yeah, bro, about that...
...I'm not sure how we can make that happen.
Let's think about it for a sec.
I mean, if we knew how to become the greatest YouTubers the world has ever known...wouldn't we have done it by now?
I know trying to build an audience can be hard, but, like,
if you just stick with it and have a good time—
I've tried! Many times! Many different channels! None of them have been successful!
But you two will teach me how to do it. That's why you're *here*...
...and you'll *never leave* until I'm the most popular creator in the world.

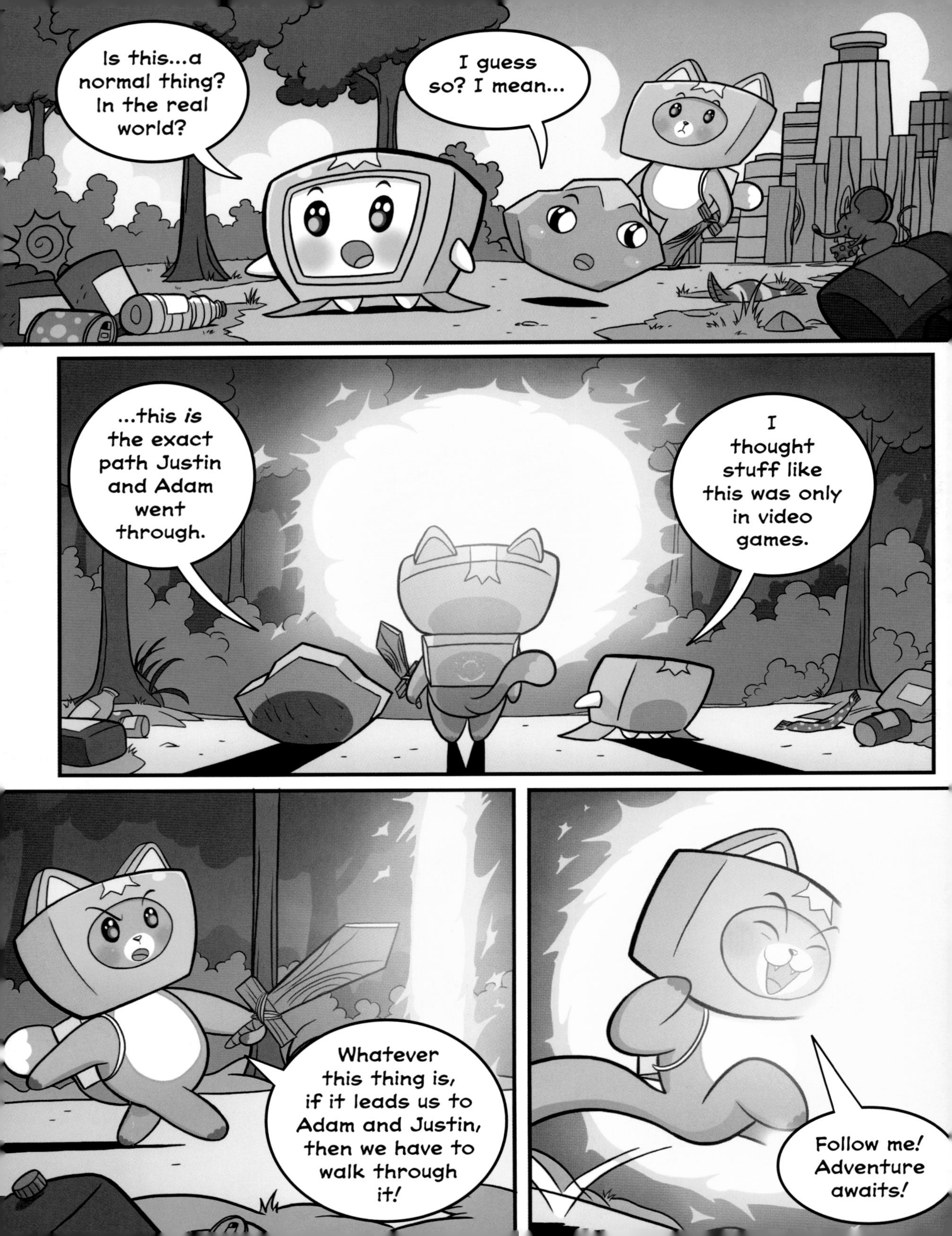
Is this...a normal thing? In the real world?
I guess so? I mean...
...this *is* the exact path Justin and Adam went through.
I thought stuff like this was only in video games.
Whatever this thing is, if it leads us to Adam and Justin, then we have to walk through it!
Follow me! Adventure awaits!

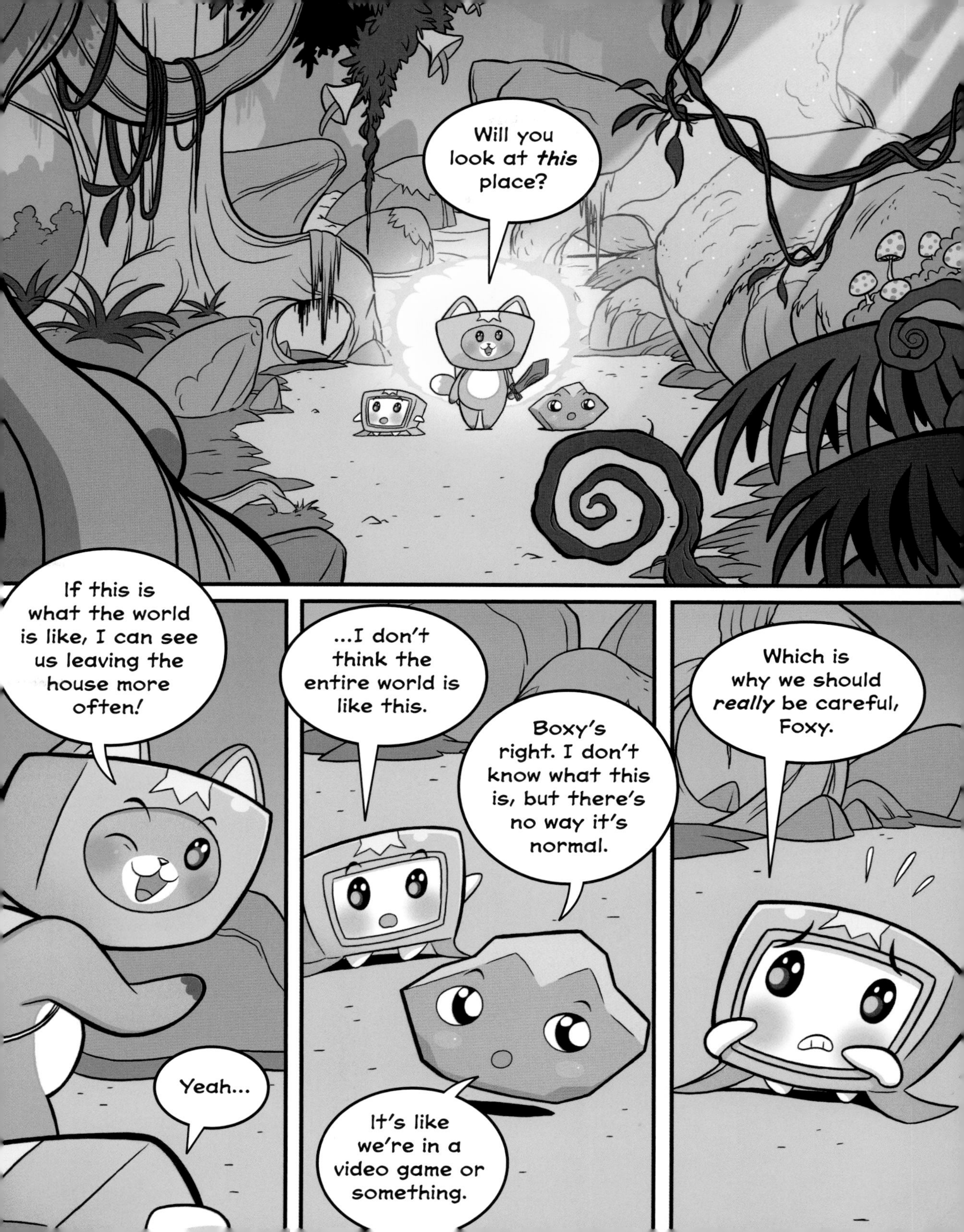
Will you look at *this* place?
If this is what the world is like, I can see us leaving the house more often!
Yeah...
...I don't think the entire world is like this.
Boxy's right. I don't know what this is, but there's no way it's normal.
It's like we're in a video game or something.
Which is why we should *really* be careful, Foxy.

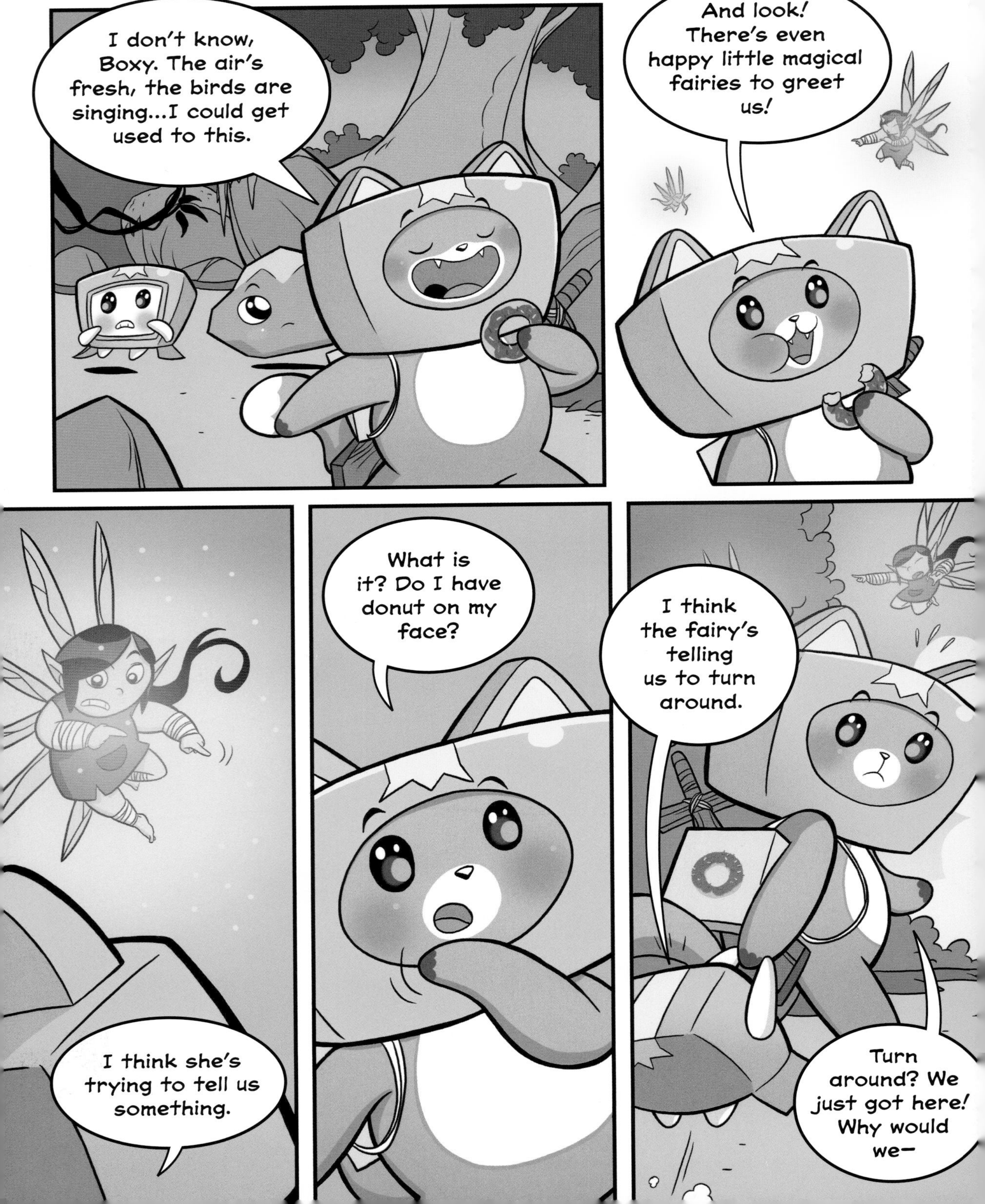
I don't know, Boxy. The air's fresh, the birds are singing...I could get used to this.
And look! There's even happy little magical fairies to greet us!
I think she's trying to tell us something.
What is it? Do I have donut on my face?
I think the fairy's telling us to turn around.
Turn around? We just got here! Why would we–

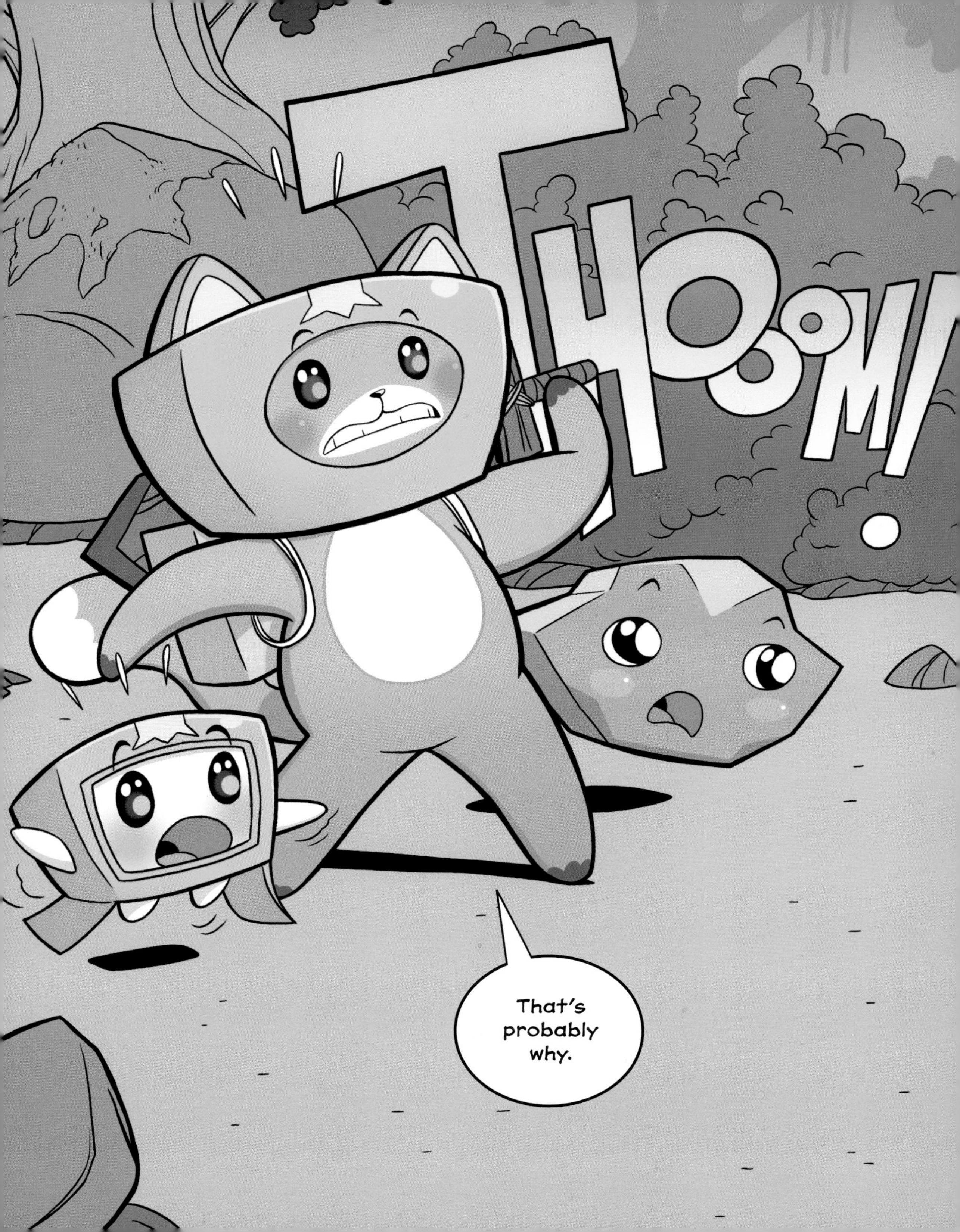
THOOOM!
That's probably why.

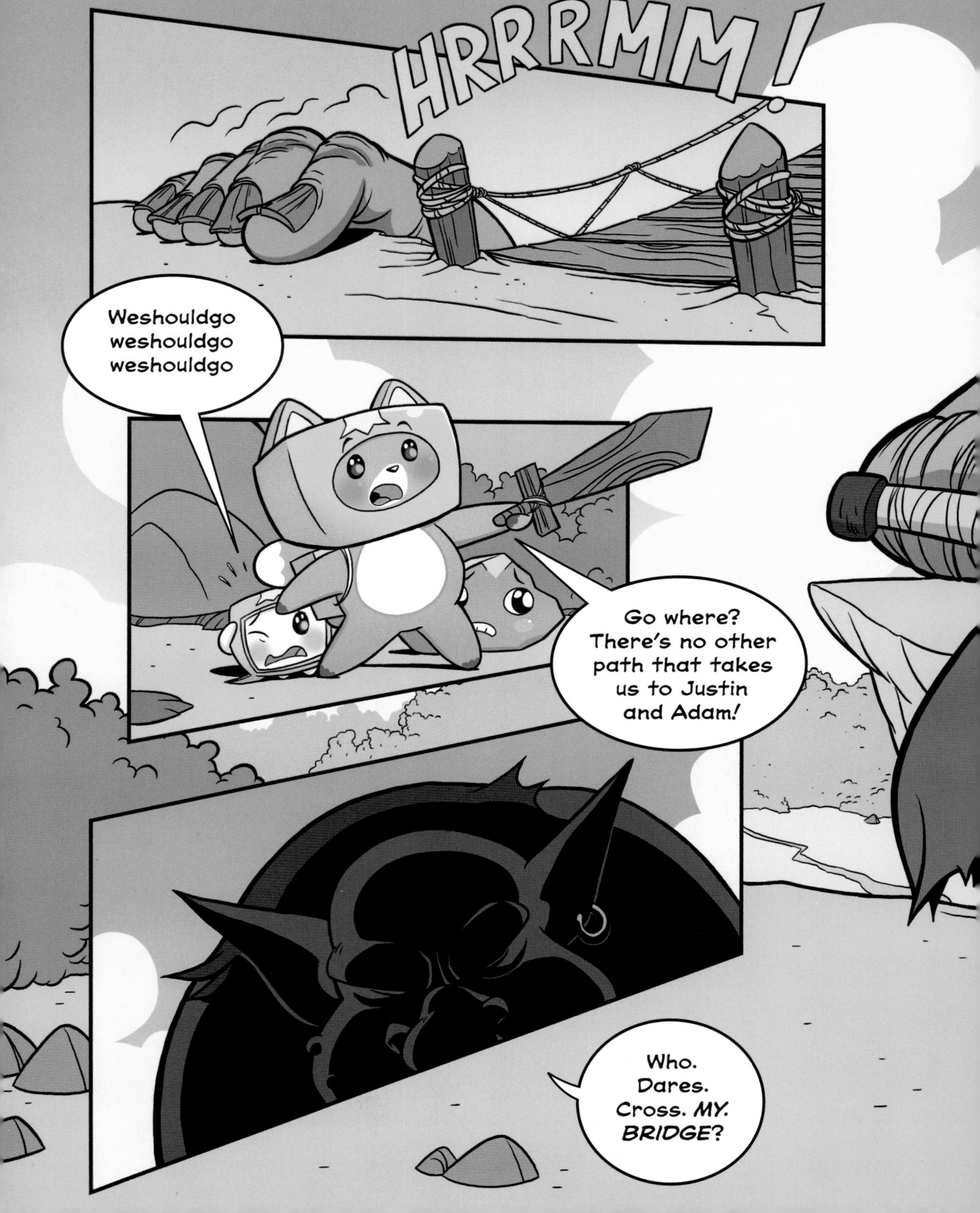
HRRRMM!
Weshouldgo weshouldgo weshouldgo
Go where? There's no other path that takes us to Justin and Adam!
Who. Dares. Cross. *MY. BRIDGE?*

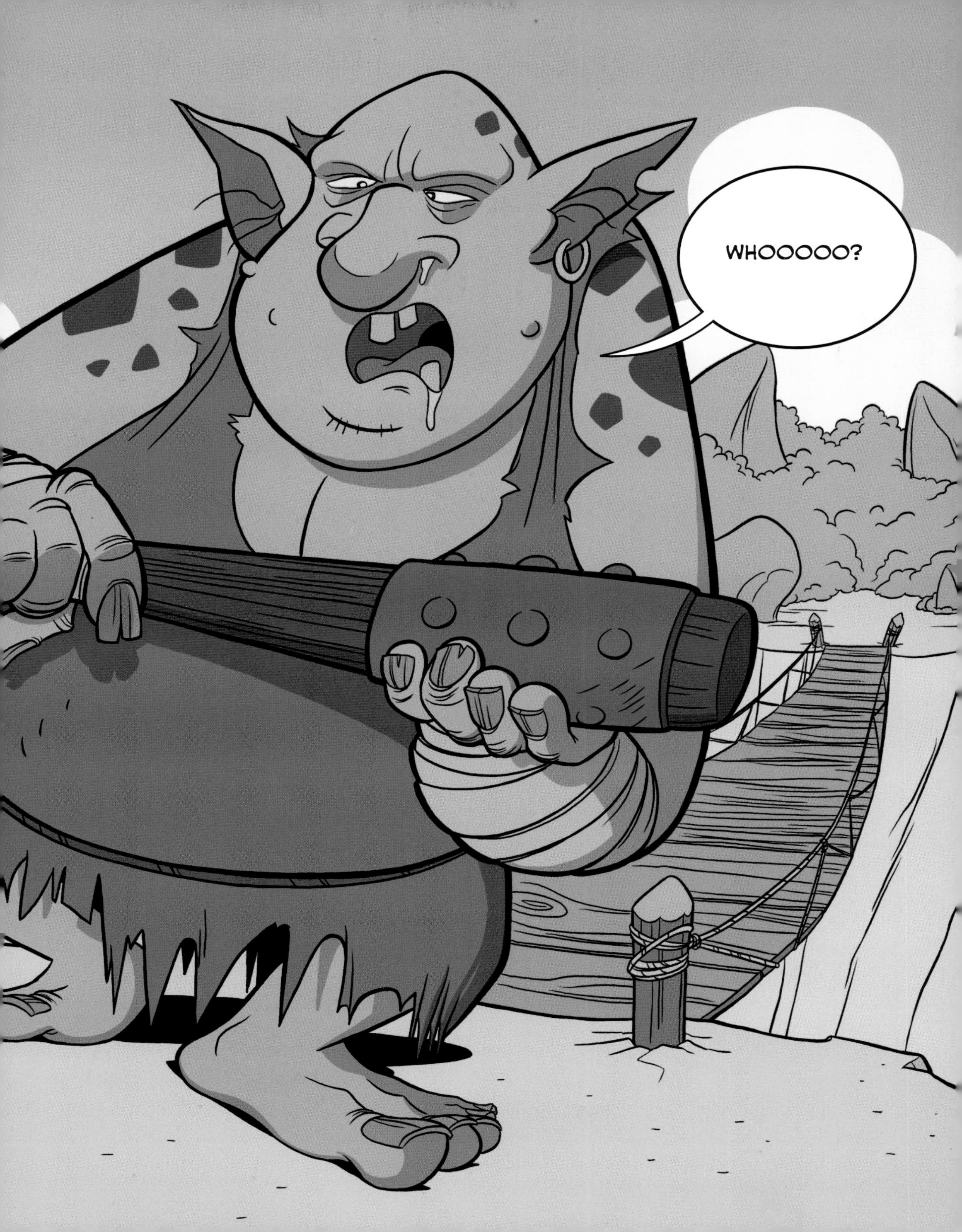
WHOOOOO?

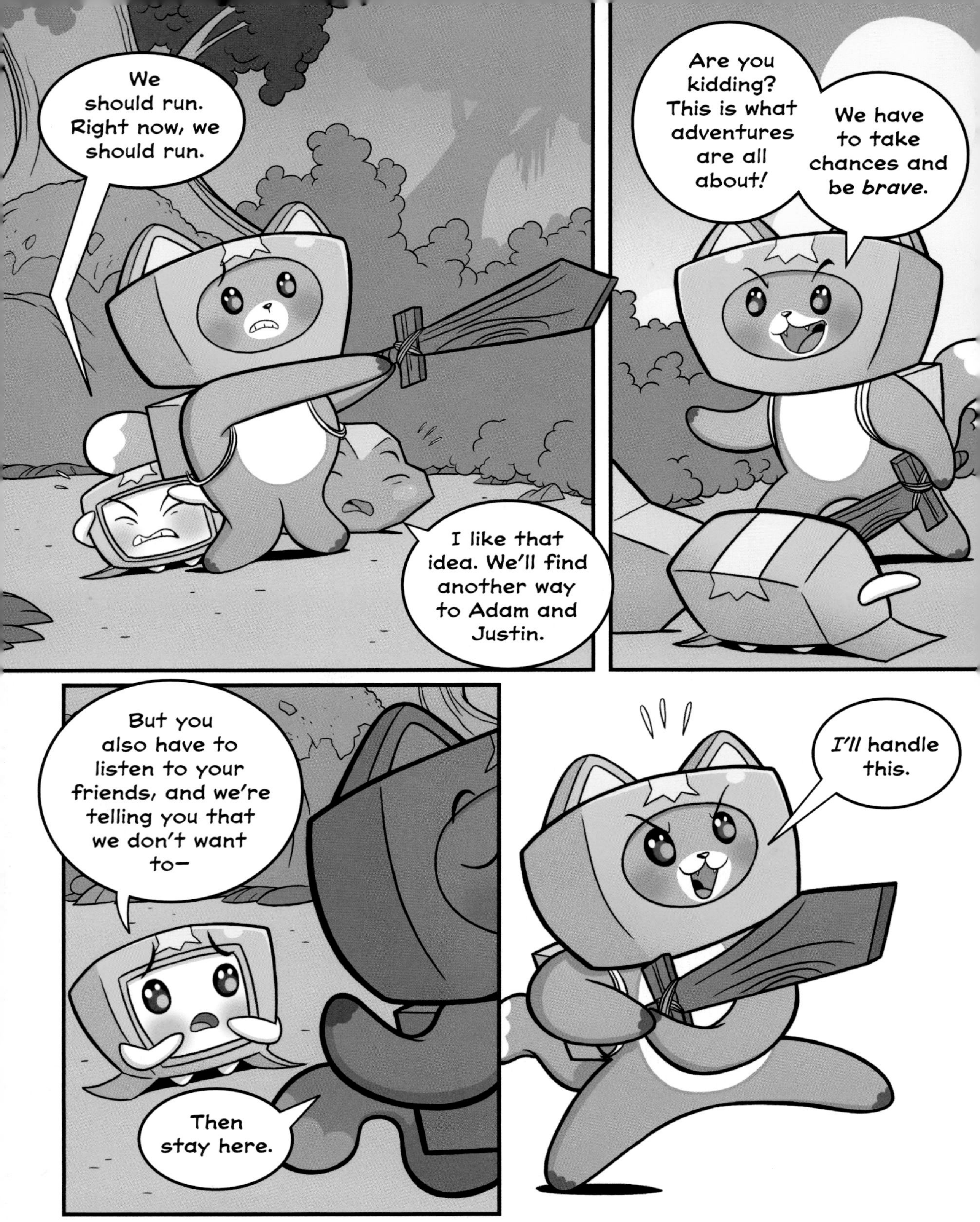
We should run. Right now, we should run.
I like that idea. We'll find another way to Adam and Justin.
Are you kidding? This is what adventures are all about!
We have to take chances and be *brave*.
But you also have to listen to your friends, and we're telling you that we don't want to—
Then stay here.
I'll handle this.

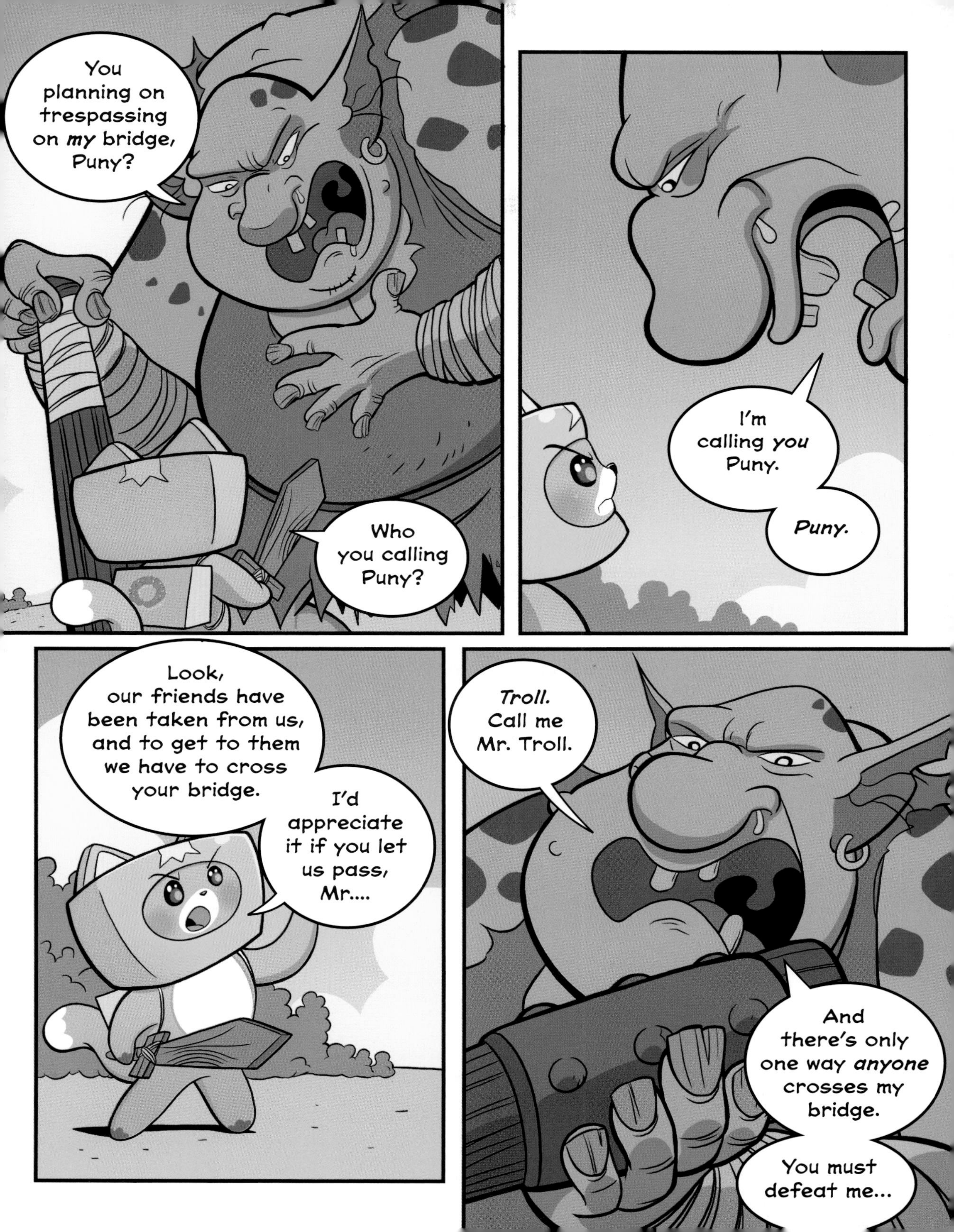
You planning on trespassing on *my* bridge, Puny?
Who you calling Puny?
I'm calling *you* Puny.
Puny.
Look, our friends have been taken from us, and to get to them we have to cross your bridge.
I'd appreciate it if you let us pass, Mr....
Troll. Call me Mr. Troll.
And there's only one way *anyone* crosses my bridge.
You must defeat me...

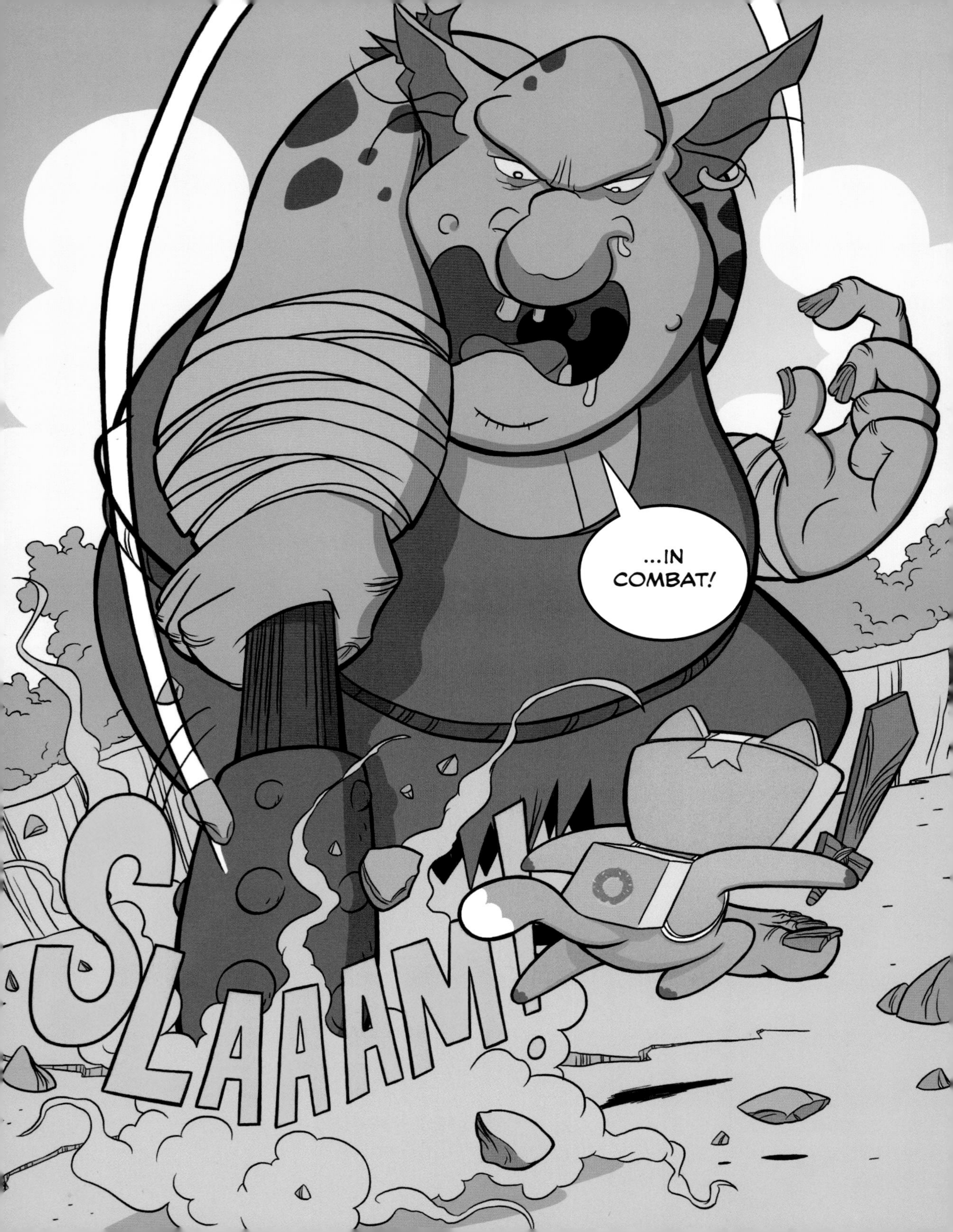
...IN COMBAT!
SLAAAM!

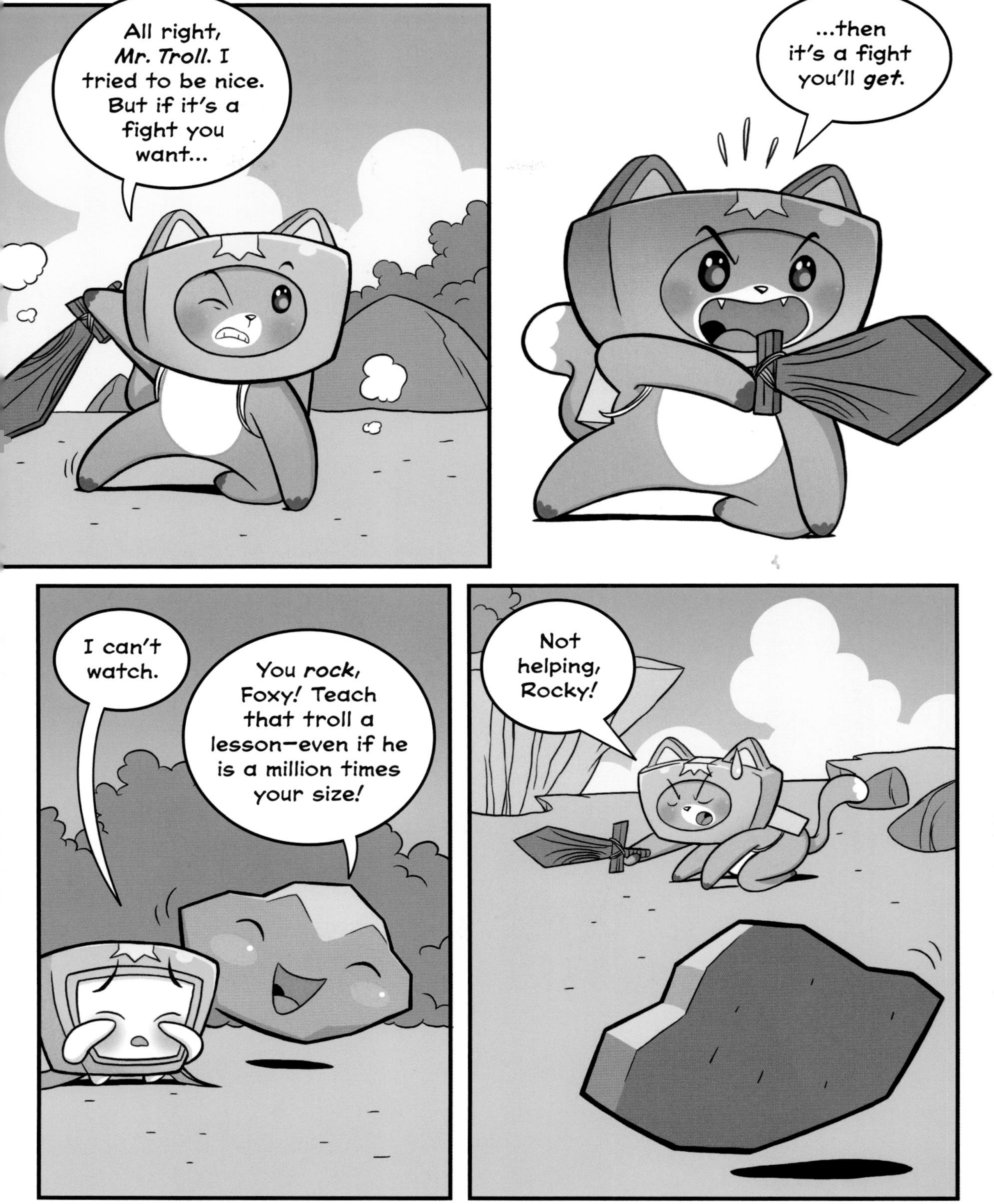
All right, *Mr. Troll*. I tried to be nice. But if it's a fight you want...
...then it's a fight you'll *get*.
I can't watch.
You *rock*, Foxy! Teach that troll a lesson—even if he is a million times your size!
Not helping, Rocky!

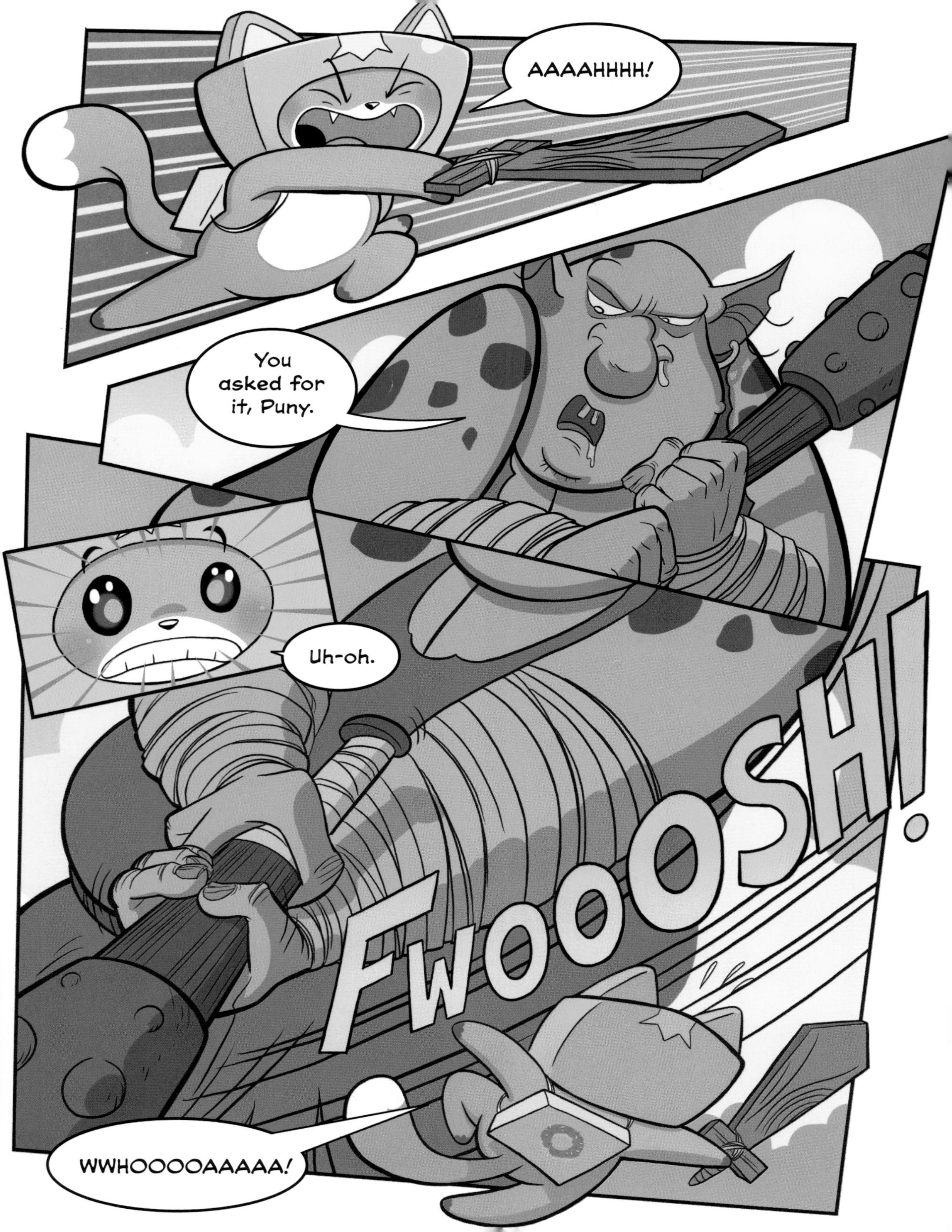
AAAAHHHH!
You asked for it, Puny.
Uh-oh.
FWOOOSH!!
WWHOOOOAAAAA!

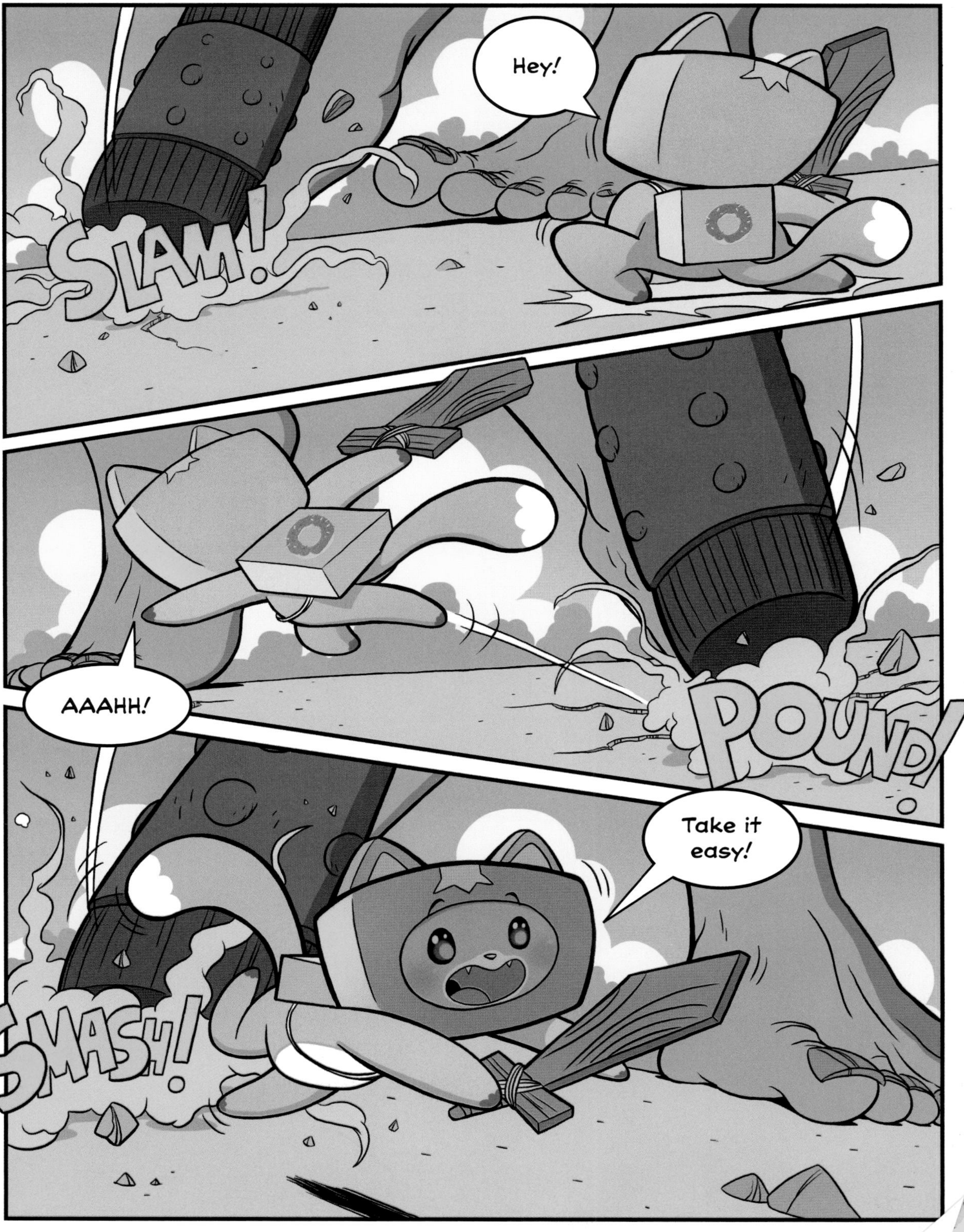

SLAM!
Hey!
AAAHH!
POUND!
Take it easy!
SMASH!

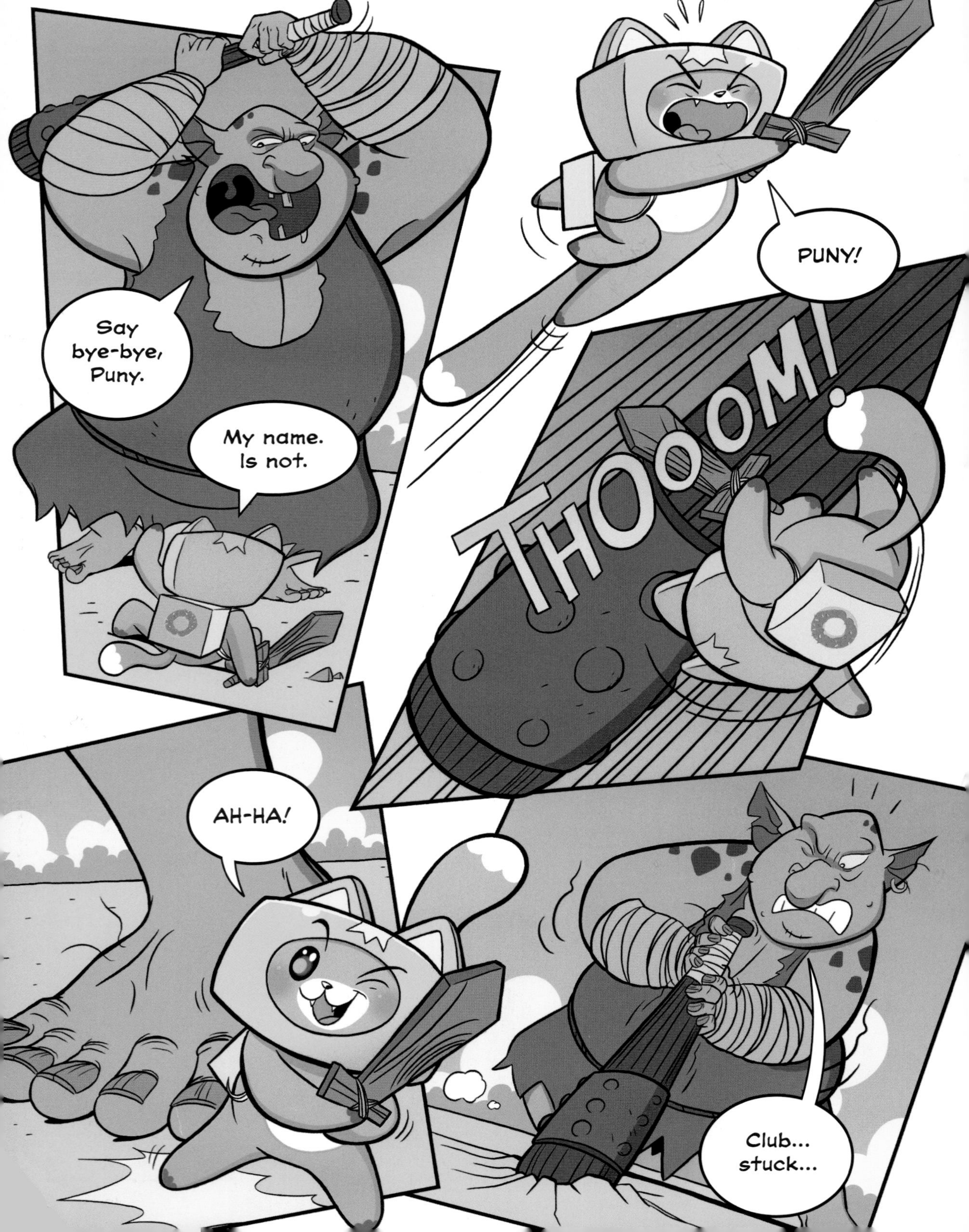
Say bye-bye, Puny.
My name. Is not.
PUNY!
THOOOM!
AH-HA!
Club... stuck...

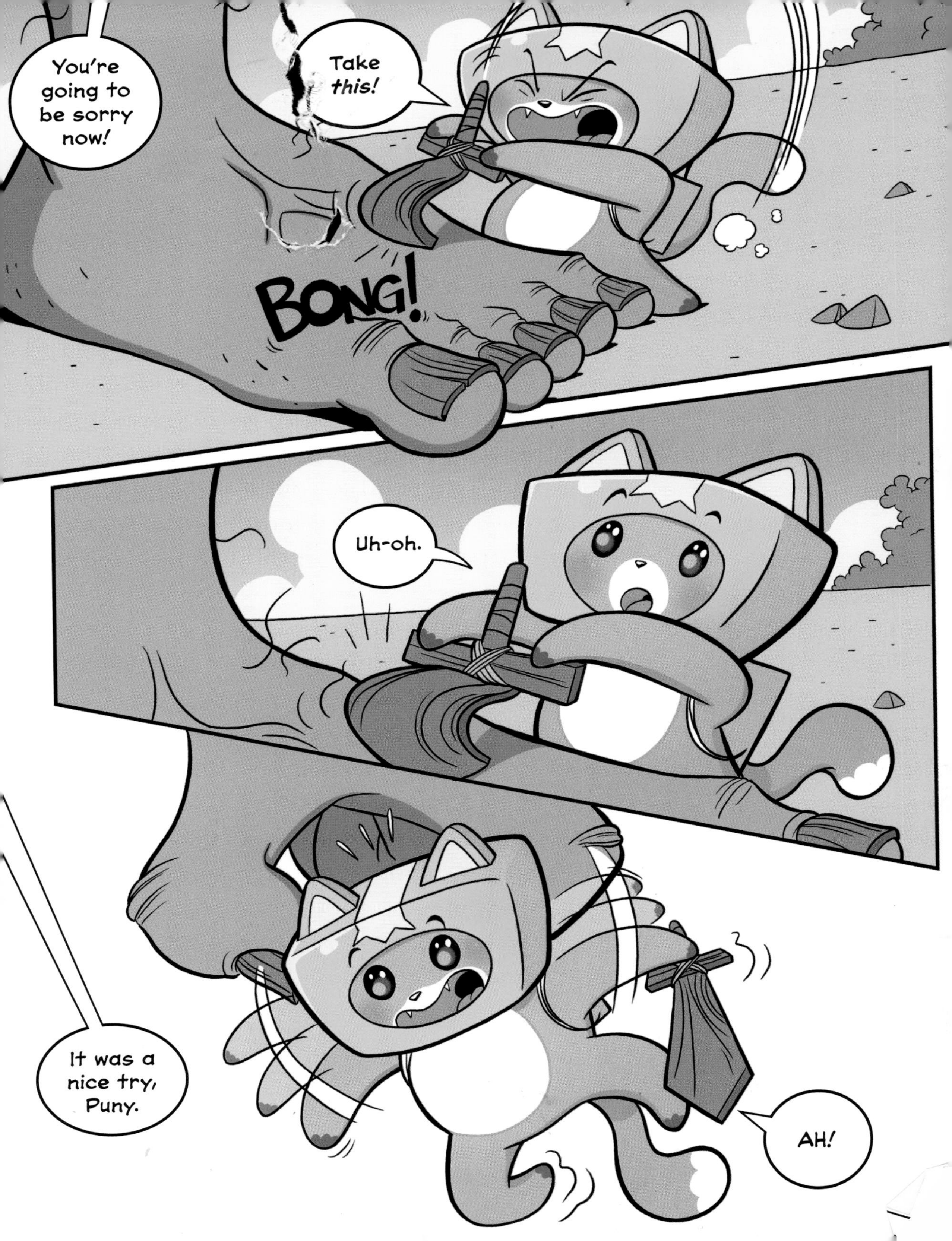
You're going to be sorry now!
Take *this!*
BONG!
Uh-oh.
It was a nice try, Puny.
AH!

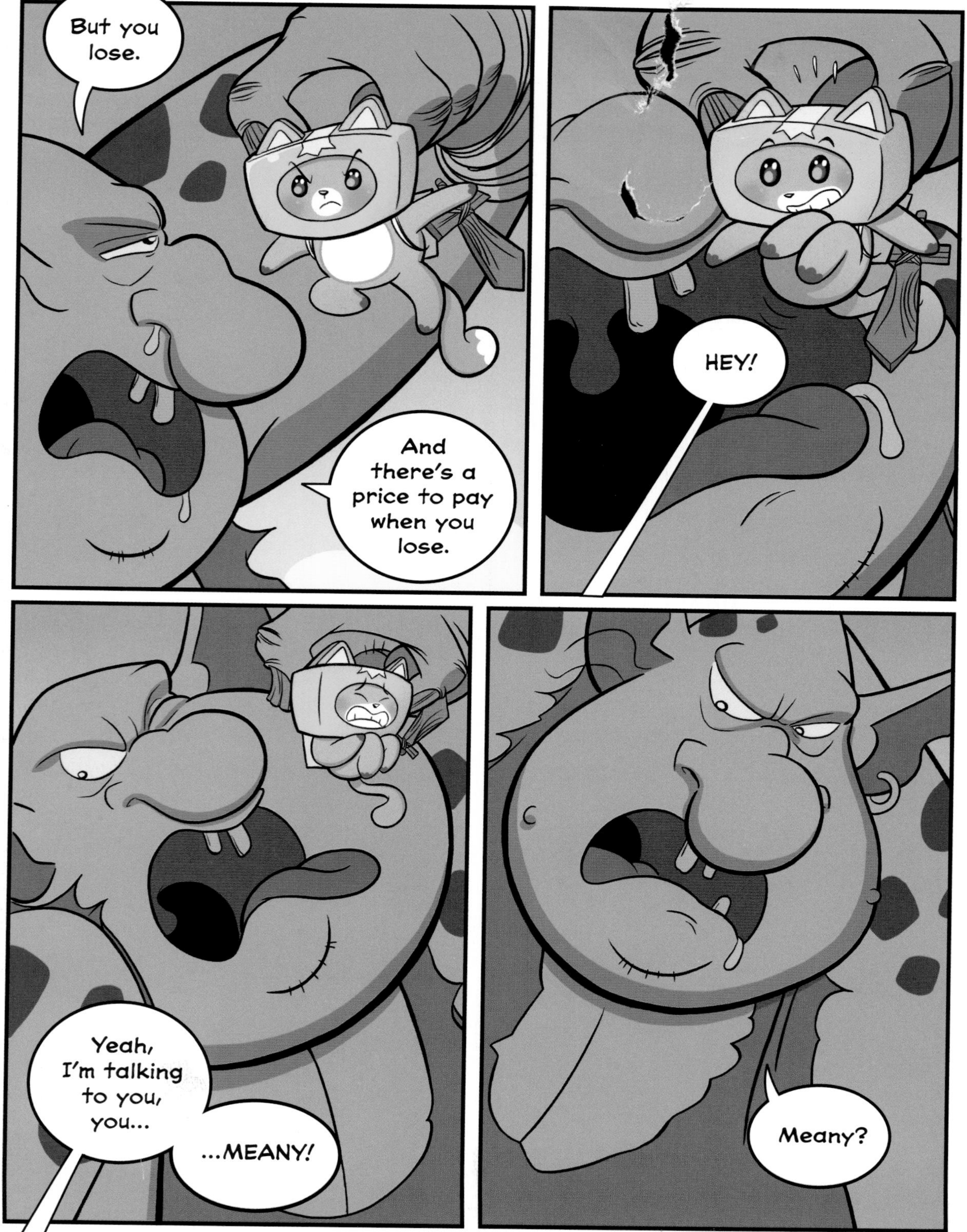
But you lose.
And there's a price to pay when you lose.
HEY!
Yeah, I'm talking to you, you...
...MEANY!
Meany?

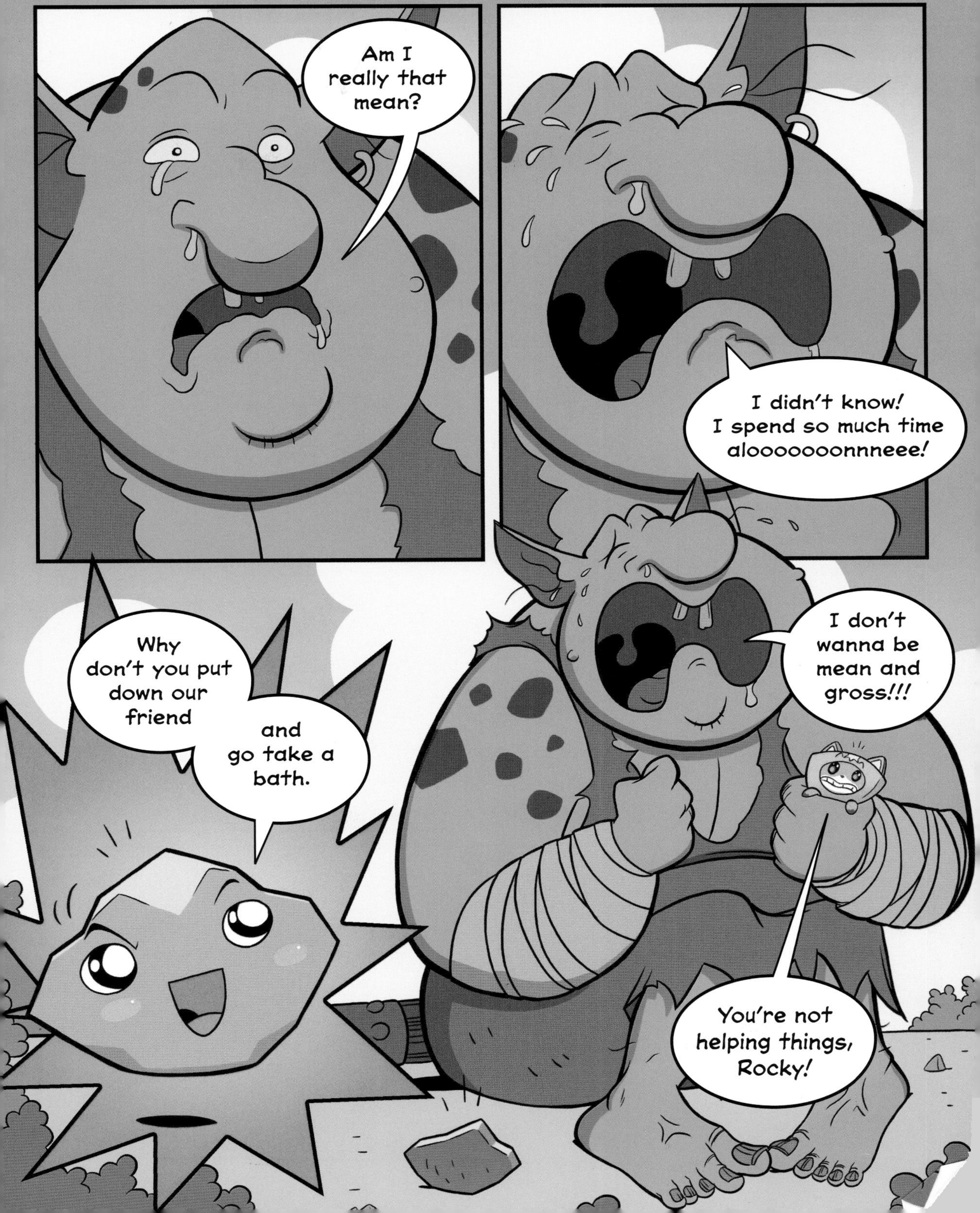
Am I really that mean?
I didn't know! I spend so much time aloooooooonnneee!
Why don't you put down our friend
and go take a bath.
I don't wanna be mean and gross!!!
You're not helping things, Rocky!

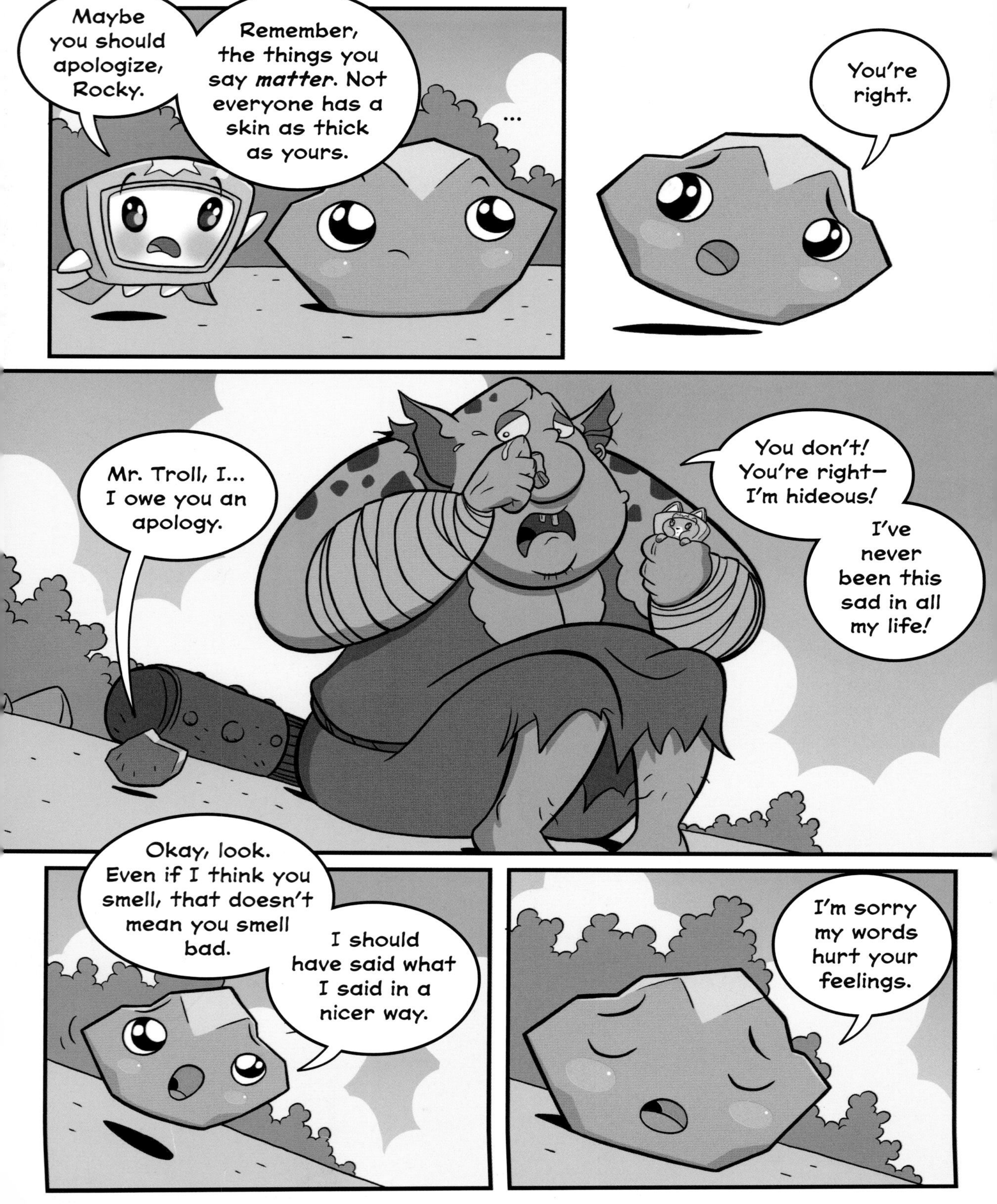
Maybe you should apologize, Rocky.
Remember, the things you say *matter*. Not everyone has a skin as thick as yours.
...
You're right.
Mr. Troll, I... I owe you an apology.
You don't! You're right— I'm hideous!
I've never been this sad in all my life!
Okay, look. Even if I think you smell, that doesn't mean you smell bad.
I should have said what I said in a nicer way.
I'm sorry my words hurt your feelings.

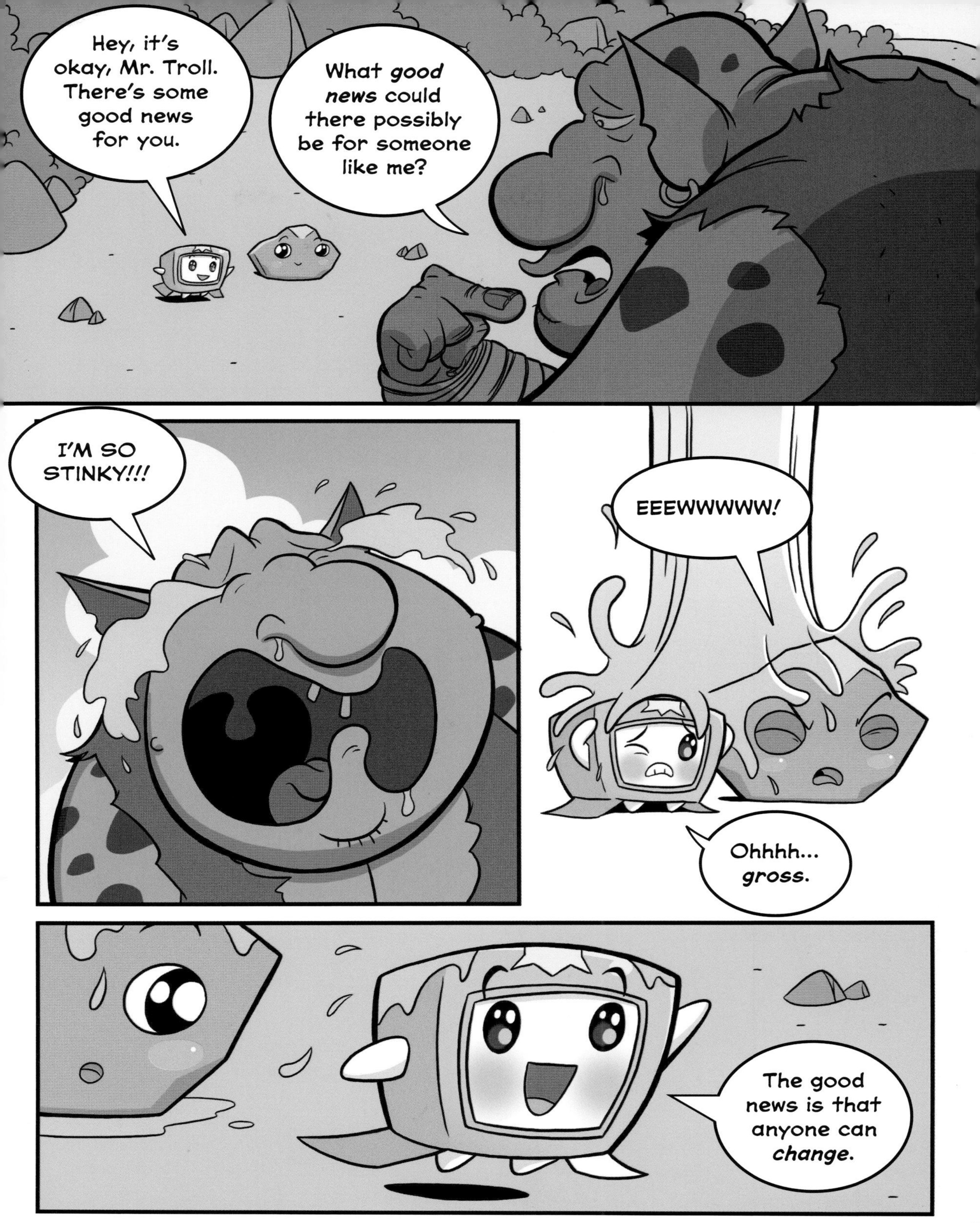

Hey, it's okay, Mr. Troll. There's some good news for you.
What *good news* could there possibly be for someone like me?
I'M SO STINKY!!!
EEEWWWWW!
Ohhhh... *gross.*
The good news is that anyone can *change*.

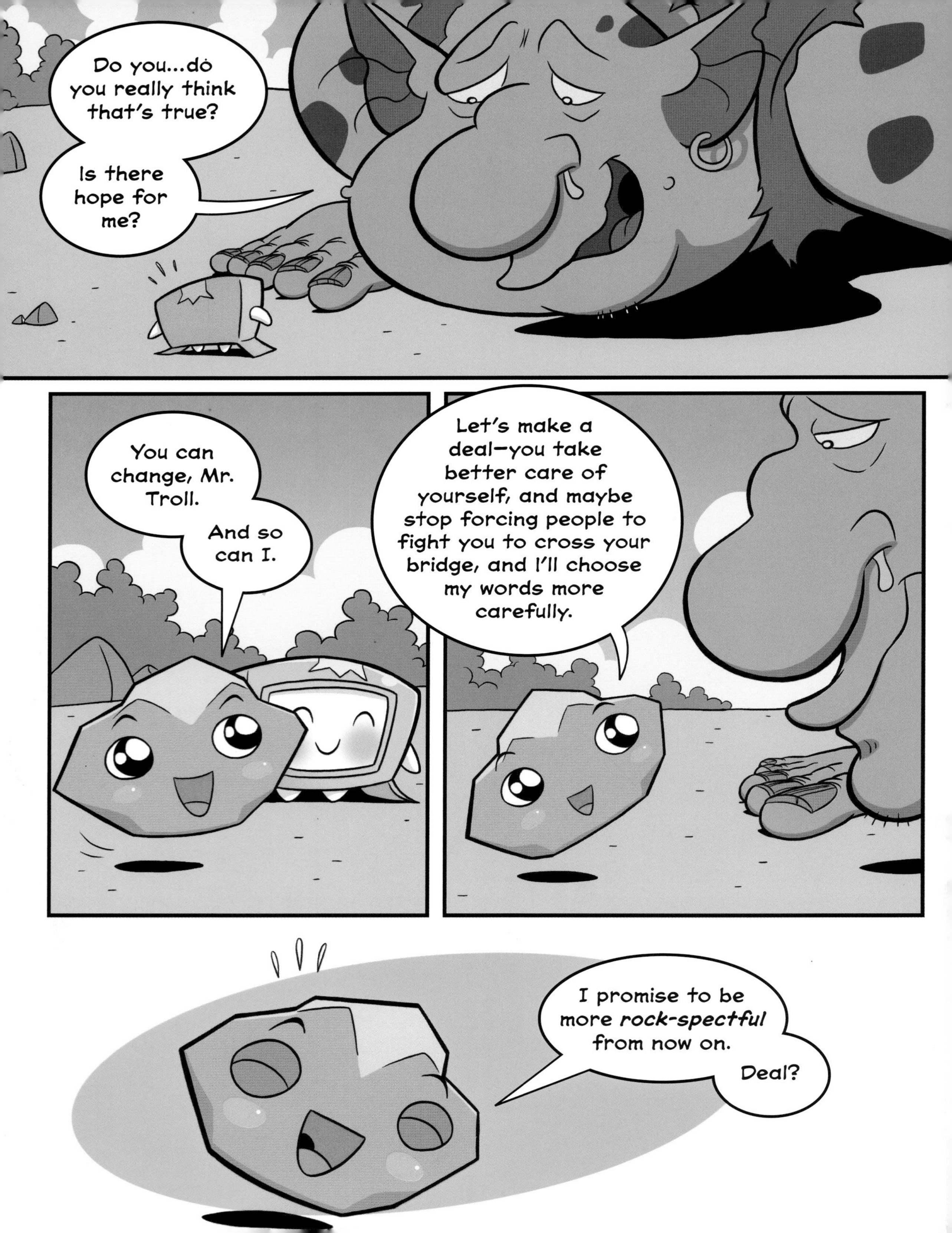
Do you...do you really think that's true?
Is there hope for me?
You can change, Mr. Troll.
And so can I.
Let's make a deal—you take better care of yourself, and maybe stop forcing people to fight you to cross your bridge, and I'll choose my words more carefully.
I promise to be more *rock-spectful* from now on.
Deal?

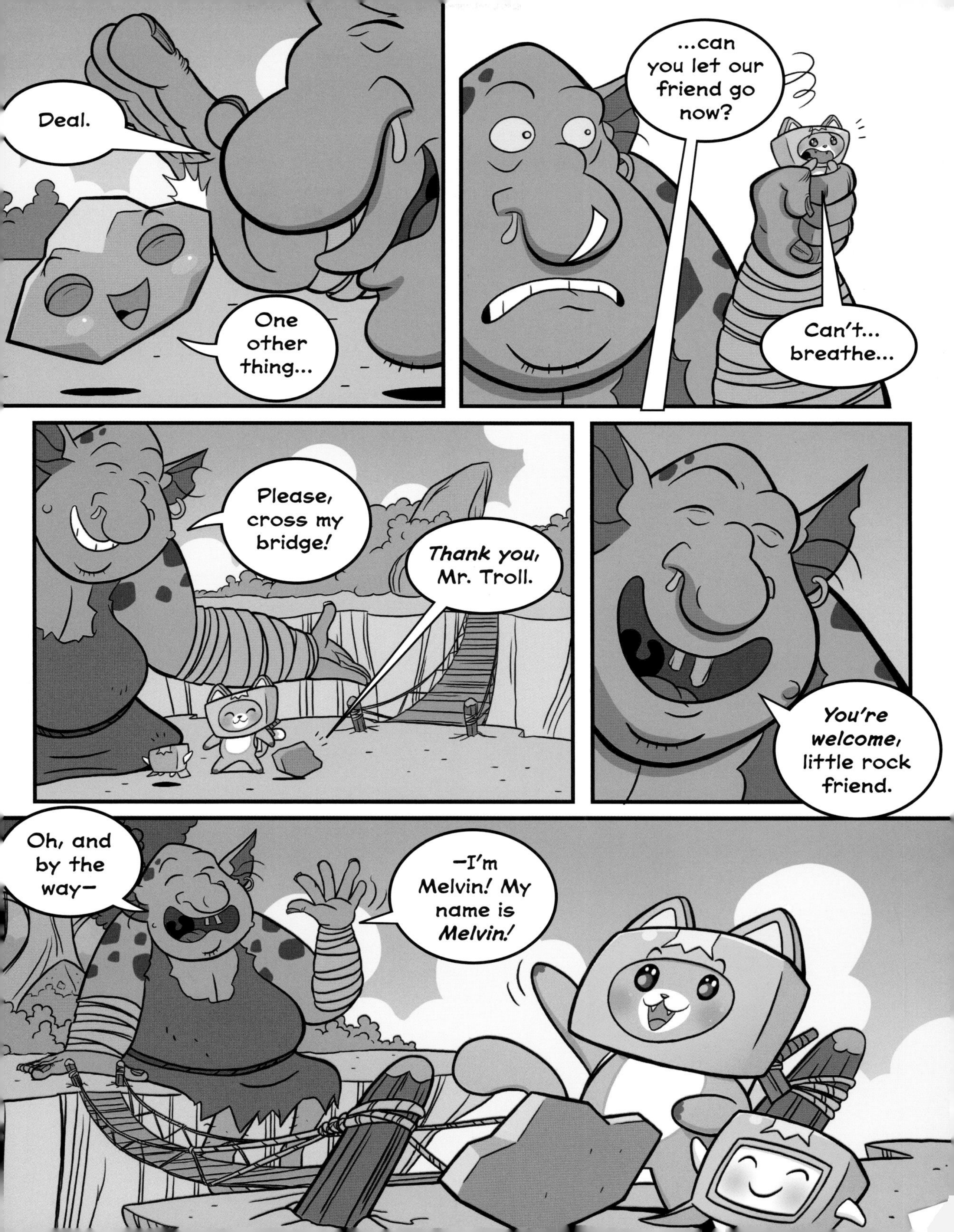
Deal.
One other thing...
...can you let our friend go now?
Can't... breathe...
Please, cross my bridge!
Thank you, Mr. Troll.
You're welcome, little rock friend.
Oh, and by the way—
—I'm Melvin! My name is *Melvin!*

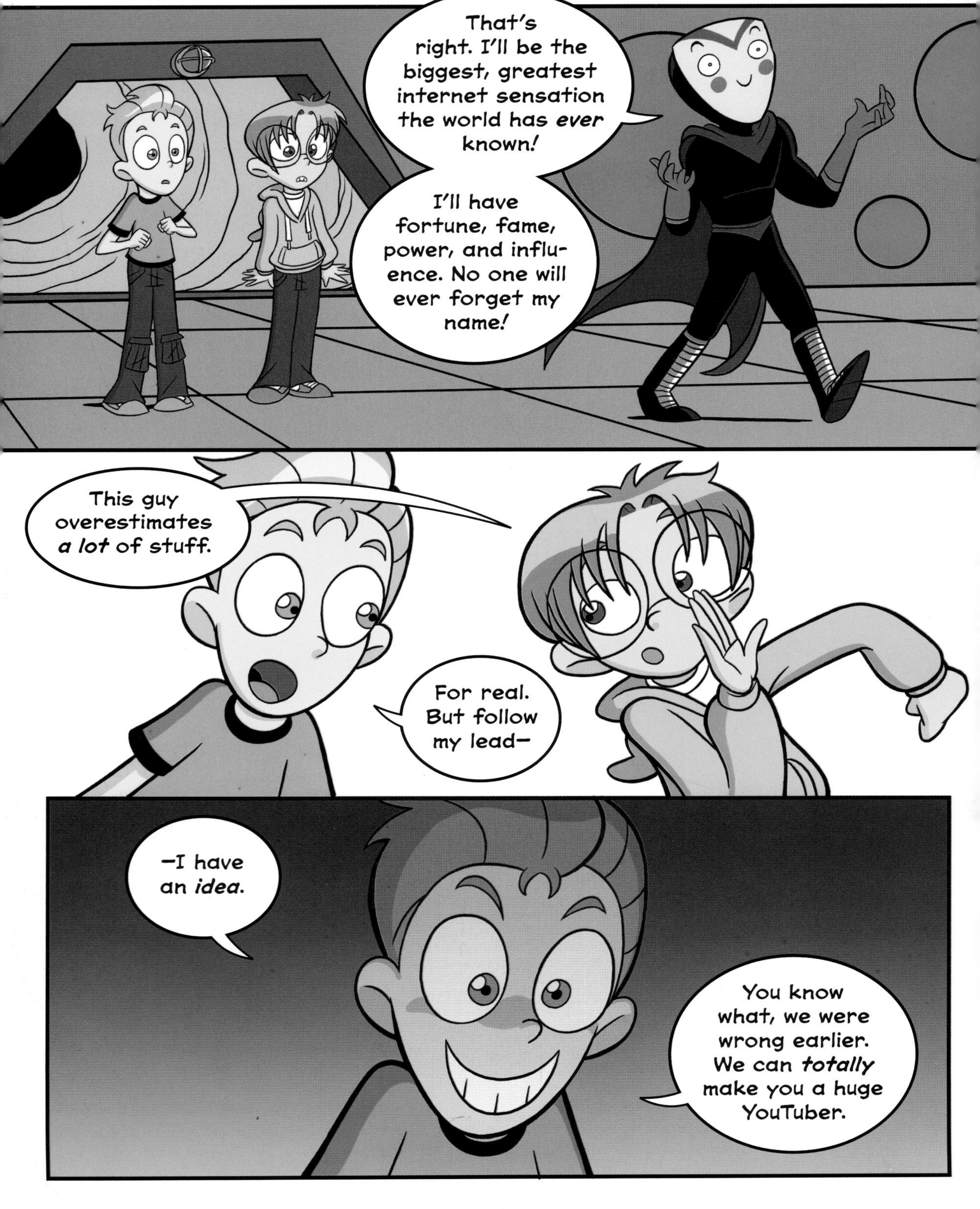
That's right. I'll be the biggest, greatest internet sensation the world has *ever* known!
I'll have fortune, fame, power, and influence. No one will ever forget my name!
This guy overestimates *a lot* of stuff.
For real. But follow my lead—
—I have an *idea*.
You know what, we were wrong earlier. We can *totally* make you a huge YouTuber.

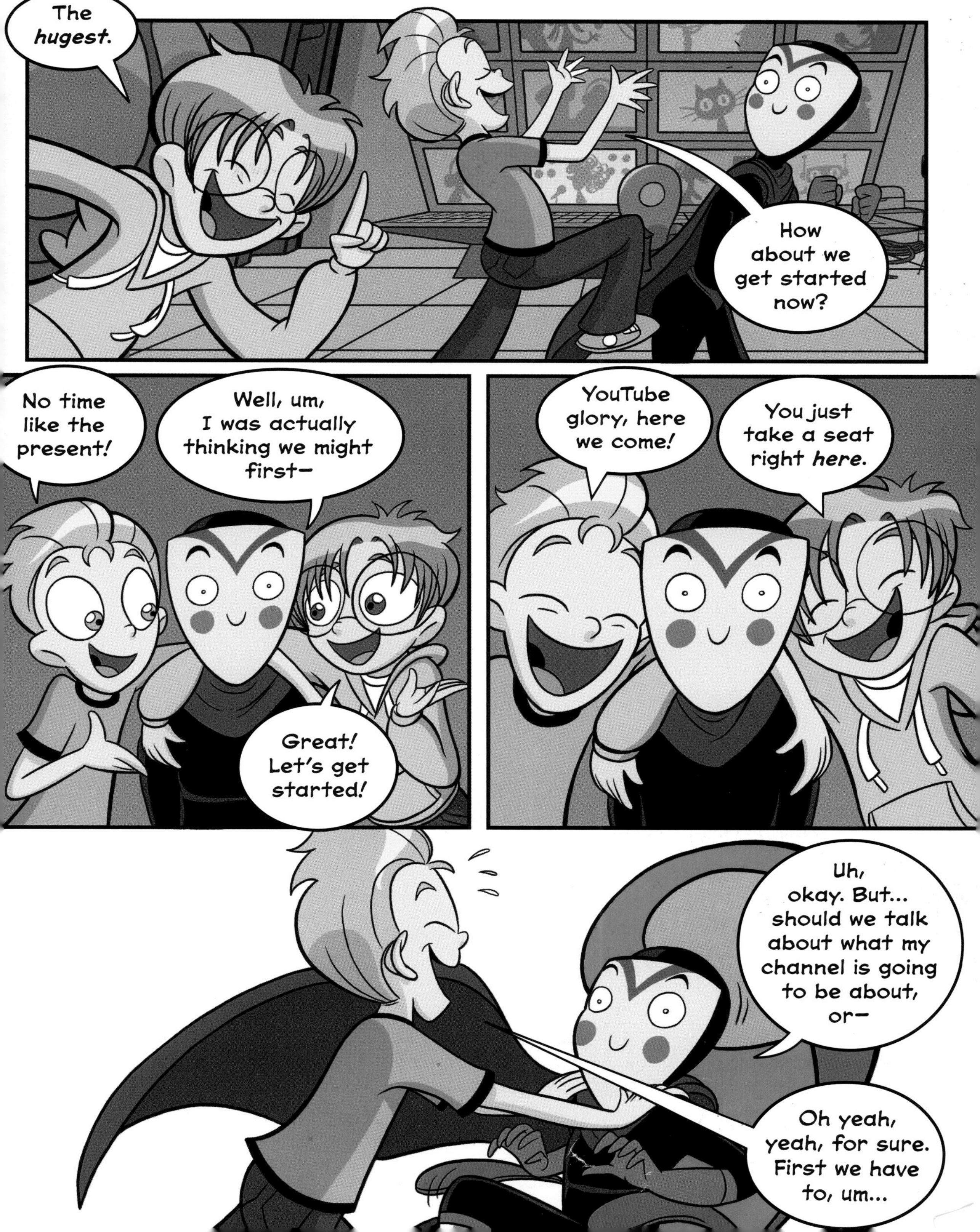
The *hugest.*
How about we get started now?
No time like the present!
Well, um, I was actually thinking we might first—
Great! Let's get started!
YouTube glory, here we come!
You just take a seat right *here.*
Uh, okay. But... should we talk about what my channel is going to be about, or—
Oh yeah, yeah, for sure. First we have to, um...

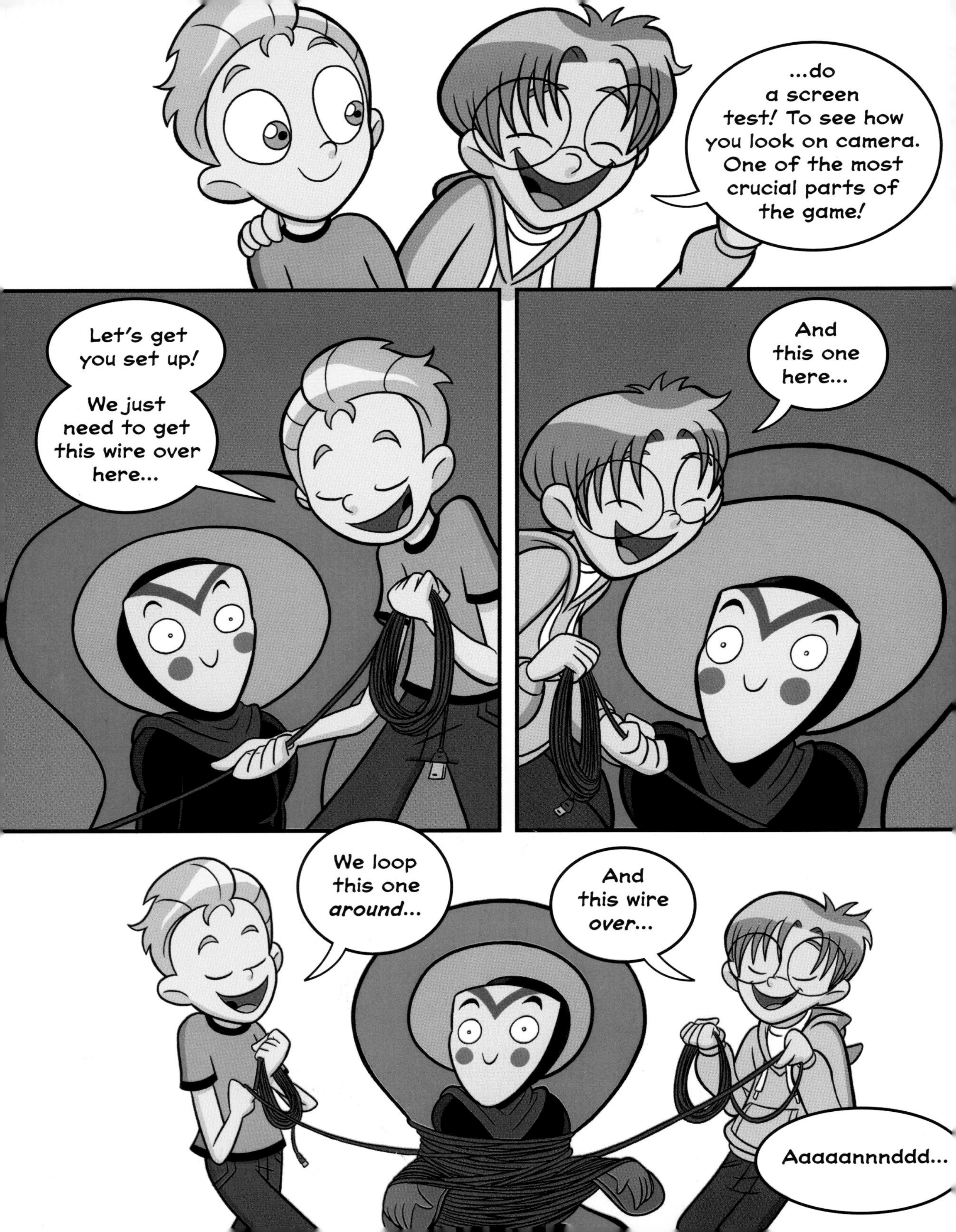
...do a screen test! To see how you look on camera. One of the most crucial parts of the game!
Let's get you set up!
We just need to get this wire over here...
And this one here...
We loop this one *around*...
And this wire *over*...
Aaaaannnddd...

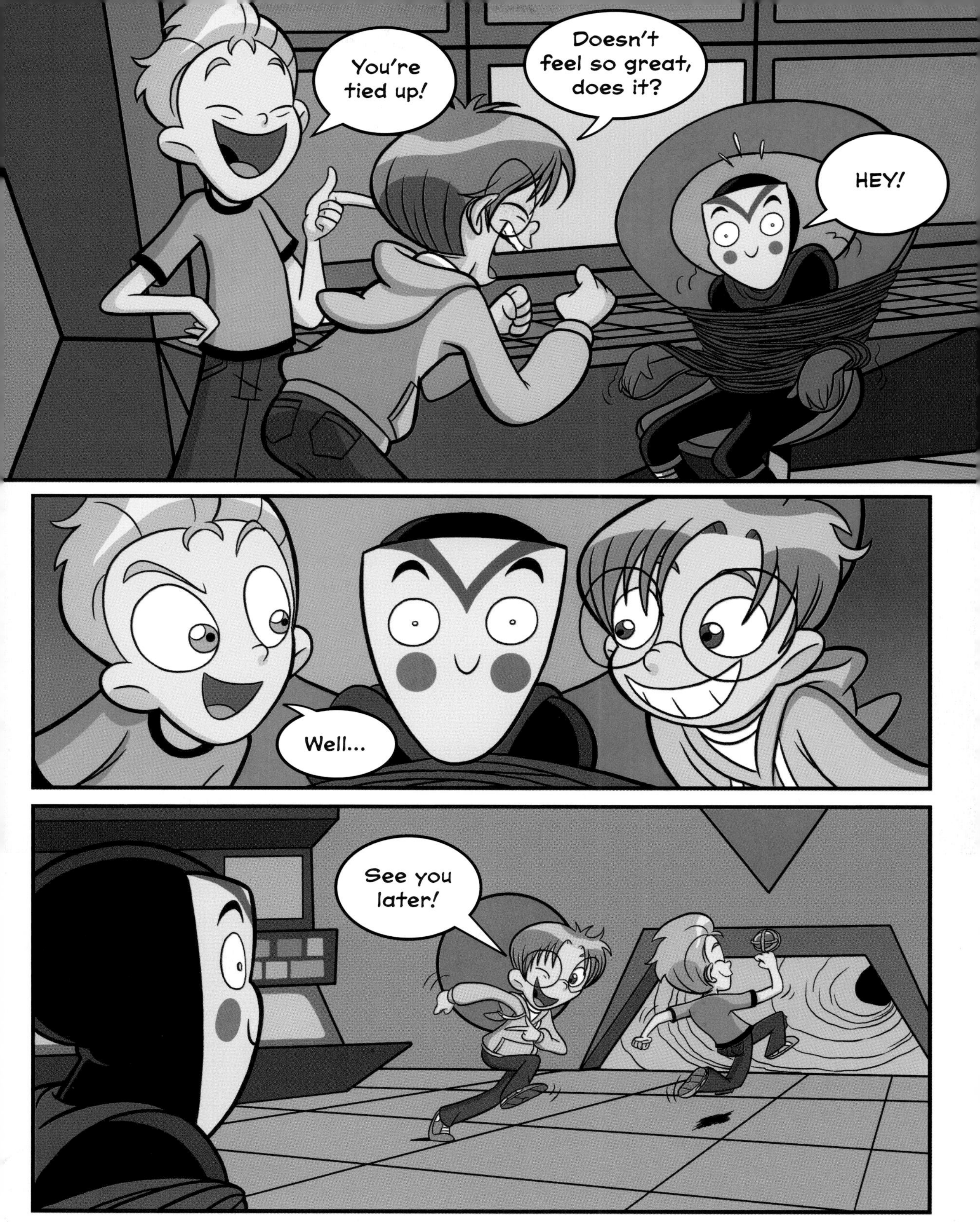
You're tied up!
Doesn't feel so great, does it?
HEY!
Well...
See you later!

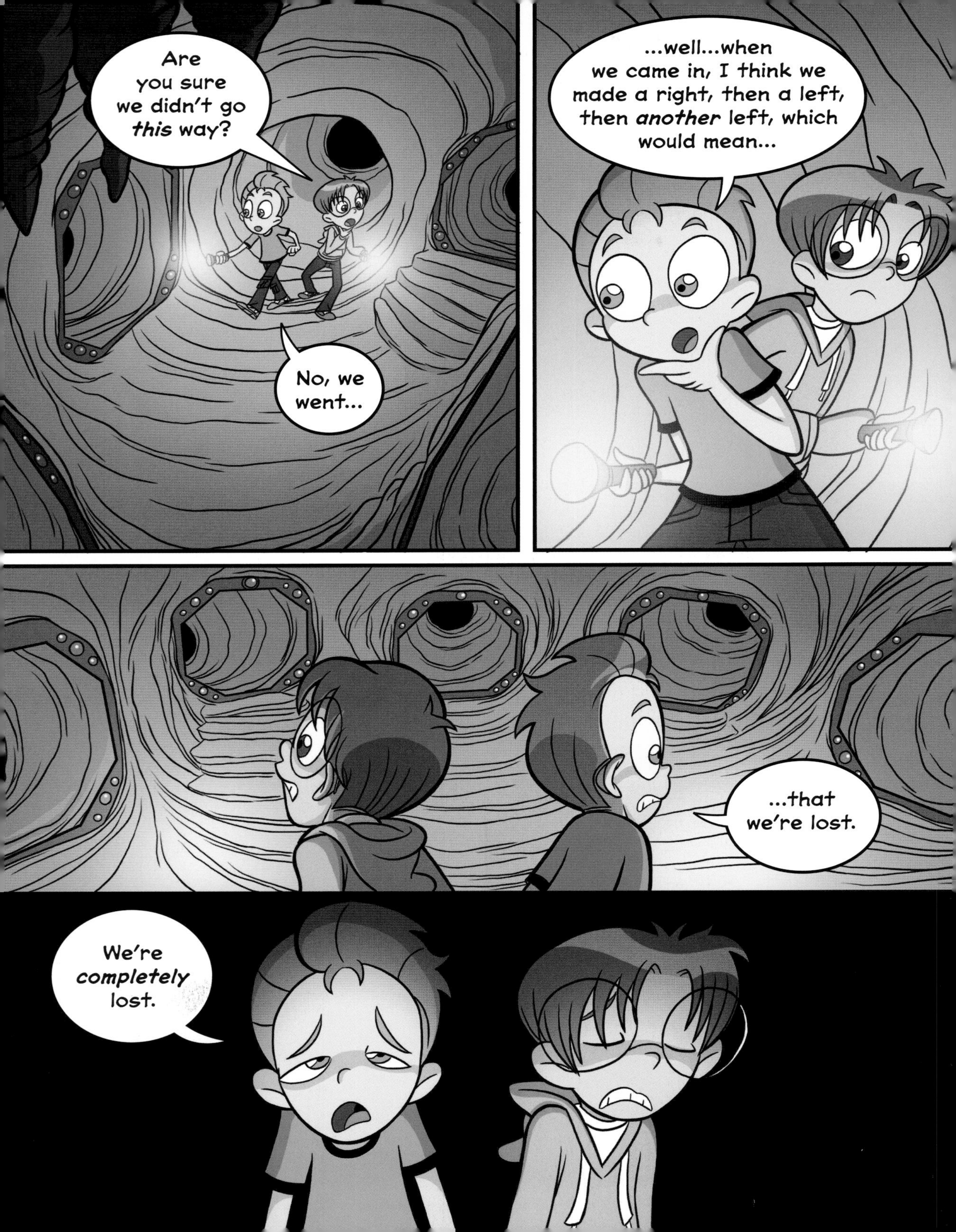
Are you sure we didn't go *this* way?
No, we went...
...well...when we came in, I think we made a right, then a left, then *another* left, which would mean...
...that we're lost.
We're *completely* lost.

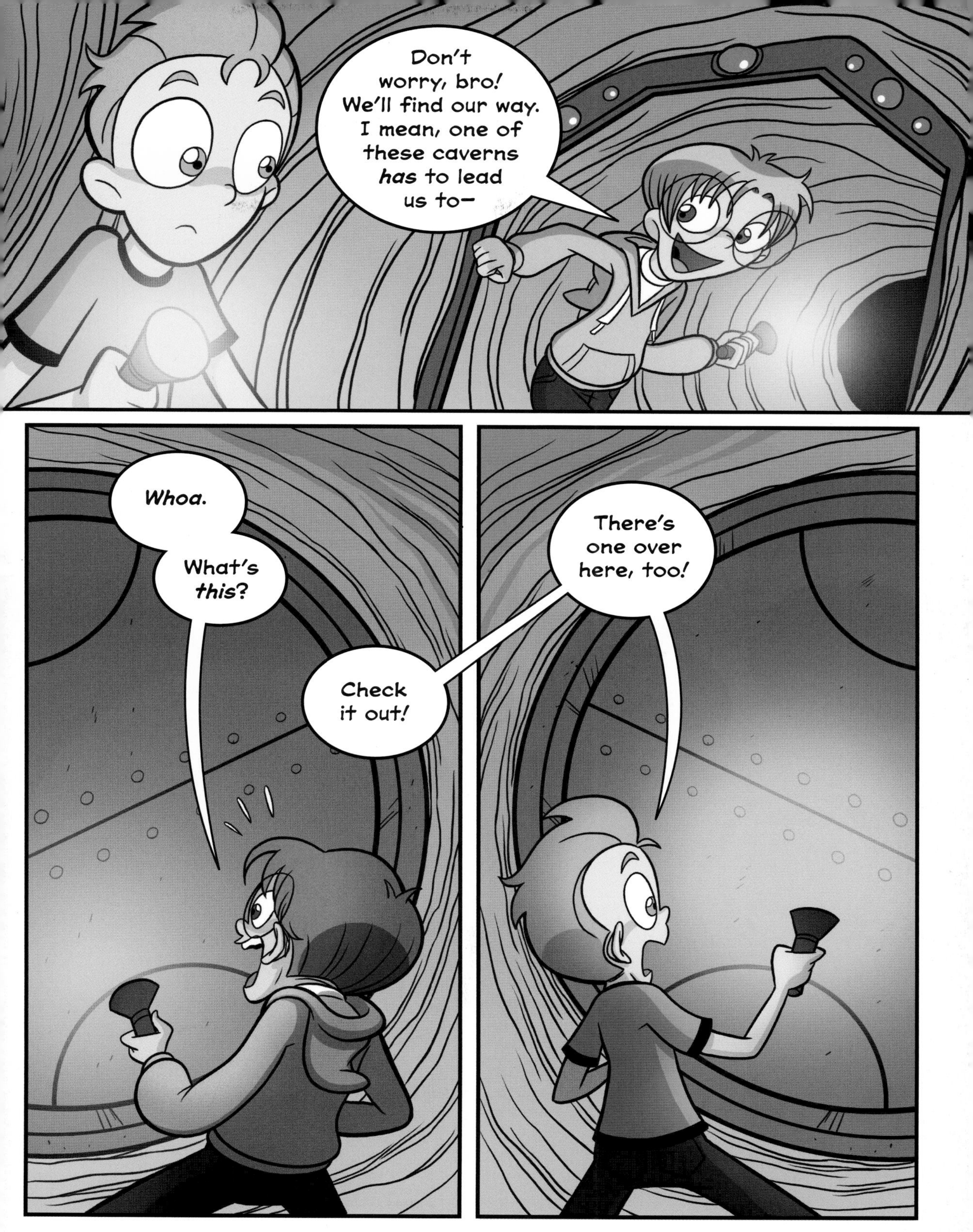
Don't worry, bro! We'll find our way. I mean, one of these caverns *has* to lead us to—
Whoa.
What's *this*?
Check it out!
There's one over here, too!

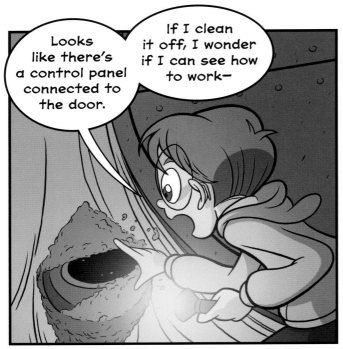

Looks like there's a control panel connected to the door.

If I clean it off, I wonder if I can see how to work—

Oh! There we go!

DOOR ACTIVATED

Do you think it's a snowmobile? I bet it's a snowmobile.

Or rocket skis. Rocket skis would be awesome!

SWOOo!

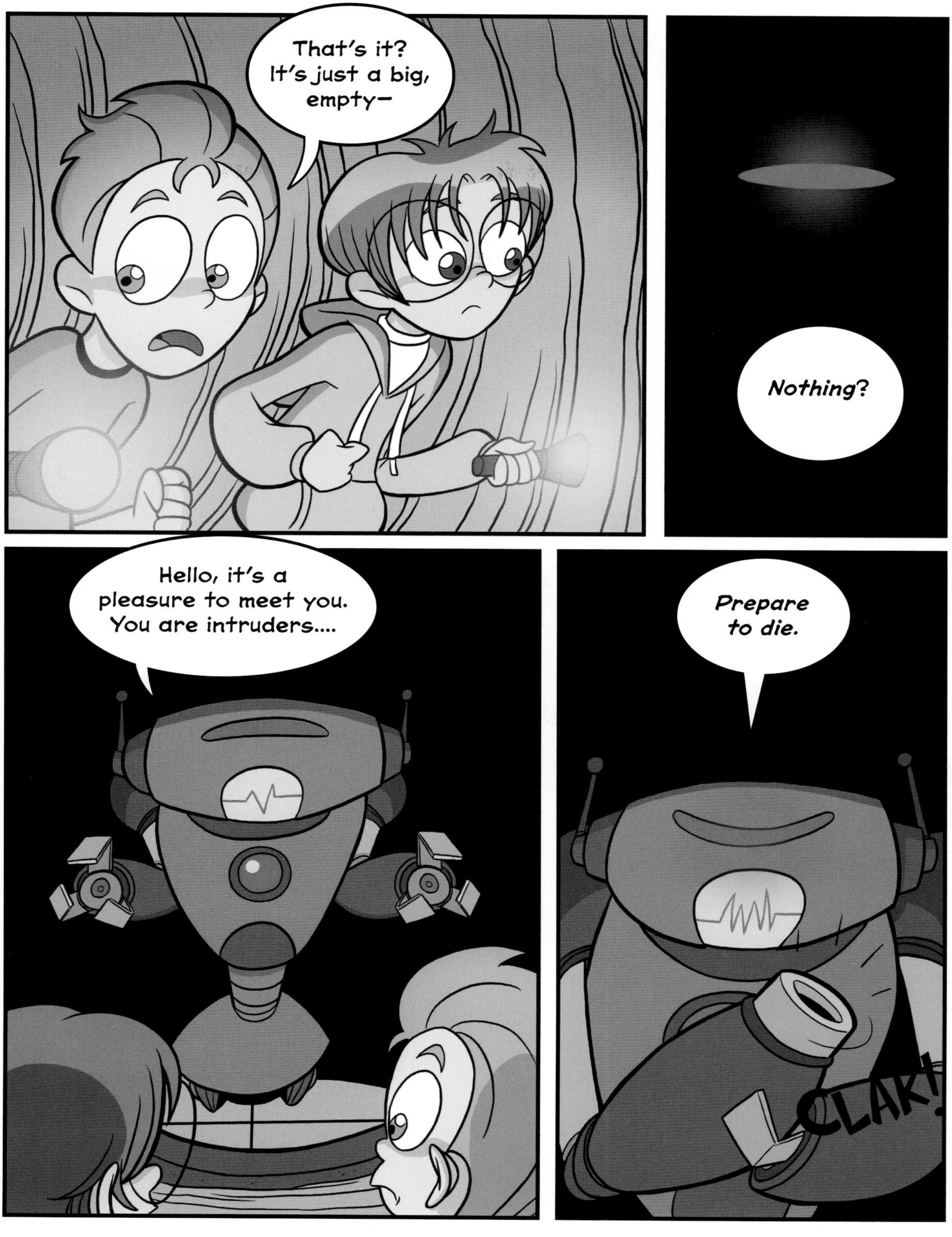
That's it? It's just a big, empty—
Nothing?
Hello, it's a pleasure to meet you. You are intruders....
Prepare to die.
CLAK!

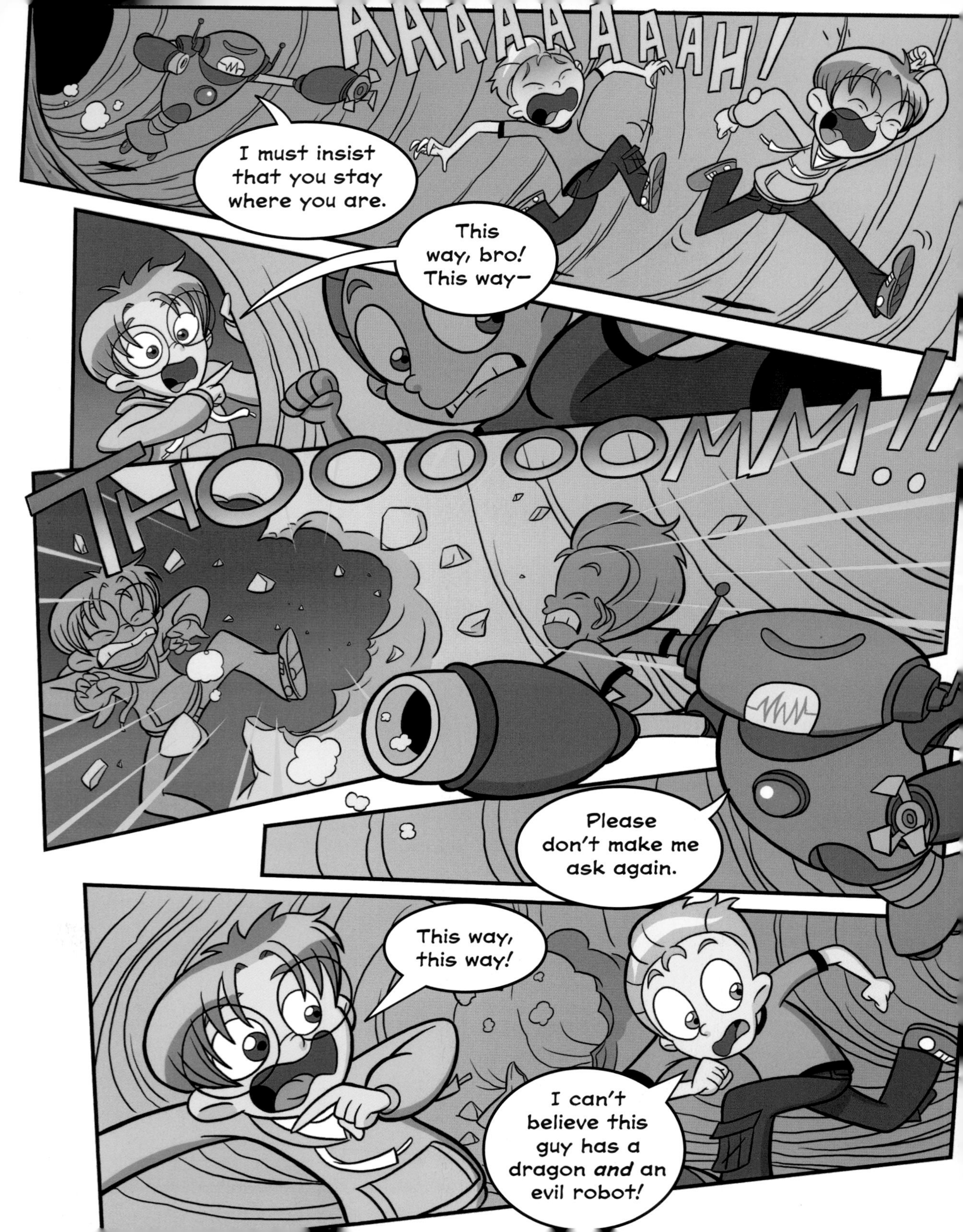
AAAAAAAAH!
I must insist that you stay where you are.
This way, bro! This way—
THOOOOOOMM!!...
Please don't make me ask again.
This way, this way!
I can't believe this guy has a dragon *and* an evil robot!

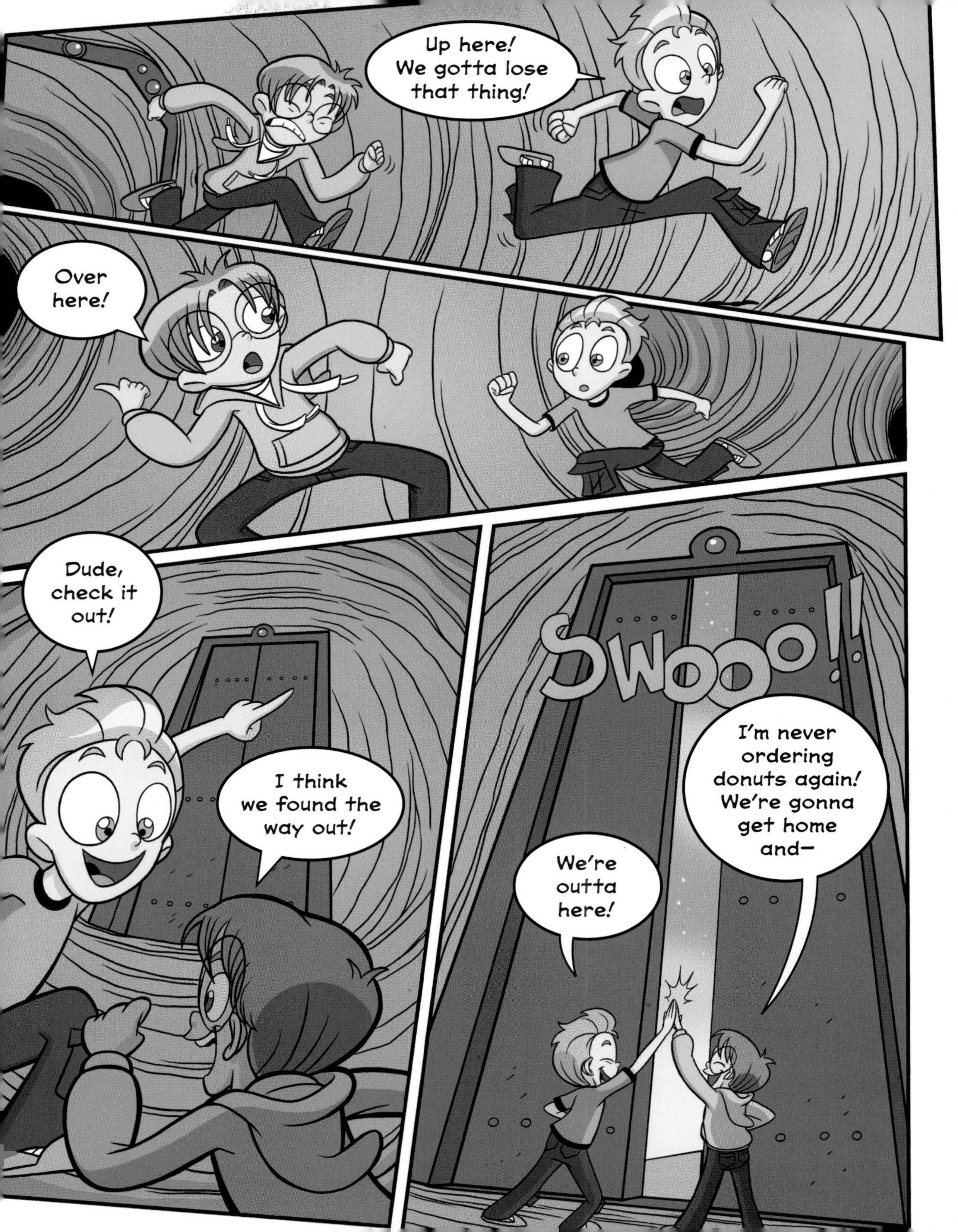
Up here! We gotta lose that thing!
Over here!
Dude, check it out!
I think we found the way out!
SWOOO!!
I'm never ordering donuts again! We're gonna get home and—
We're outta here!

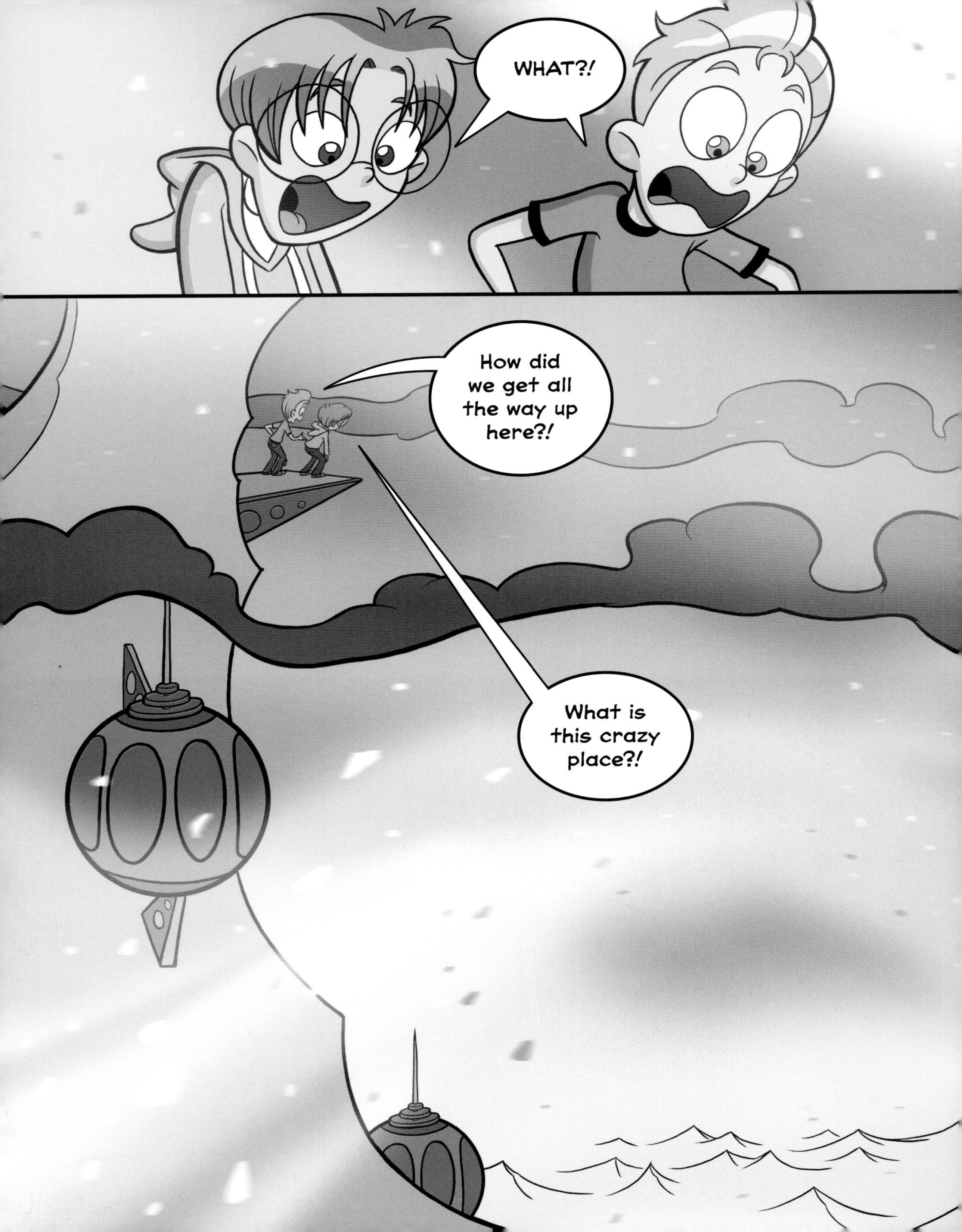
WHAT?!
How did we get all the way up here?!
What is this crazy place?!

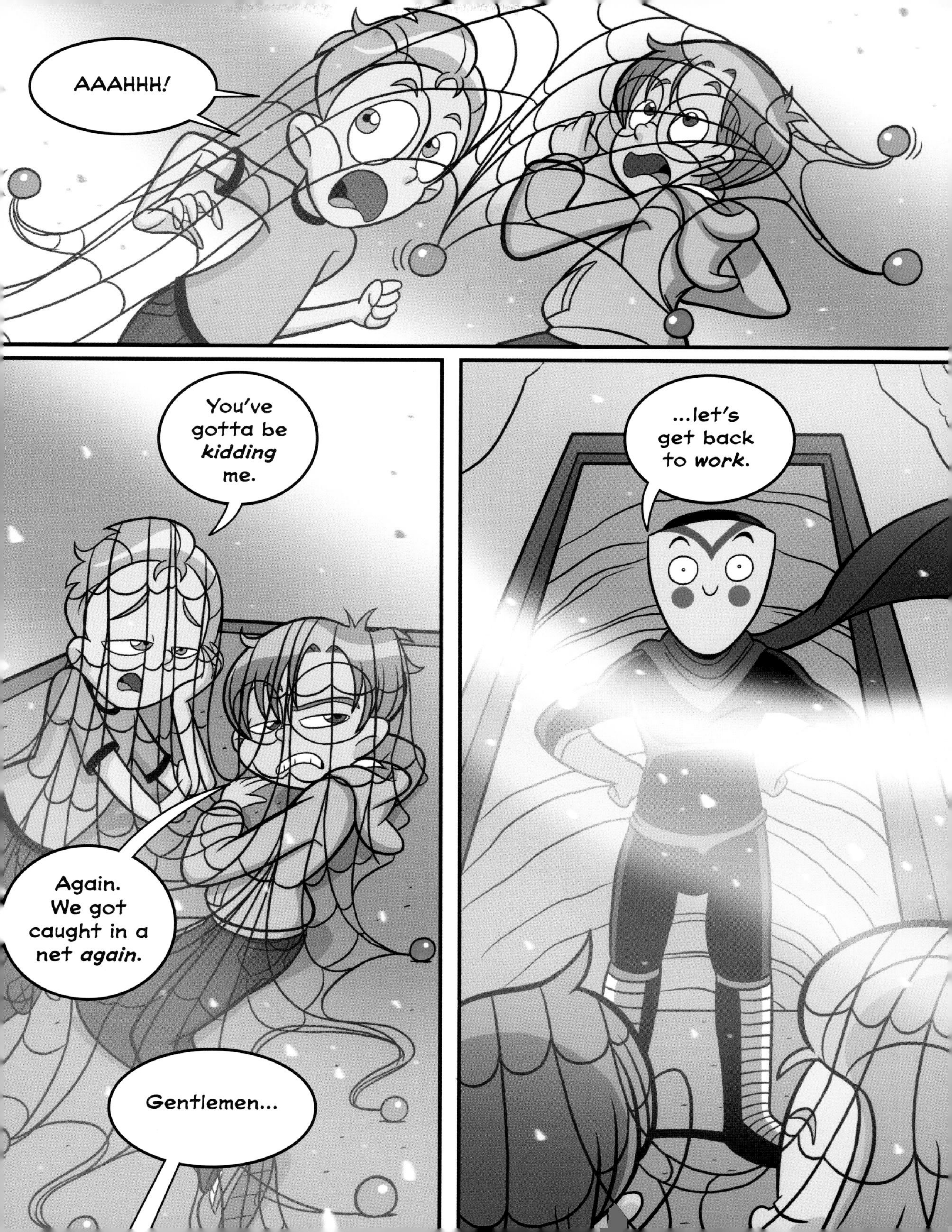
AAAHHH!
You've gotta be *kidding* me.
Again. We got caught in a net *again*.
Gentlemen...
...let's get back to *work*.

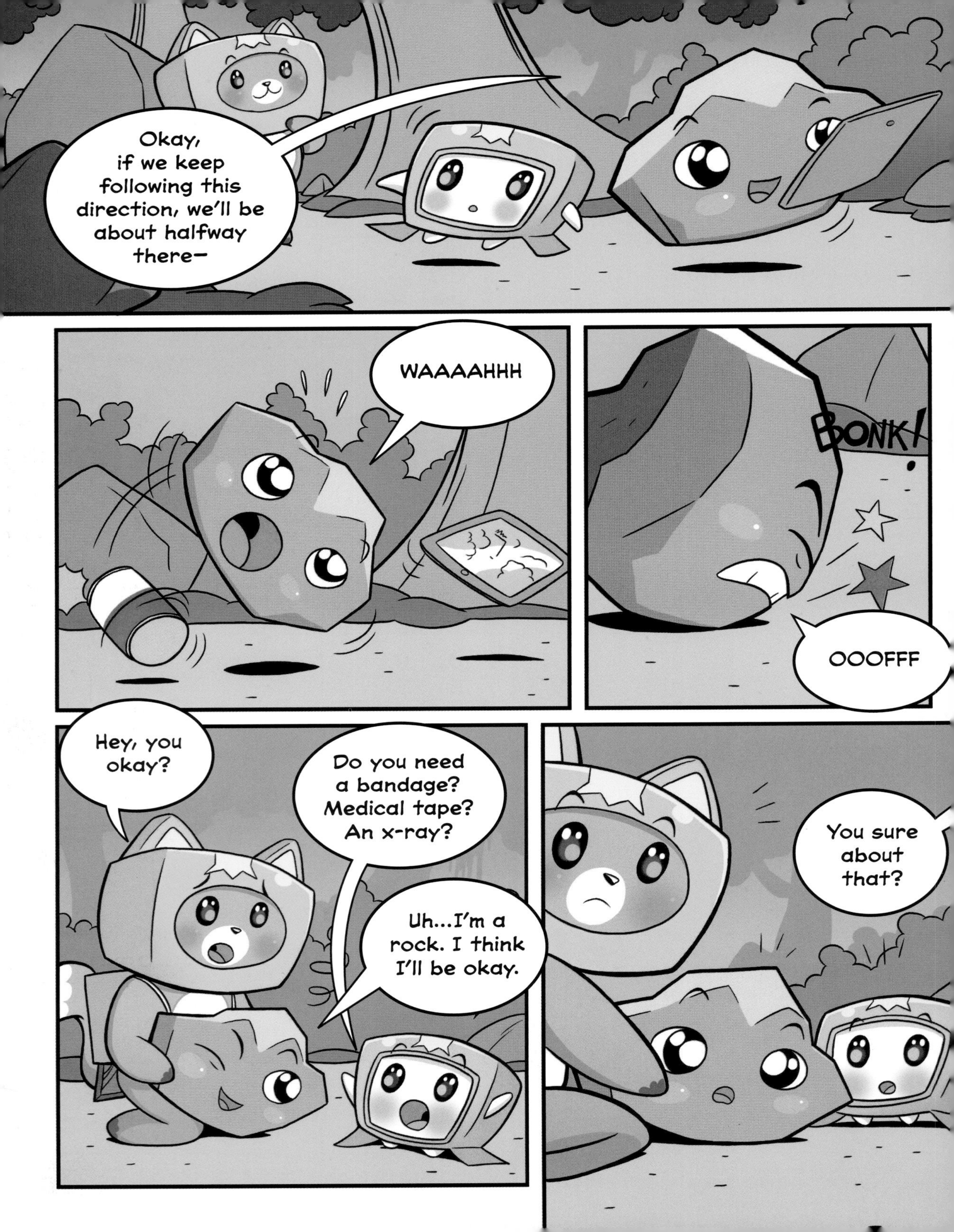
Okay, if we keep following this direction, we'll be about halfway there–
WAAAAHHH
BONK!
OOOFFF
Hey, you okay?
Do you need a bandage? Medical tape? An x-ray?
Uh...I'm a rock. I think I'll be okay.
You sure about that?

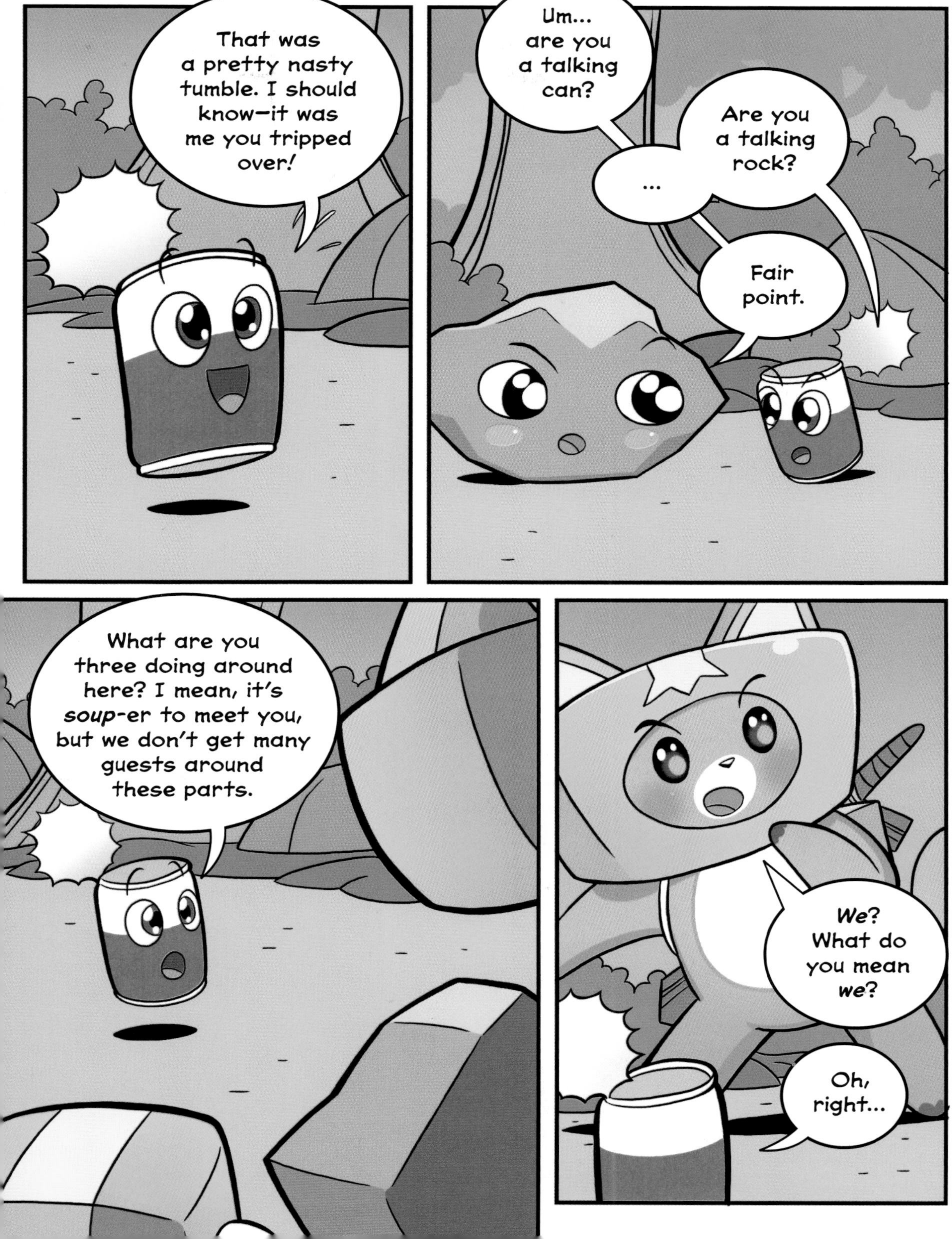
That was a pretty nasty tumble. I should know—it was me you tripped over!
Um... are you a talking can?
Are you a talking rock?
...
Fair point.
What are you three doing around here? I mean, it's *soup*-er to meet you, but we don't get many guests around these parts.
We? What do you mean *we*?
Oh, right...

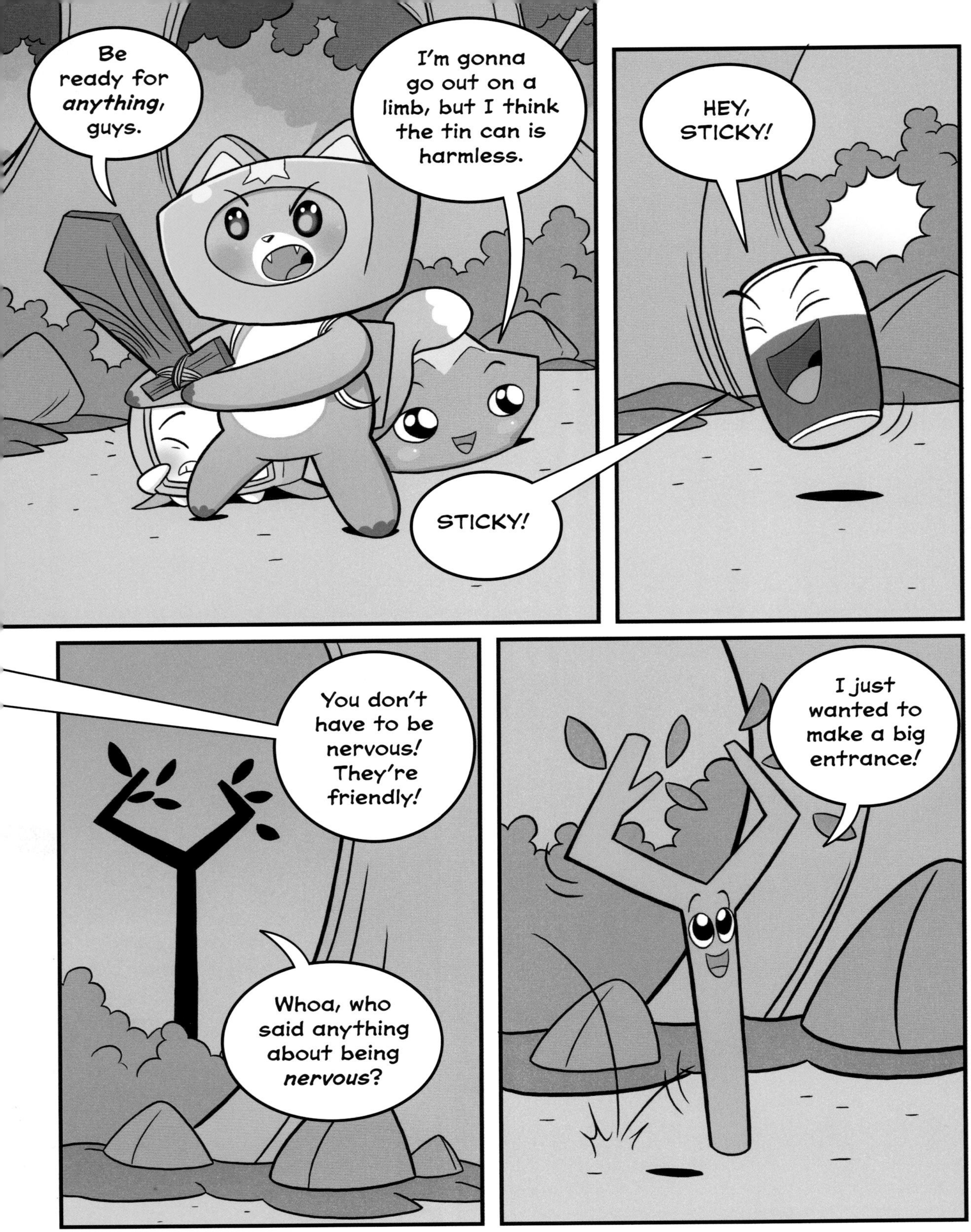

Be ready for *anything*, guys.
I'm gonna go out on a limb, but I think the tin can is harmless.
STICKY!
HEY, STICKY!
You don't have to be nervous! They're friendly!
Whoa, who said anything about being *nervous*?
I just wanted to make a big entrance!

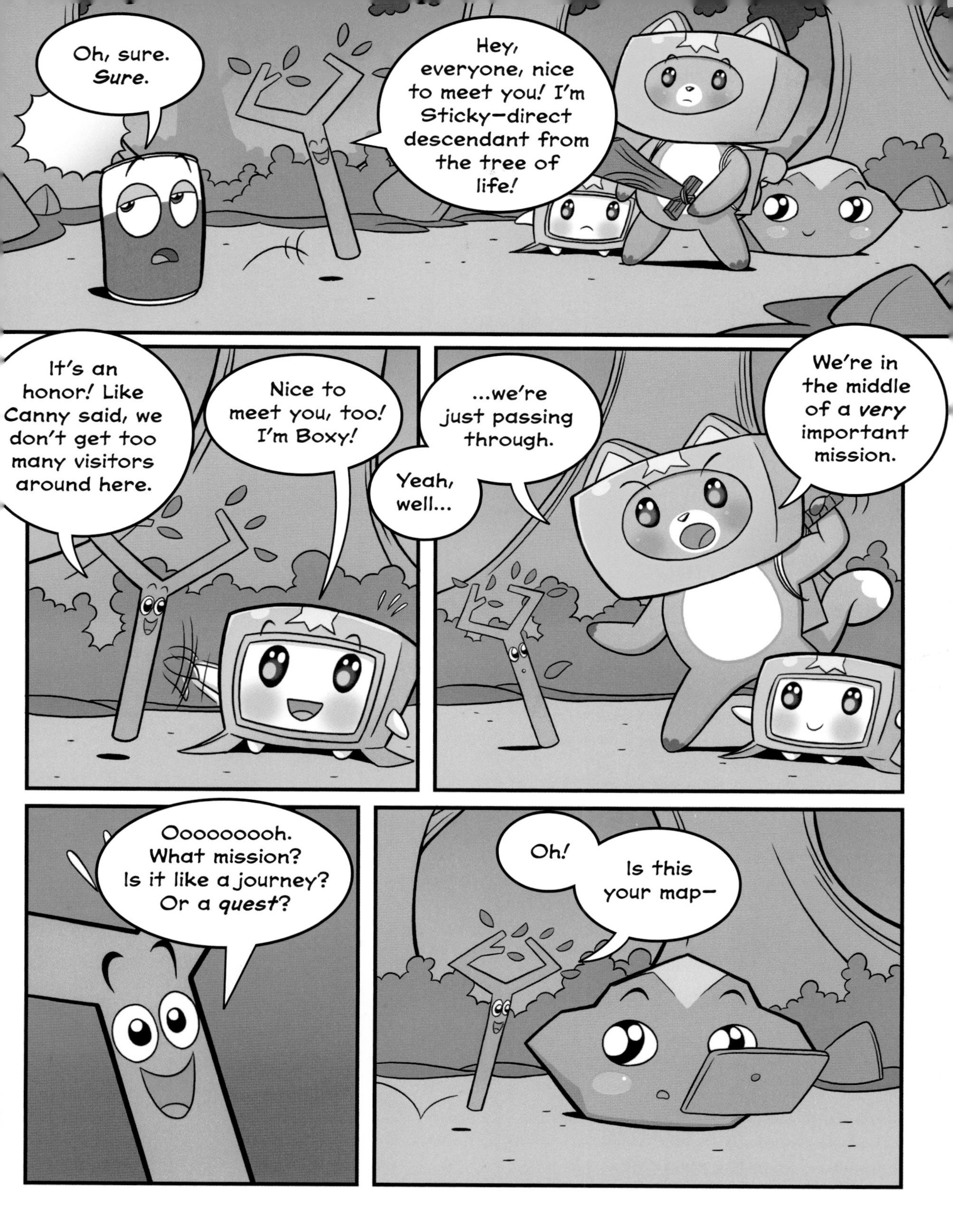
Oh, sure. *Sure.*
Hey, everyone, nice to meet you! I'm Sticky—direct descendant from the tree of life!
It's an honor! Like Canny said, we don't get too many visitors around here.
Nice to meet you, too! I'm Boxy!
Yeah, well...
...we're just passing through.
We're in the middle of a *very* important mission.
Oooooooh. What mission? Is it like a journey? Or a *quest*?
Oh!
Is this your map—

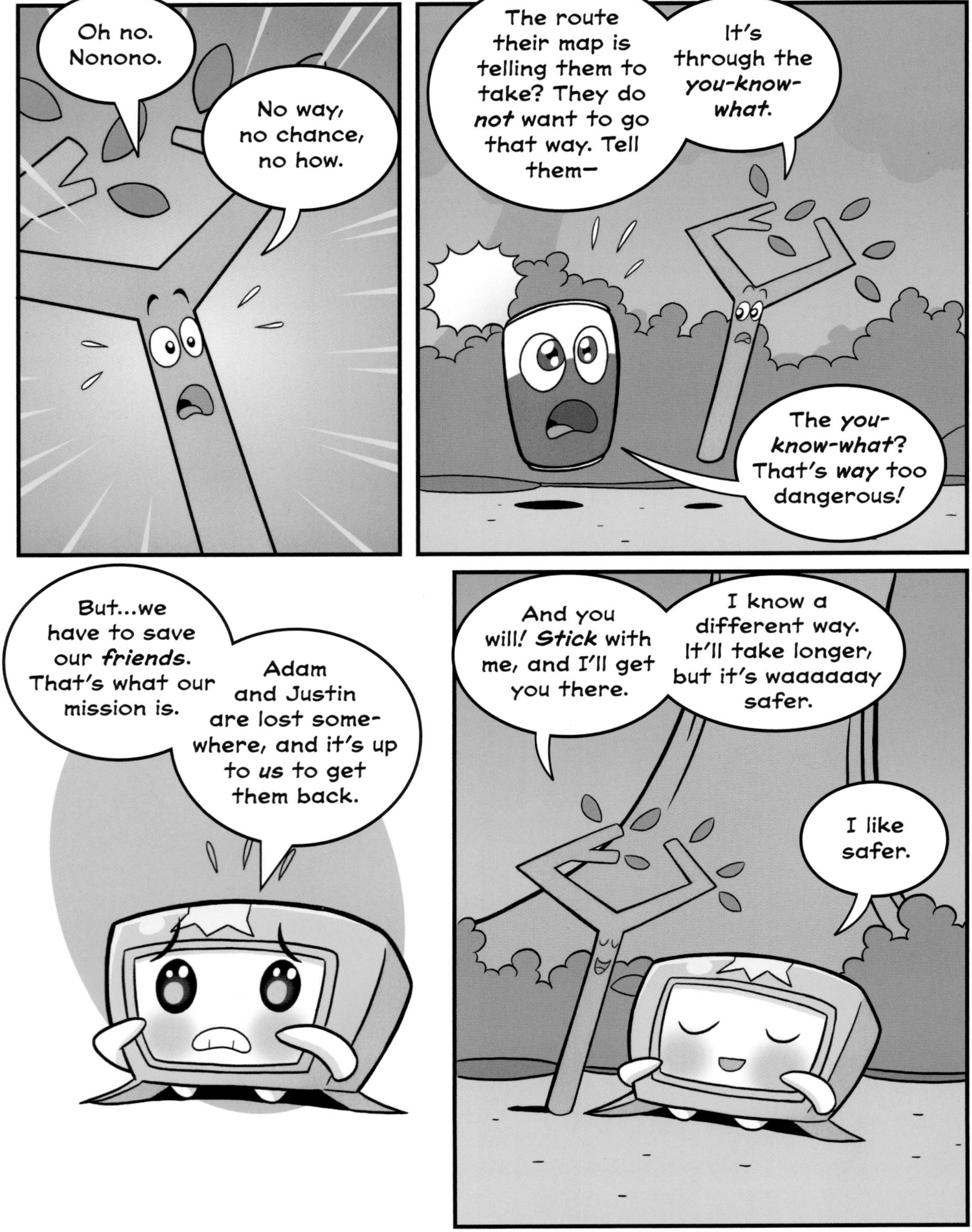
Oh no. Nonono.
No way, no chance, no how.
The route their map is telling them to take? They do *not* want to go that way. Tell them—
It's through the *you-know-what*.
The *you-know-what*? That's *way* too dangerous!
But...we have to save our *friends*. That's what our mission is.
Adam and Justin are lost somewhere, and it's up to *us* to get them back.
And you will! *Stick* with me, and I'll get you there.
I know a different way. It'll take longer, but it's waaaaaay safer.
I like safer.

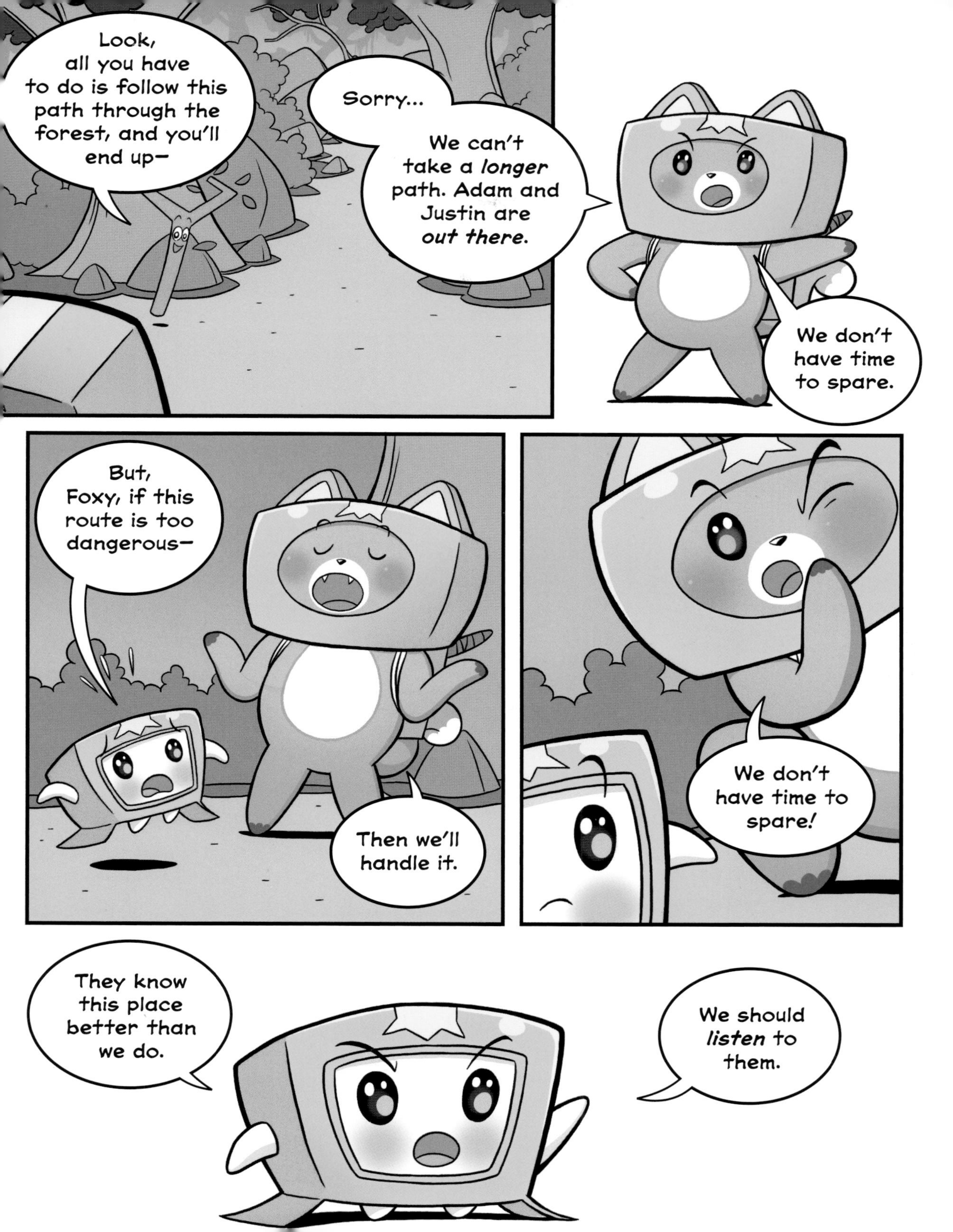

Look, all you have to do is follow this path through the forest, and you'll end up—
Sorry...
We can't take a *longer* path. Adam and Justin are *out there.*
We don't have time to spare.
But, Foxy, if this route is too dangerous—
Then we'll handle it.
We don't have time to spare!
They know this place better than we do.
We should *listen* to them.

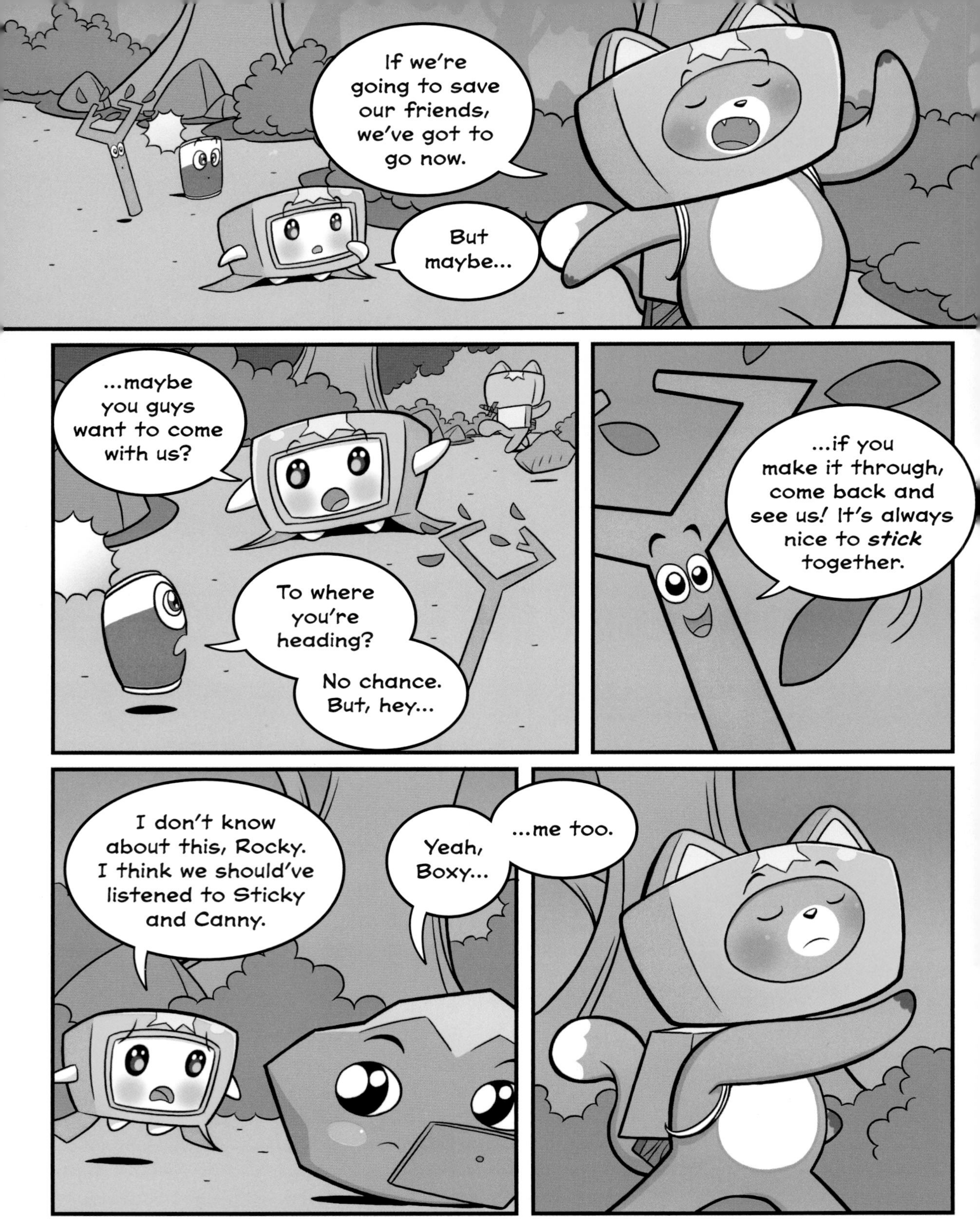
If we're going to save our friends, we've got to go now.
But maybe...
...maybe you guys want to come with us?
To where you're heading?
No chance. But, hey...
...if you make it through, come back and see us! It's always nice to *stick* together.
I don't know about this, Rocky. I think we should've listened to Sticky and Canny.
Yeah, Boxy...
...me too.

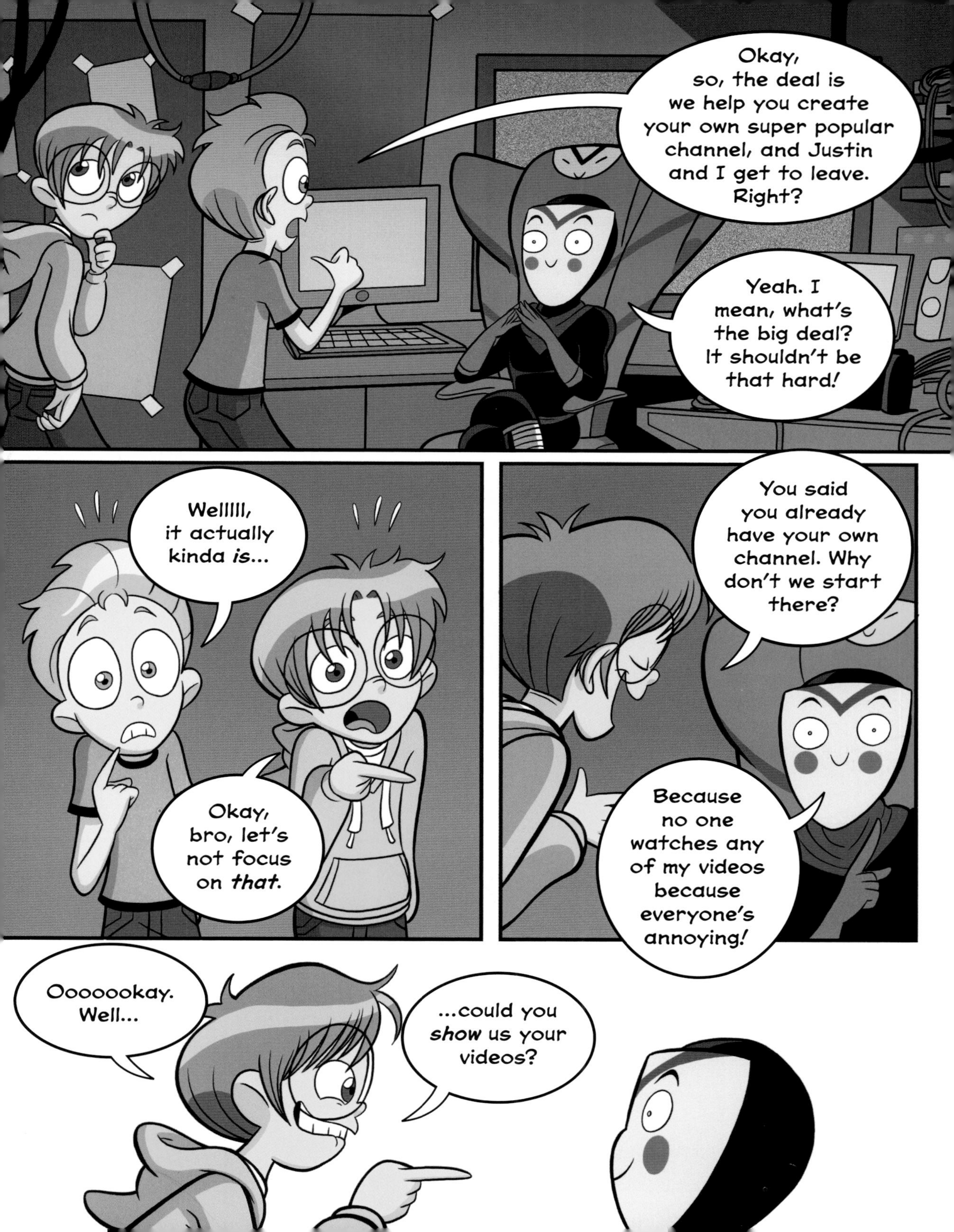
Okay, so, the deal is we help you create your own super popular channel, and Justin and I get to leave. Right?
Yeah. I mean, what's the big deal? It shouldn't be that hard!
Welllll, it actually kinda *is*...
Okay, bro, let's not focus on *that*.
You said you already have your own channel. Why don't we start there?
Because no one watches any of my videos because everyone's annoying!
Ooooookay. Well...
...could you *show* us your videos?

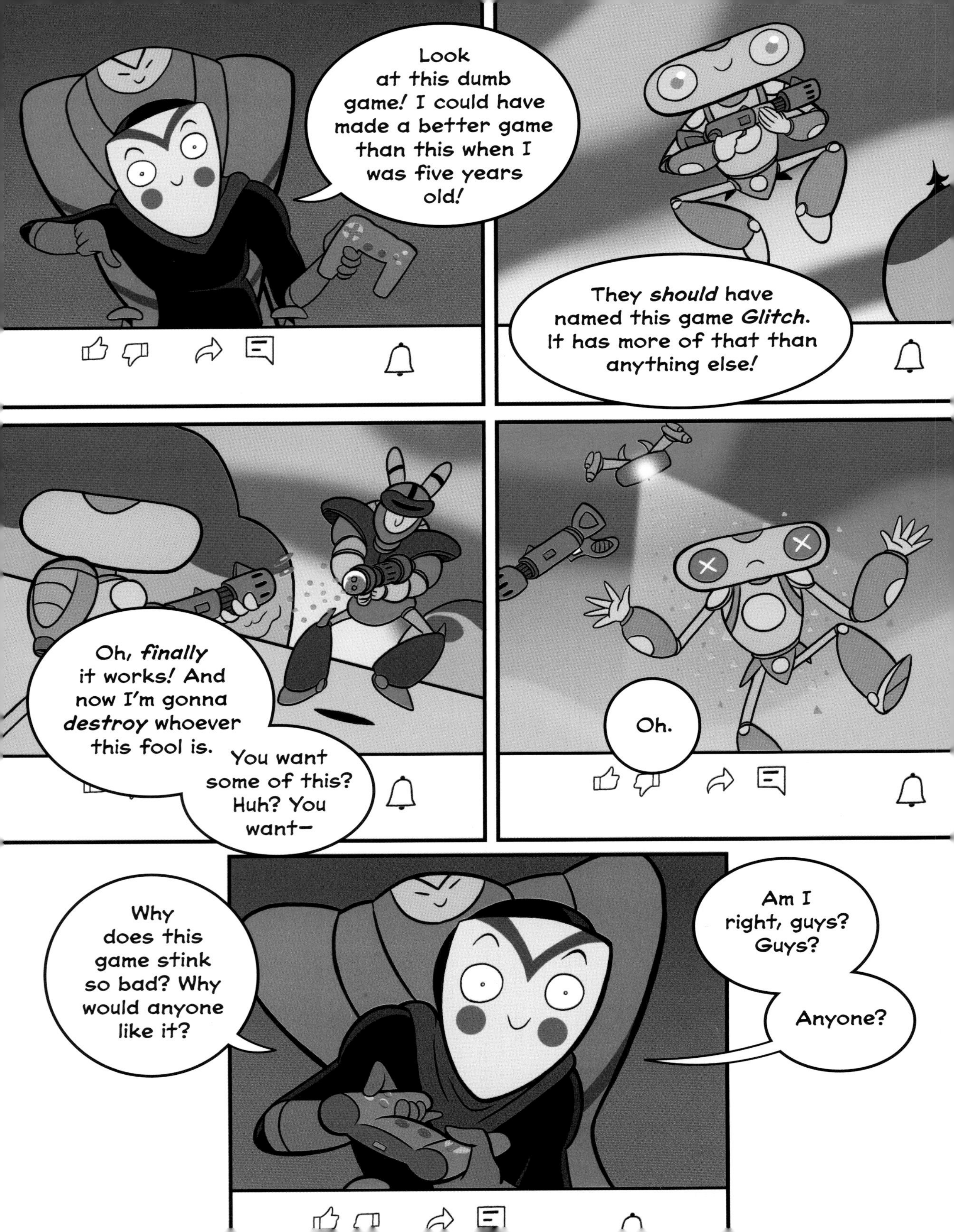
Look at this dumb game! I could have made a better game than this when I was five years old!
They *should* have named this game *Glitch*. It has more of that than anything else!
Oh, *finally* it works! And now I'm gonna *destroy* whoever this fool is.
You want some of this? Huh? You want—
Oh.
Why does this game stink so bad? Why would anyone like it?
Am I right, guys? Guys?
Anyone?

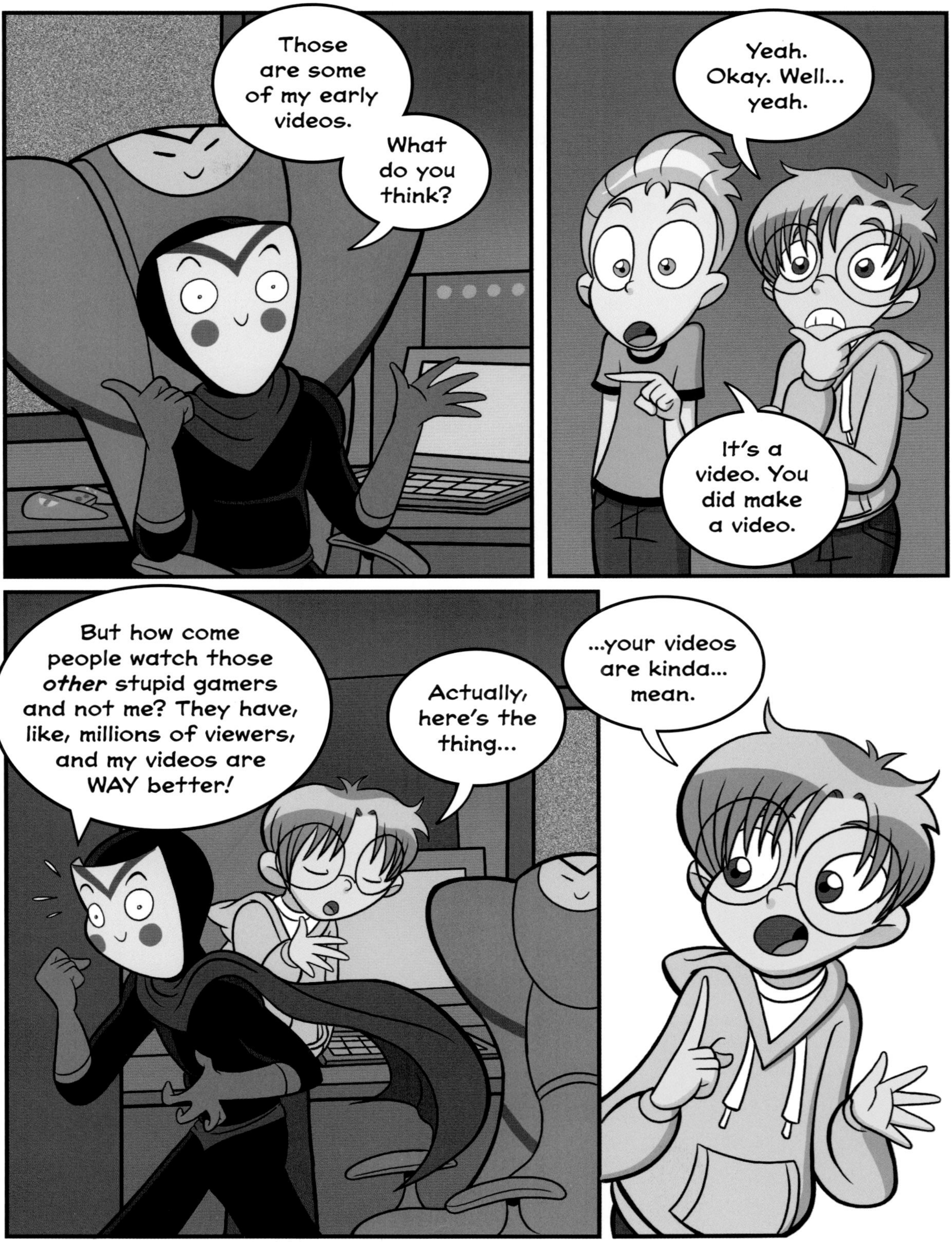
Those are some of my early videos.
What do you think?
Yeah. Okay. Well... yeah.
It's a video. You did make a video.
But how come people watch those *other* stupid gamers and not me? They have, like, millions of viewers, and my videos are WAY better!
Actually, here's the thing...
...your videos are kinda... mean.

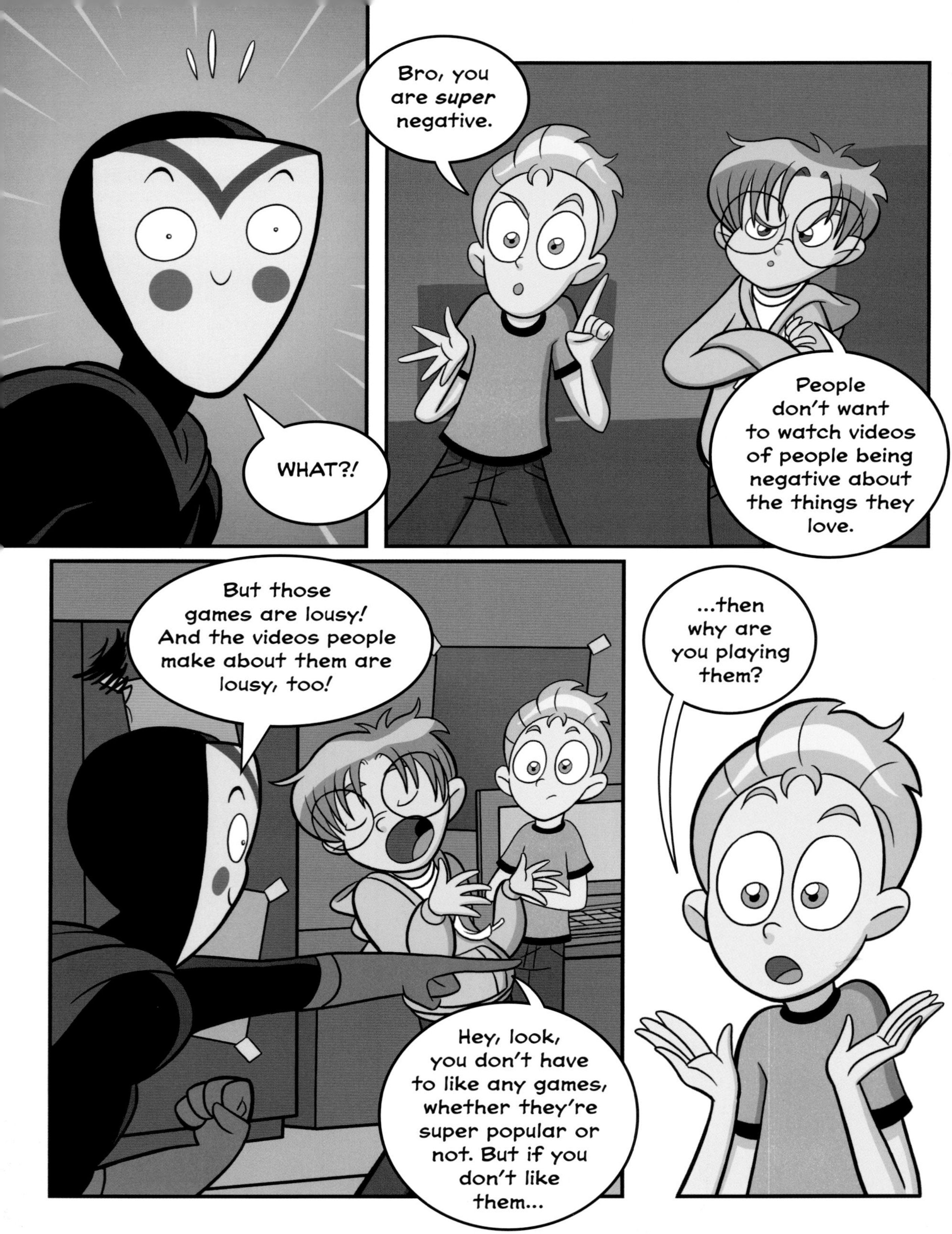
WHAT?!
Bro, you are *super* negative.
People don't want to watch videos of people being negative about the things they love.
But those games are lousy! And the videos people make about them are lousy, too!
Hey, look, you don't have to like any games, whether they're super popular or not. But if you don't like them...
...then why are you playing them?

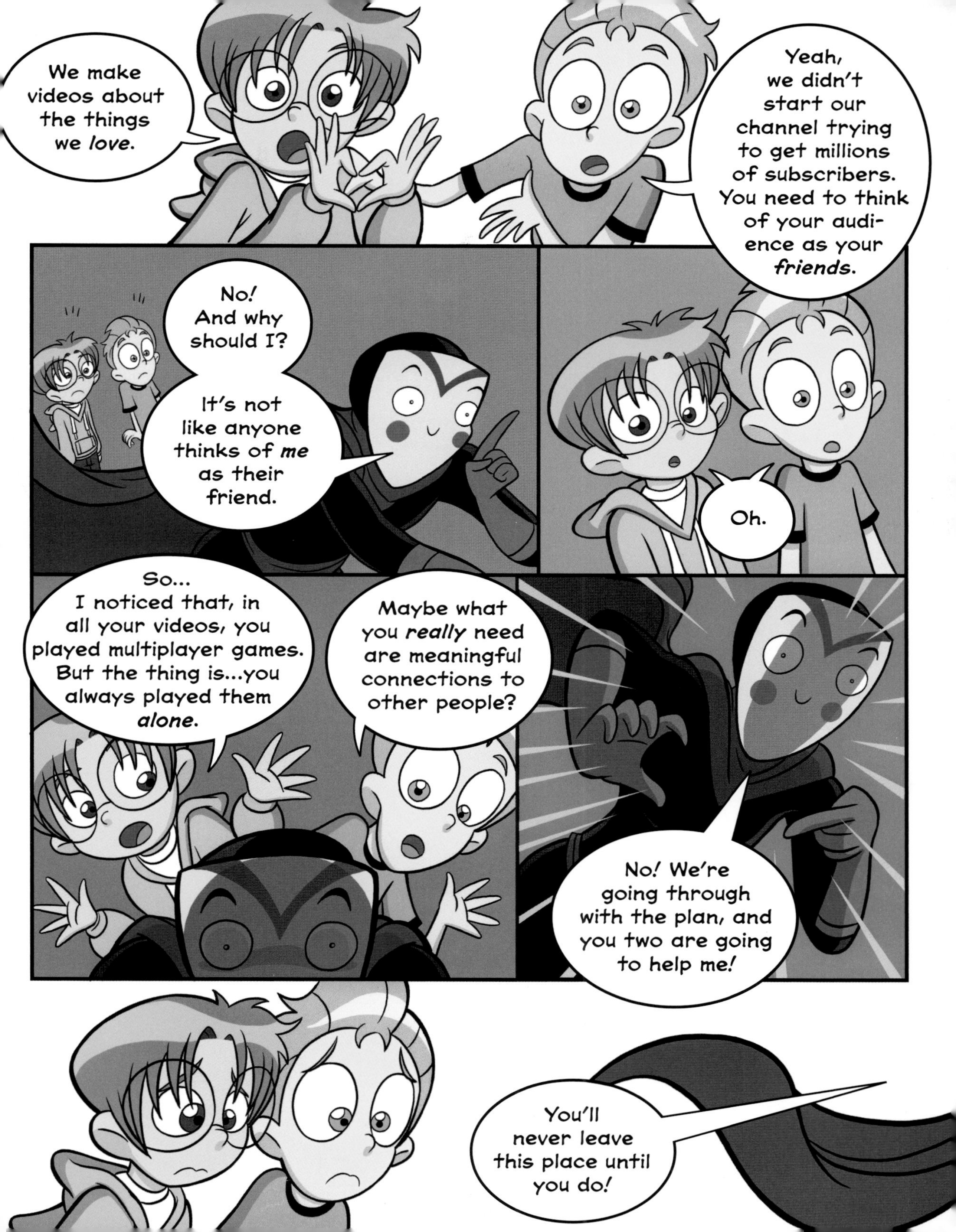
We make videos about the things we *love*.
Yeah, we didn't start our channel trying to get millions of subscribers. You need to think of your audience as your ***friends***.
No! And why should I?
It's not like anyone thinks of *me* as their friend.
Oh.
So... I noticed that, in all your videos, you played multiplayer games. But the thing is...you always played them ***alone***.
Maybe what you ***really*** need are meaningful connections to other people?
No! We're going through with the plan, and you two are going to help me!
You'll never leave this place until you do!

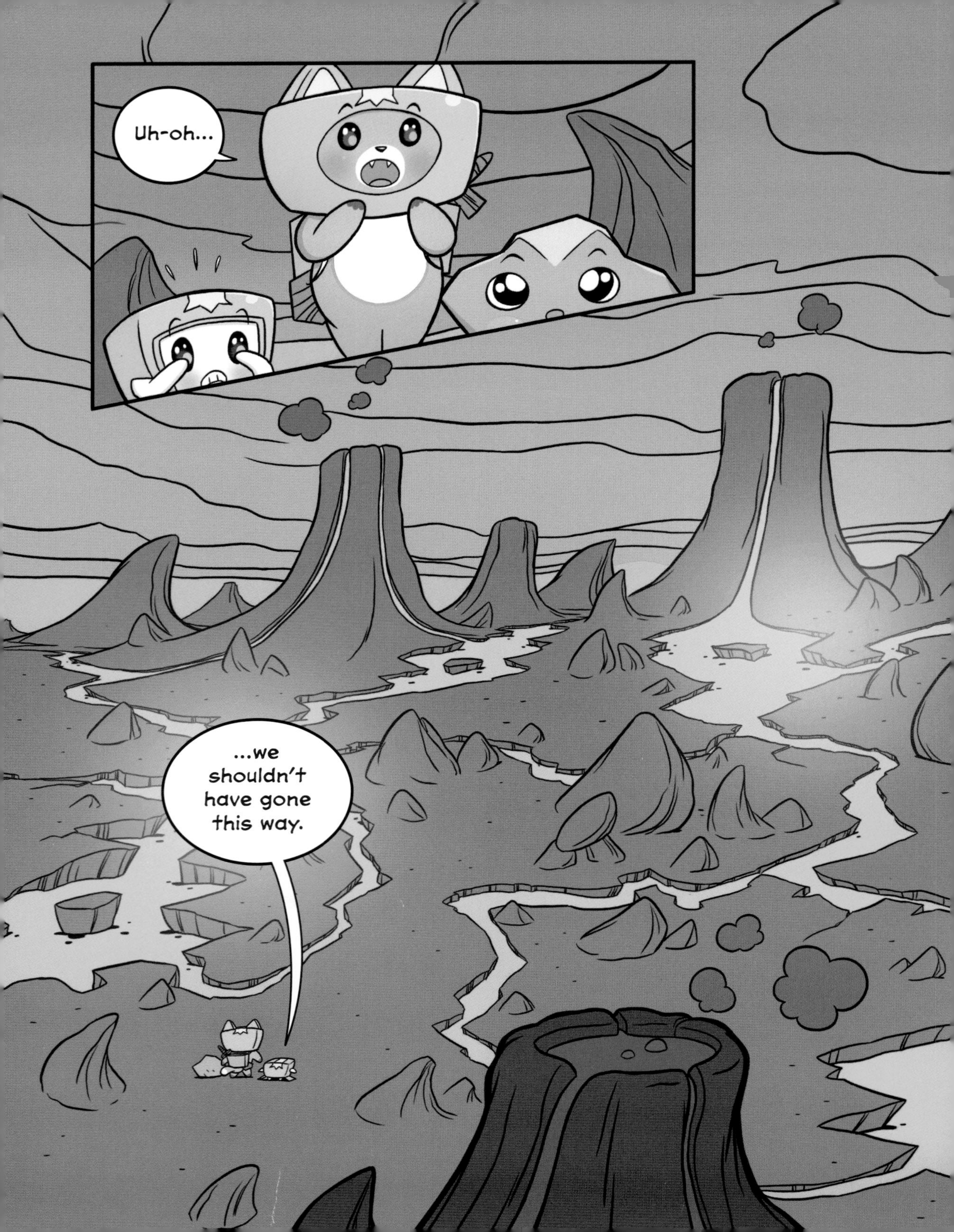
Uh-oh...
...we shouldn't have gone this way.

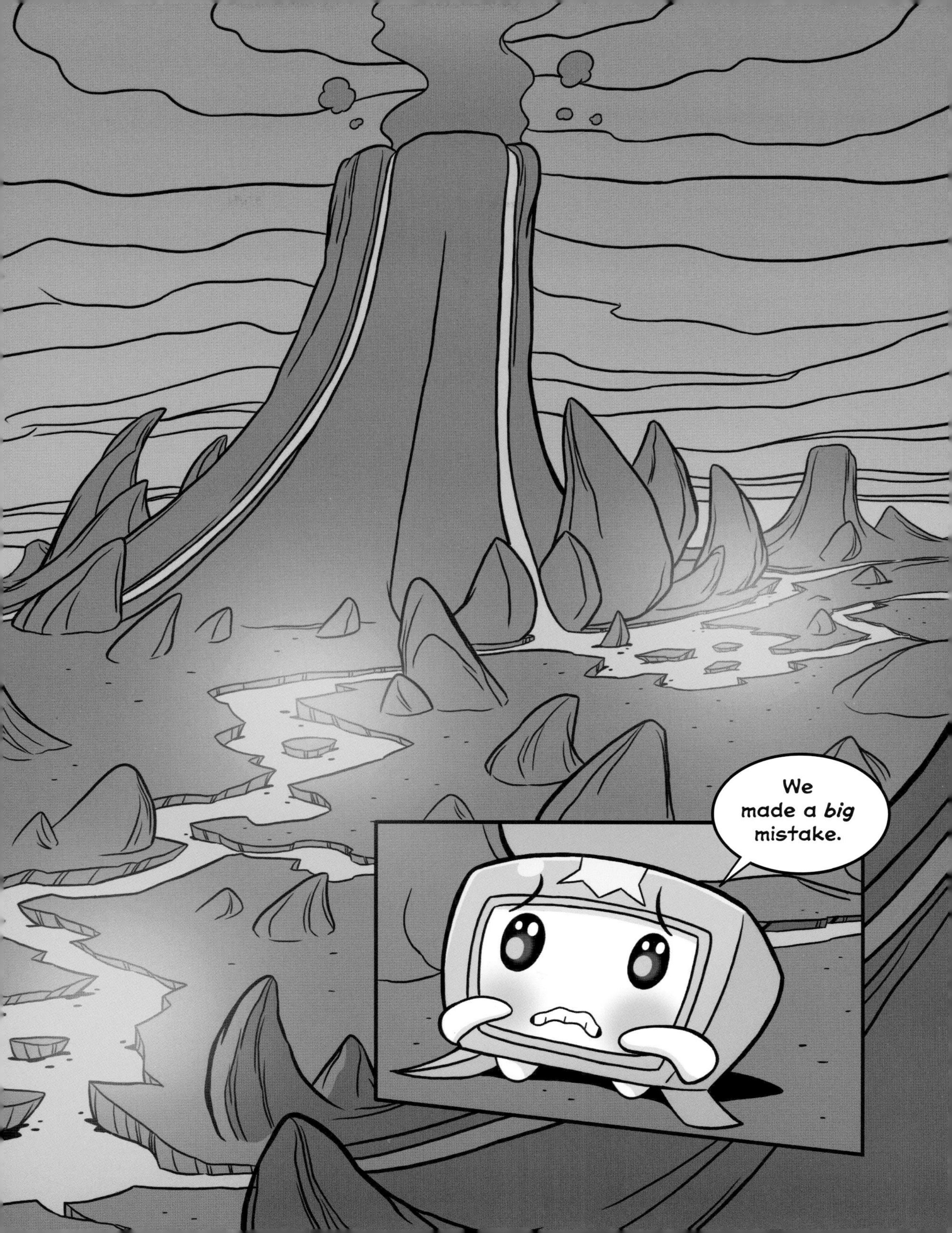
We made a *big* mistake.

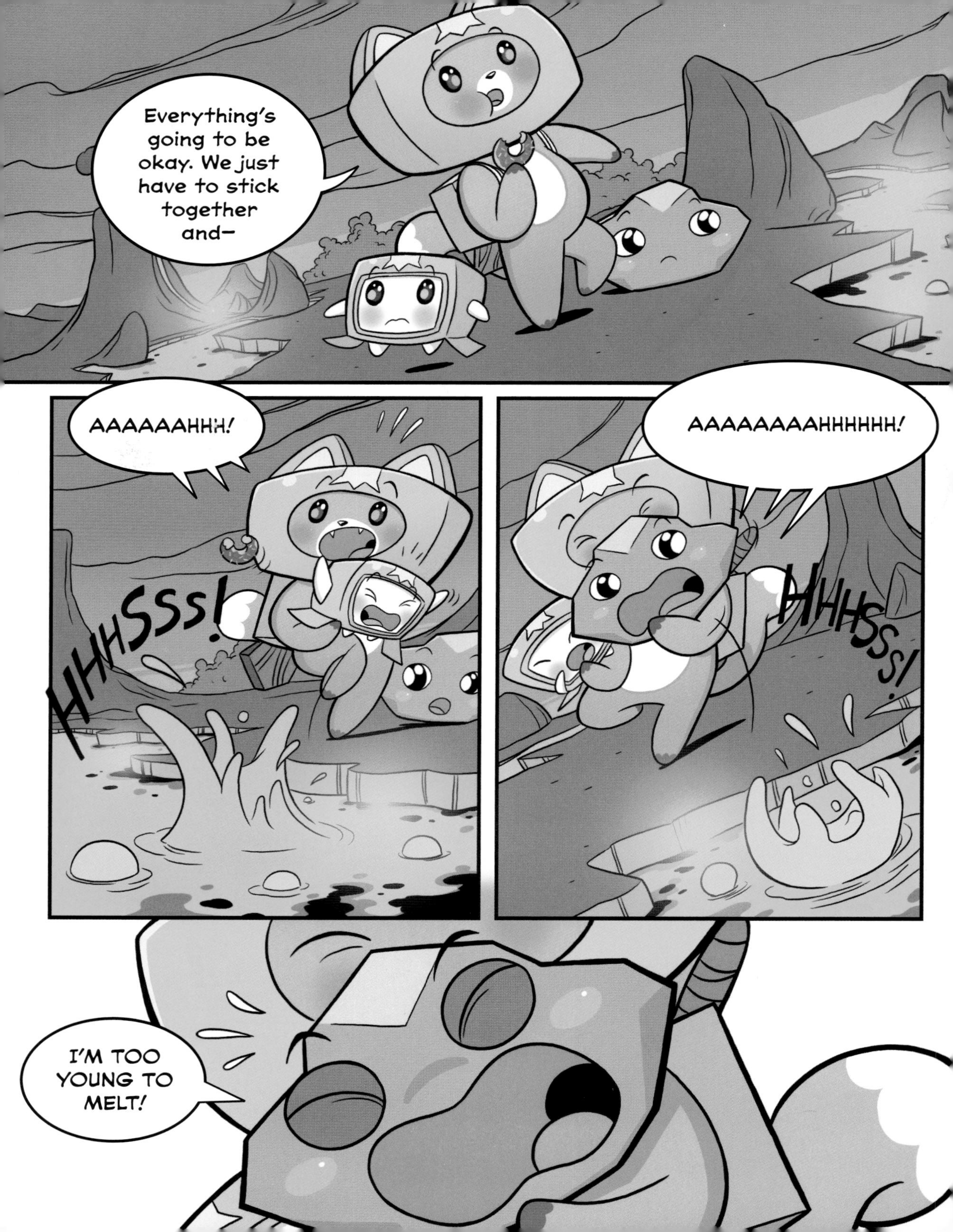
Everything's going to be okay. We just have to stick together and–
AAAAAAHHH!
HHHSSS!
AAAAAAAAHHHHHH!
HHHSSS!
I'M TOO YOUNG TO MELT!

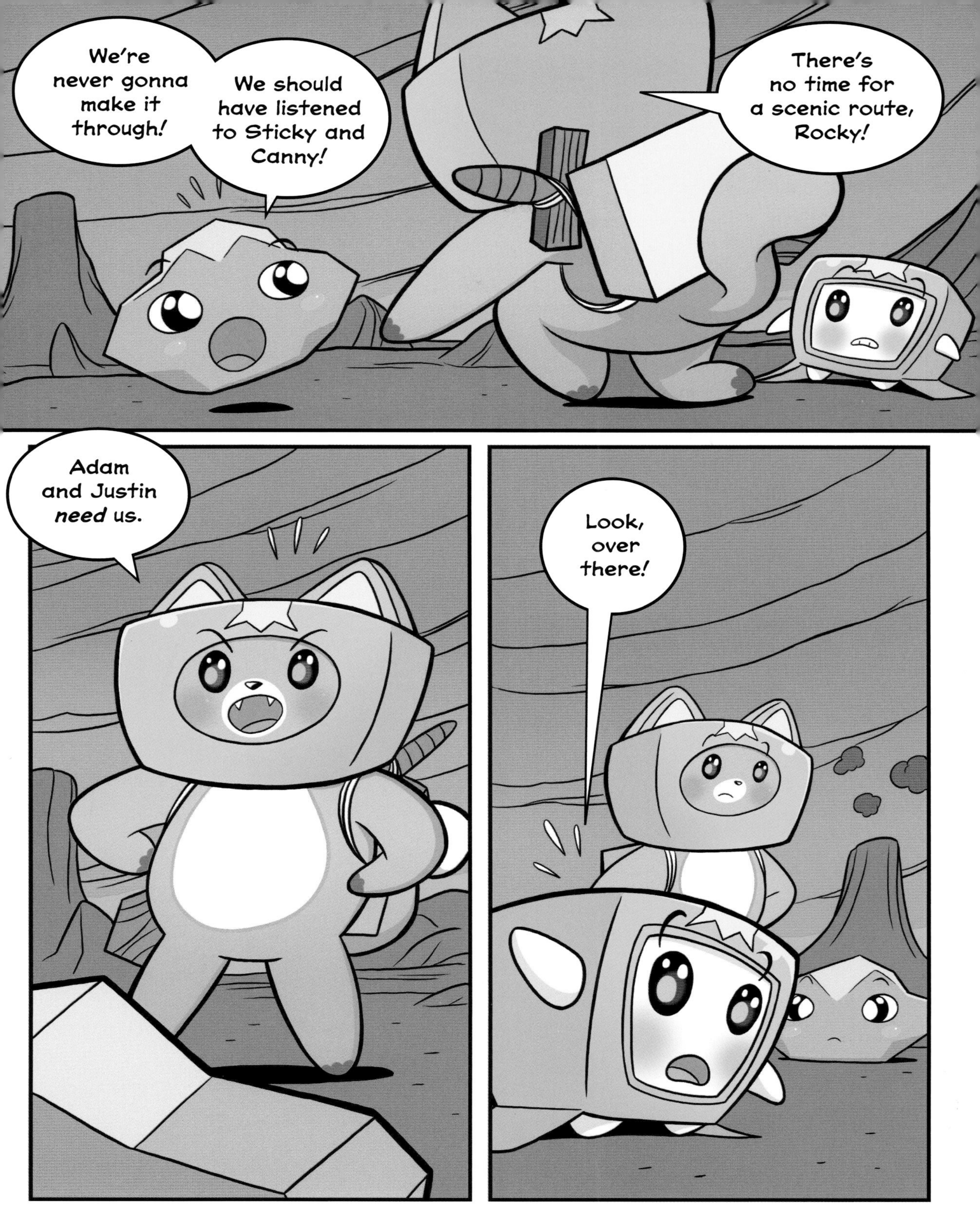
We're never gonna make it through!
We should have listened to Sticky and Canny!
There's no time for a scenic route, Rocky!
Adam and Justin *need* us.
Look, over there!

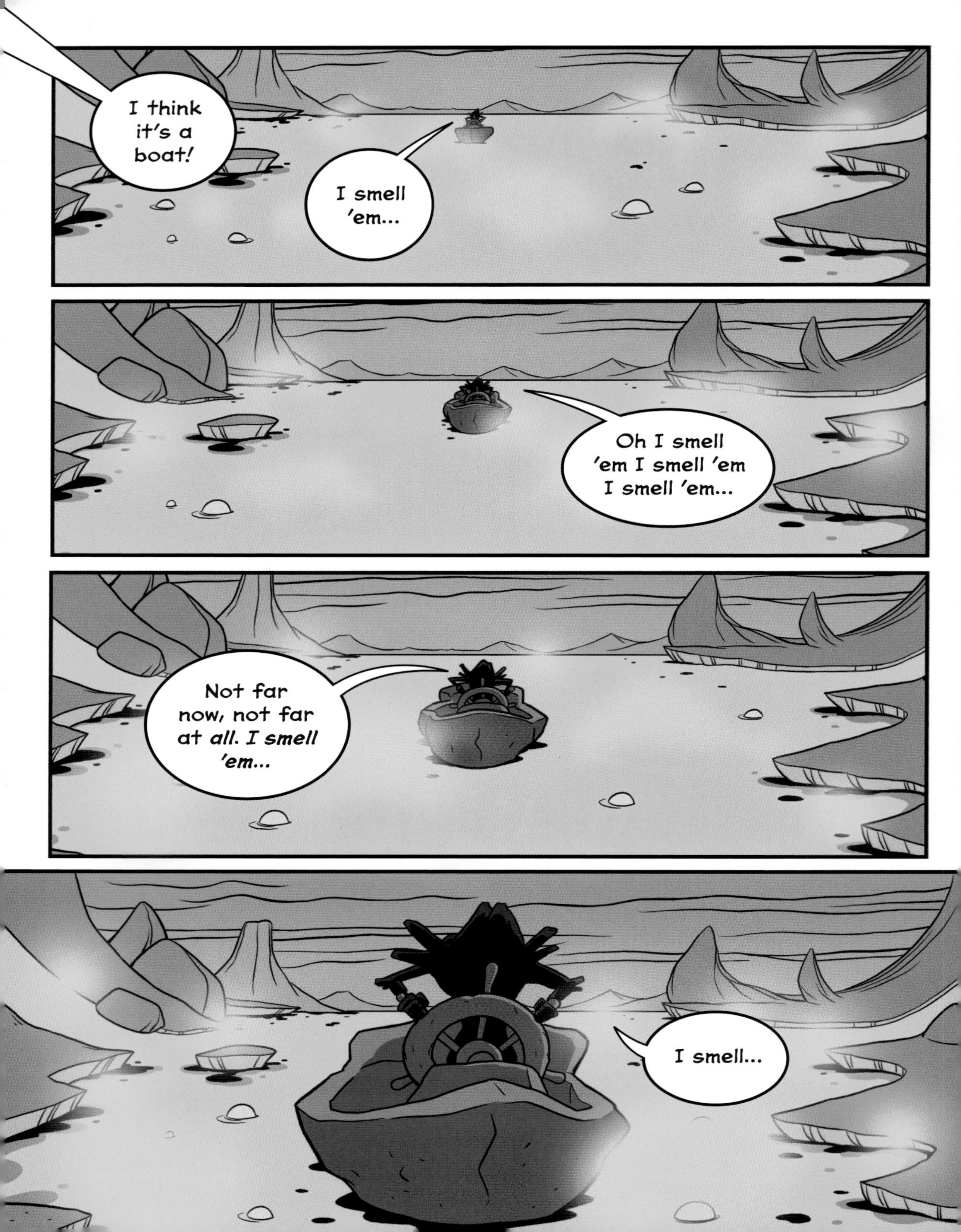
I think it's a boat!
I smell 'em...
Oh I smell 'em I smell 'em I smell 'em...
Not far now, not far at *all. I smell 'em...*
I smell...

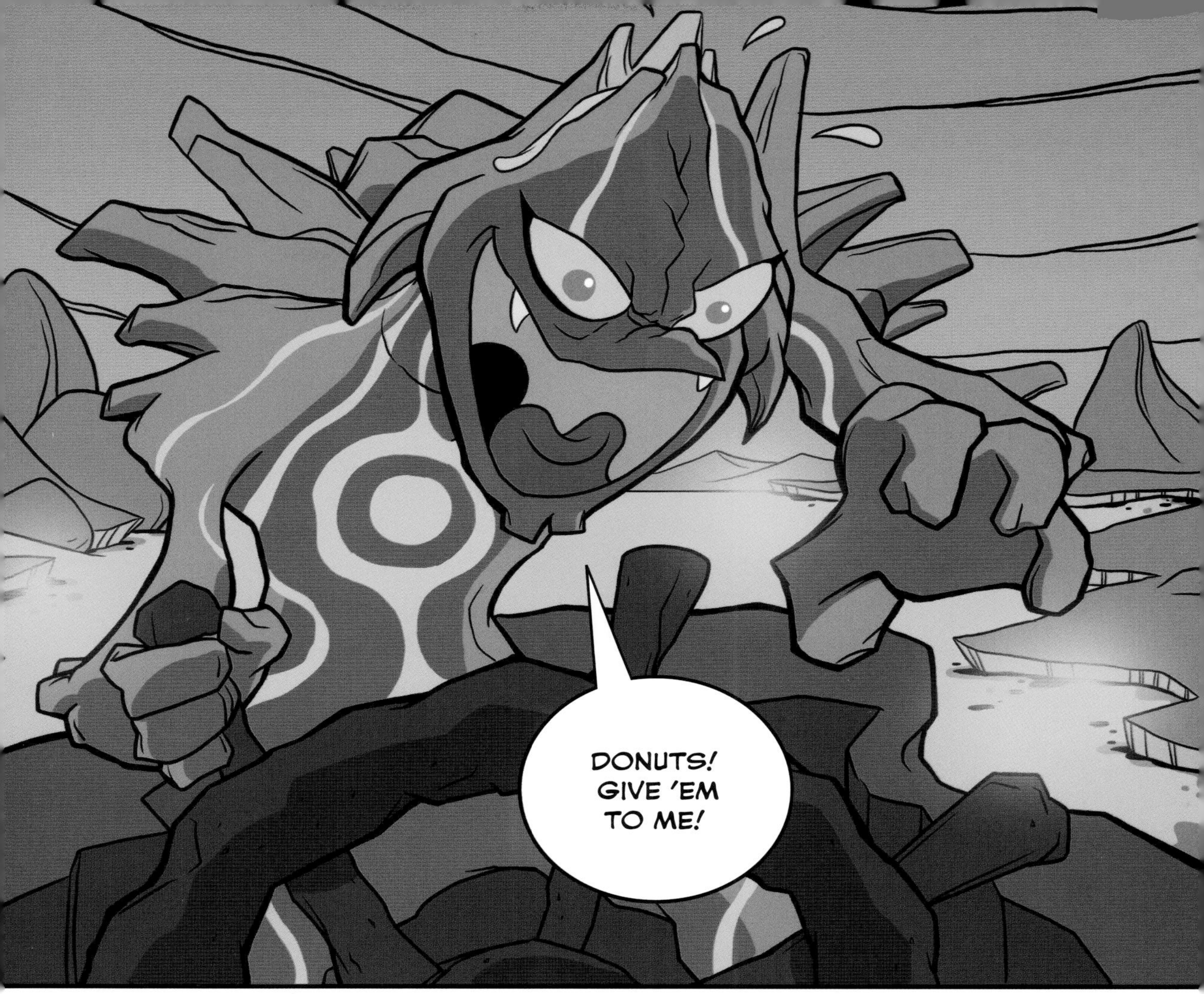
DONUTS!
GIVE 'EM
TO ME!

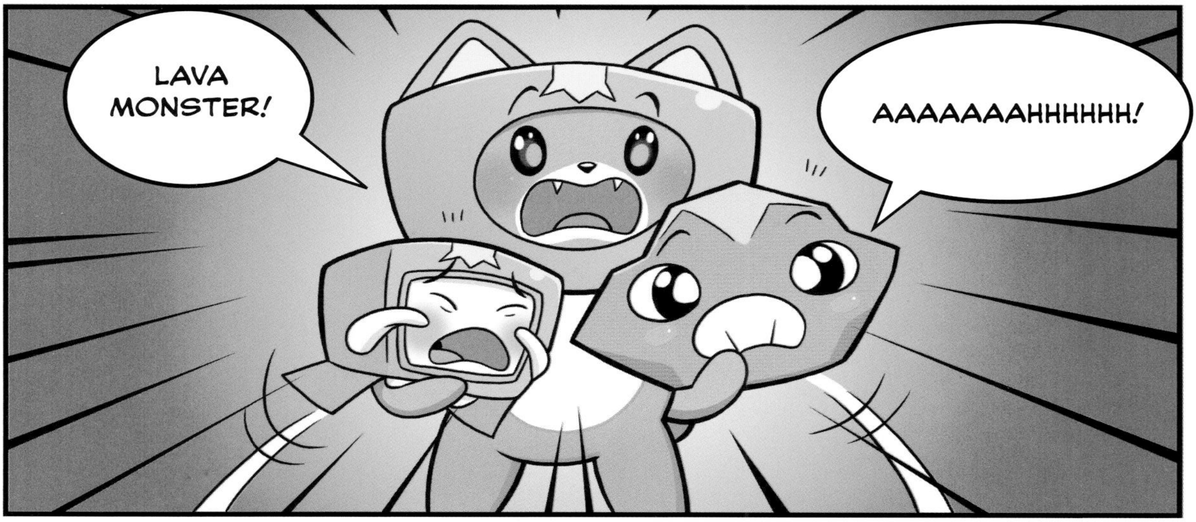
LAVA
MONSTER!
AAAAAAAHHHHHH!

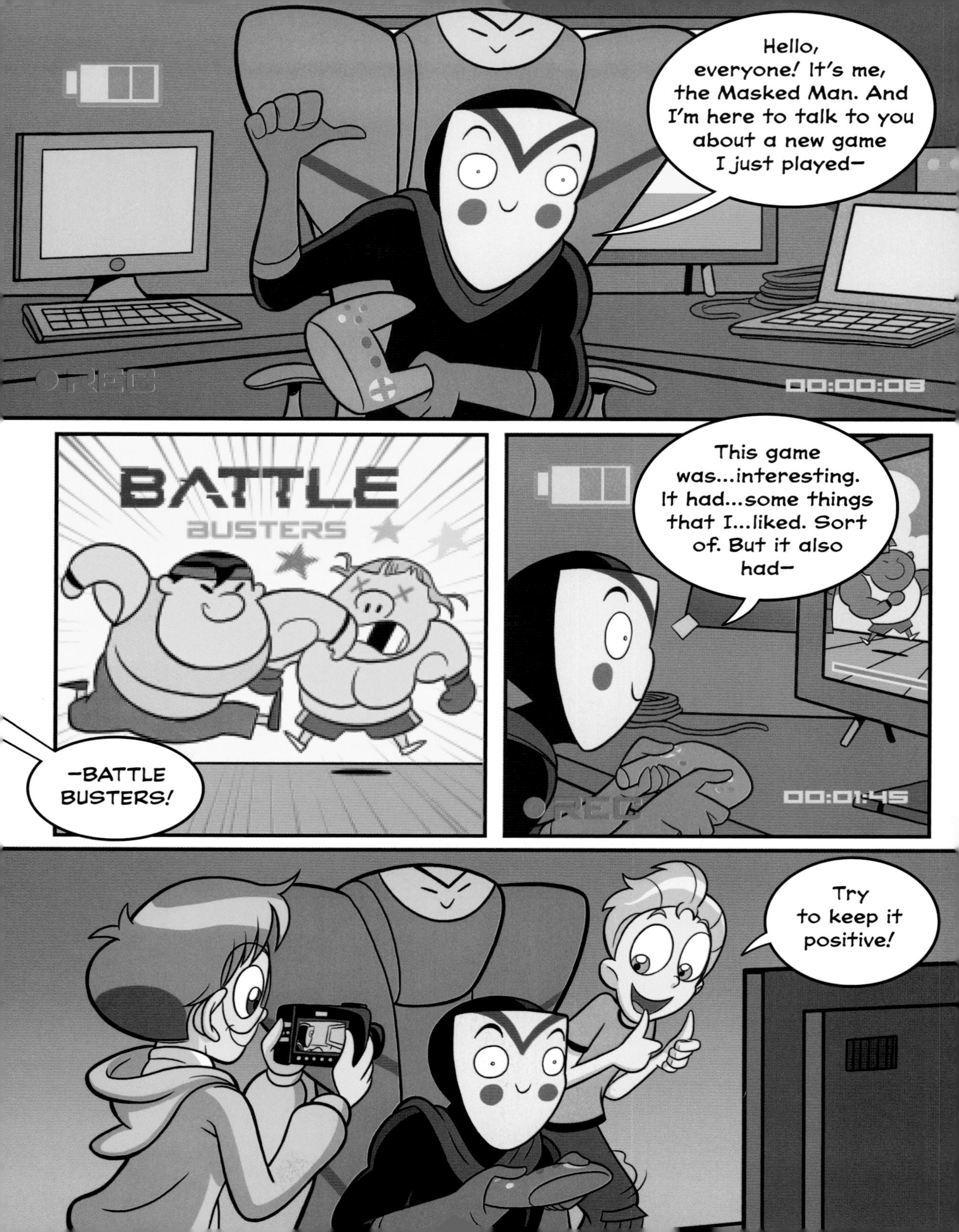
Hello, everyone! It's me, the Masked Man. And I'm here to talk to you about a new game I just played—
REC
00:00:08
BATTLE BUSTERS
—BATTLE BUSTERS!
This game was...interesting. It had...some things that I...liked. Sort of. But it also had—
REC
00:01:45
Try to keep it positive!

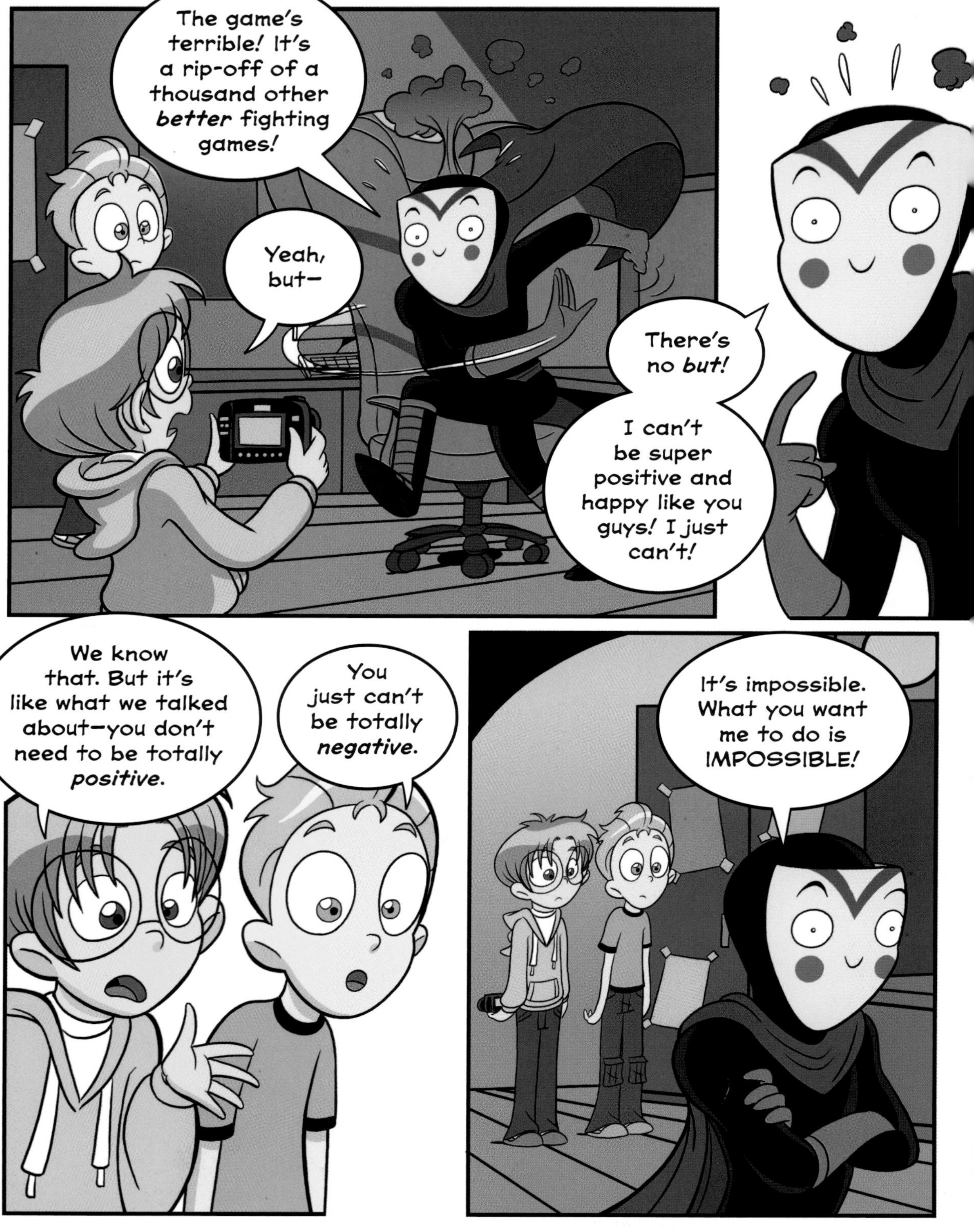
The game's terrible! It's a rip-off of a thousand other *better* fighting games!
Yeah, but—
There's no *but*!
I can't be super positive and happy like you guys! I just can't!
We know that. But it's like what we talked about—you don't need to be totally *positive*.
You just can't be totally *negative*.
It's impossible. What you want me to do is IMPOSSIBLE!

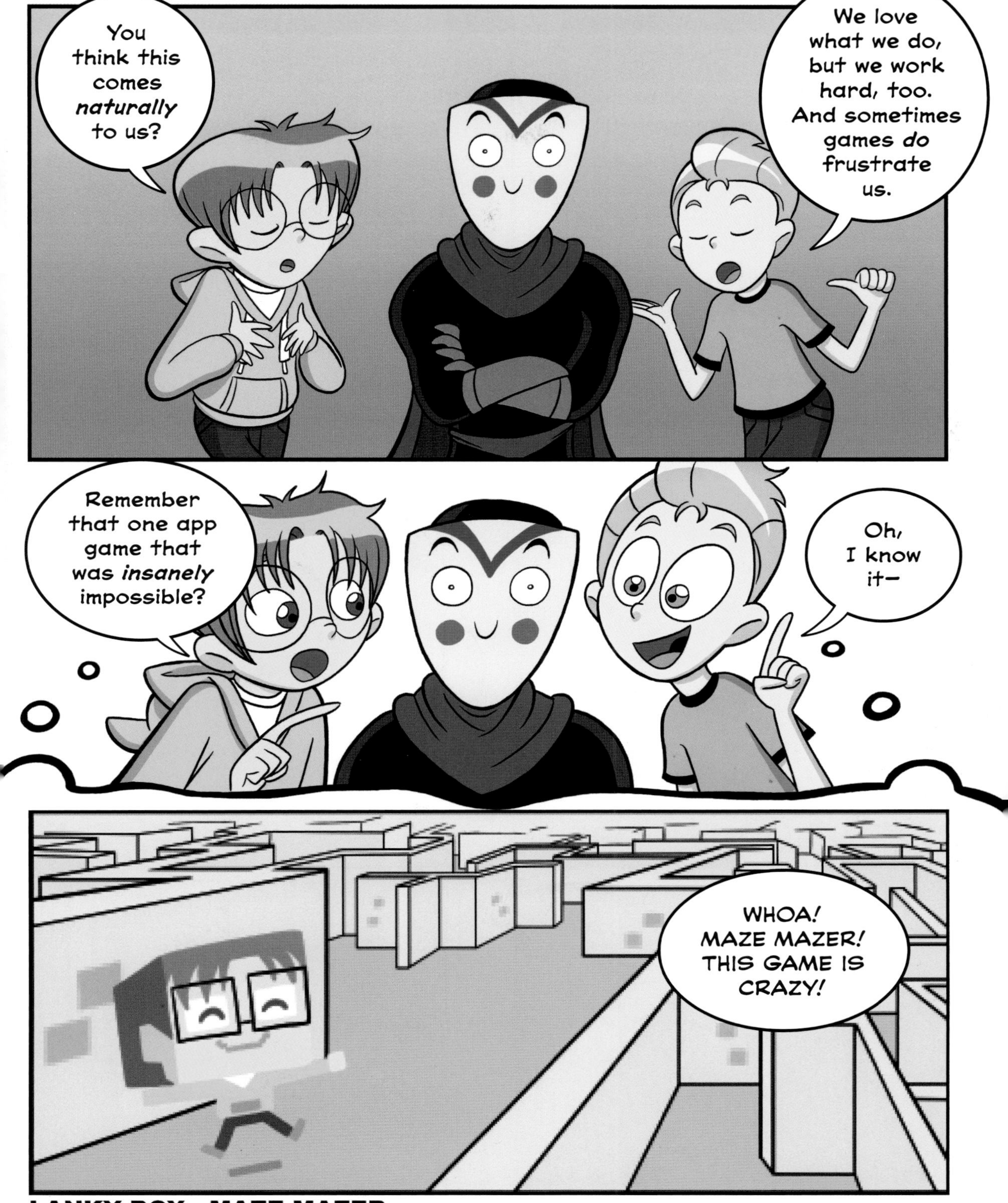
You think this comes *naturally* to us?
We love what we do, but we work hard, too. And sometimes games *do* frustrate us.
Remember that one app game that was *insanely* impossible?
Oh, I know it–
WHOA! MAZE MAZER! THIS GAME IS CRAZY!

LANKY BOX - MAZE MAZER

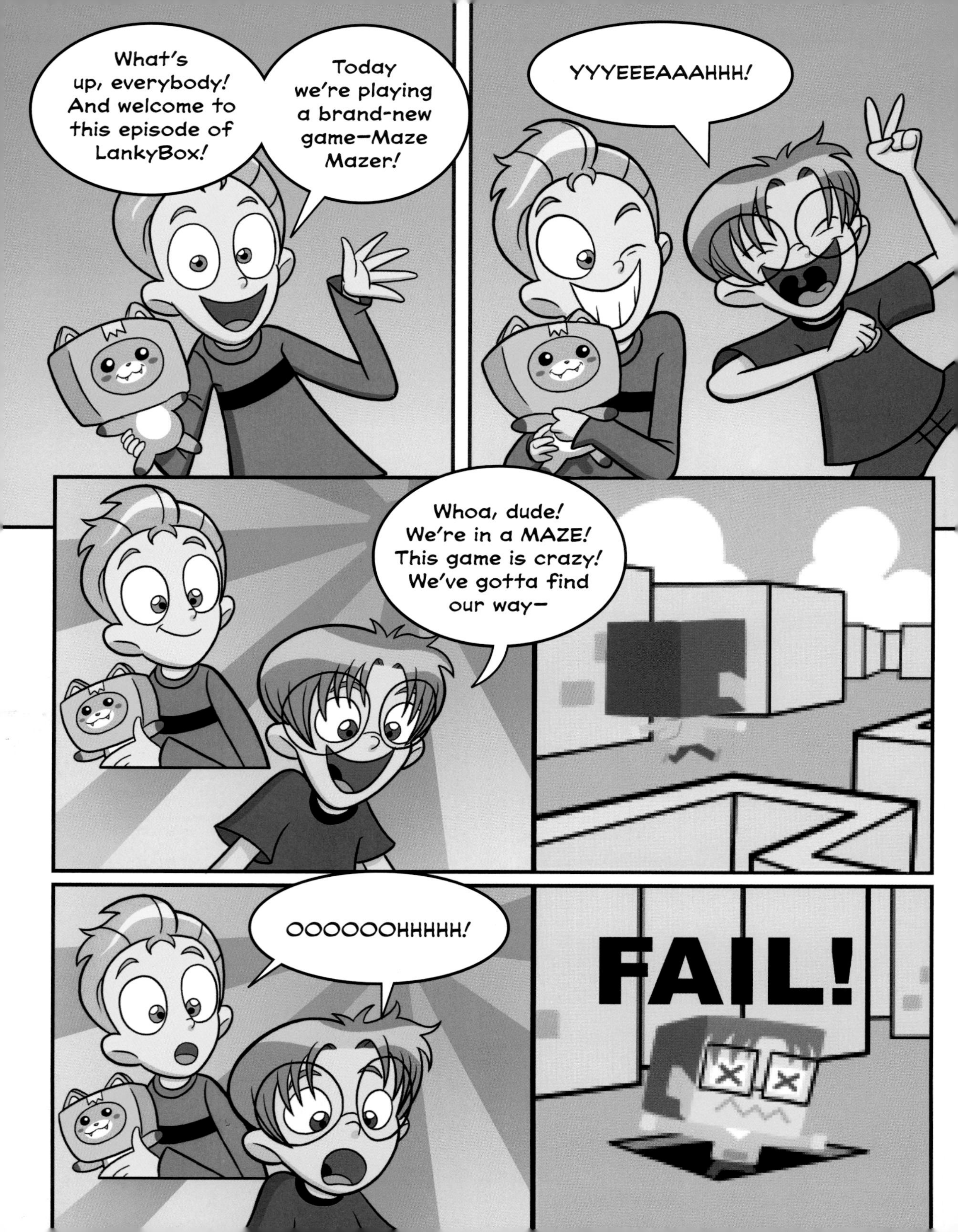
What's up, everybody! And welcome to this episode of LankyBox!
Today we're playing a brand-new game—Maze Mazer!
YYYEEEAAAHHH!
Whoa, dude! We're in a MAZE! This game is crazy! We've gotta find our way—
OOOOOOHHHHH!
FAIL!

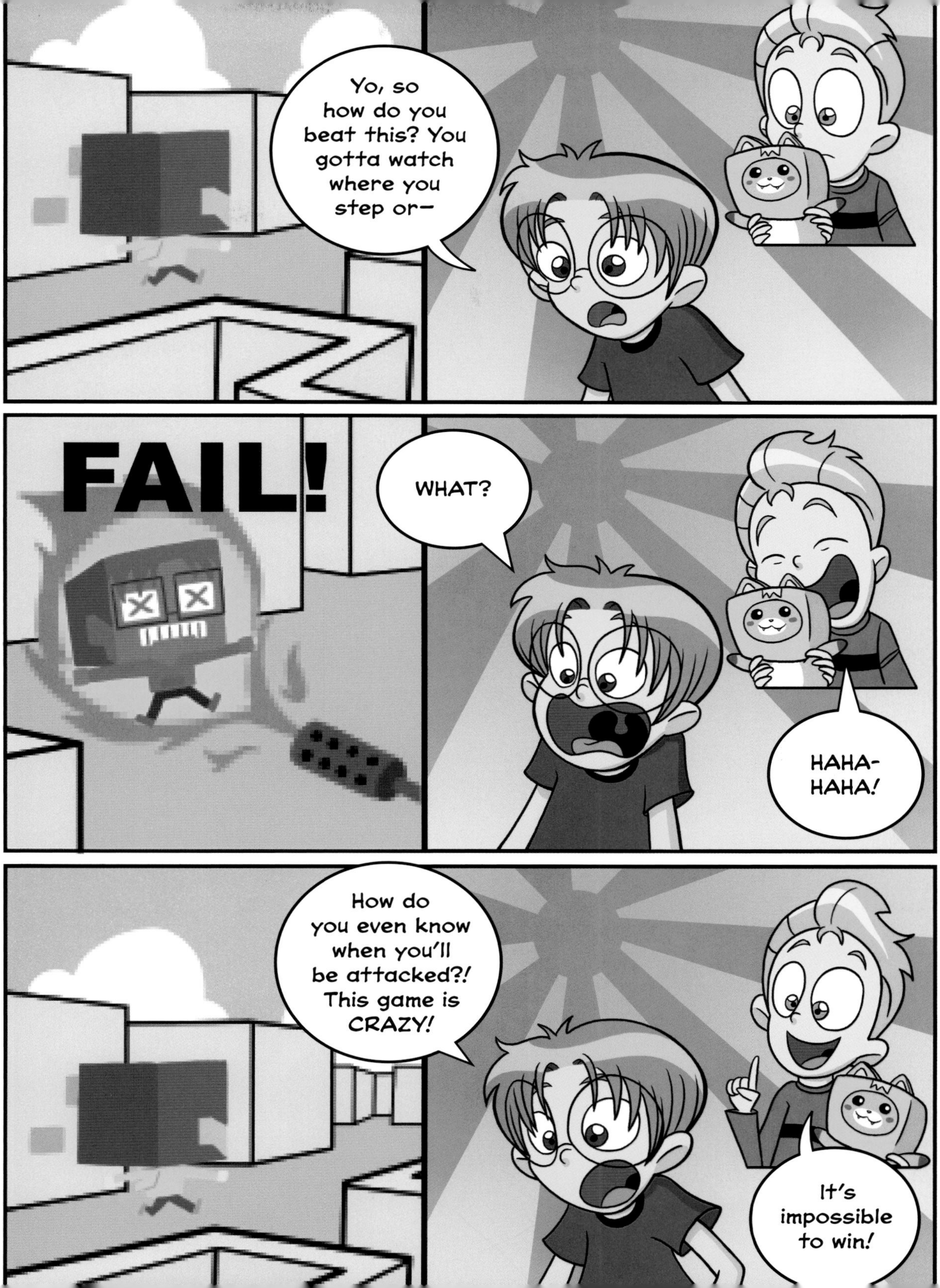
Yo, so how do you beat this? You gotta watch where you step or—
FAIL!
WHAT?
HAHA-HAHA!
How do you even know when you'll be attacked?! This game is CRAZY!
It's impossible to win!

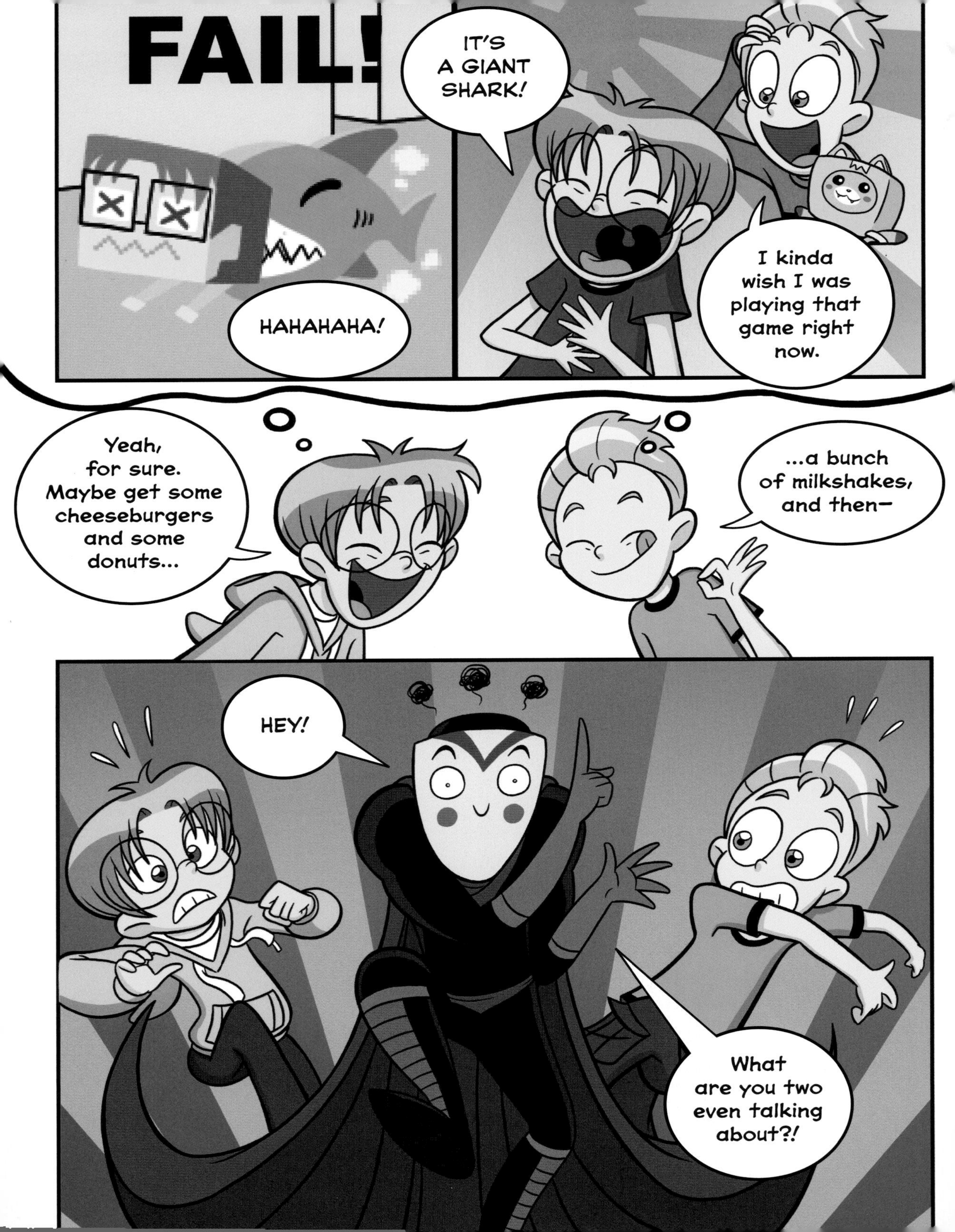
FAIL!
IT'S A GIANT SHARK!
HAHAHAHA!
I kinda wish I was playing that game right now.
Yeah, for sure. Maybe get some cheeseburgers and some donuts...
...a bunch of milkshakes, and then—
HEY!
What are you two even talking about?!

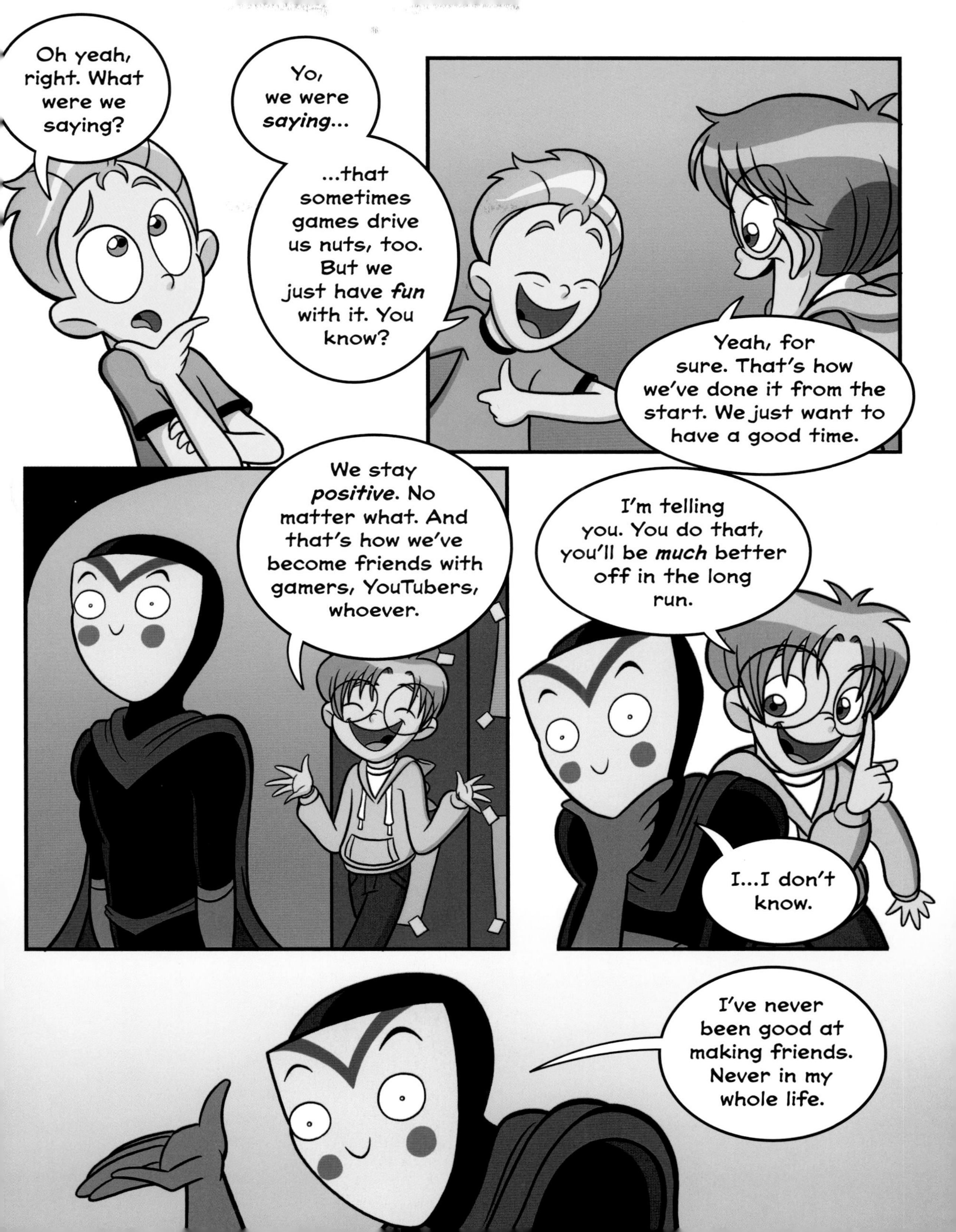
Oh yeah, right. What were we saying?
Yo, we were *saying*...
...that sometimes games drive us nuts, too. But we just have *fun* with it. You know?
Yeah, for sure. That's how we've done it from the start. We just want to have a good time.
We stay *positive*. No matter what. And that's how we've become friends with gamers, YouTubers, whoever.
I'm telling you. You do that, you'll be *much* better off in the long run.
I...I don't know.
I've never been good at making friends. Never in my whole life.

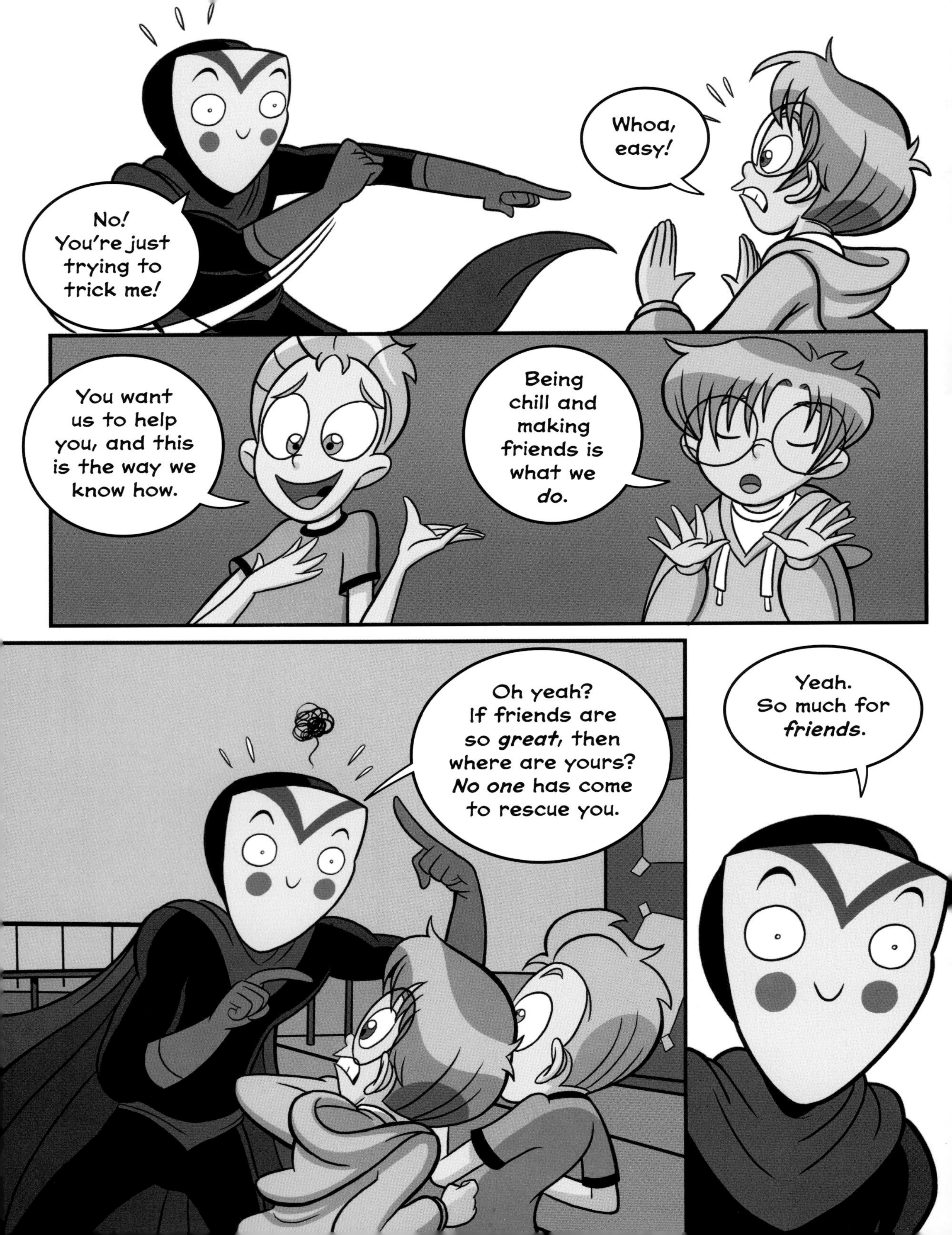
Whoa, easy!
No! You're just trying to trick me!
You want us to help you, and this is the way we know how.
Being chill and making friends is what we *do.*
Oh yeah? If friends are so *great*, then where are yours? *No one* has come to rescue you.
Yeah. So much for *friends*.

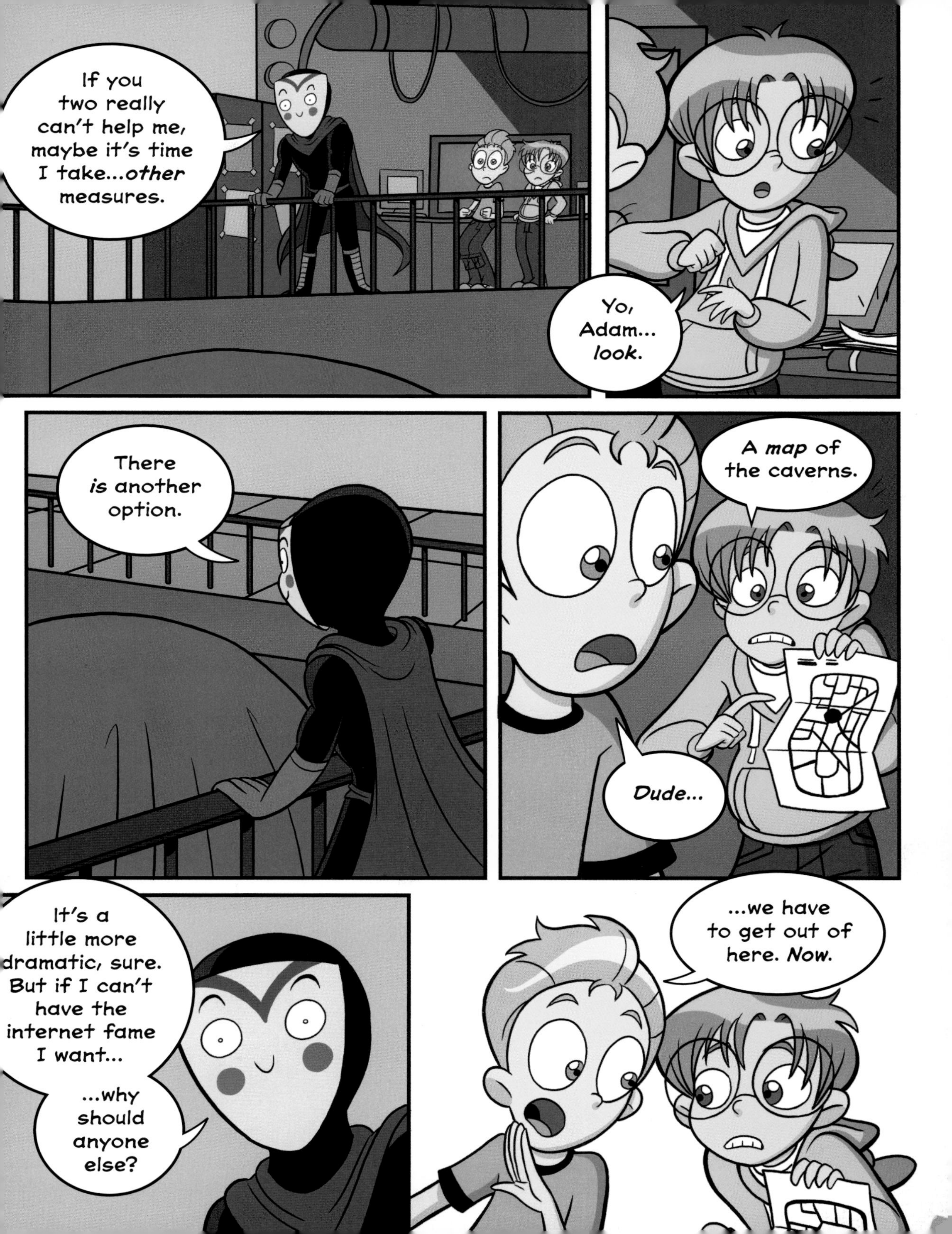
If you two really can't help me, maybe it's time I take...*other* measures.
Yo, Adam... *look*.
There *is* another option.
A *map* of the caverns.
Dude...
It's a little more dramatic, sure. But if I can't have the internet fame I want...
...why should anyone else?
...we have to get out of here. *Now*.

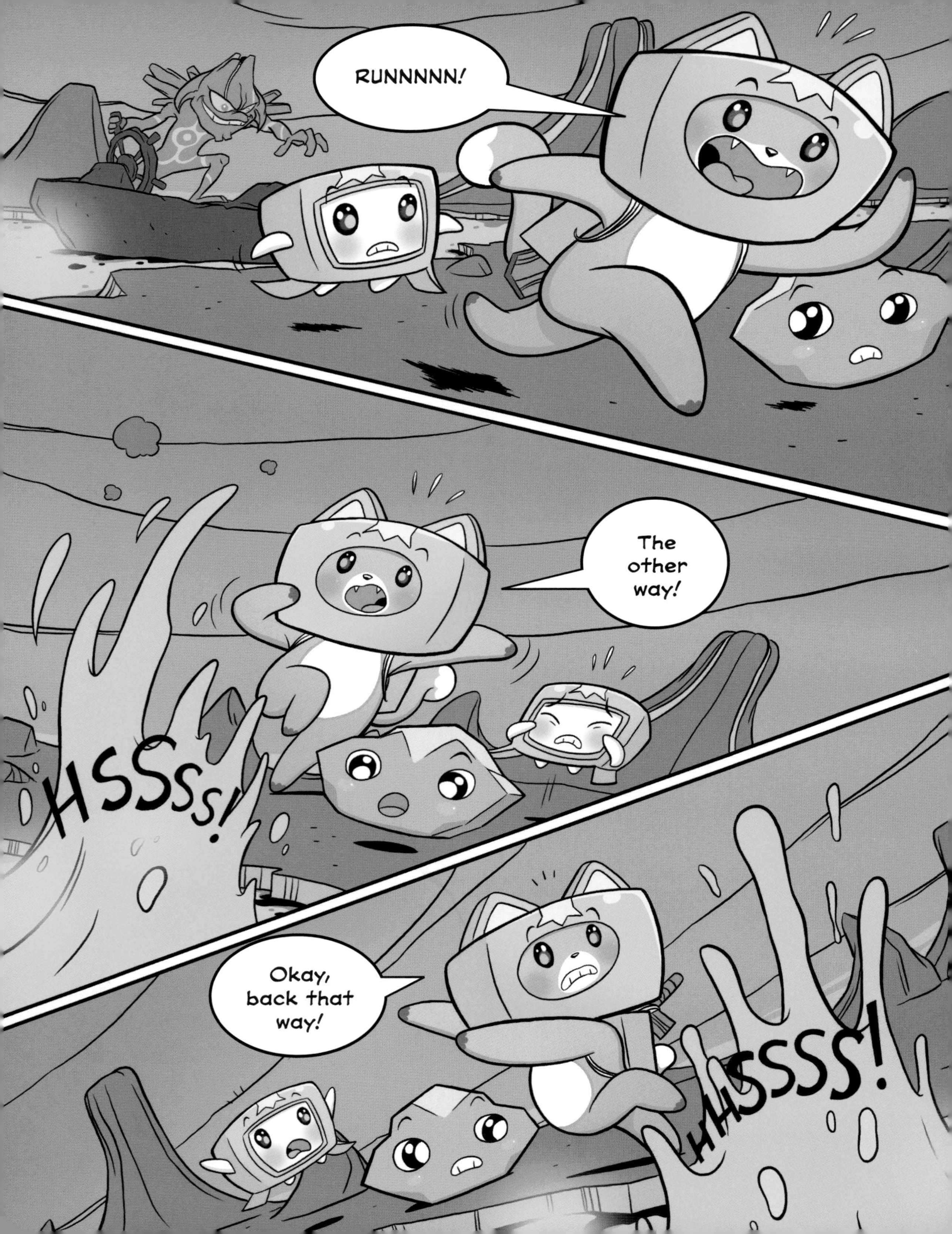
RUNNNNN!
The other way!
HSSSs!
Okay, back that way!
HSSSS!

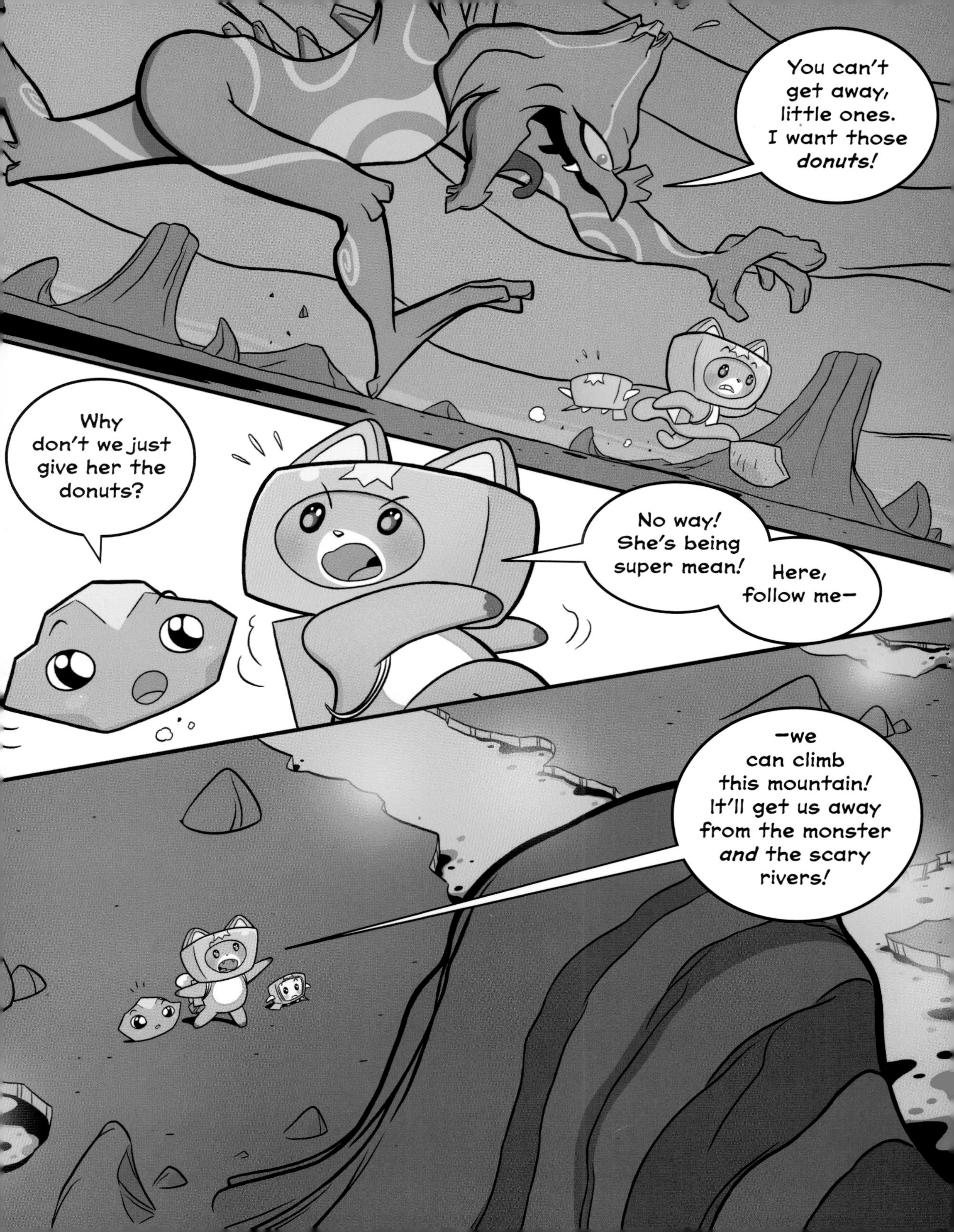
You can't get away, little ones. I want those *donuts!*
Why don't we just give her the donuts?
No way! She's being super mean!
Here, follow me—
—we can climb this mountain! It'll get us away from the monster *and* the scary rivers!

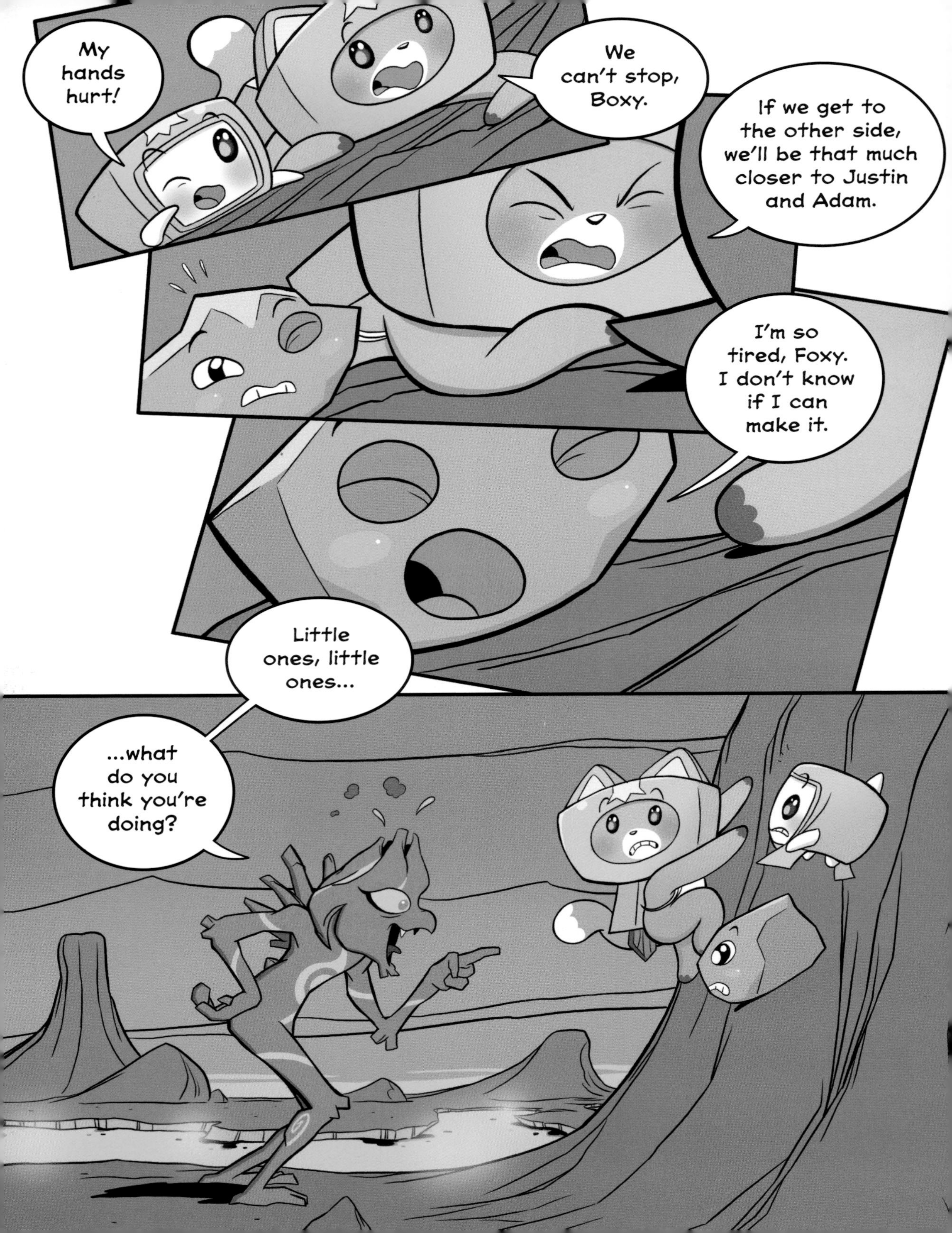
My hands hurt!
We can't stop, Boxy.
If we get to the other side, we'll be that much closer to Justin and Adam.
I'm so tired, Foxy. I don't know if I can make it.
Little ones, little ones...
...what do you think you're doing?

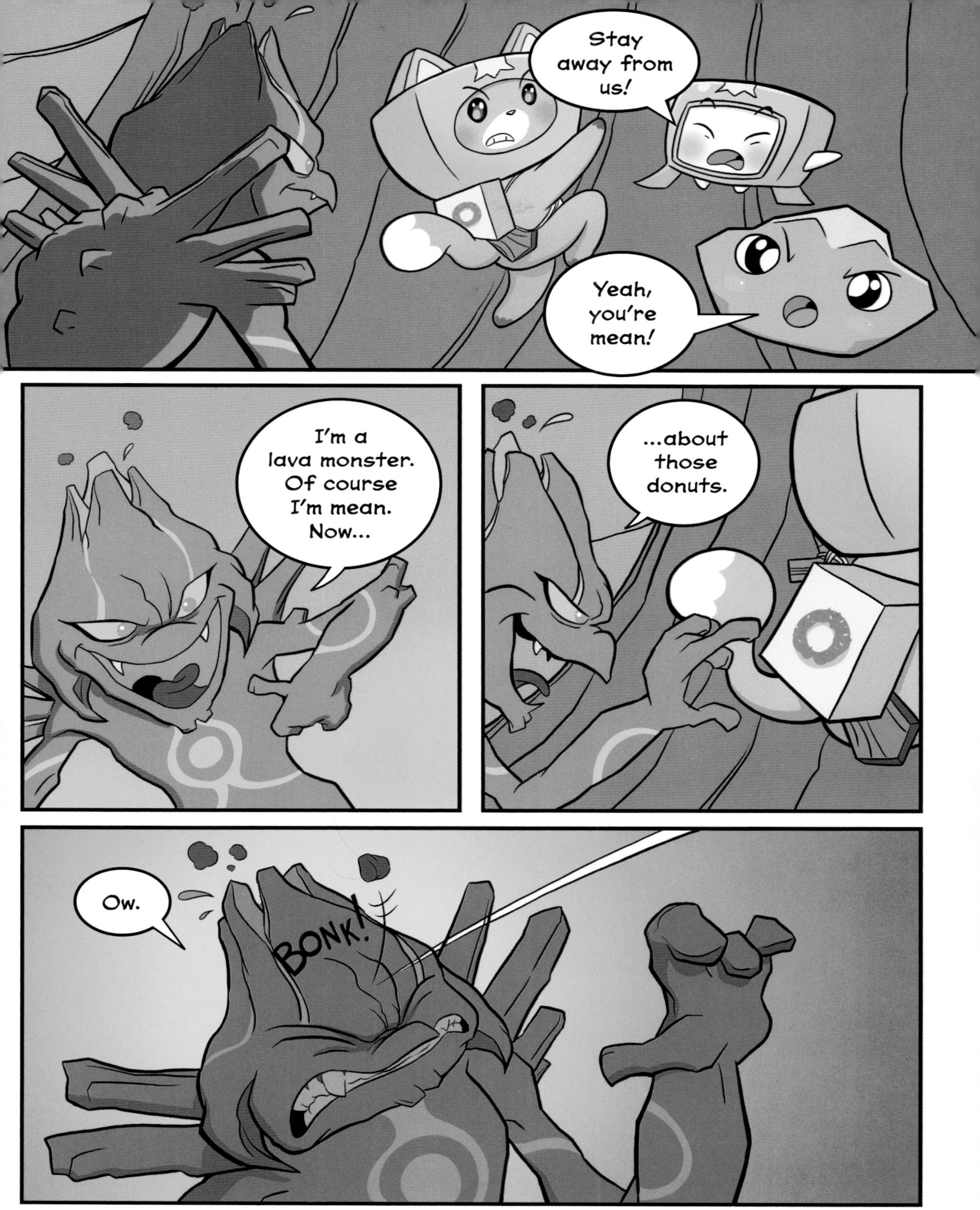
Stay away from us!
Yeah, you're mean!
I'm a lava monster. Of course I'm mean. Now...
...about those donuts.
Ow.
BONK!

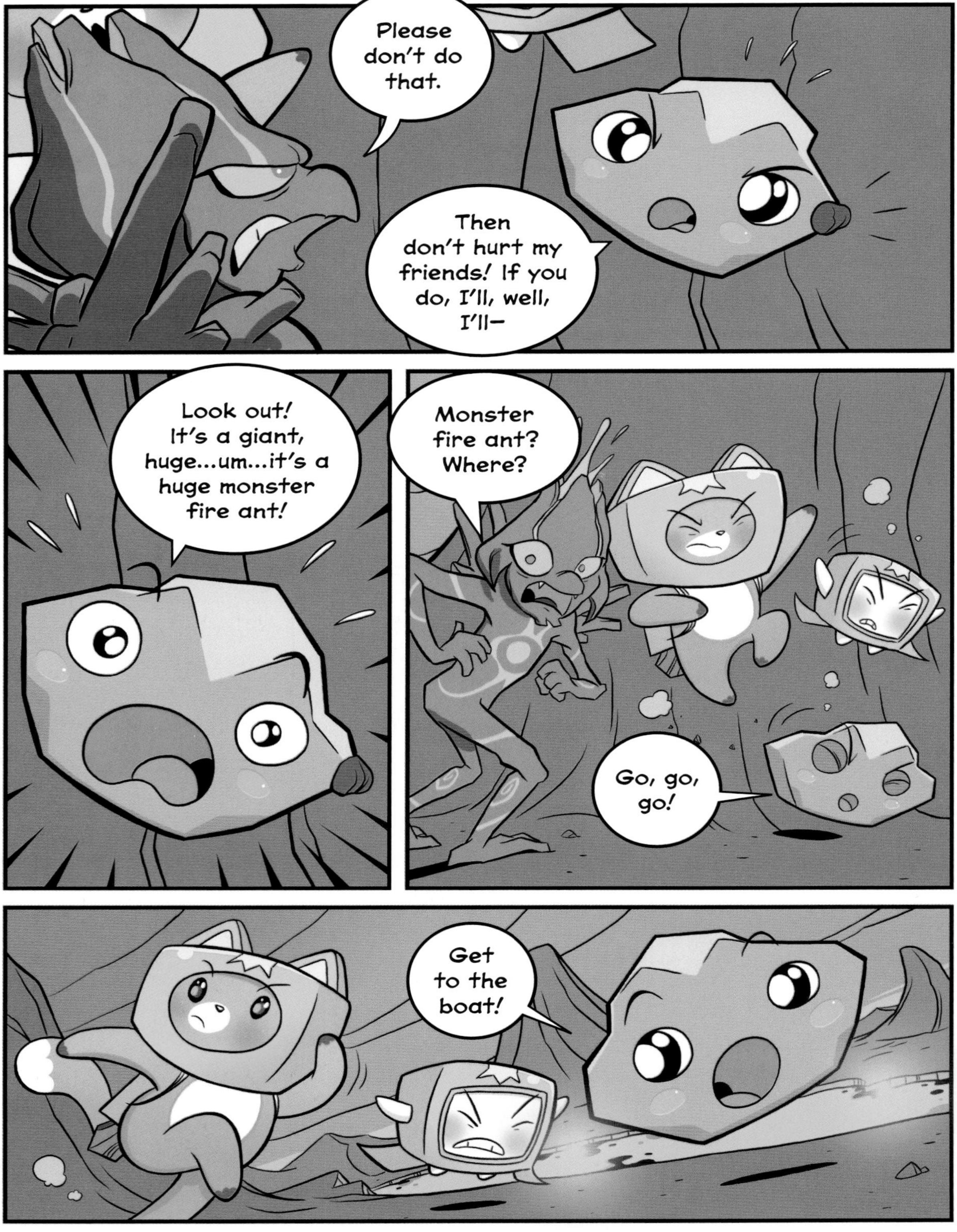
Please don't do that.
Then don't hurt my friends! If you do, I'll, well, I'll—
Look out! It's a giant, huge...um...it's a huge monster fire ant!
Monster fire ant? Where?
Go, go, go!
Get to the boat!

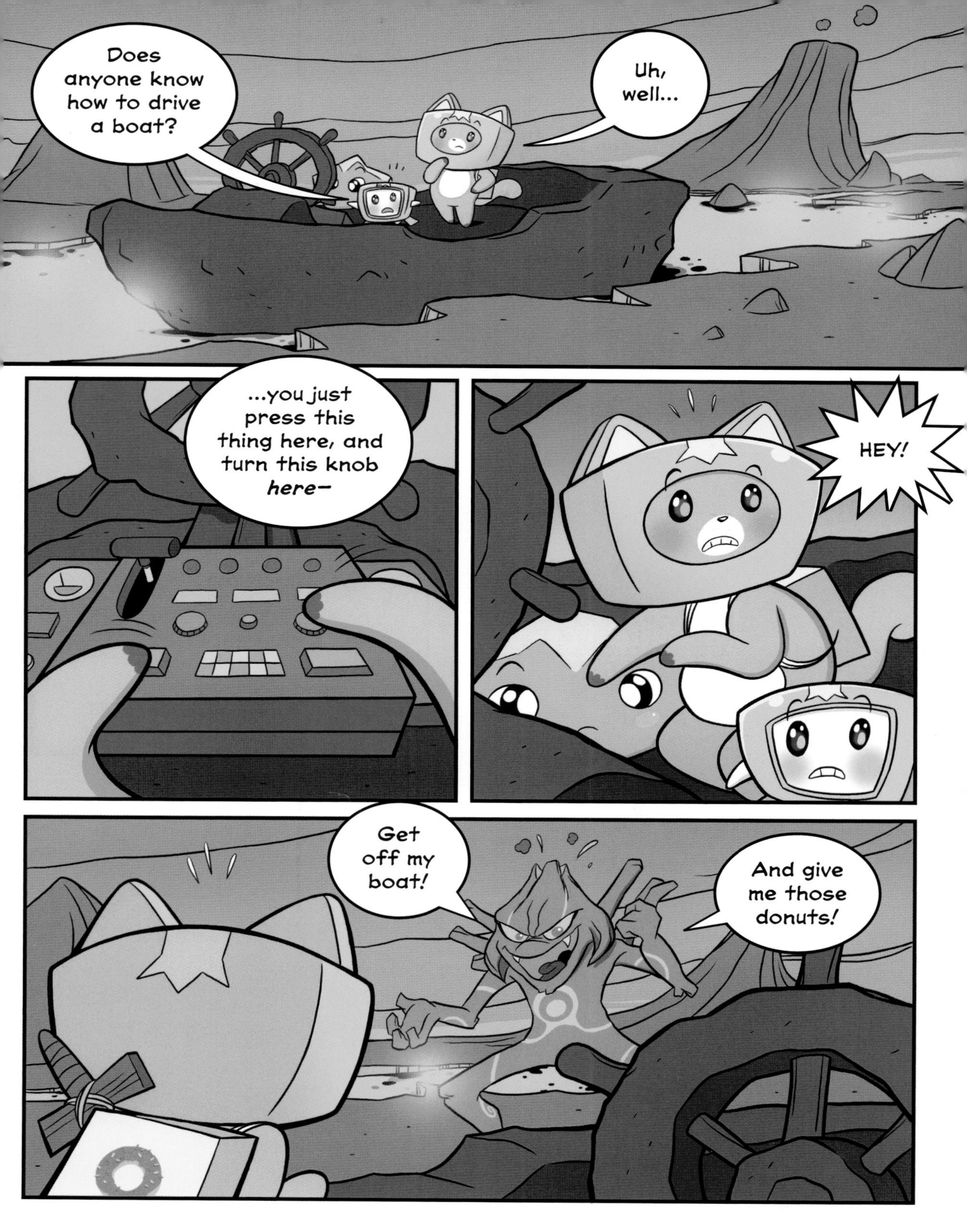
Does anyone know how to drive a boat?
Uh, well...
...you just press this thing here, and turn this knob *here*—
HEY!
Get off my boat!
And give me those donuts!

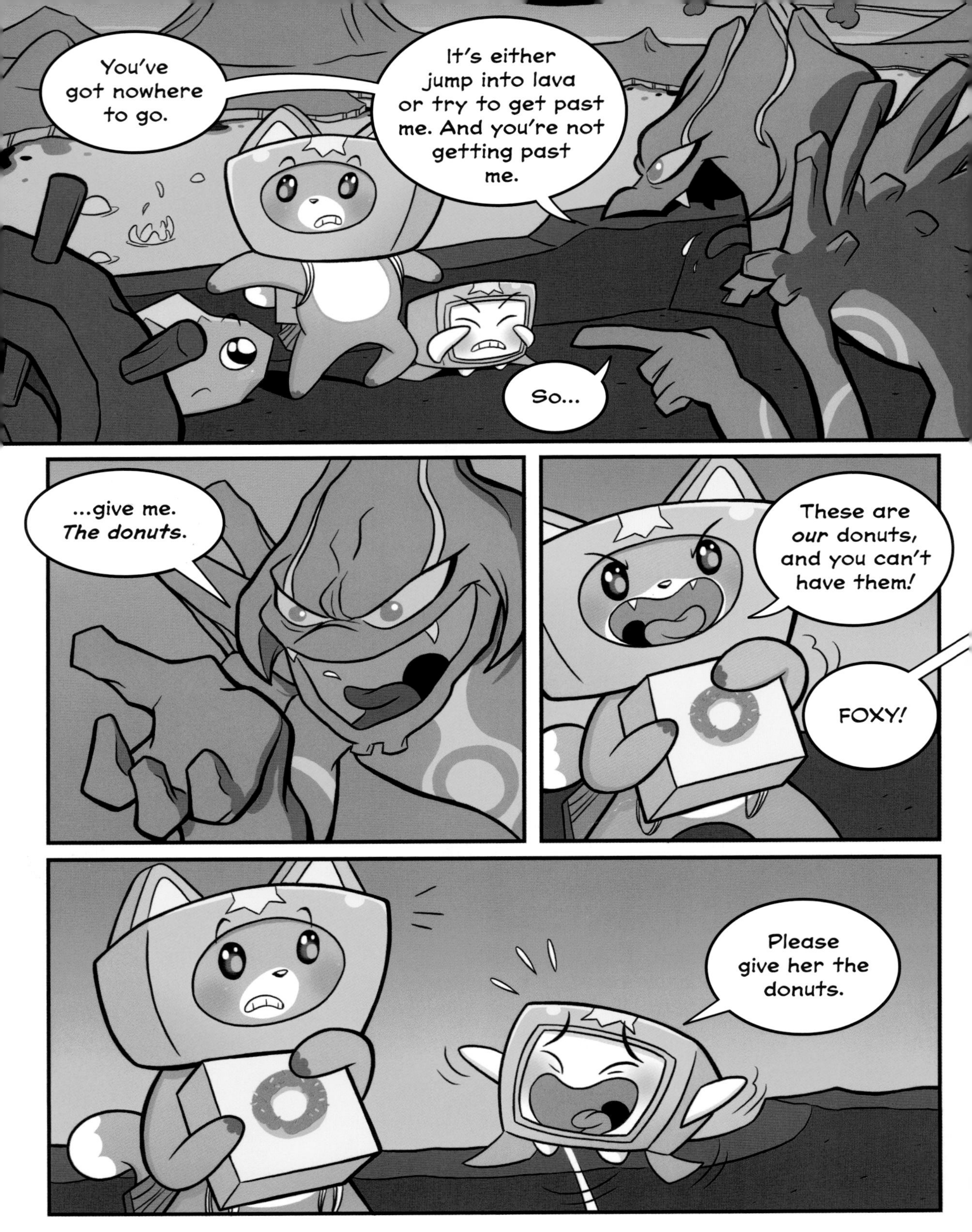
You've got nowhere to go.
It's either jump into lava or try to get past me. And you're not getting past me.
So...
...give me. *The donuts.*
These are *our* donuts, and you can't have them!
FOXY!
Please give her the donuts.

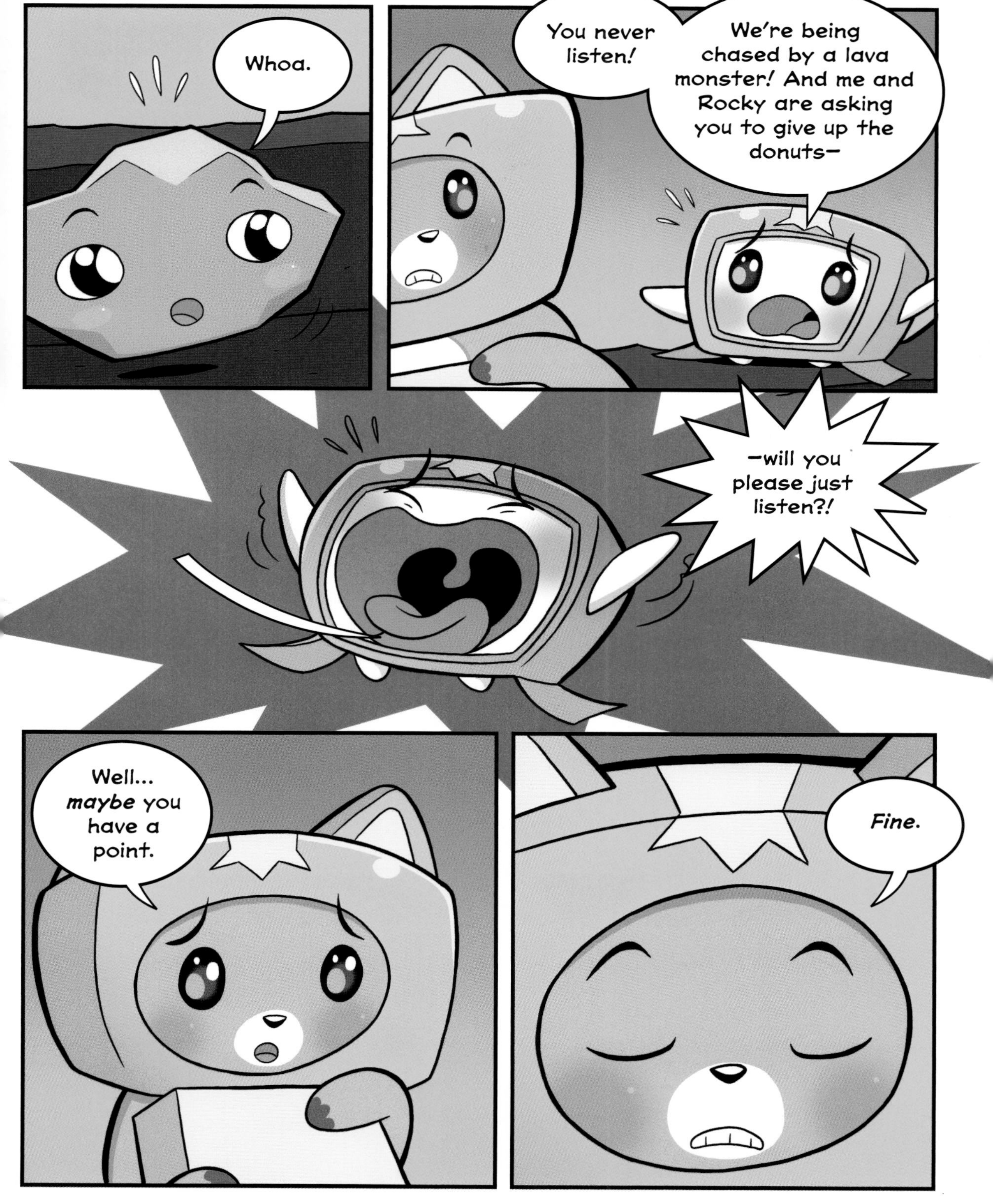
Whoa.
You never listen!
We're being chased by a lava monster! And me and Rocky are asking you to give up the donuts—
—will you please just listen?!
Well... *maybe* you have a point.
Fine.

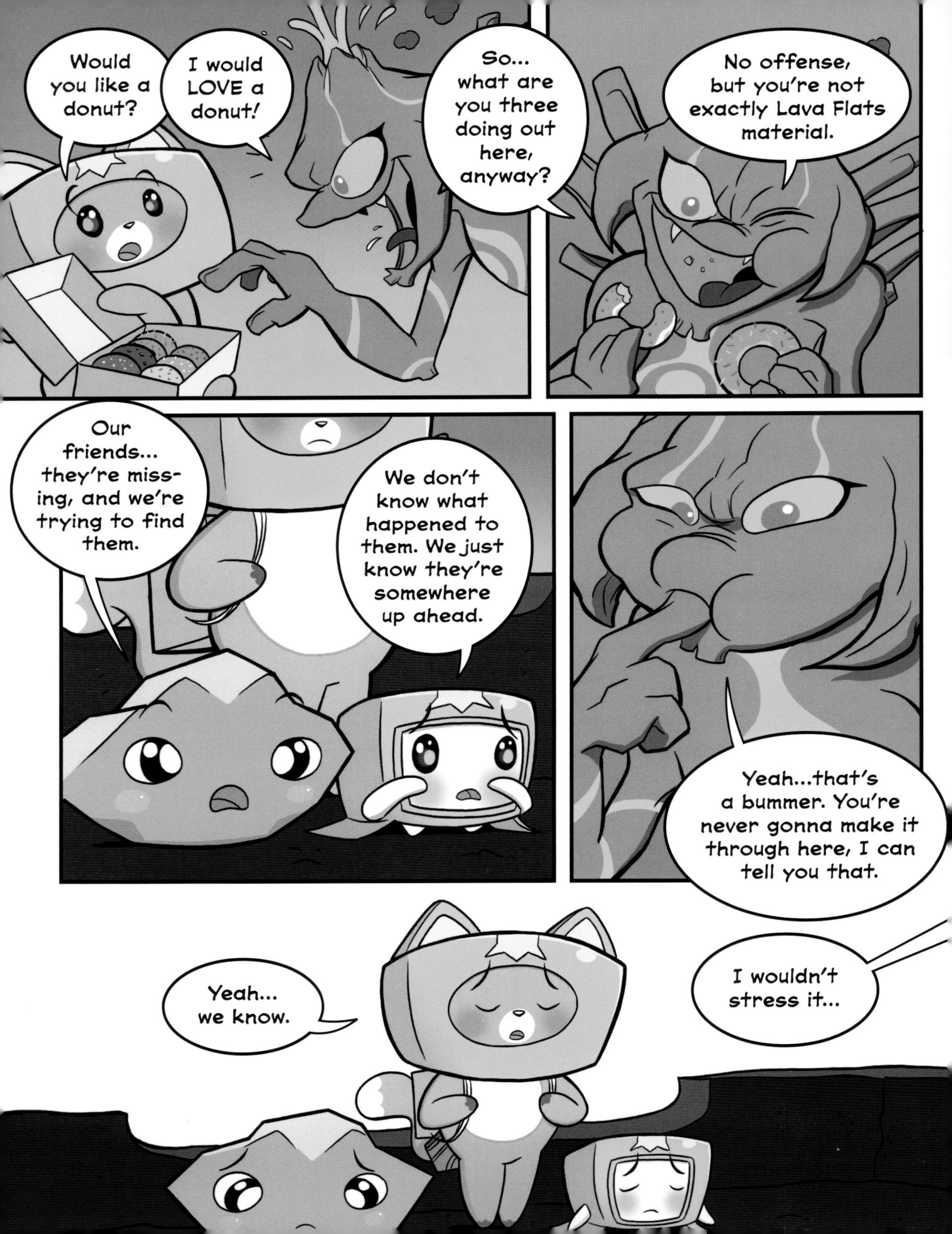
Would you like a donut?
I would LOVE a donut!
So... what are you three doing out here, anyway?
No offense, but you're not exactly Lava Flats material.
Our friends... they're missing, and we're trying to find them.
We don't know what happened to them. We just know they're somewhere up ahead.
Yeah...that's a bummer. You're never gonna make it through here, I can tell you that.
Yeah... we know.
I wouldn't stress it...

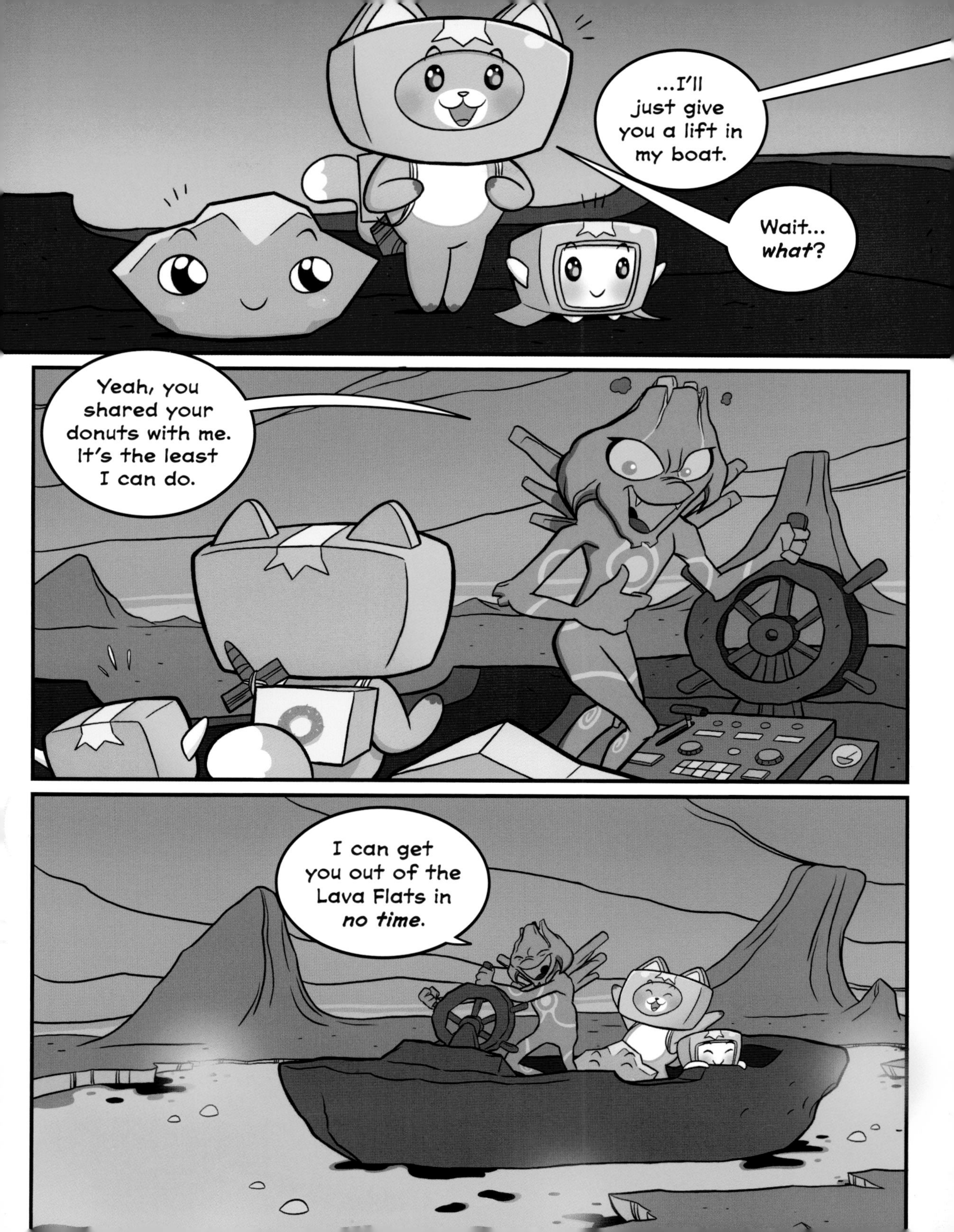
...I'll just give you a lift in my boat.
Wait... *what*?
Yeah, you shared your donuts with me. It's the least I can do.
I can get you out of the Lava Flats in *no time*.

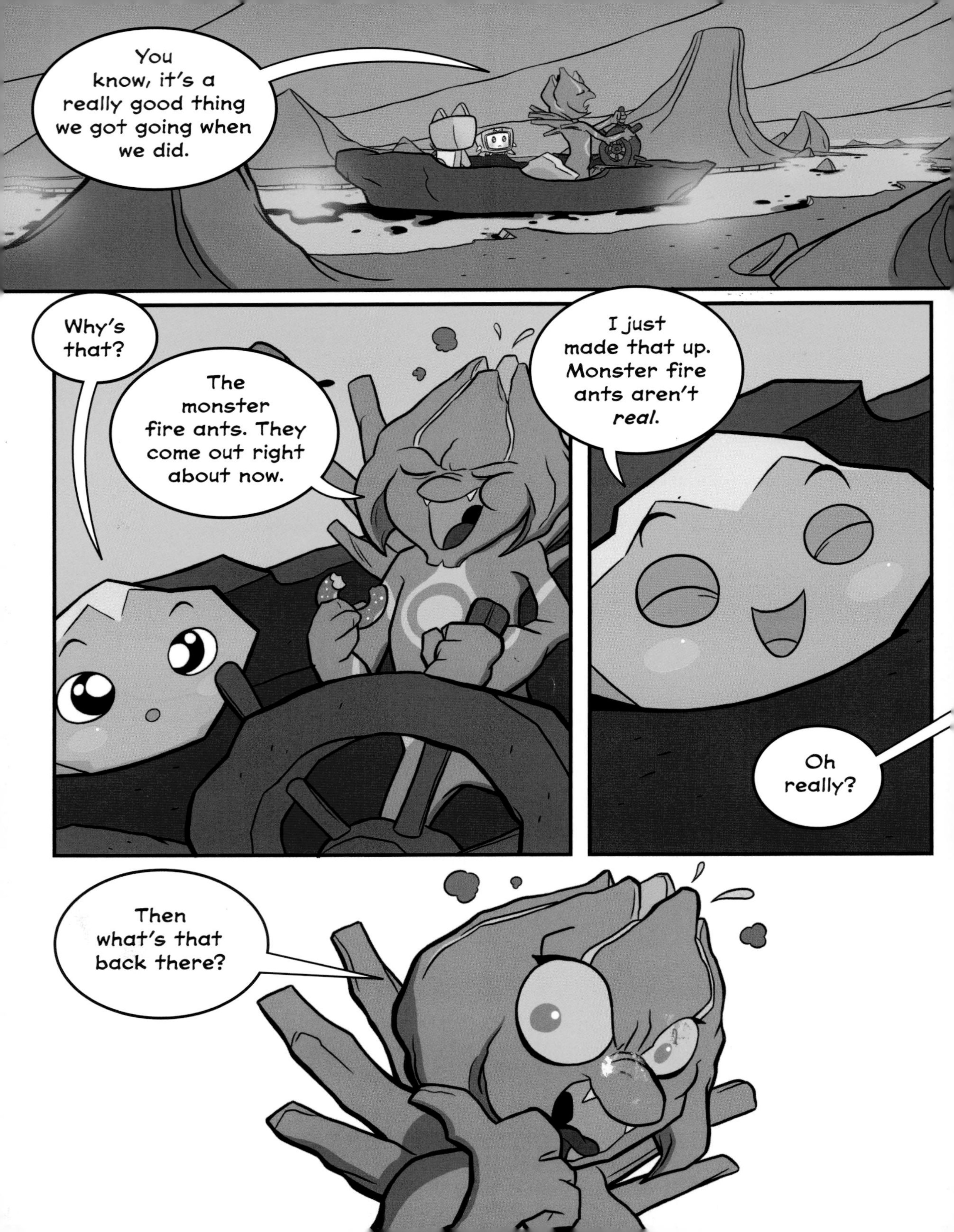
You know, it's a really good thing we got going when we did.
Why's that?
The monster fire ants. They come out right about now.
I just made that up. Monster fire ants aren't *real*.
Oh really?
Then what's that back there?

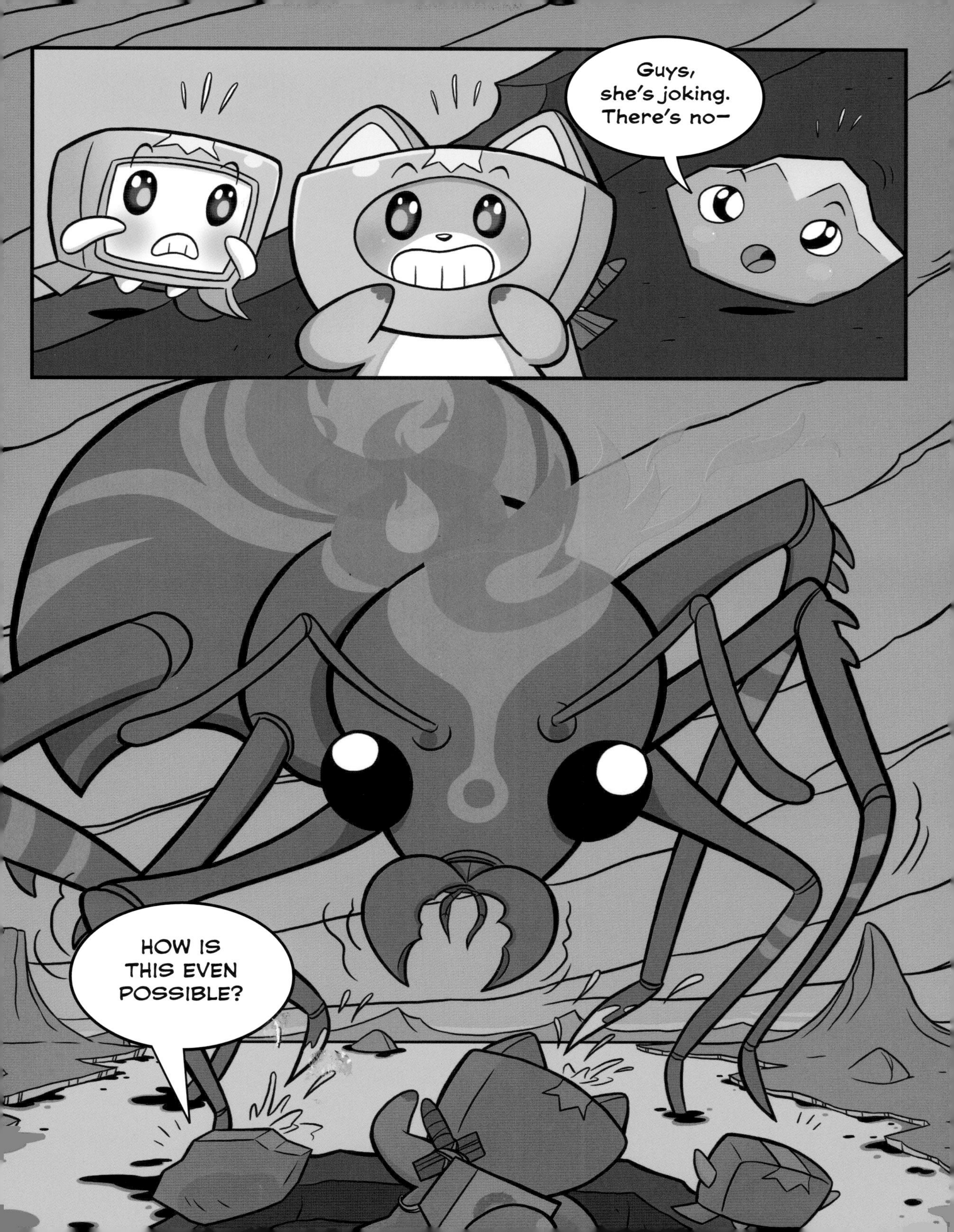
Guys, she's joking. There's no—
HOW IS THIS EVEN POSSIBLE?

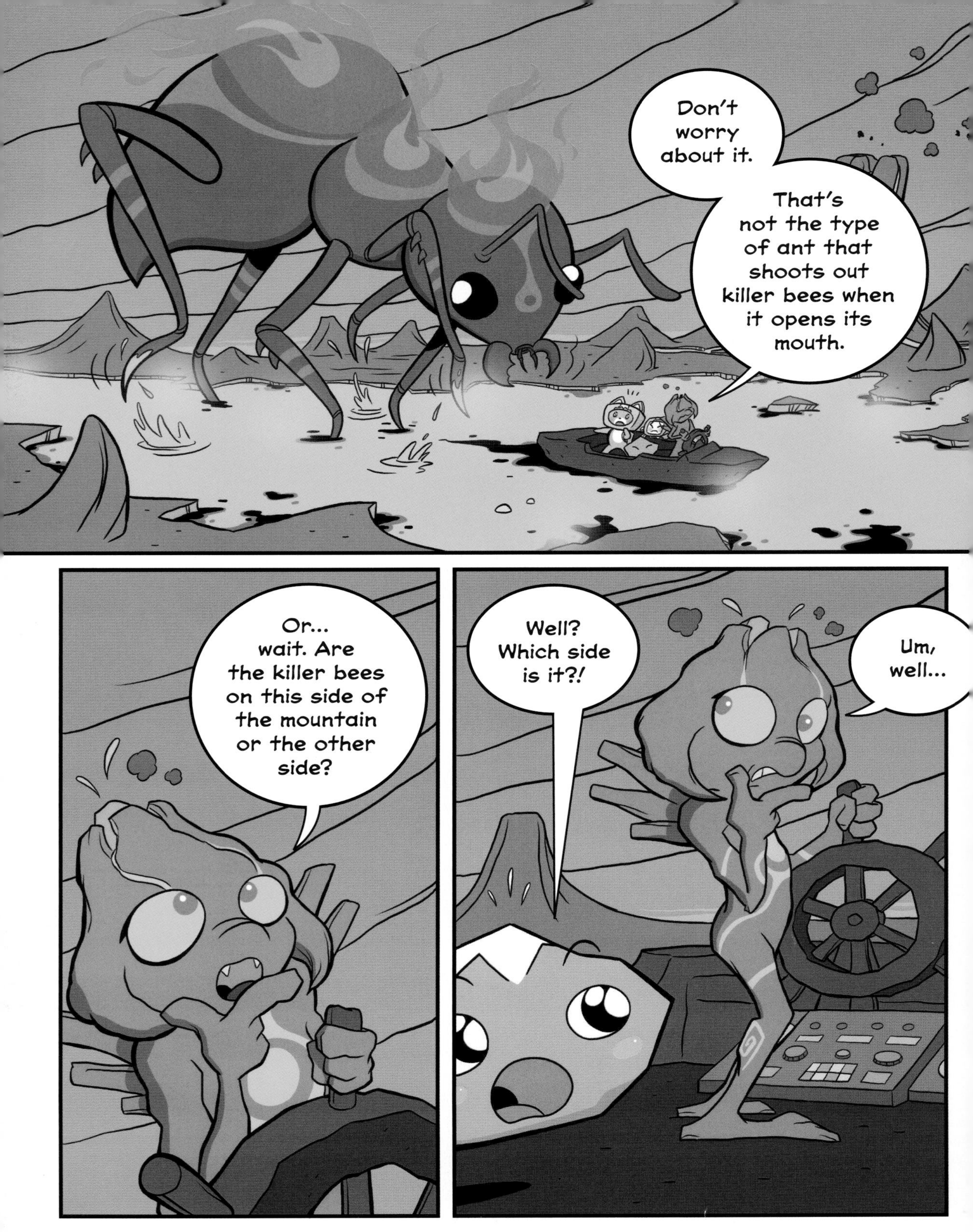
Don't worry about it.
That's not the type of ant that shoots out killer bees when it opens its mouth.
Or... wait. Are the killer bees on this side of the mountain or the other side?
Well? Which side is it?!
Um, well...

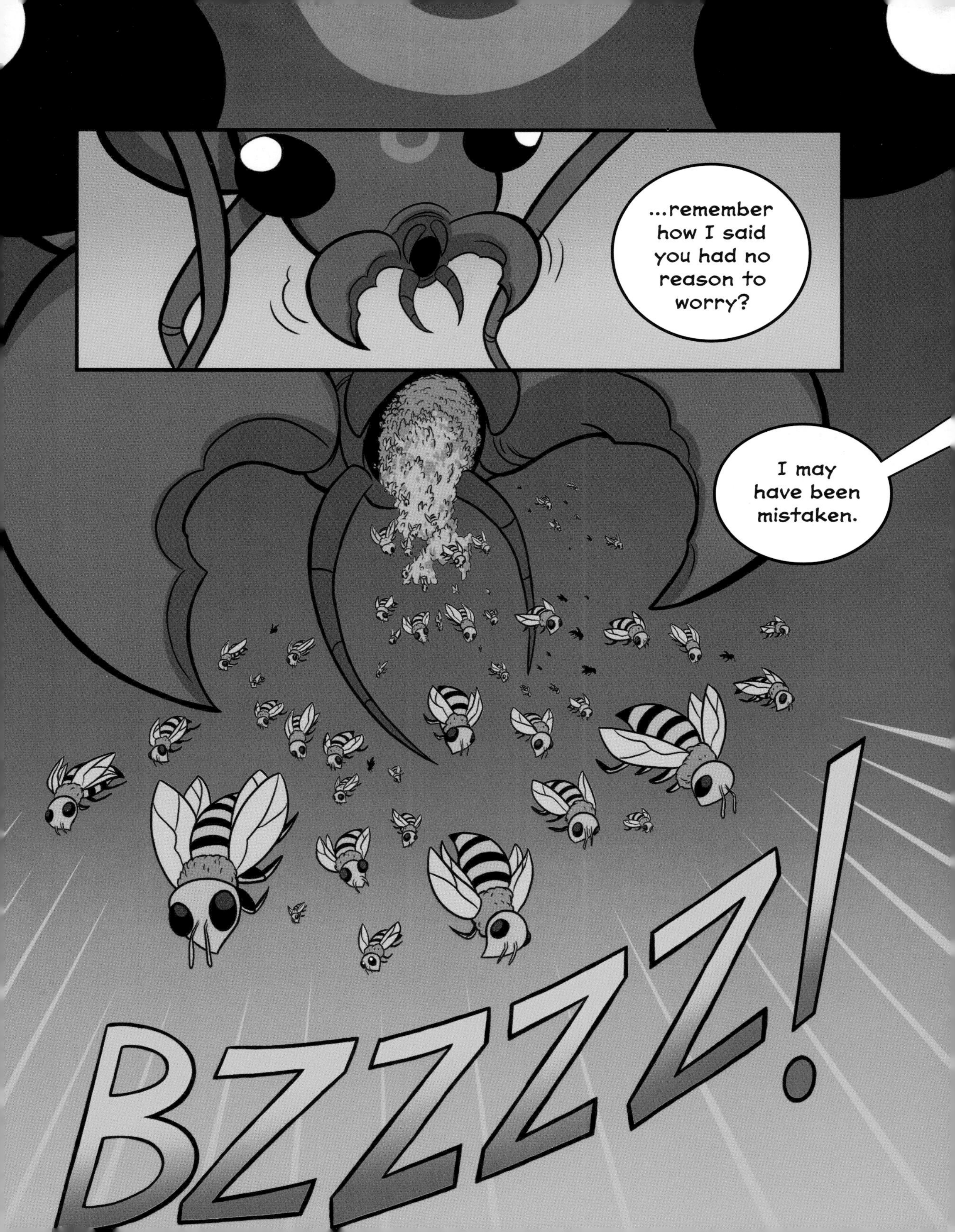
...remember how I said you had no reason to worry?
I may have been mistaken.
BZZZZ!

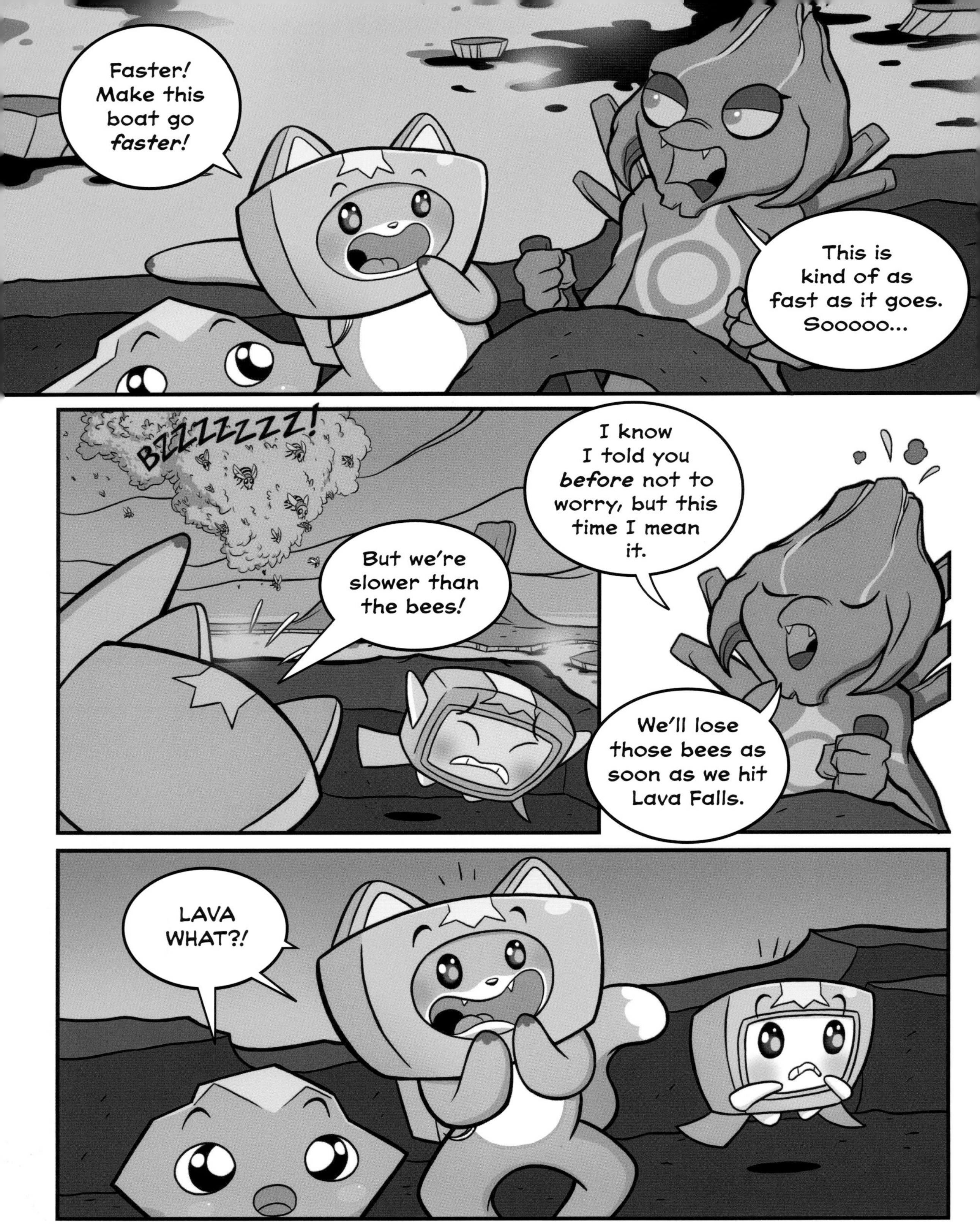
Faster! Make this boat go faster!
This is kind of as fast as it goes. Sooooo...
BZZZZZZZ!
But we're slower than the bees!
I know I told you before not to worry, but this time I mean it.
We'll lose those bees as soon as we hit Lava Falls.
LAVA WHAT?!

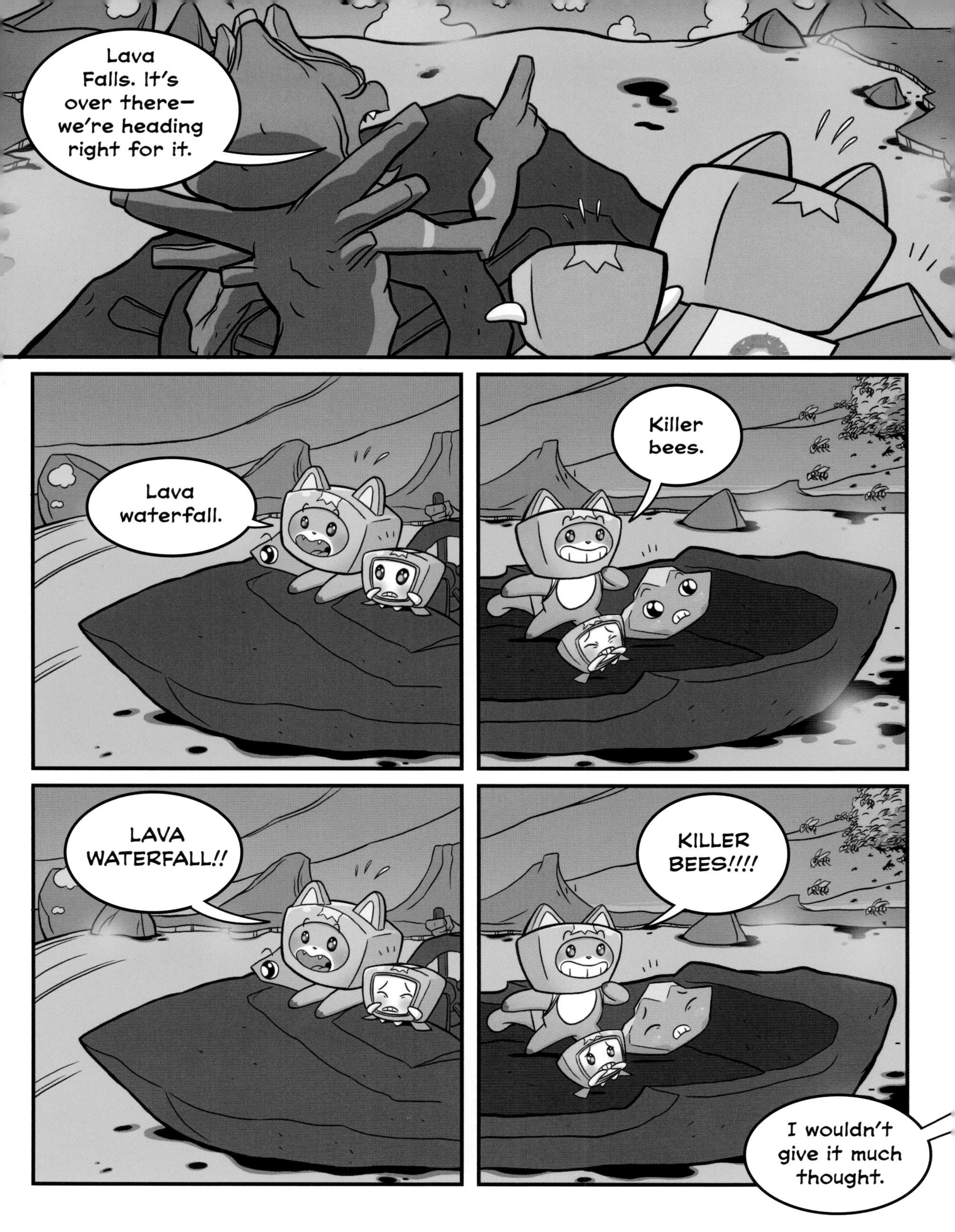
Lava Falls. It's over there—we're heading right for it.
Lava waterfall.
Killer bees.
LAVA WATERFALL!!
KILLER BEES!!!!
I wouldn't give it much thought.

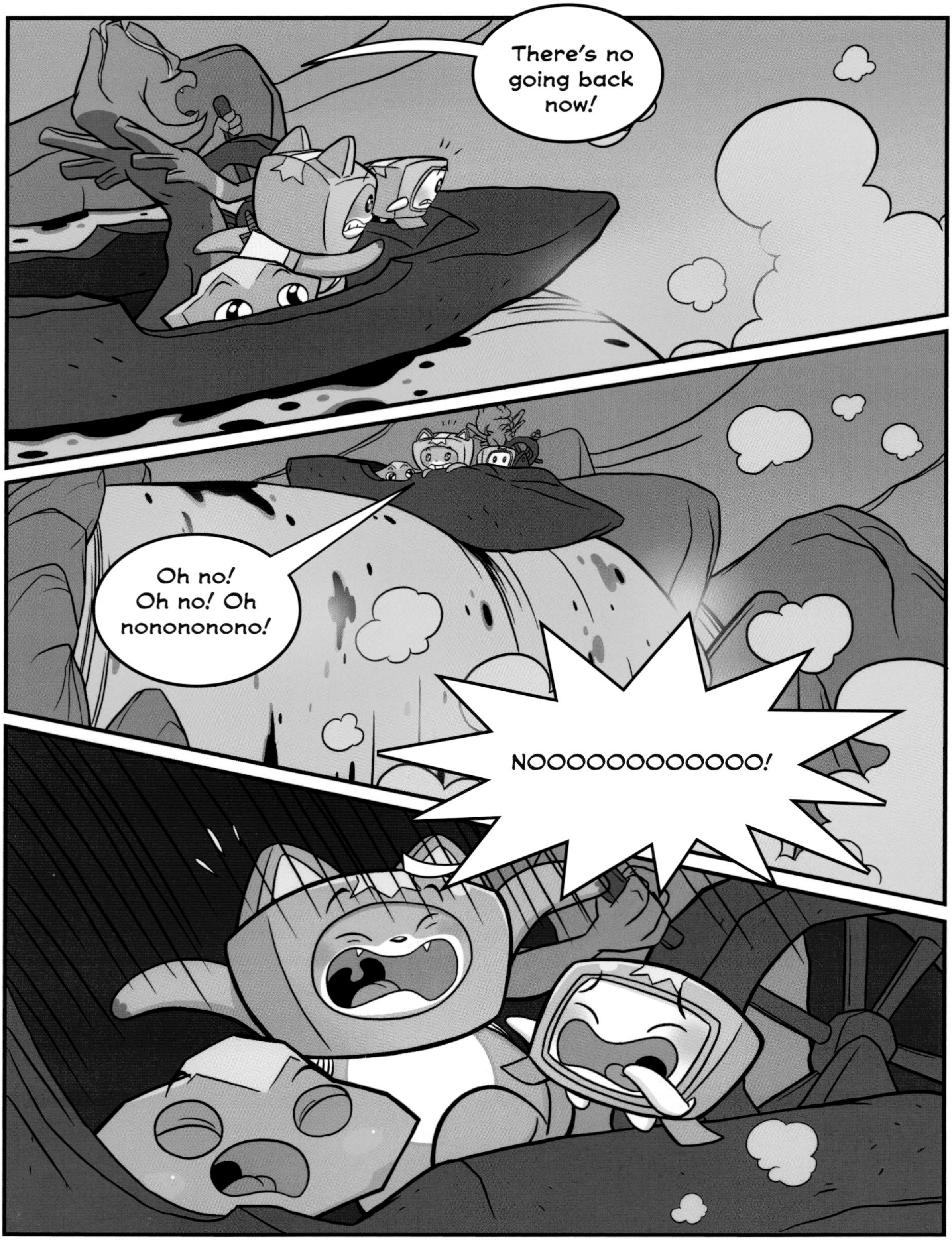
There's no going back now!
Oh no! Oh no! Oh nonononono!
NOOOOOOOOOOOO!

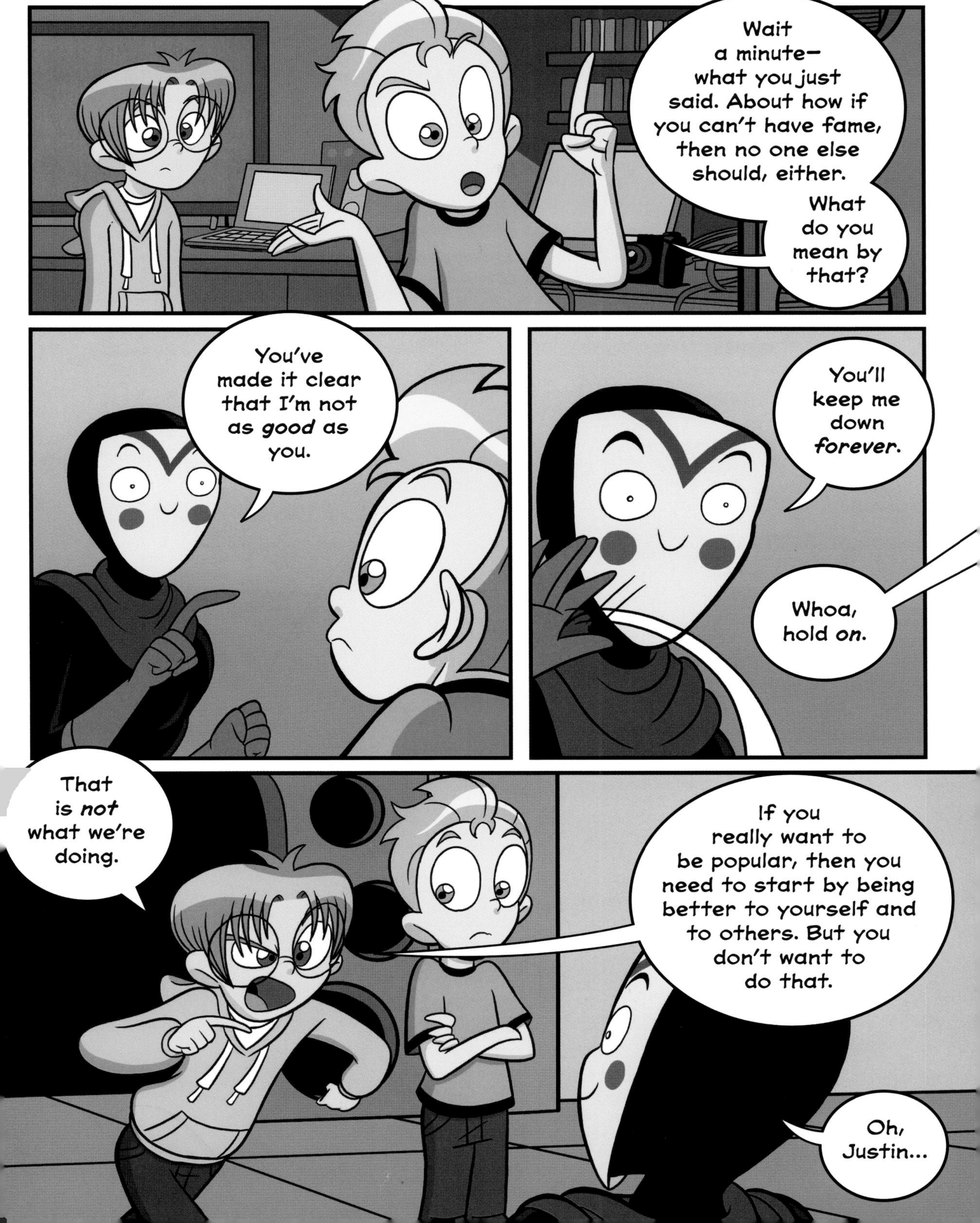
Wait a minute—what you just said. About how if you can't have fame, then no one else should, either.
What do you mean by that?
You've made it clear that I'm not as *good* as you.
You'll keep me down *forever*.
Whoa, hold *on*.
That is *not* what we're doing.
If you really want to be popular, then you need to start by being better to yourself and to others. But you don't want to do that.
Oh, Justin...

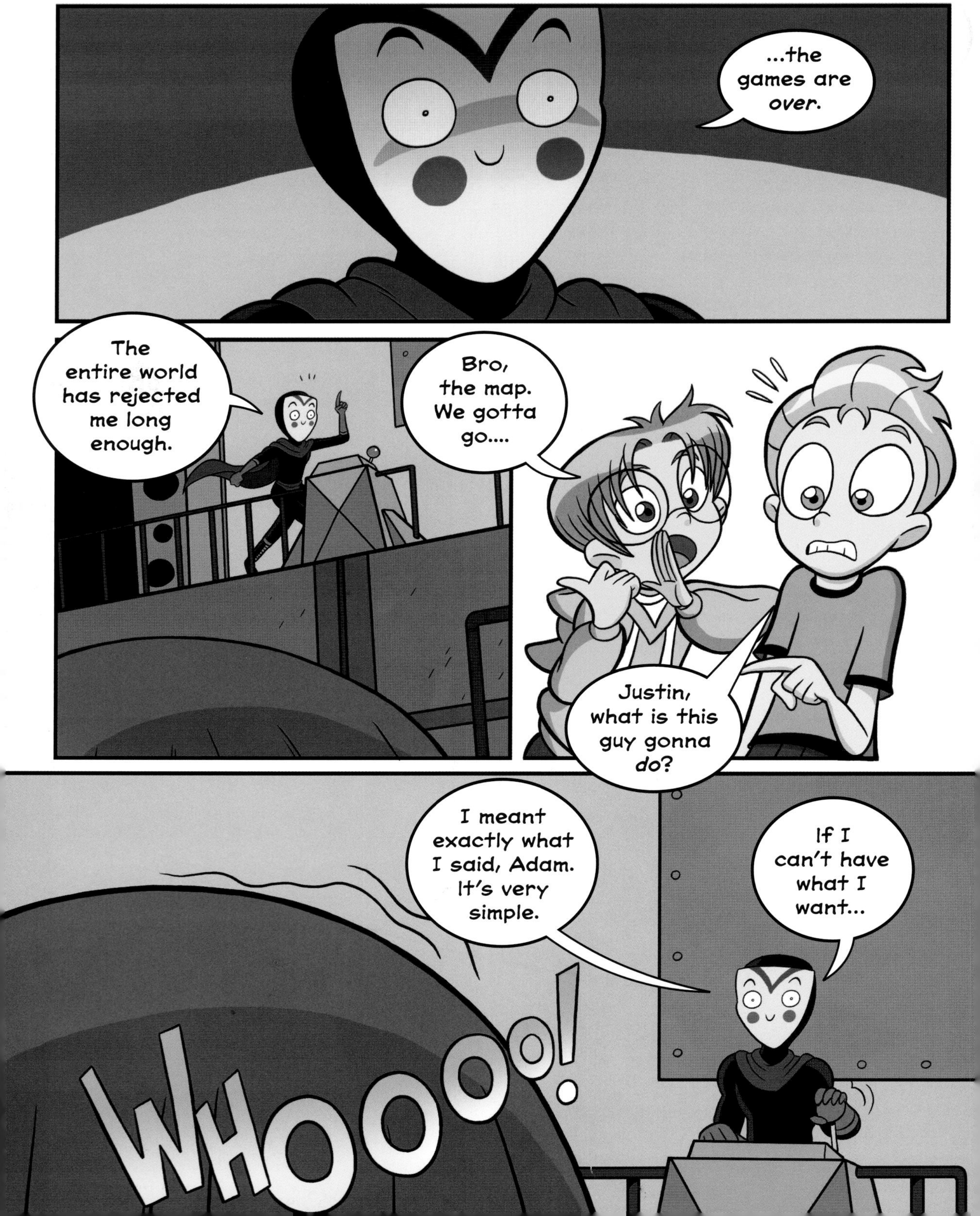
...the games are over.
The entire world has rejected me long enough.
Bro, the map. We gotta go....
Justin, what is this guy gonna do?
I meant exactly what I said, Adam. It's very simple.
If I can't have what I want...
WHOOOO!

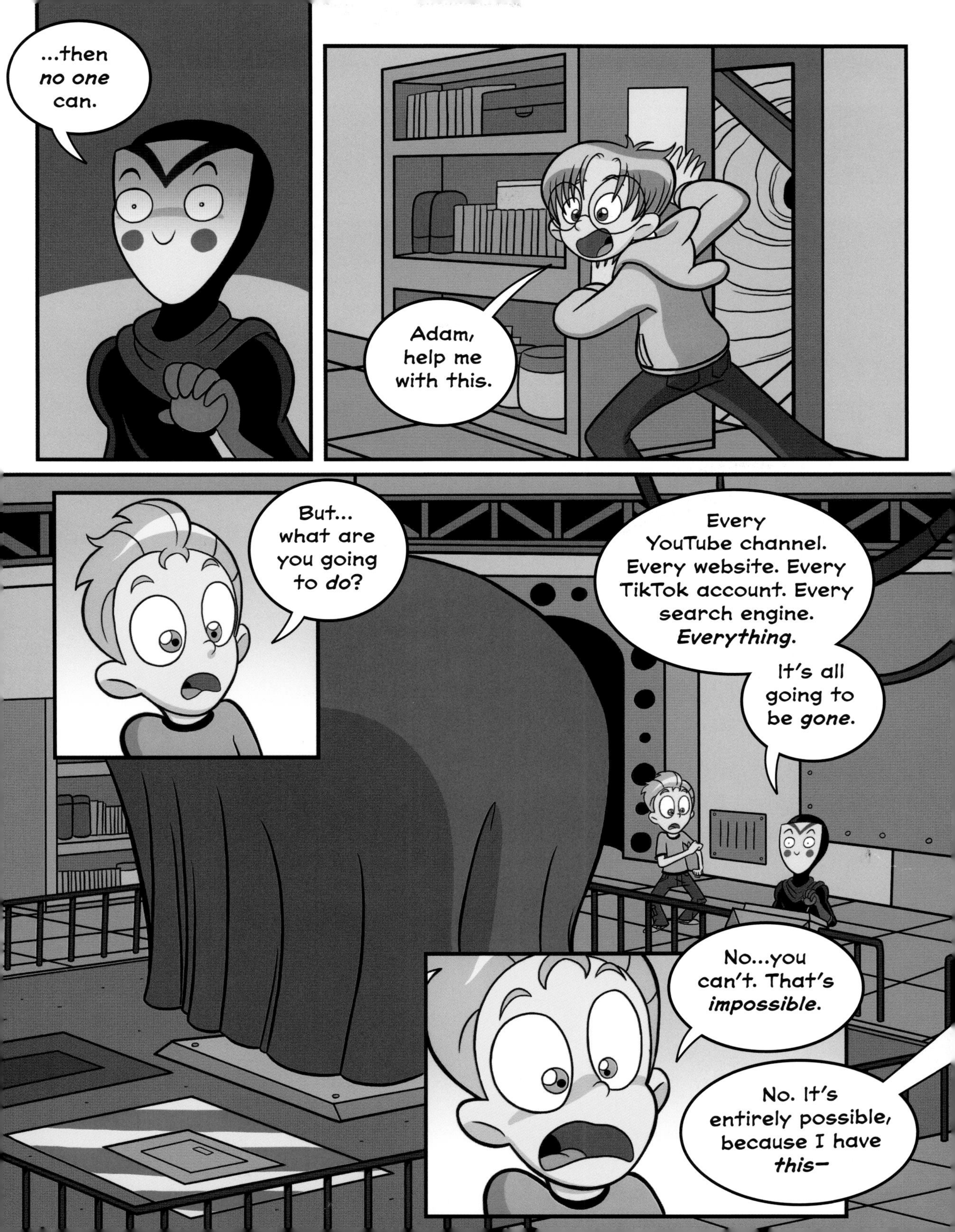
...then *no one* can.
Adam, help me with this.
But... what are you going to *do*?
Every YouTube channel. Every website. Every TikTok account. Every search engine. *Everything*.
It's all going to be *gone*.
No...you can't. That's *impossible*.
No. It's entirely possible, because I have *this*—

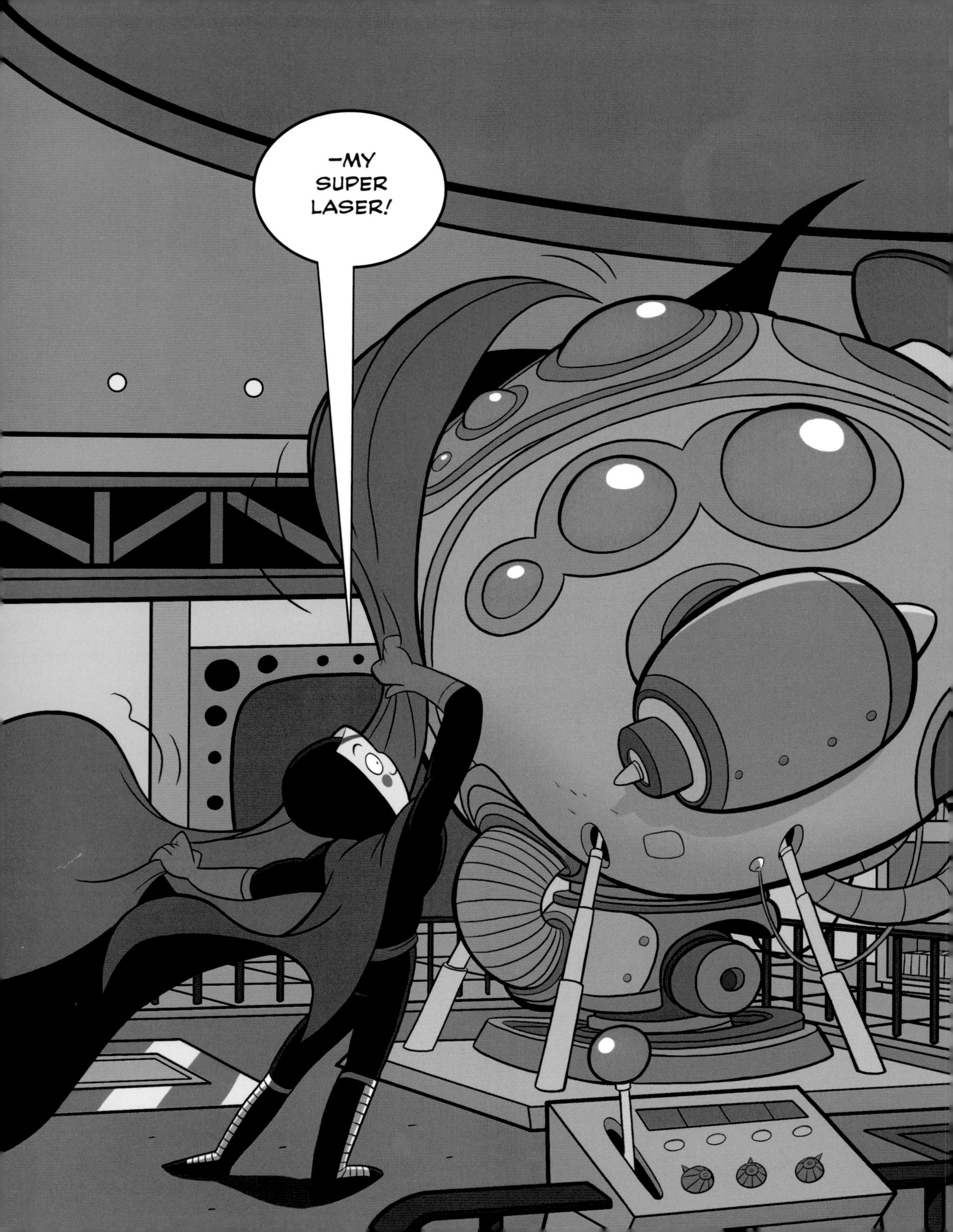
—MY SUPER LASER!

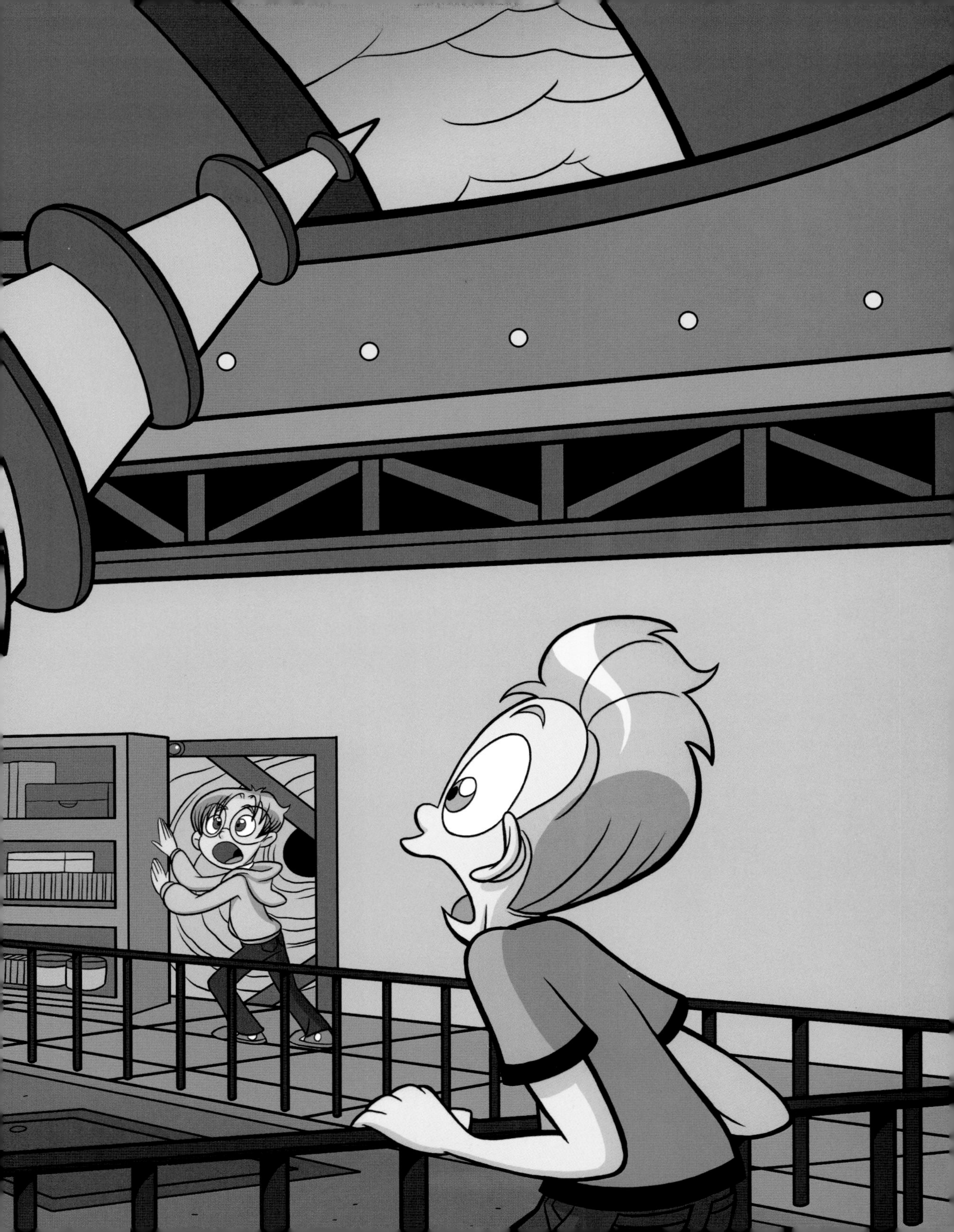

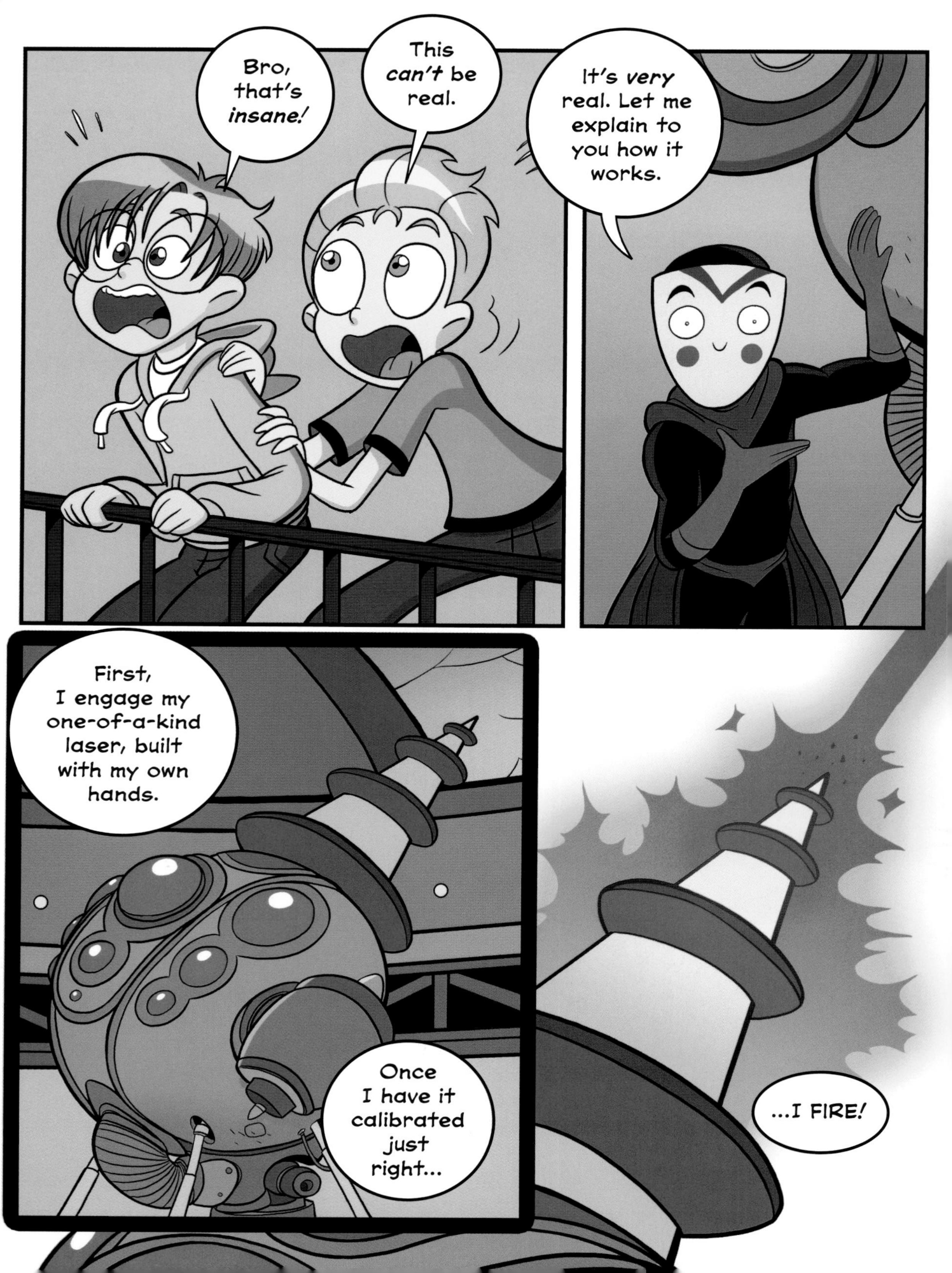
Bro, that's *insane!*
This *can't* be real.
It's *very* real. Let me explain to you how it works.
First, I engage my one-of-a-kind laser, built with my own hands.
Once I have it calibrated just right...
...I FIRE!

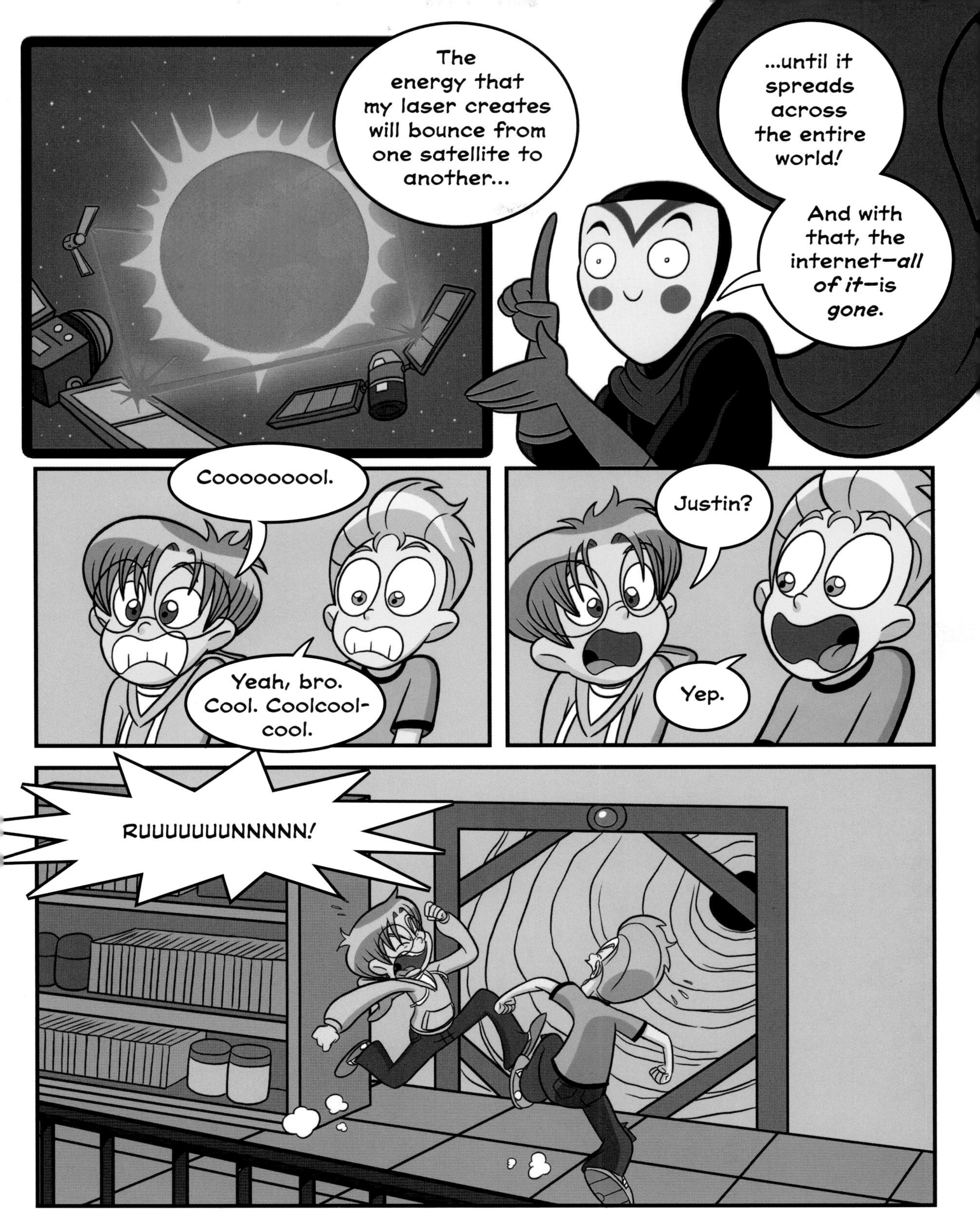
The energy that my laser creates will bounce from one satellite to another...
...until it spreads across the entire world!
And with that, the internet—*all of it*—is *gone*.
Cooooooool.
Yeah, bro. Cool. Coolcool-cool.
Justin?
Yep.
RUUUUUUUNNNNN!

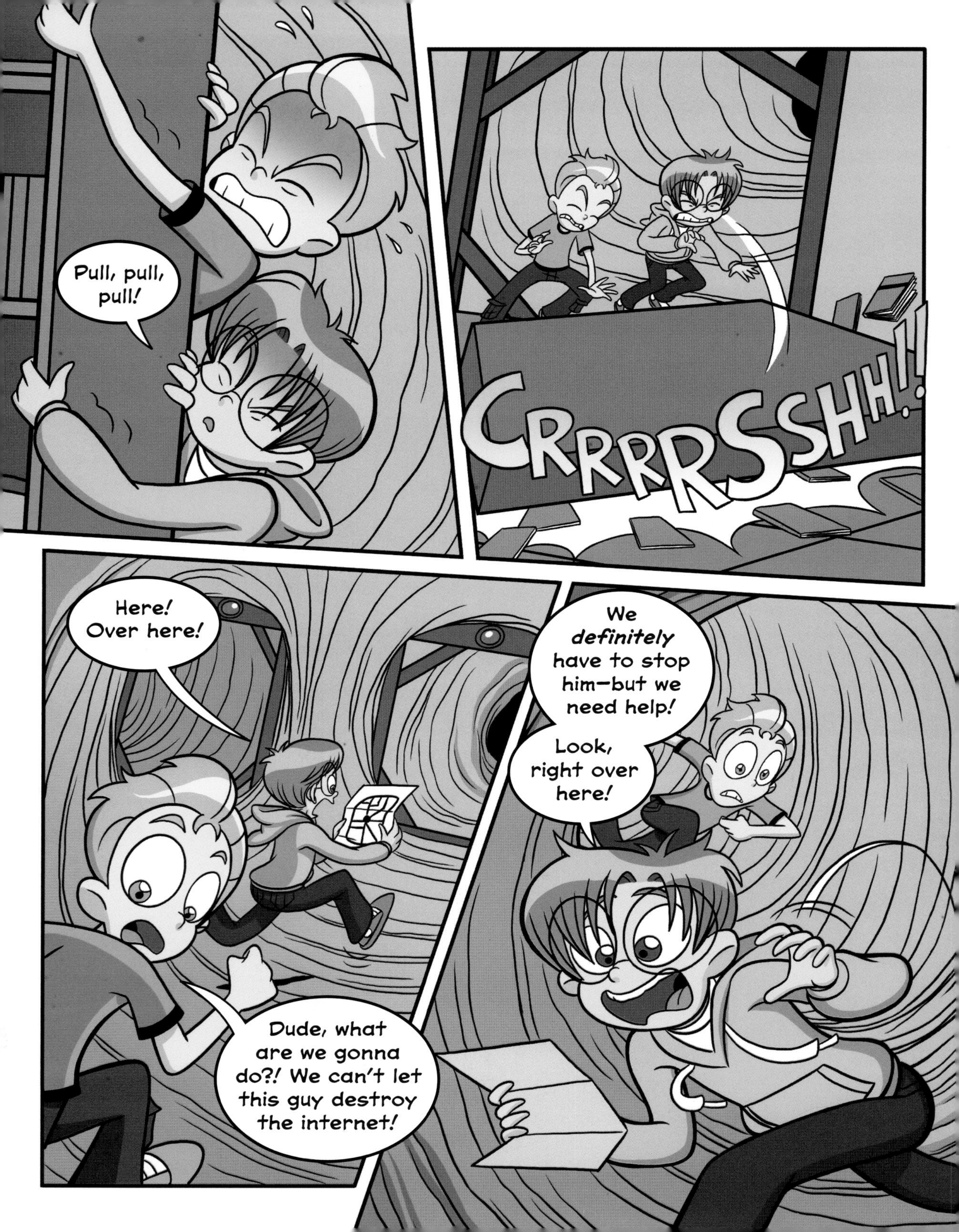
Pull, pull, pull!
CRRRRSSHH!!!
Here! Over here!
Dude, what are we gonna do?! We can't let this guy destroy the internet!
We *definitely* have to stop him—but we need help!
Look, right over here!

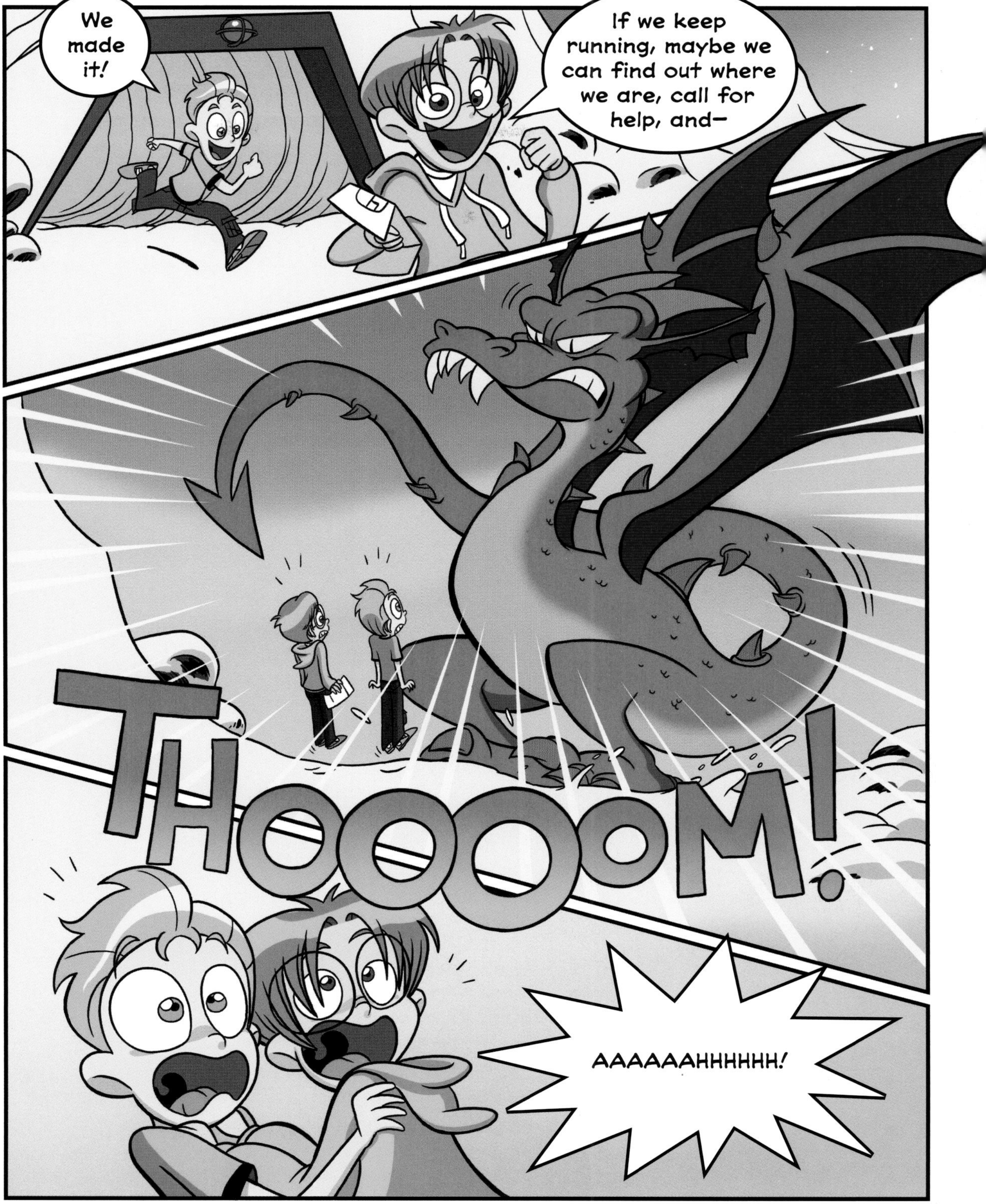
We made it!
If we keep running, maybe we can find out where we are, call for help, and—
THOOOOM!
AAAAAAHHHHHH!

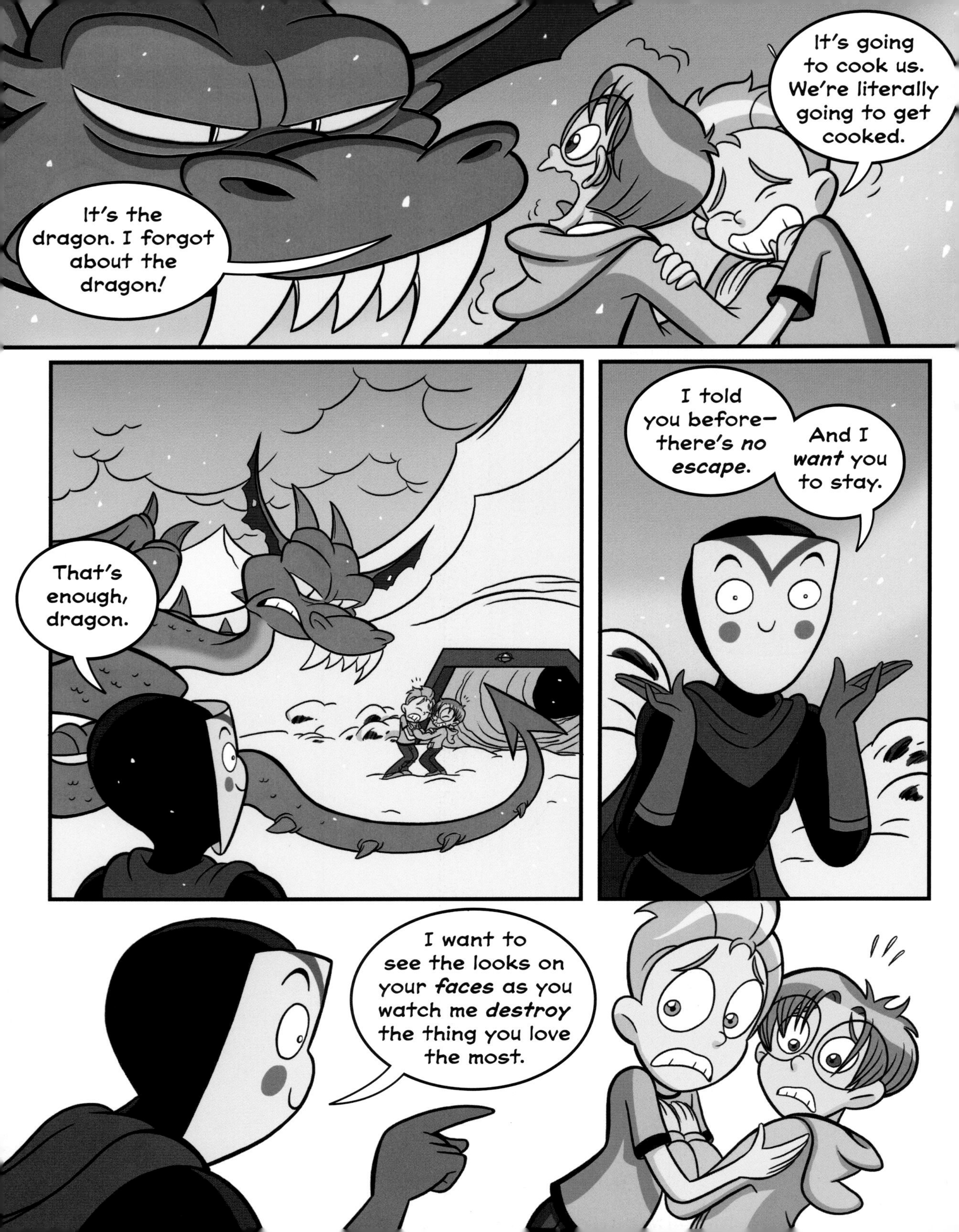
It's the dragon. I forgot about the dragon!
It's going to cook us. We're literally going to get cooked.
That's enough, dragon.
I told you before—there's *no escape*.
And I *want* you to stay.
I want to see the looks on your *faces* as you watch me *destroy* the thing you love the most.

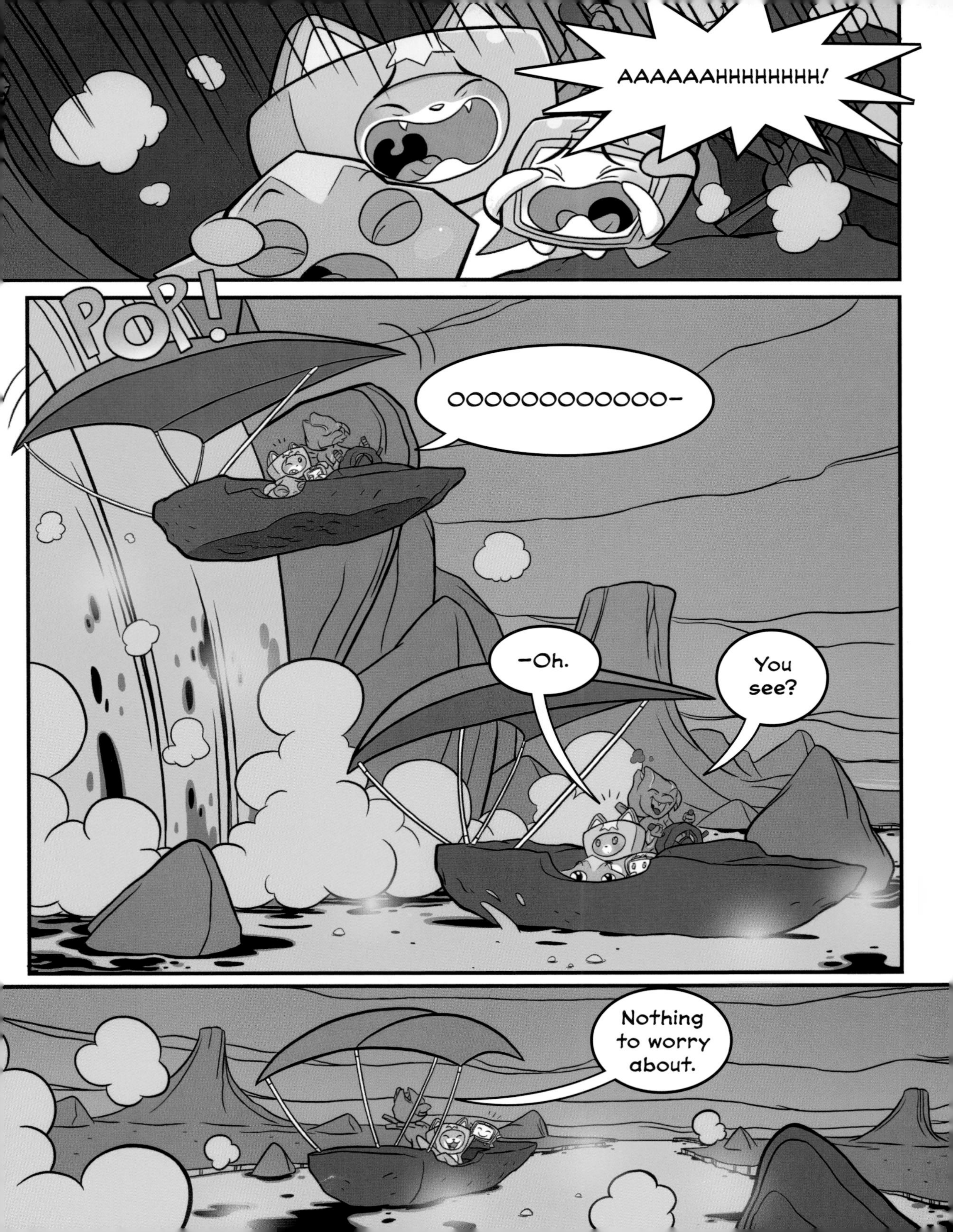
AAAAAAHHHHHHHH!
POP!
OOOOOOOOOOOO-
-Oh.
You see?
Nothing to worry about.

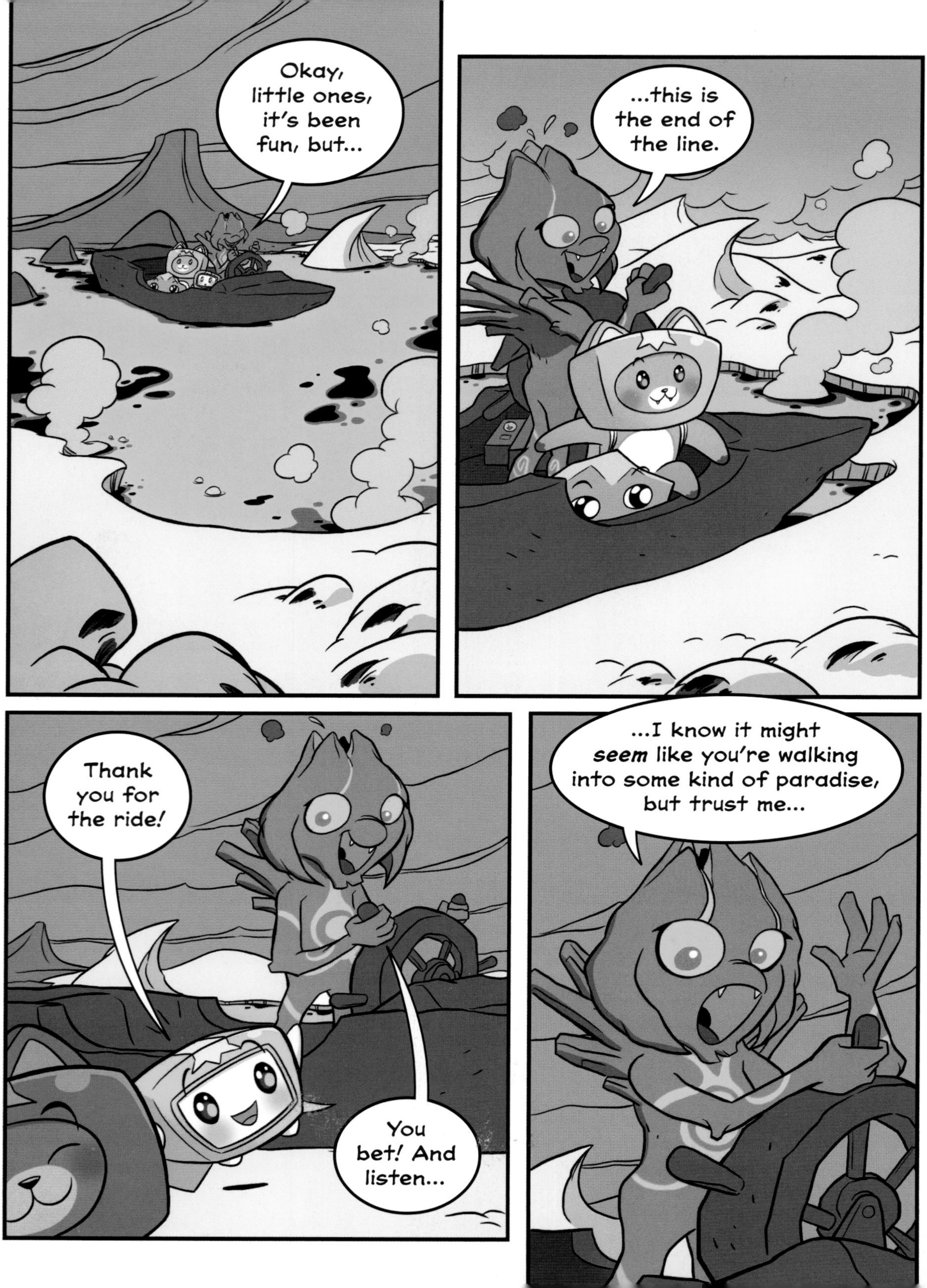
Okay, little ones, it's been fun, but...
...this is the end of the line.
Thank you for the ride!
You bet! And listen...
...I know it might *seem* like you're walking into some kind of paradise, but trust me...

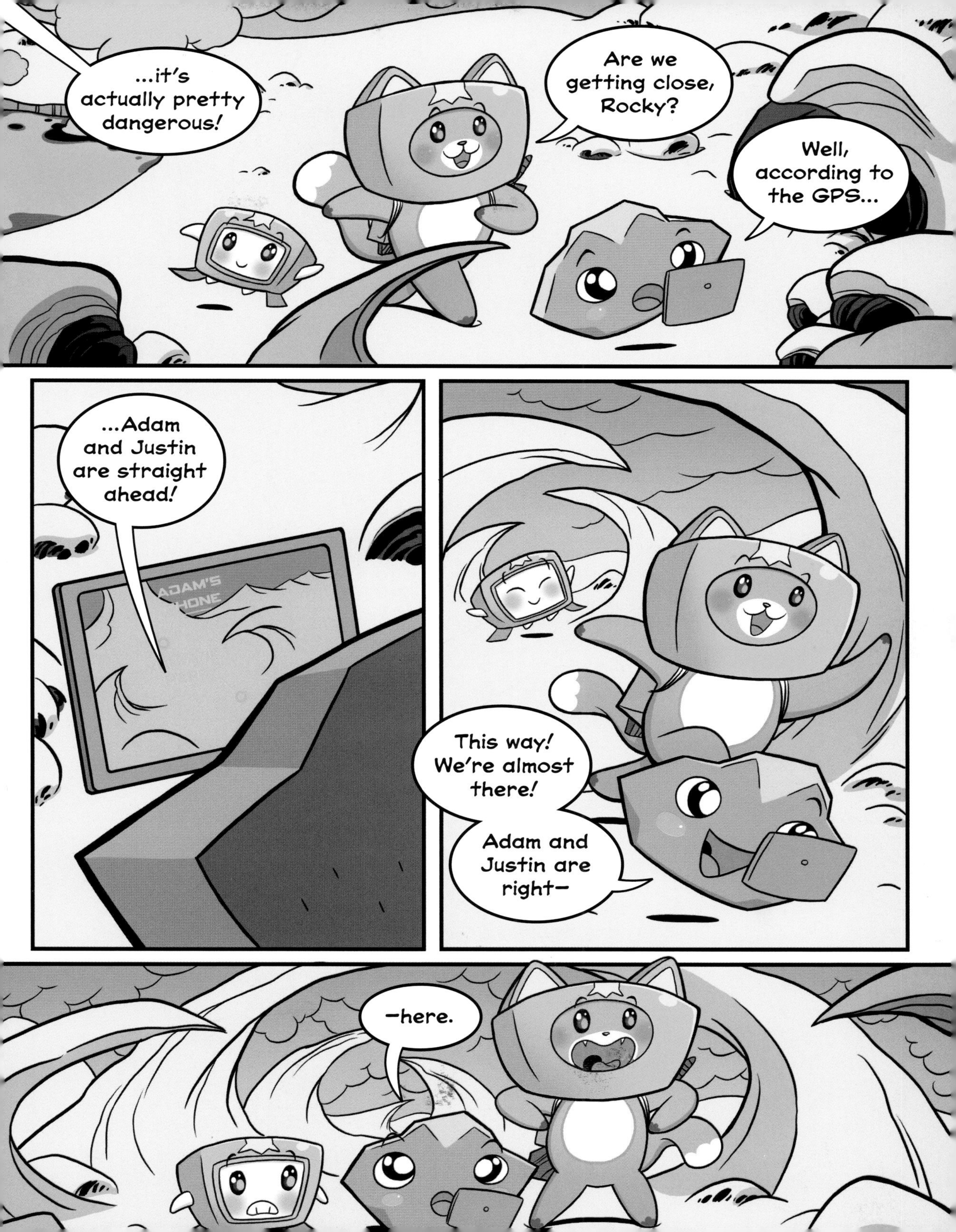
...it's actually pretty dangerous!
Are we getting close, Rocky?
Well, according to the GPS...
...Adam and Justin are straight ahead!
ADAM'S PHONE
This way! We're almost there!
Adam and Justin are right—
—here.

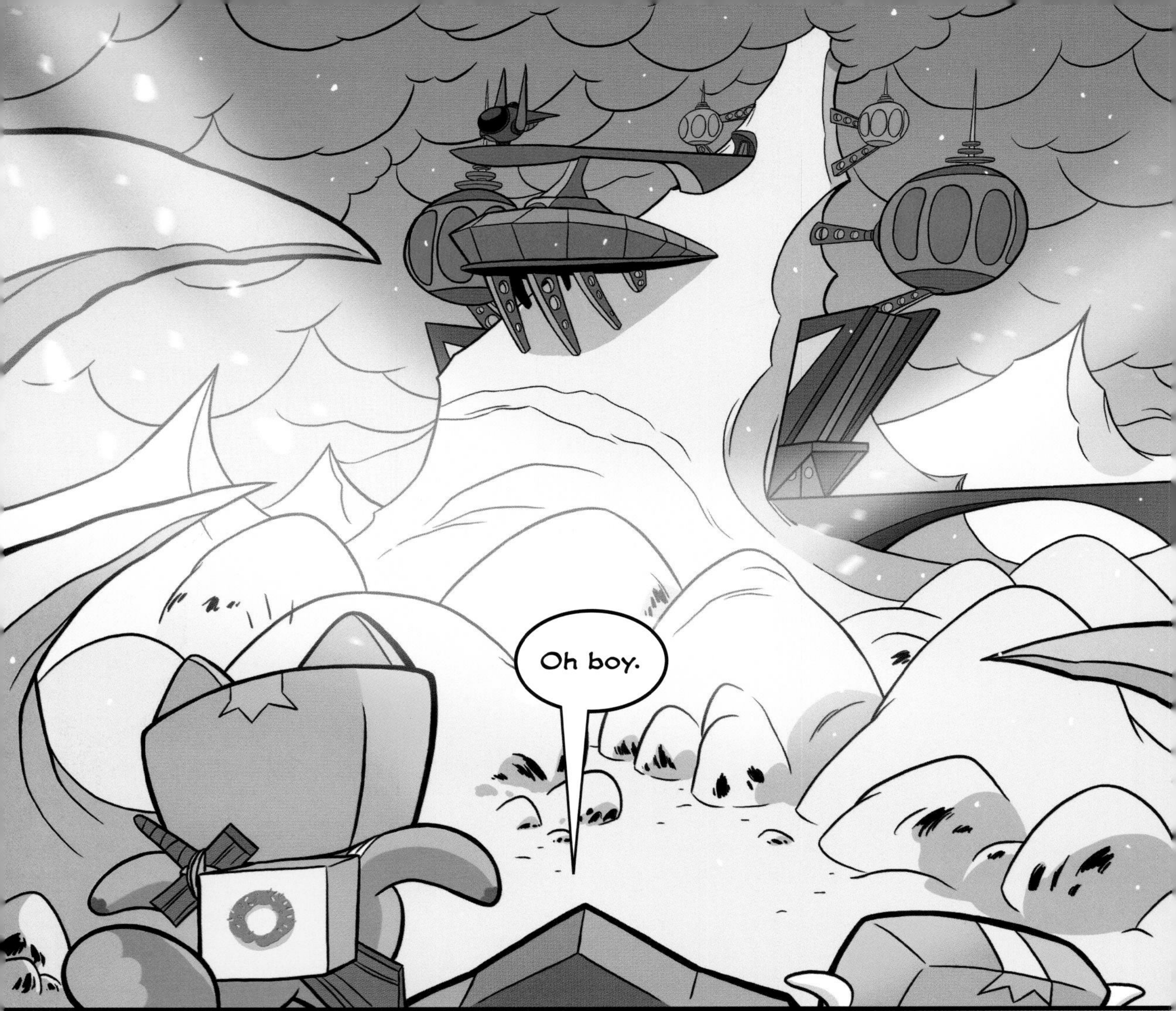
Oh boy.

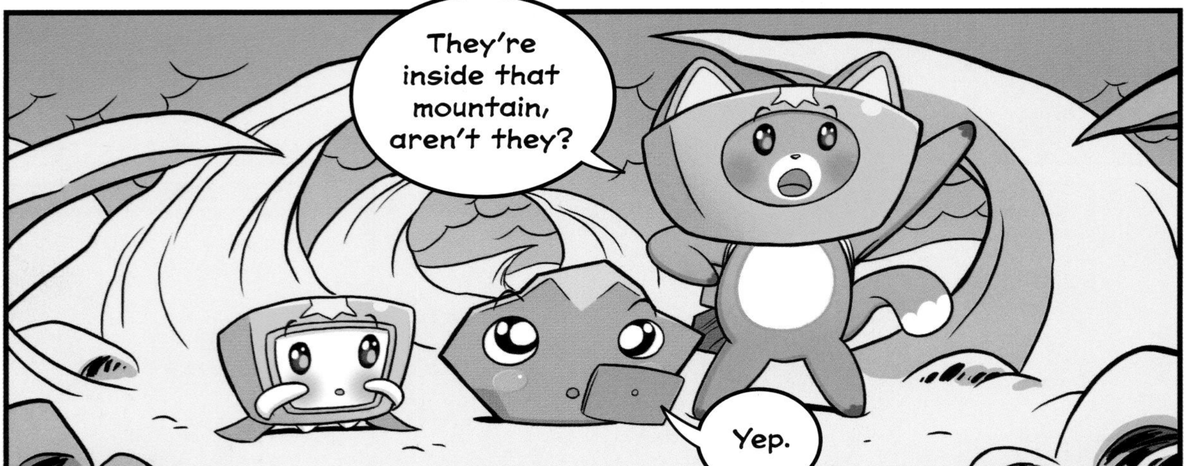
They're inside that mountain, aren't they?
Yep.

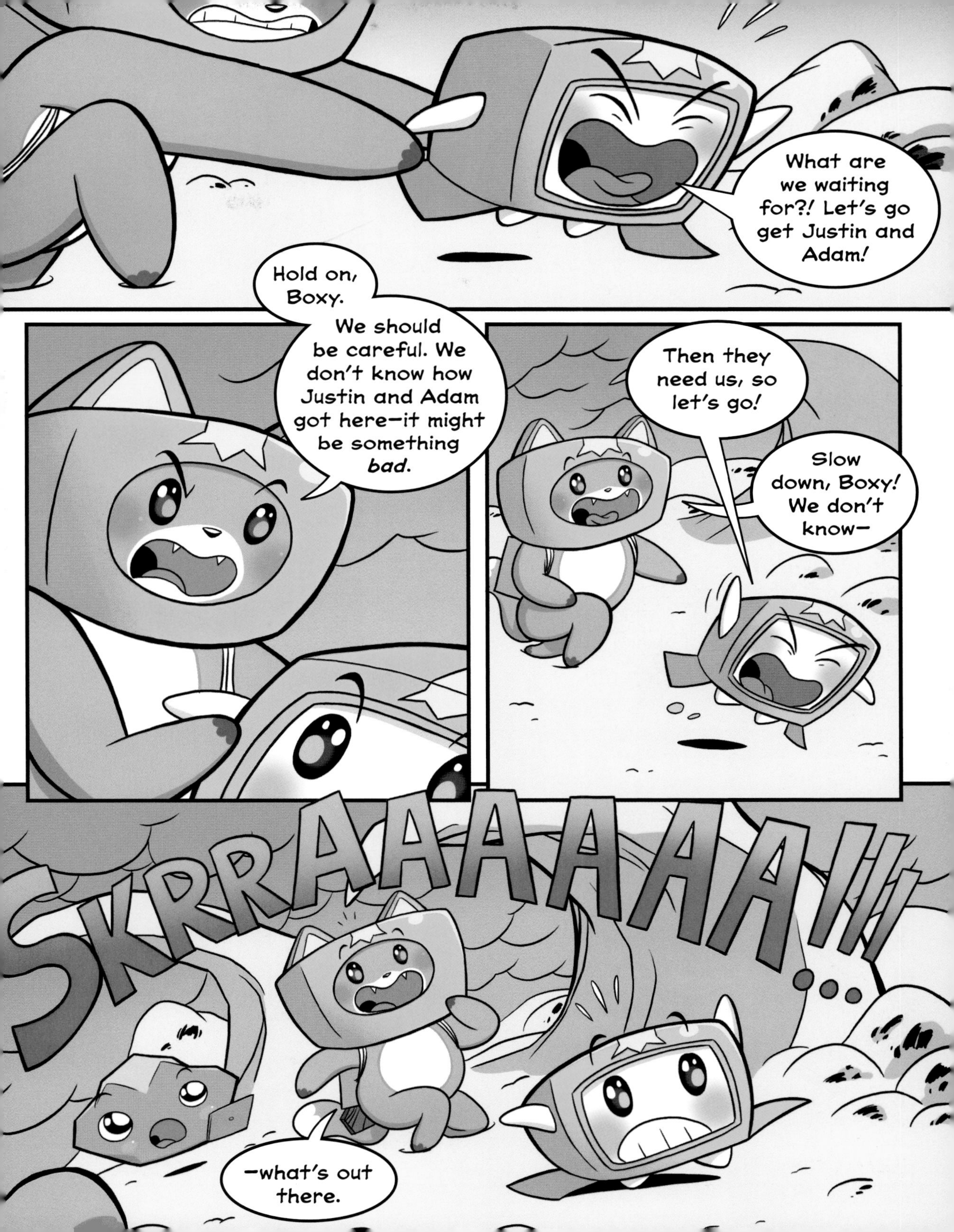

What are we waiting for?! Let's go get Justin and Adam!
Hold on, Boxy.
We should be careful. We don't know how Justin and Adam got here—it might be something *bad*.
Then they need us, so let's go!
Slow down, Boxy! We don't know—
SKRRAAAAAAA!!!...
—what's out there.

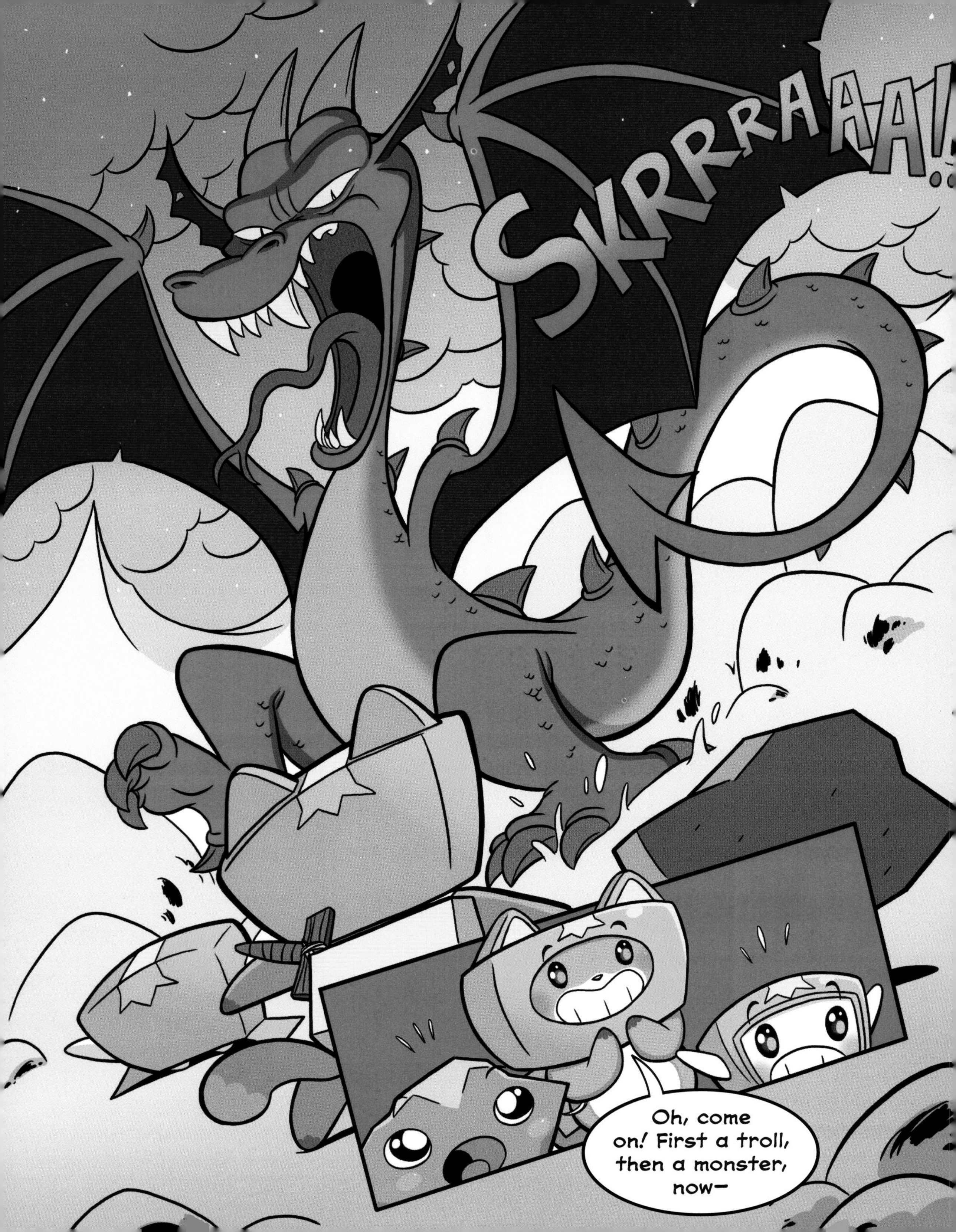
SKRRRAAA!!
Oh, come on! First a troll, then a monster, now—

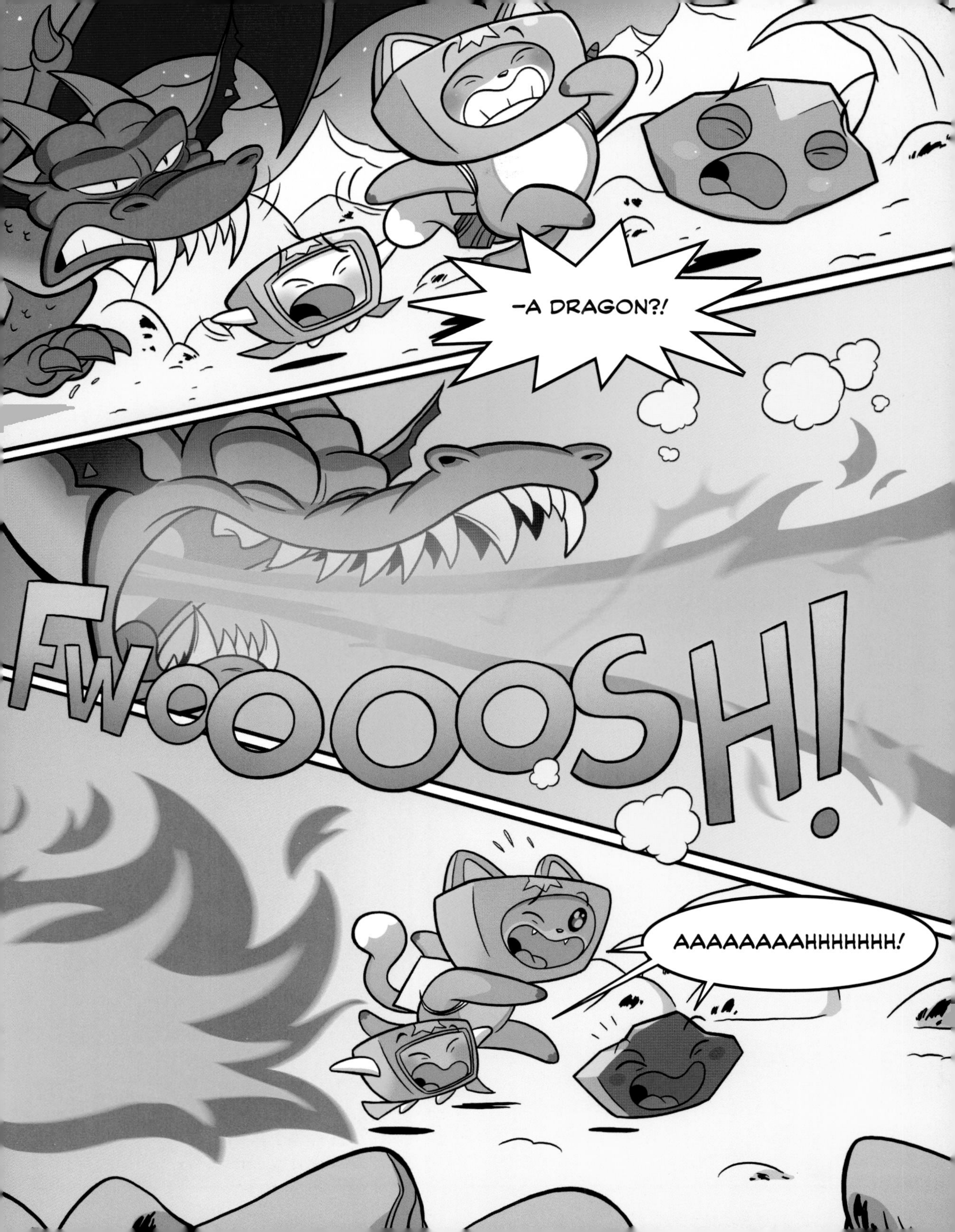
–A DRAGON?!
FWOOOOSH!
AAAAAAAAHHHHHHH!

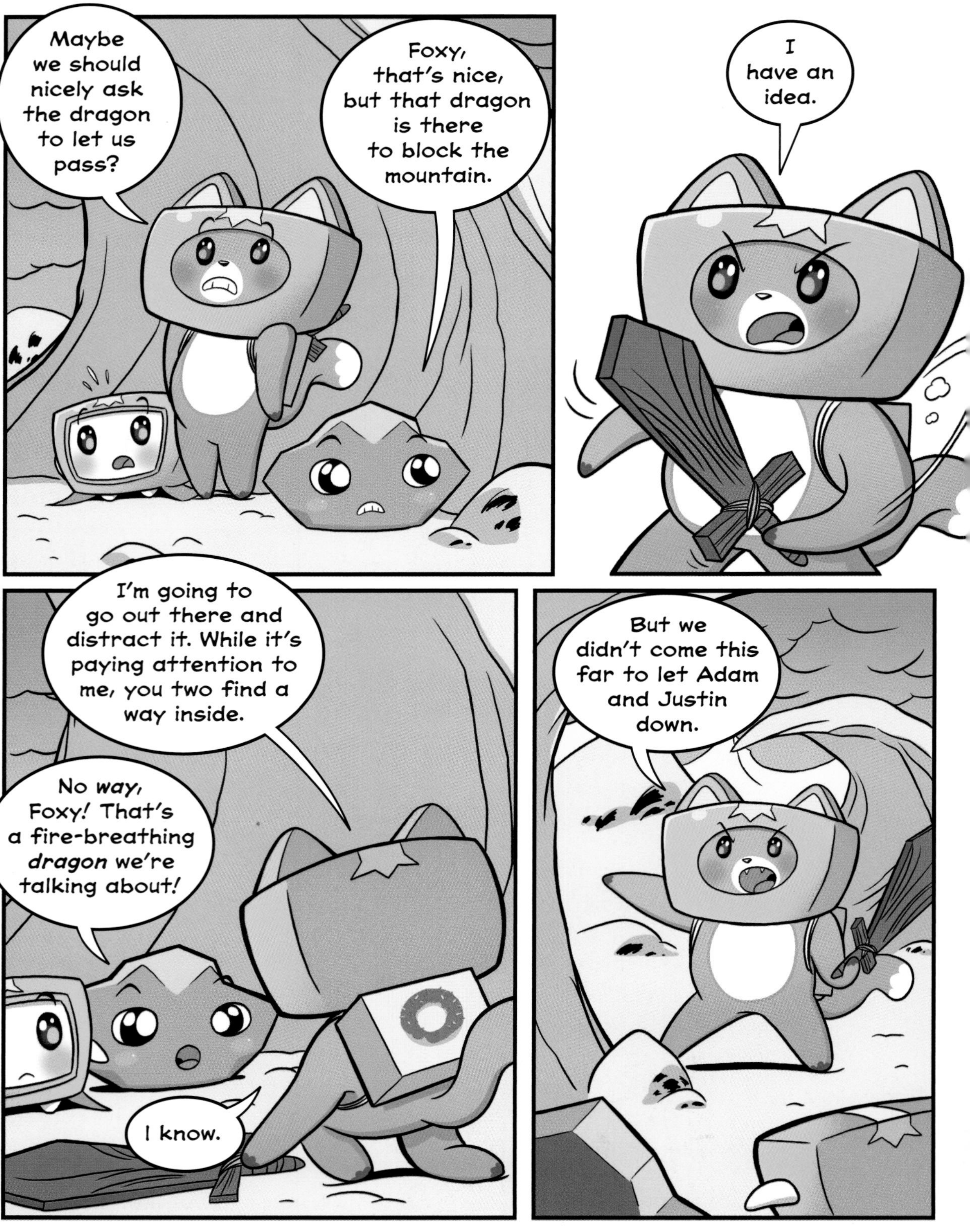
Maybe we should nicely ask the dragon to let us pass?
Foxy, that's nice, but that dragon is there to block the mountain.
I have an idea.
I'm going to go out there and distract it. While it's paying attention to me, you two find a way inside.
No *way*, Foxy! That's a fire-breathing *dragon* we're talking about!
I know.
But we didn't come this far to let Adam and Justin down.

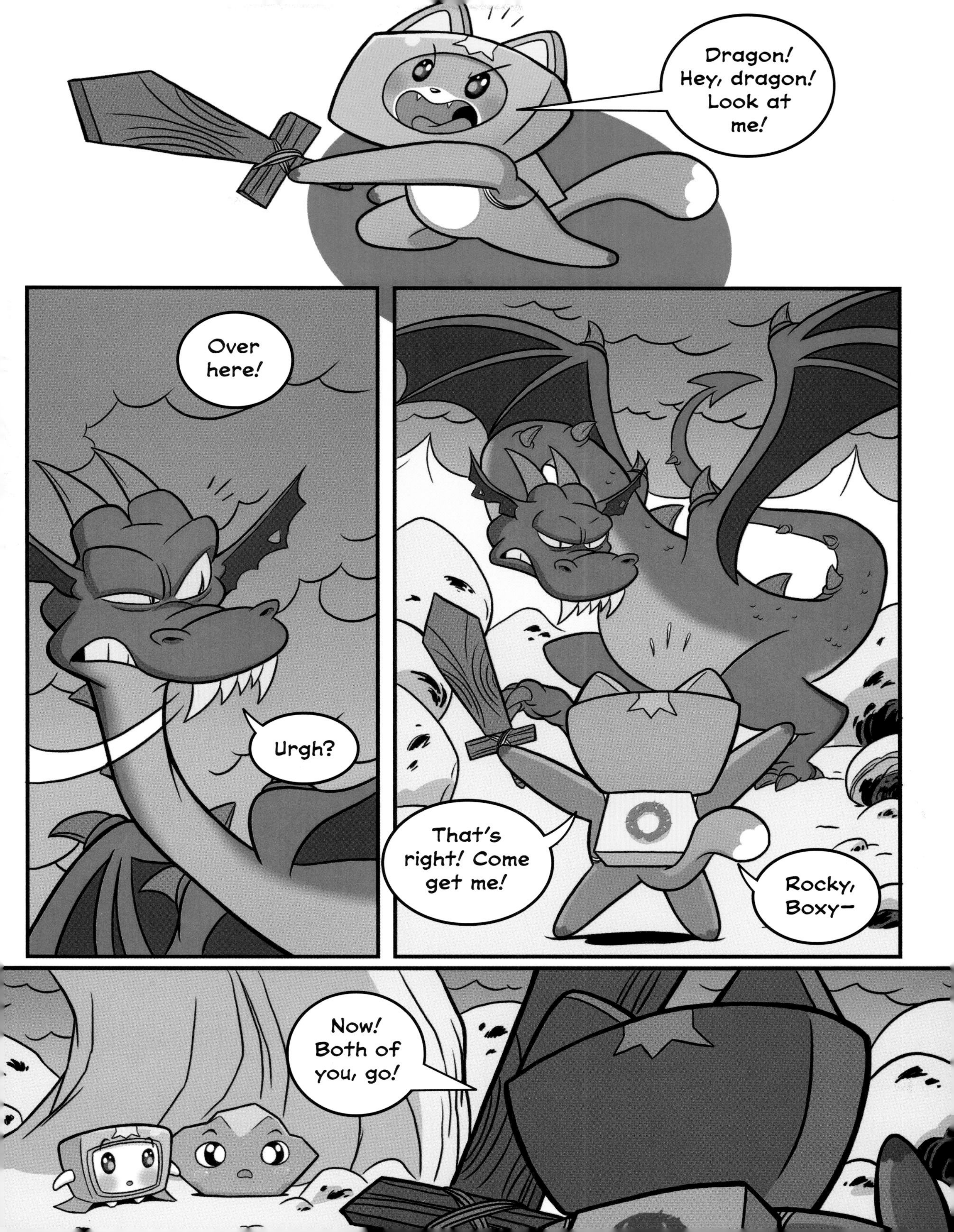
Dragon! Hey, dragon! Look at me!
Over here!
Urgh?
That's right! Come get me!
Rocky, Boxy—
Now! Both of you, go!

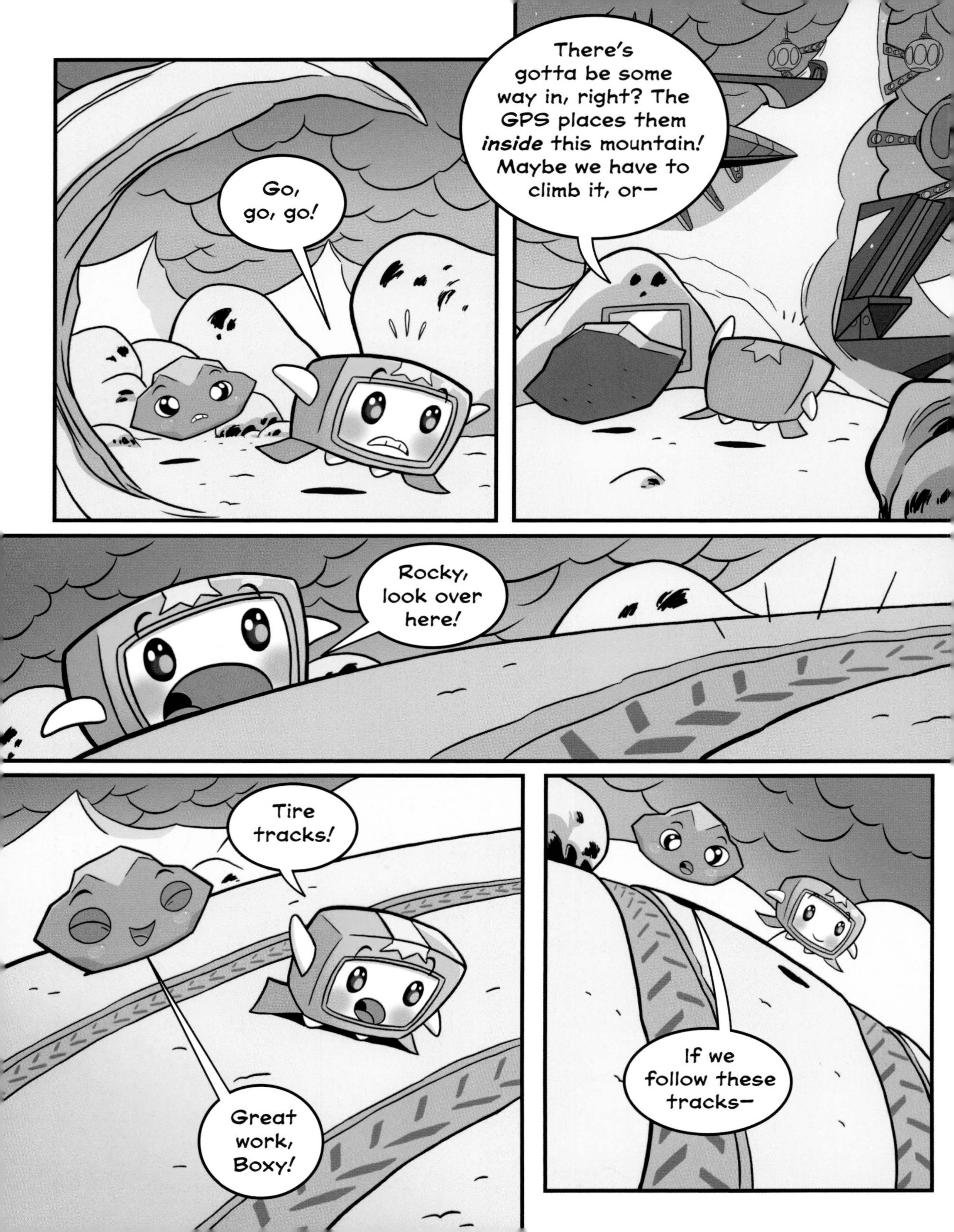
Go, go, go!
There's gotta be some way in, right? The GPS places them *inside* this mountain! Maybe we have to climb it, or—
Rocky, look over here!
Tire tracks!
Great work, Boxy!
If we follow these tracks—

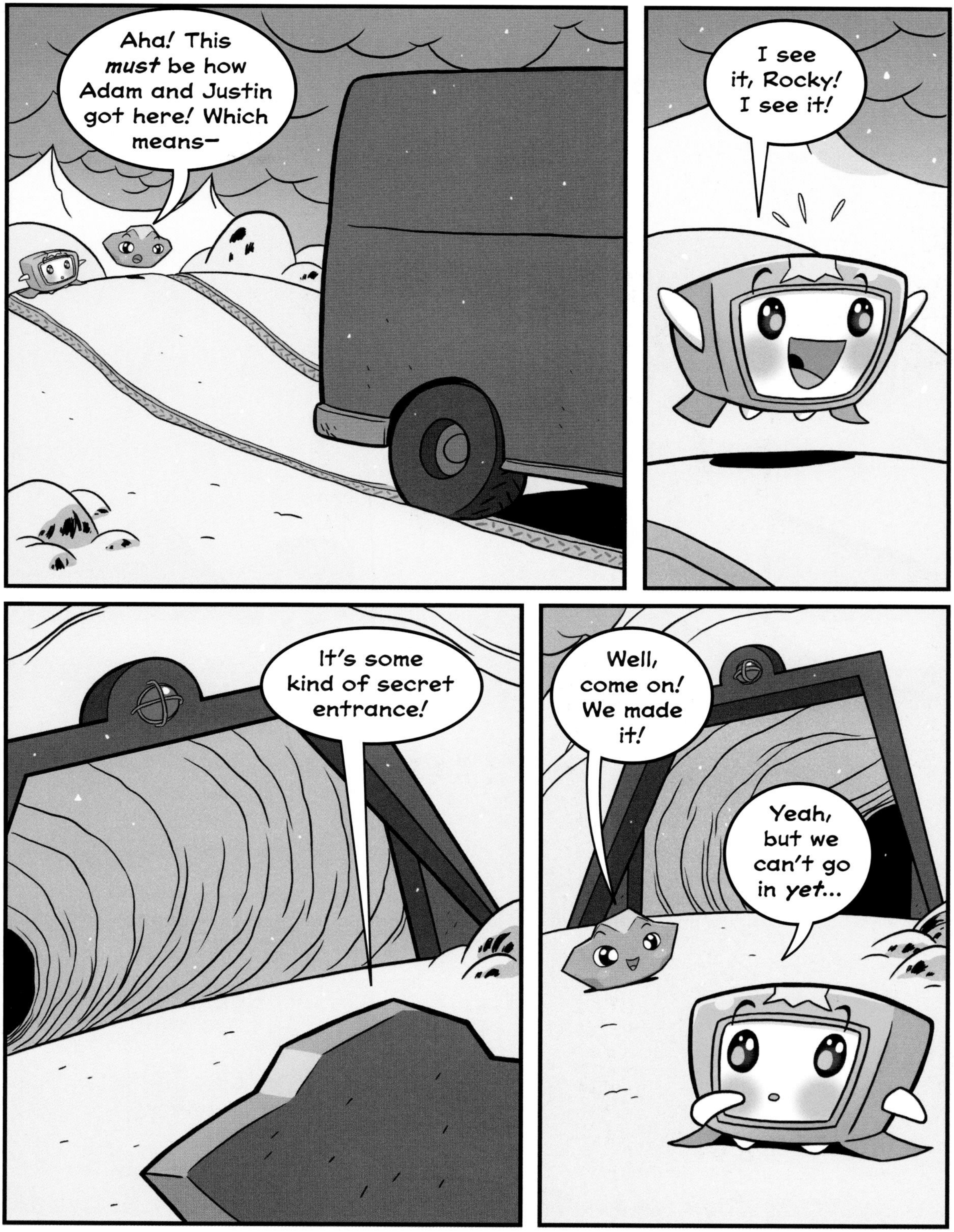
Aha! This *must* be how Adam and Justin got here! Which means—
I see it, Rocky! I see it!
It's some kind of secret entrance!
Well, come on! We made it!
Yeah, but we can't go in *yet*...

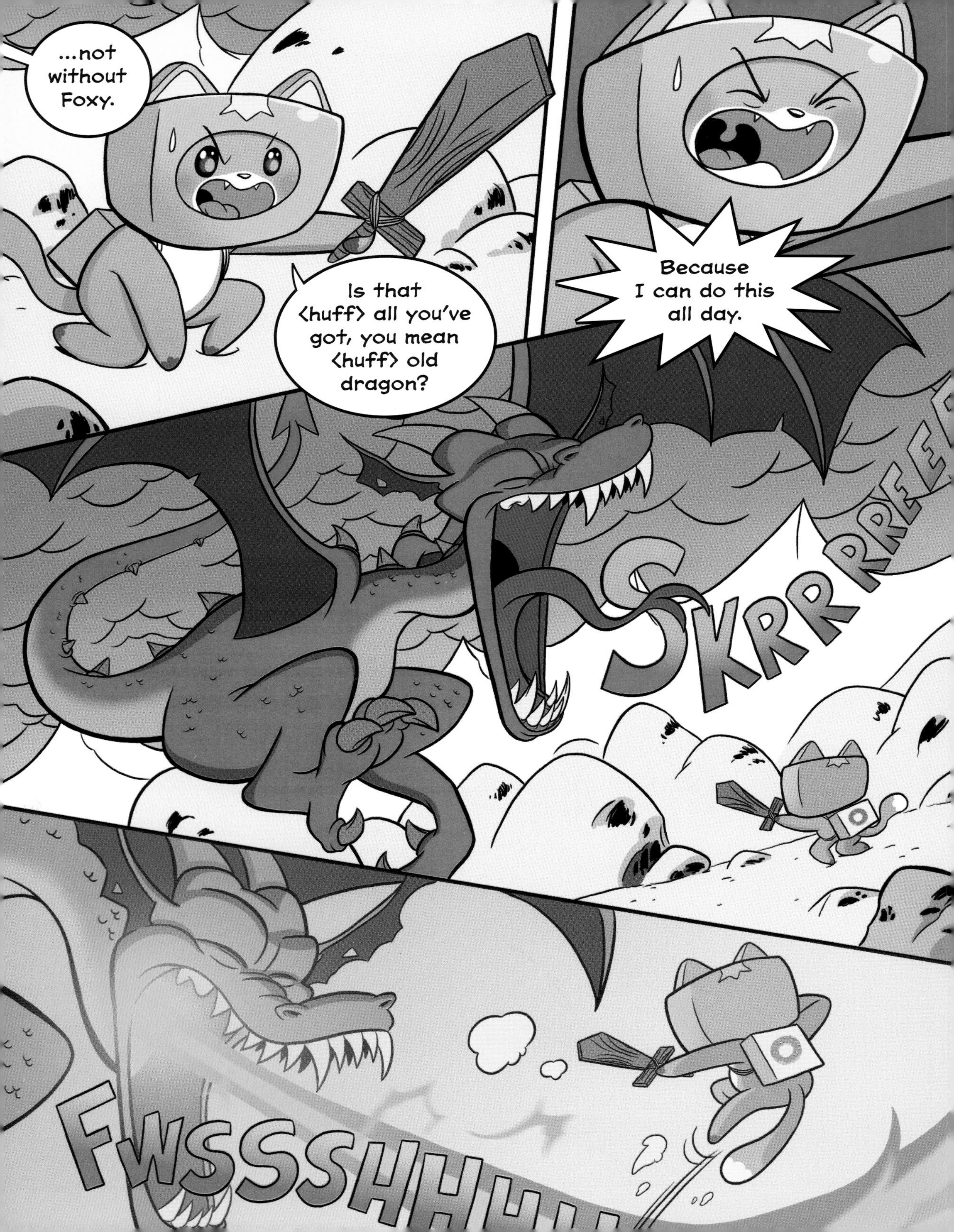
...not without Foxy.
Is that <huff> all you've got, you mean <huff> old dragon?
Because I can do this all day.
SKRRREEE
FWSSSHHH

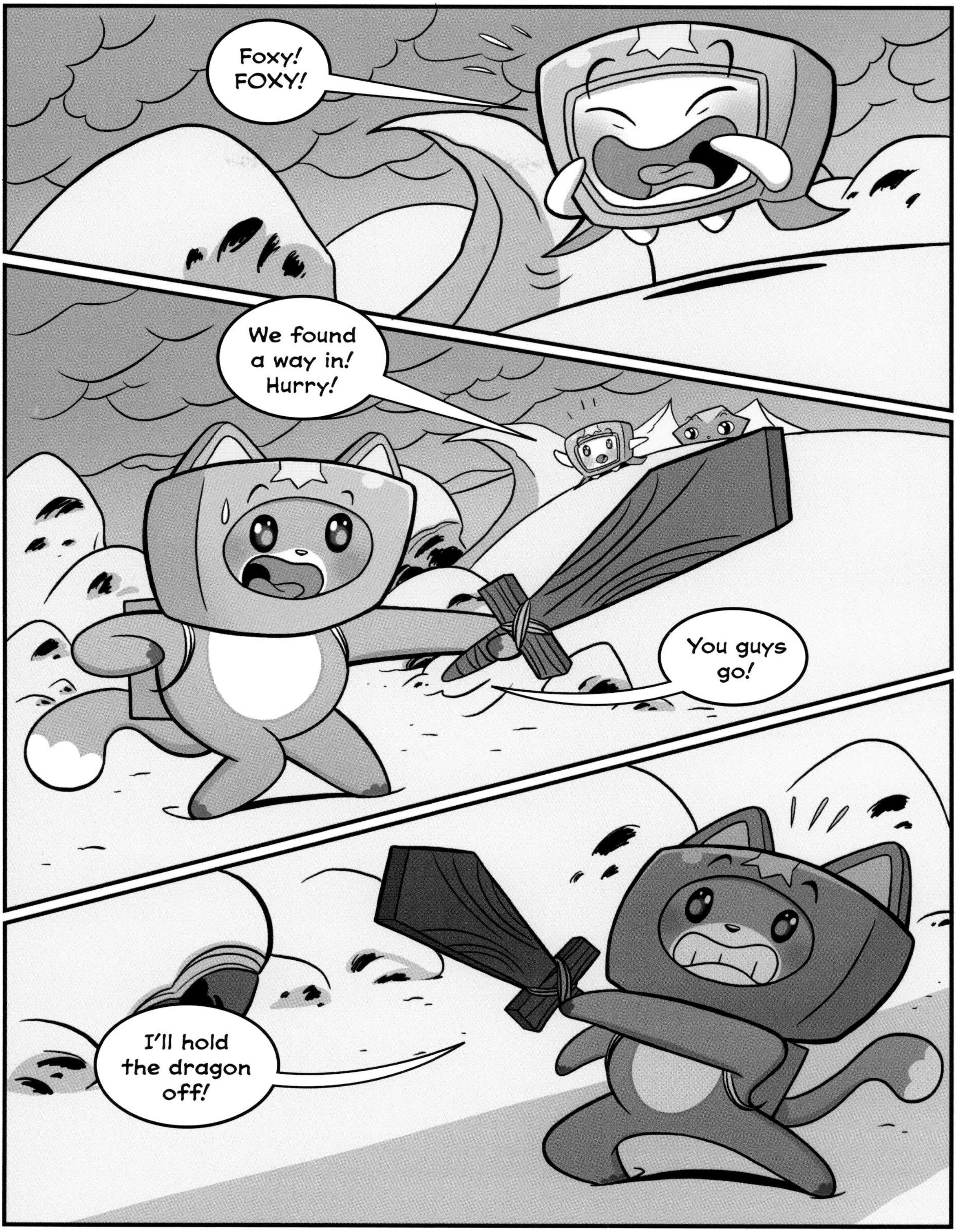
Foxy! FOXY!
We found a way in! Hurry!
You guys go!
I'll hold the dragon off!

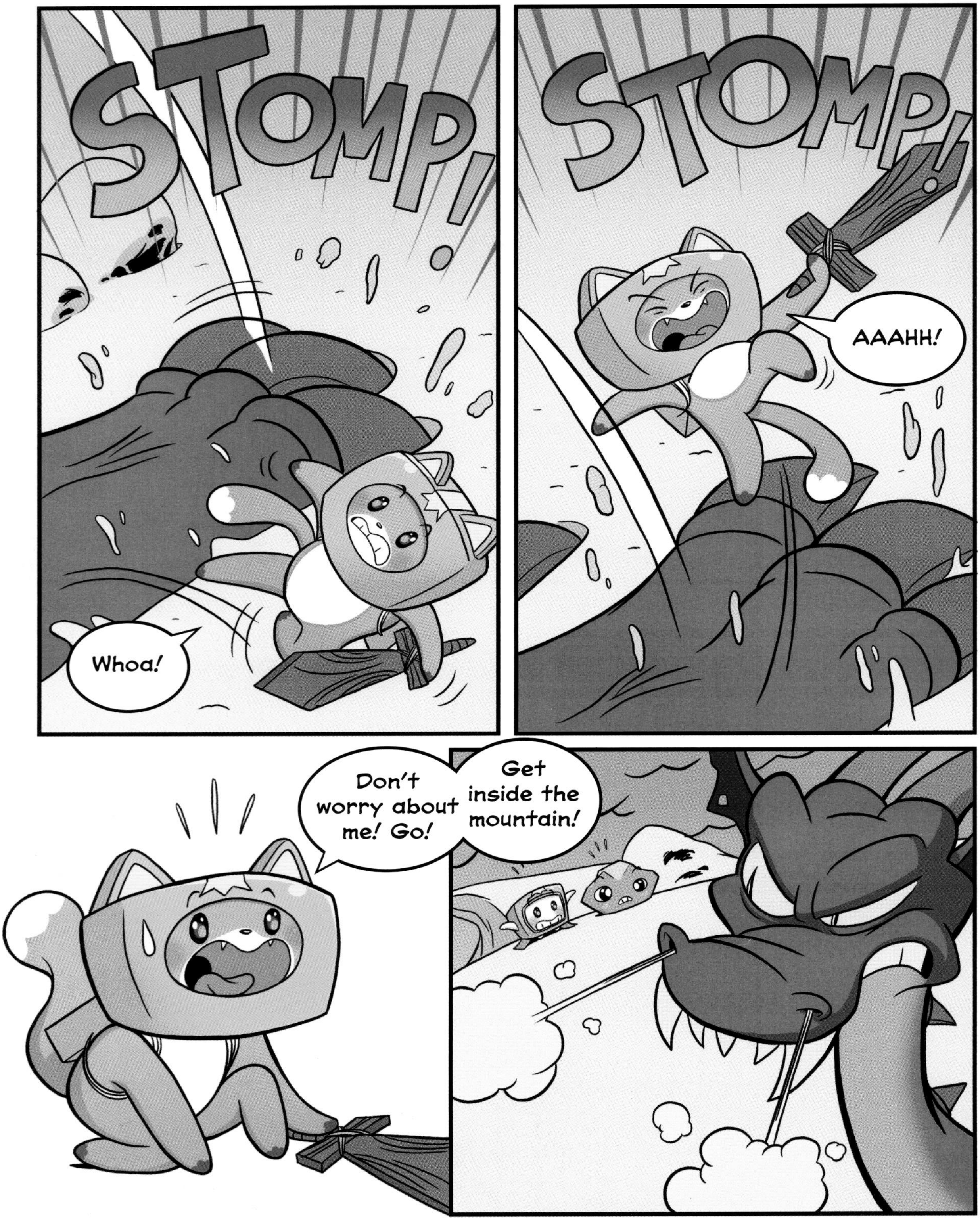
STOMP!
Whoa!
STOMP!
AAAHH!
Don't worry about me! Go!
Get inside the mountain!

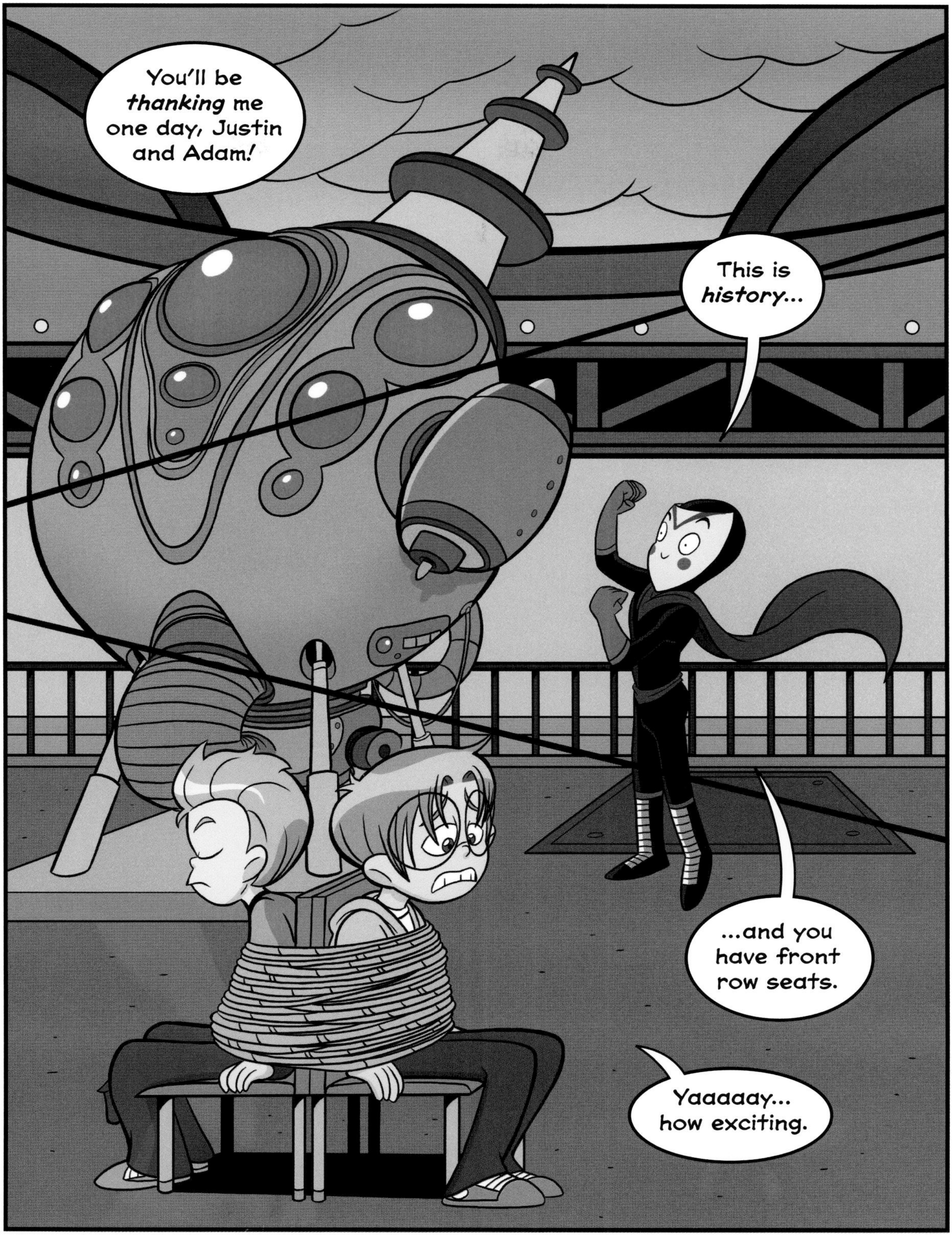
You'll be *thinking* me one day, Justin and Adam!
This is *history*...
...and you have front row seats.
Yaaaaay... how exciting.

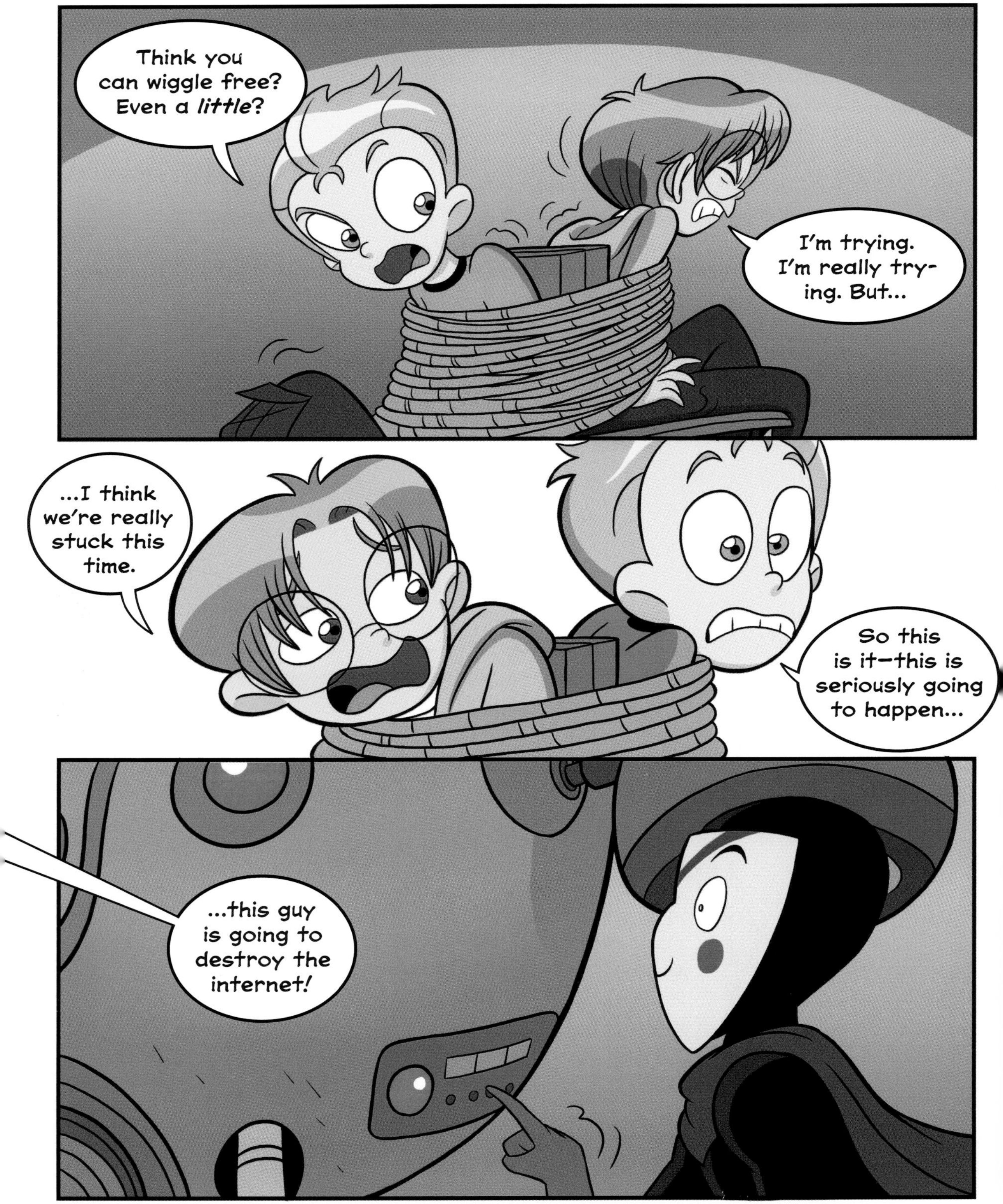
Think you can wiggle free? Even a *little*?
I'm trying. I'm really try-ing. But...
...I think we're really stuck this time.
So this is it—this is seriously going to happen...
...this guy is going to destroy the internet!

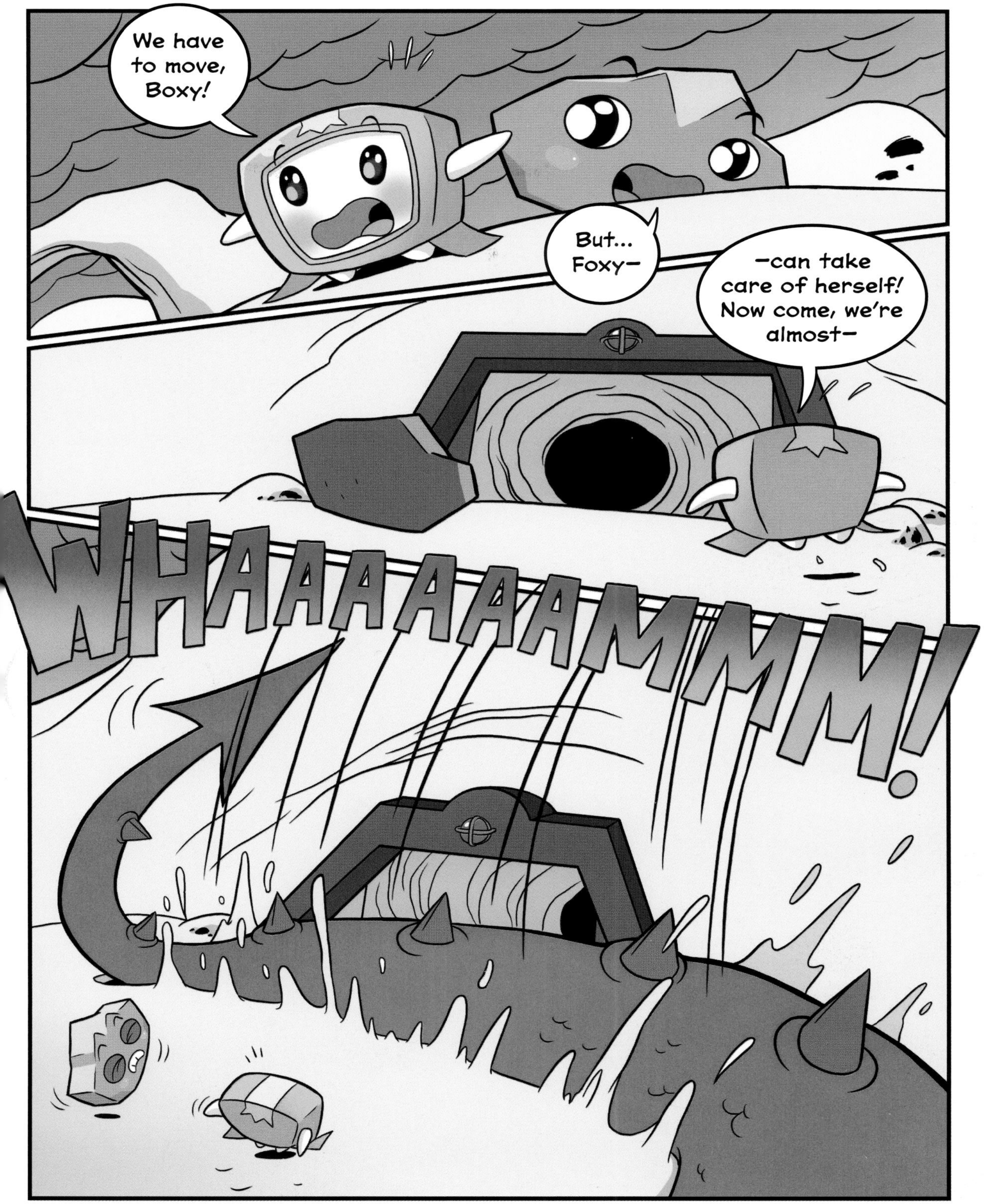
We have to move, Boxy!
But... Foxy—
—can take care of herself! Now come, we're almost—
WHAAAAAAAMMMM!

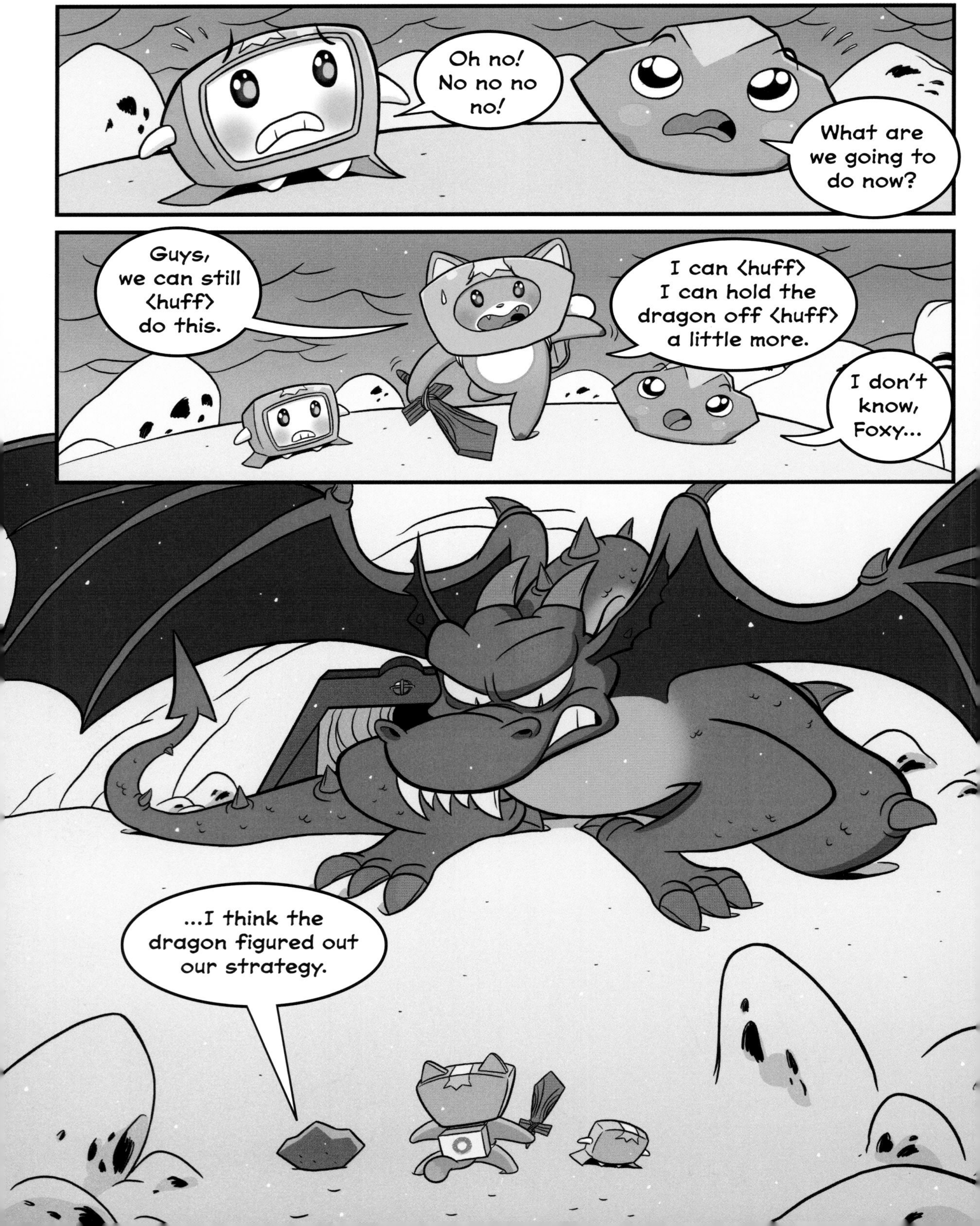
Oh no! No no no no!
What are we going to do now?
Guys, we can still <huff> do this.
I can <huff> I can hold the dragon off <huff> a little more.
I don't know, Foxy...
...I think the dragon figured out our strategy.

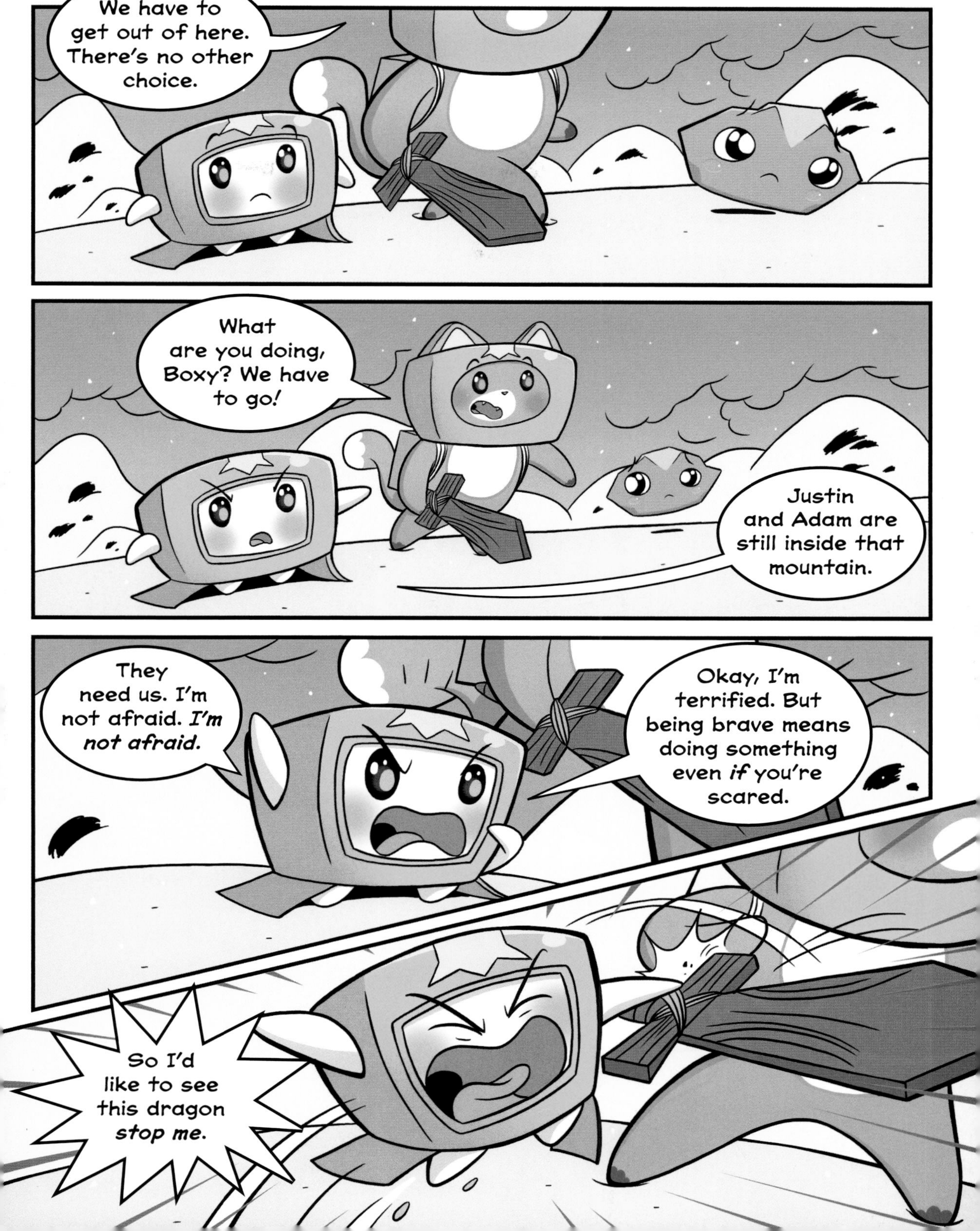
We have to get out of here. There's no other choice.
What are you doing, Boxy? We have to go!
Justin and Adam are still inside that mountain.
They need us. I'm not afraid. *I'm not afraid.*
Okay, I'm terrified. But being brave means doing something even *if* you're scared.
So I'd like to see this dragon *stop me*.

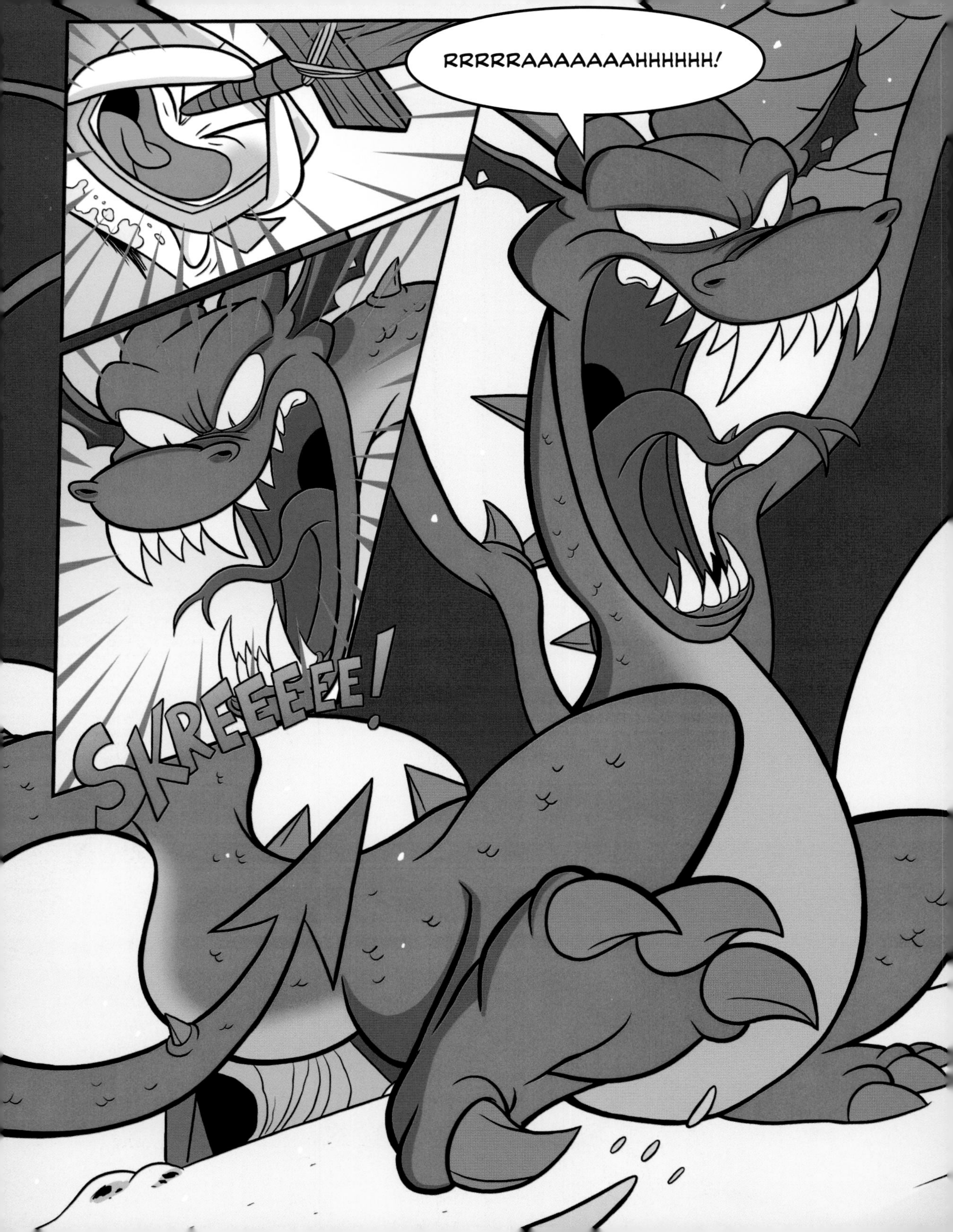
RRRRRAAAAAAAAHHHHHH!
SKREEEEEE!

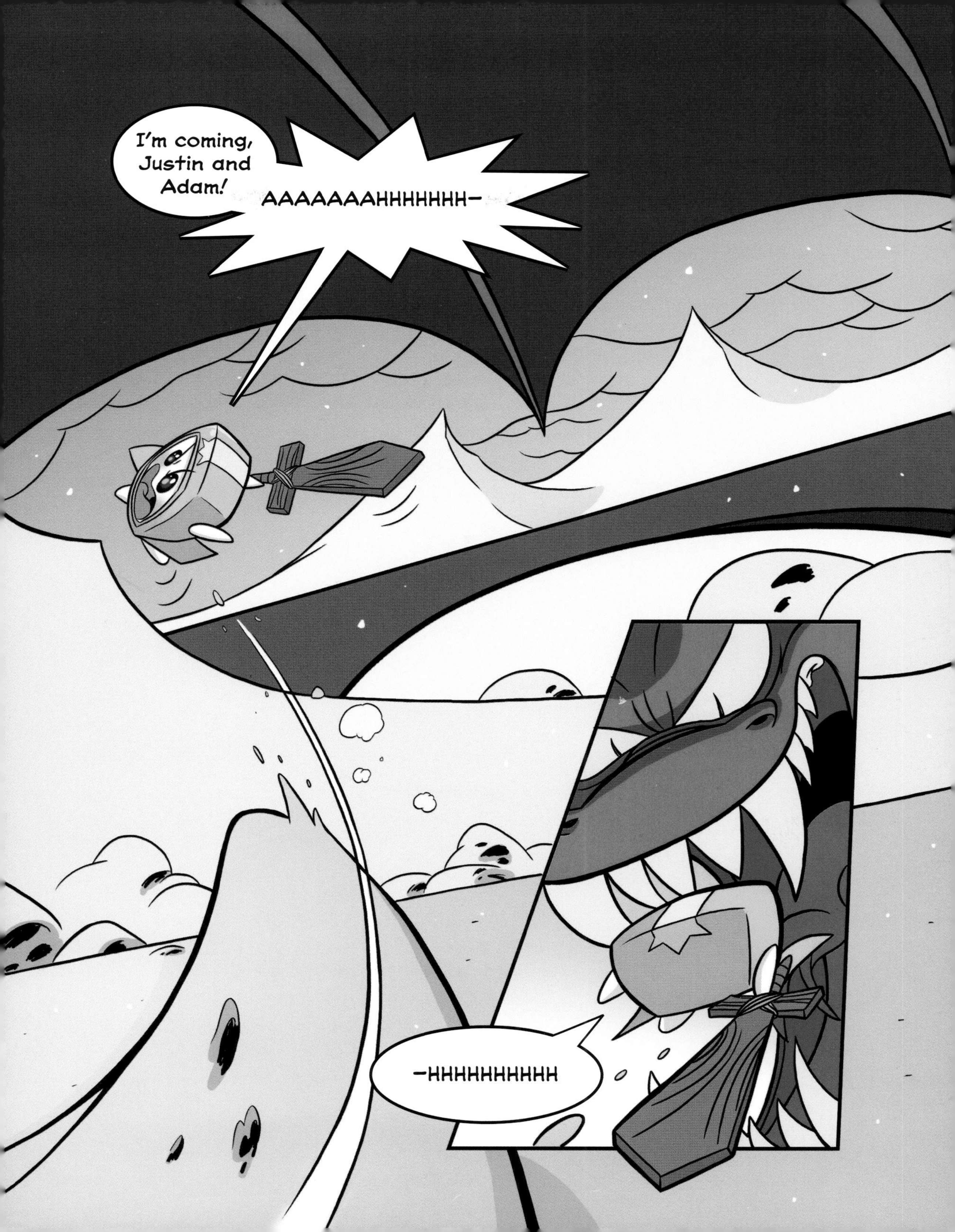
I'm coming, Justin and Adam!
AAAAAAAHHHHHHH–
–HHHHHHHHHH

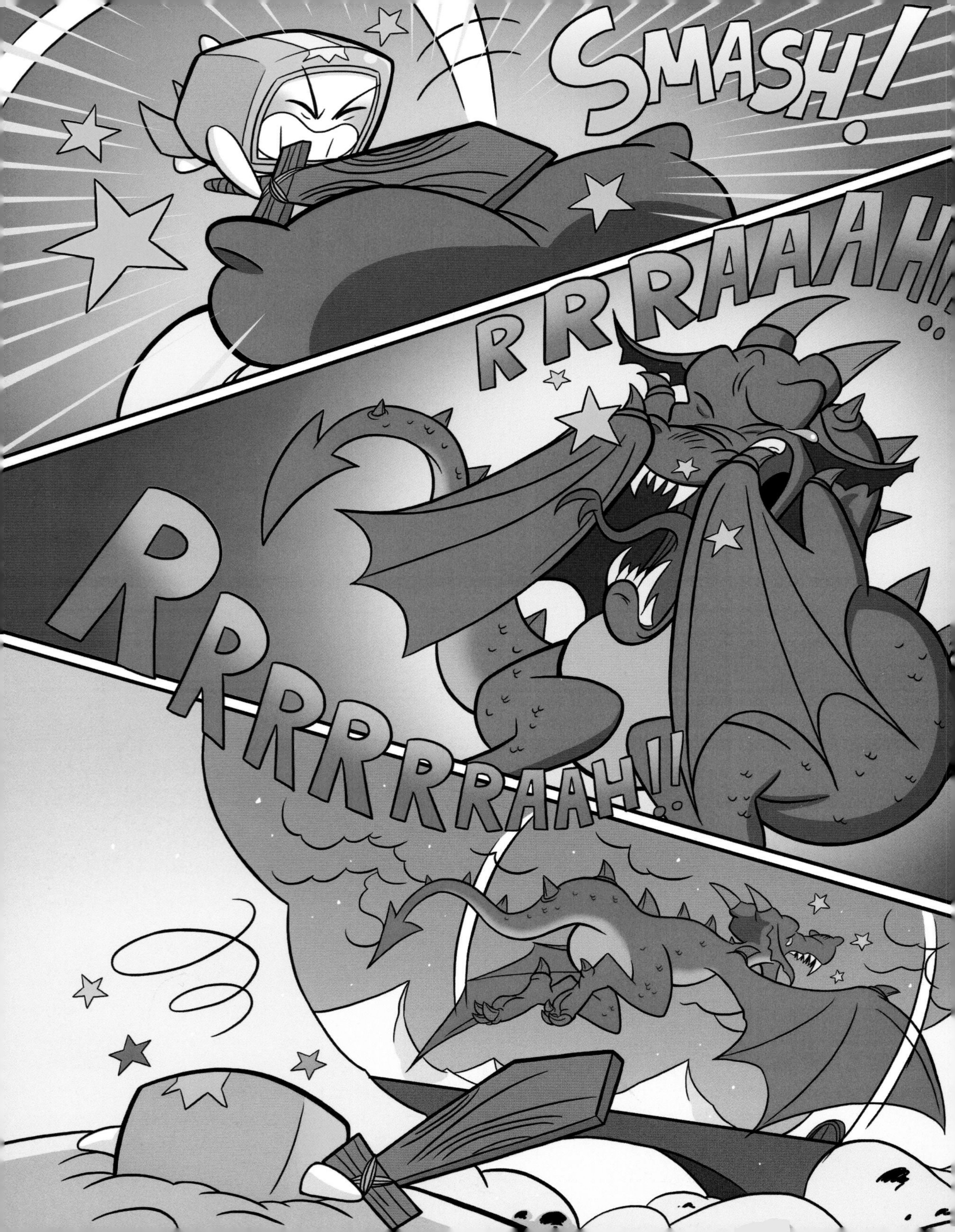
SMASH!
RRRAAAAH!!
RRRRRRRRAAH!!

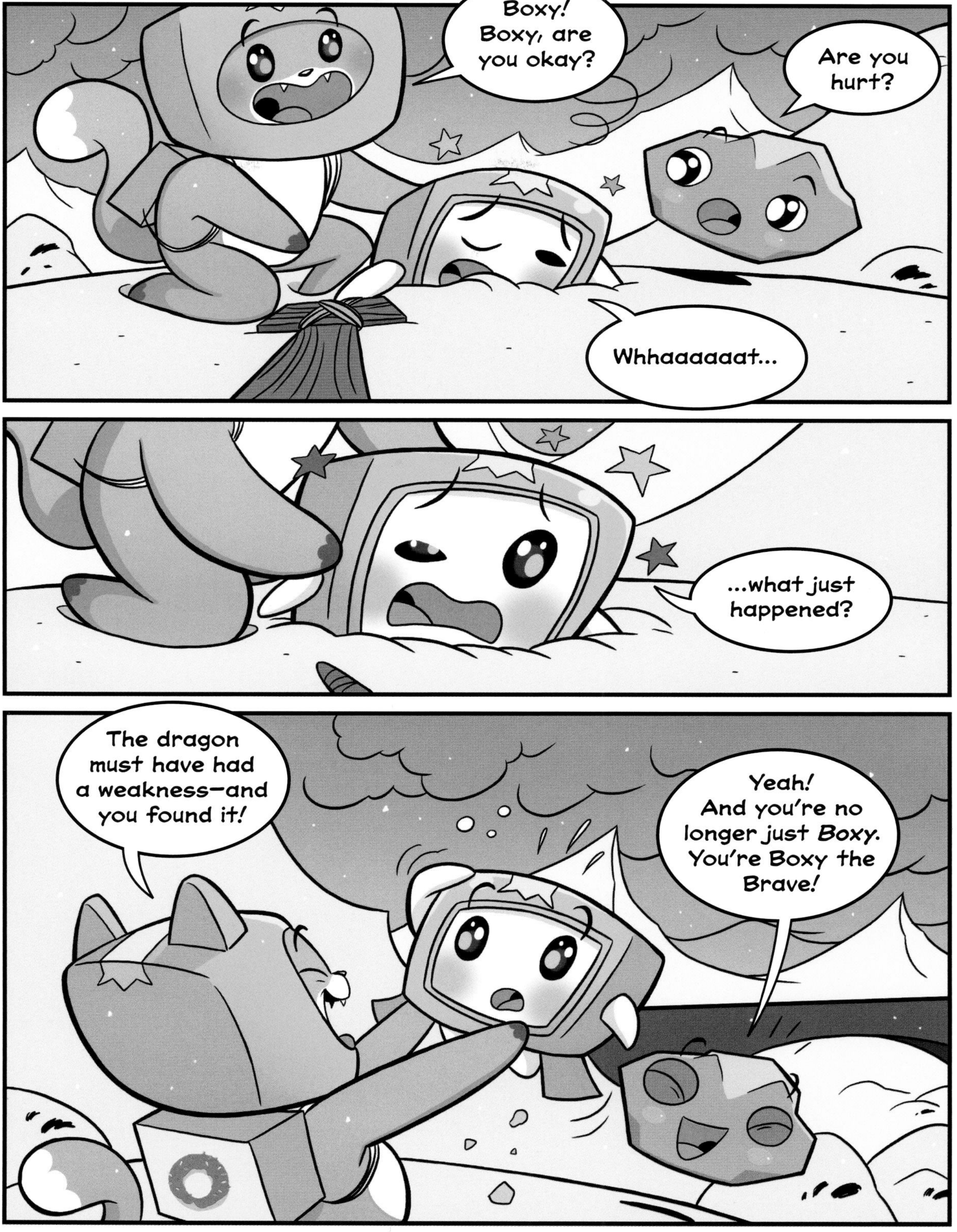
Boxy! Boxy, are you okay?
Are you hurt?
Whhaaaaaat...
...what just happened?
The dragon must have had a weakness—and you found it!
Yeah! And you're no longer just *Boxy.* You're Boxy the Brave!

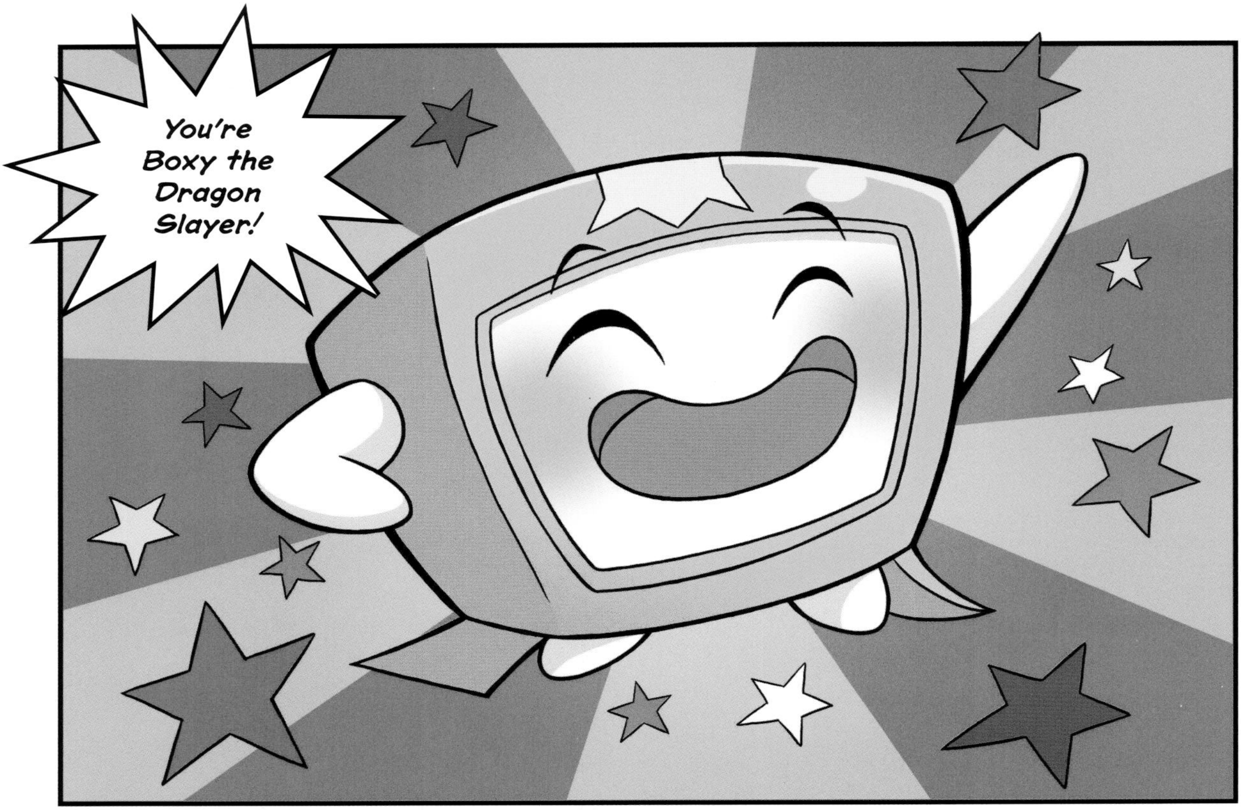
You're Boxy the Dragon Slayer!

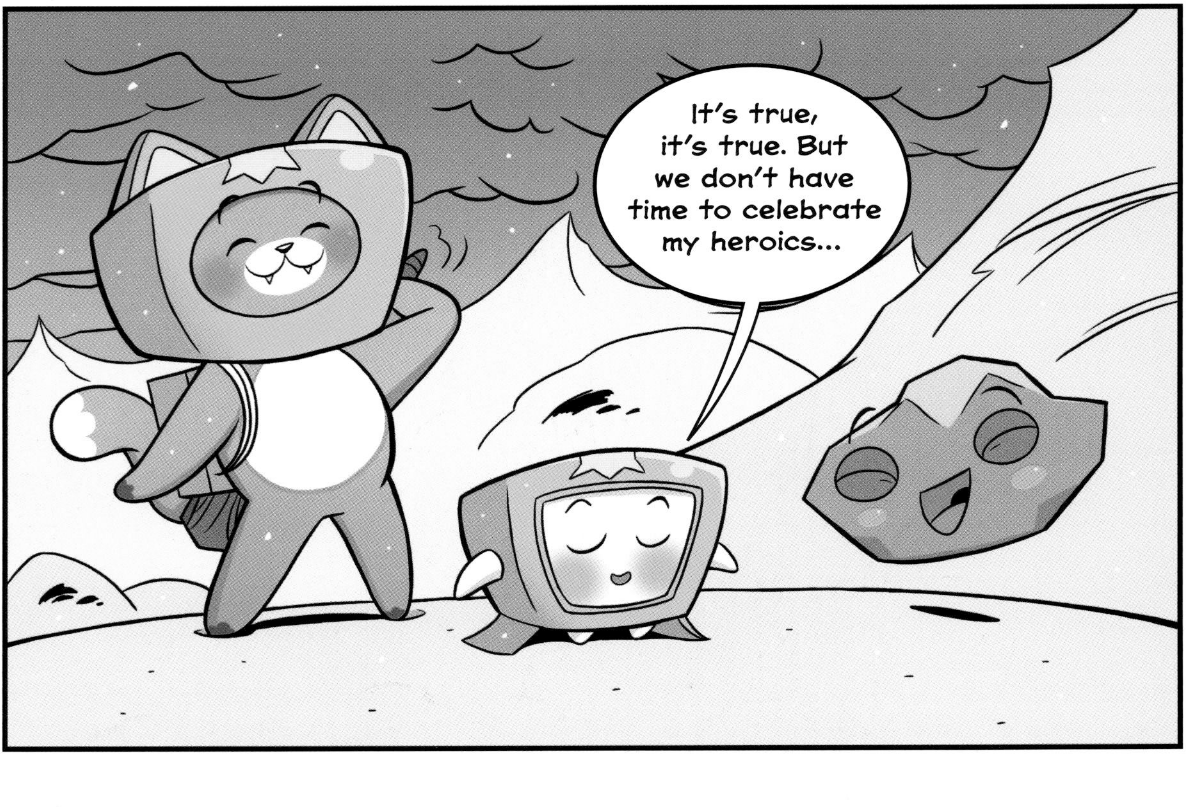
It's true, it's true. But we don't have time to celebrate my heroics...

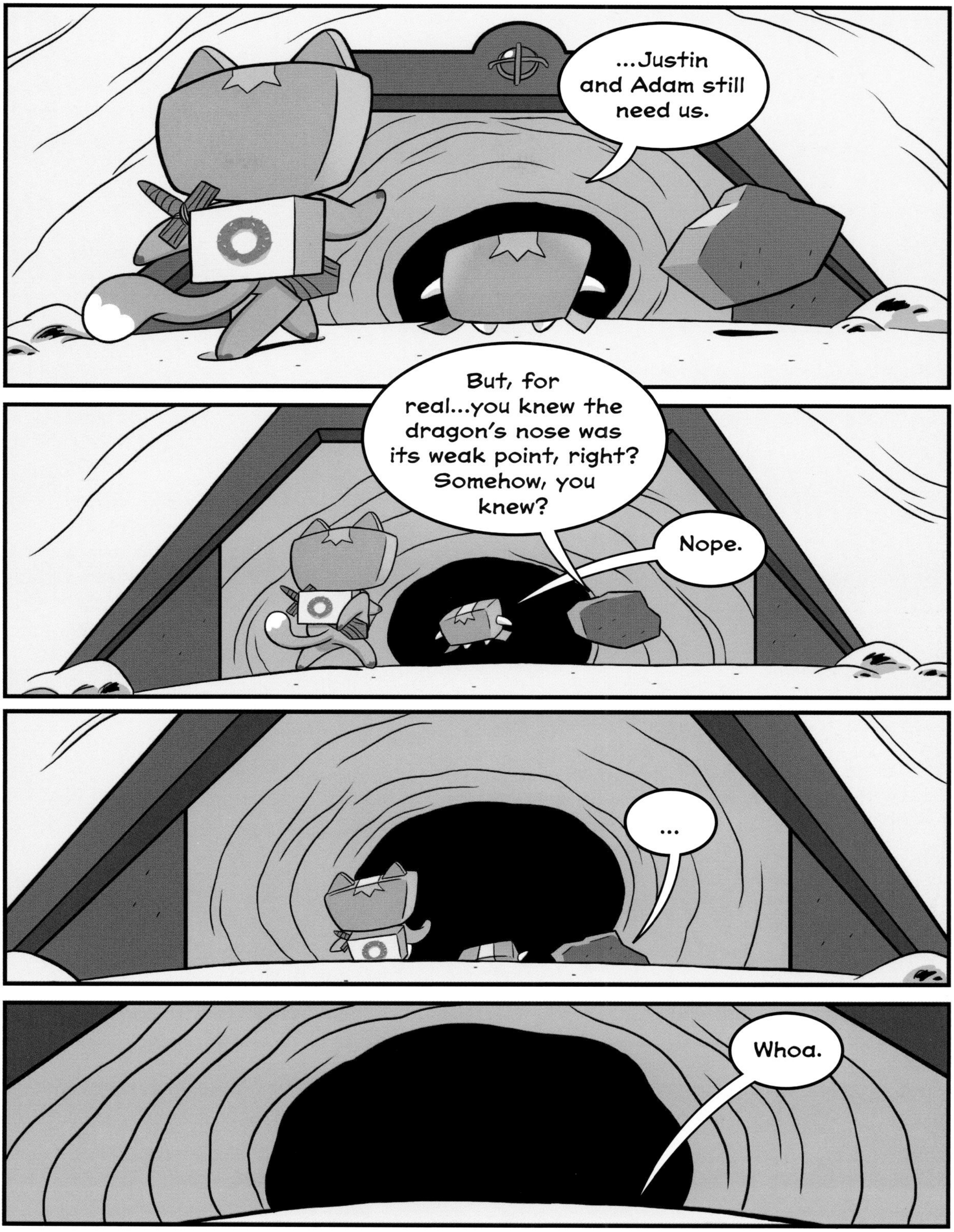
...Justin and Adam still need us.
But, for real...you knew the dragon's nose was its weak point, right? Somehow, you knew?
Nope.
...
Whoa.

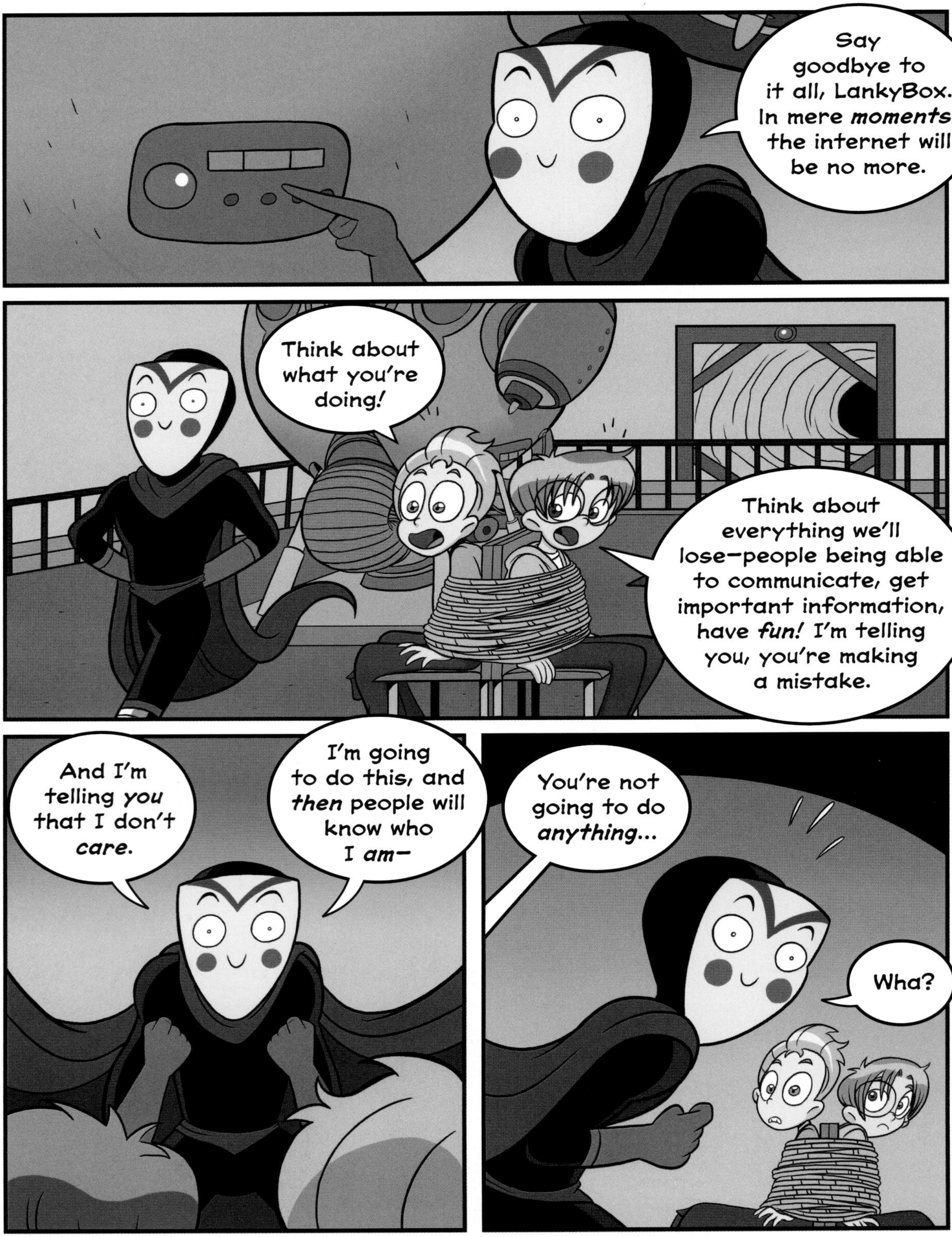
Say goodbye to it all, LankyBox. In mere *moments*, the internet will be no more.
Think about what you're doing!
Think about everything we'll lose—people being able to communicate, get important information, have *fun!* I'm telling you, you're making a mistake.
And I'm telling *you* that I don't *care*.
I'm going to do this, and *then* people will know who I *am*—
You're not going to do *anything*...
Wha?

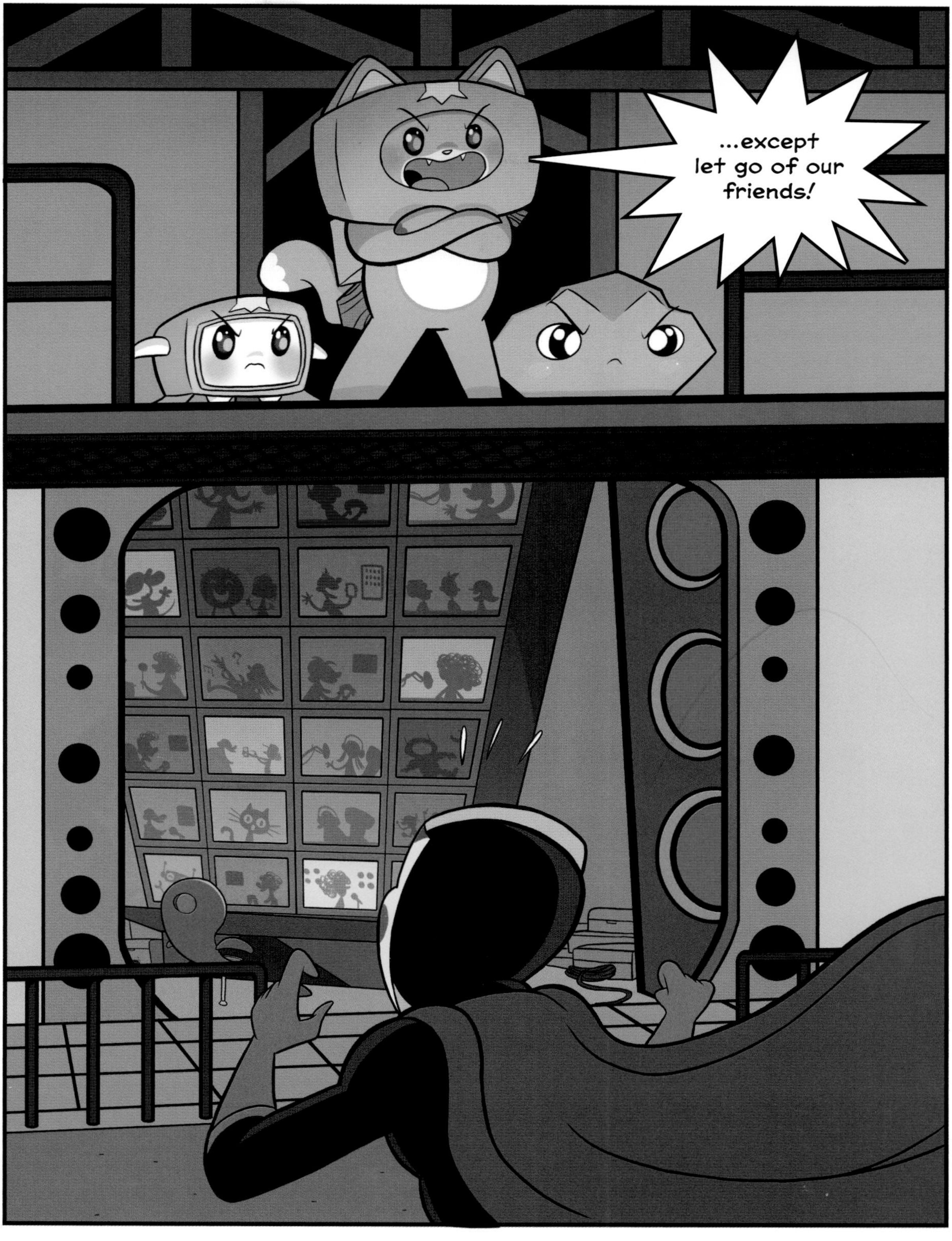
...except
let go of our
friends!

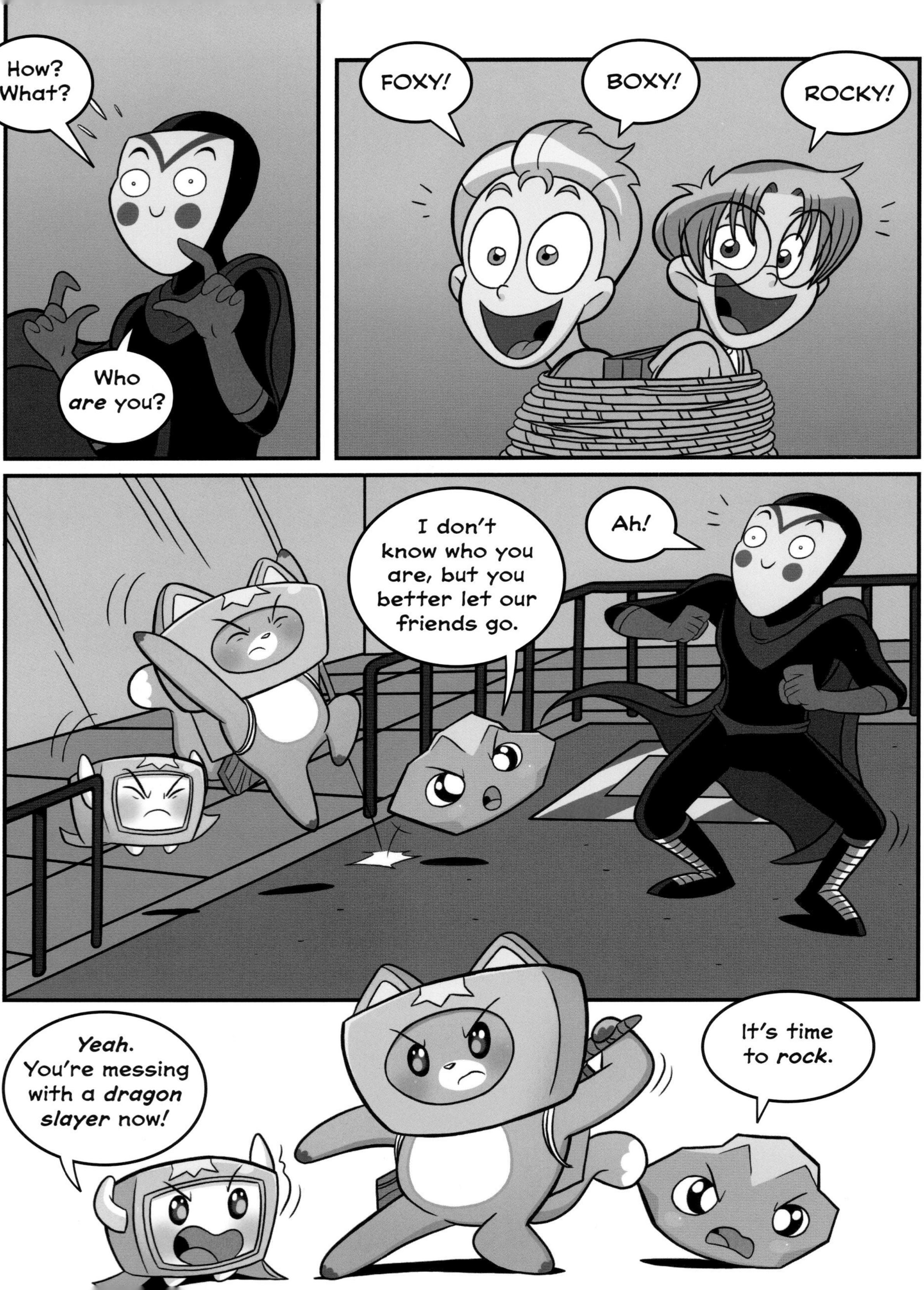
How? What?
Who *are* you?
FOXY!
BOXY!
ROCKY!
I don't know who you are, but you better let our friends go.
Ah!
Yeah. You're messing with a *dragon slayer* now!
It's time to *rock*.

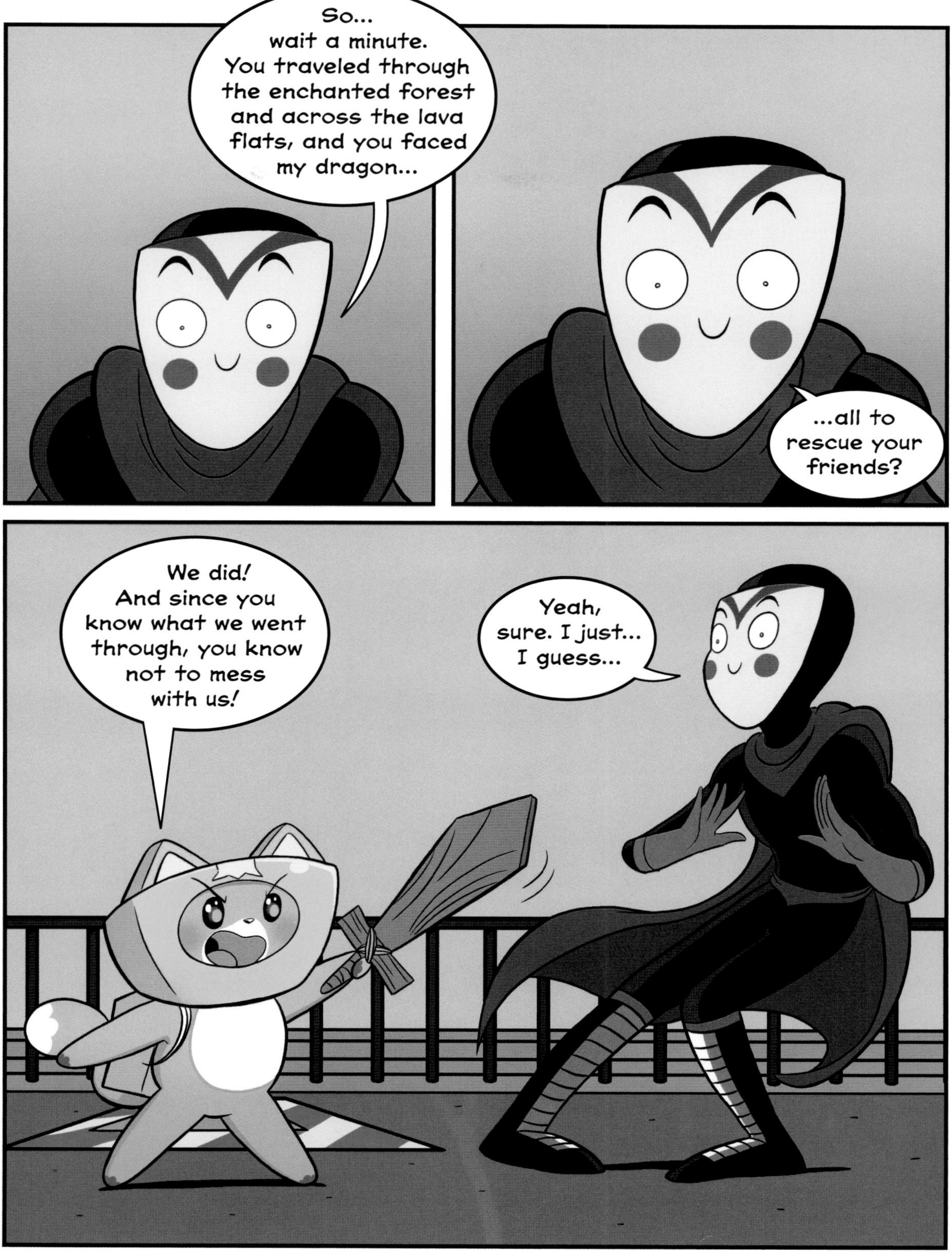
So... wait a minute. You traveled through the enchanted forest and across the lava flats, and you faced my dragon...
...all to rescue your friends?
We did! And since you know what we went through, you know not to mess with us!
Yeah, sure. I just... I guess...

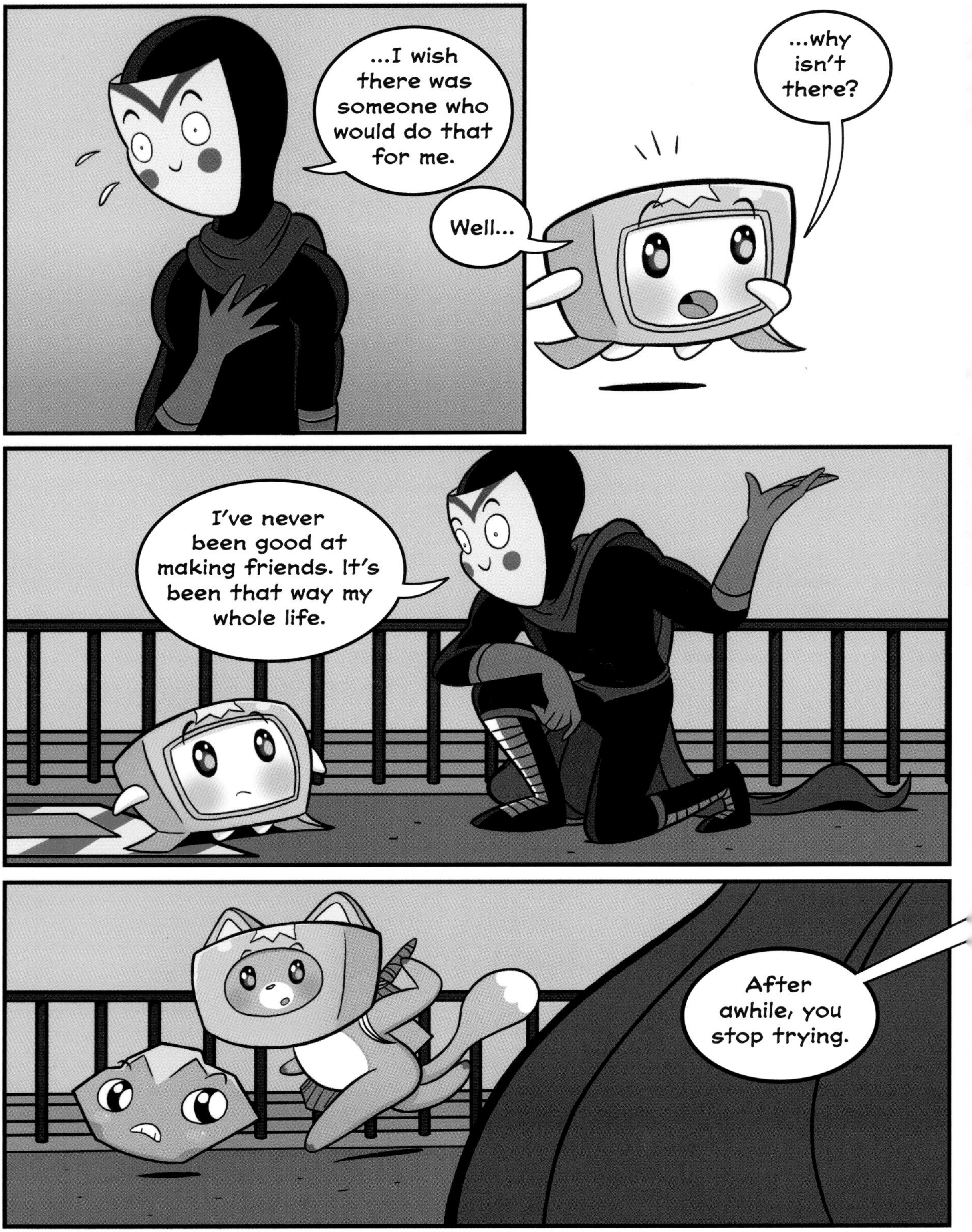
...I wish there was someone who would do that for me.
Well...
...why isn't there?
I've never been good at making friends. It's been that way my whole life.
After awhile, you stop trying.

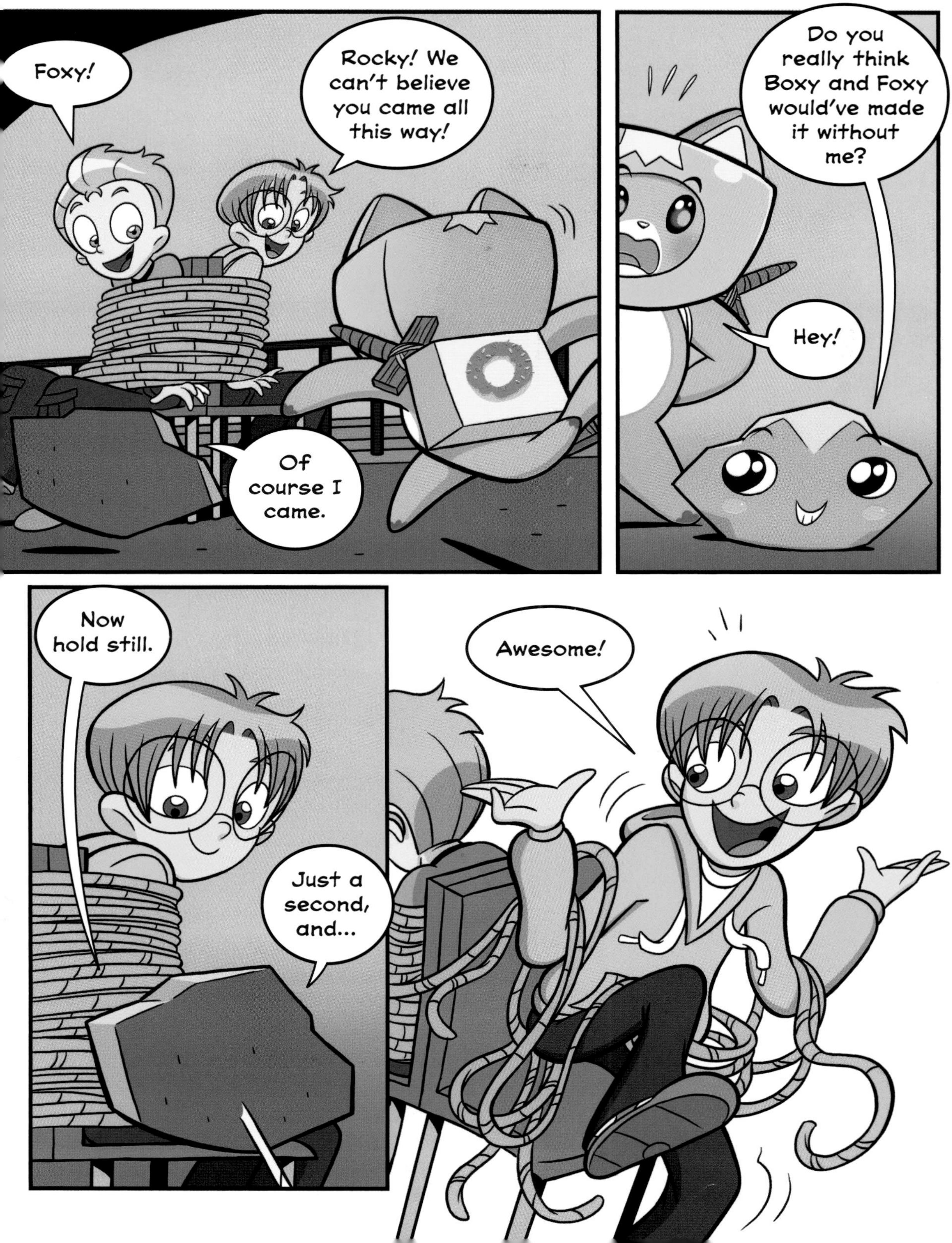
Foxy!
Rocky! We can't believe you came all this way!
Of course I came.
Do you really think Boxy and Foxy would've made it without me?
Hey!
Now hold still.
Just a second, and...
Awesome!

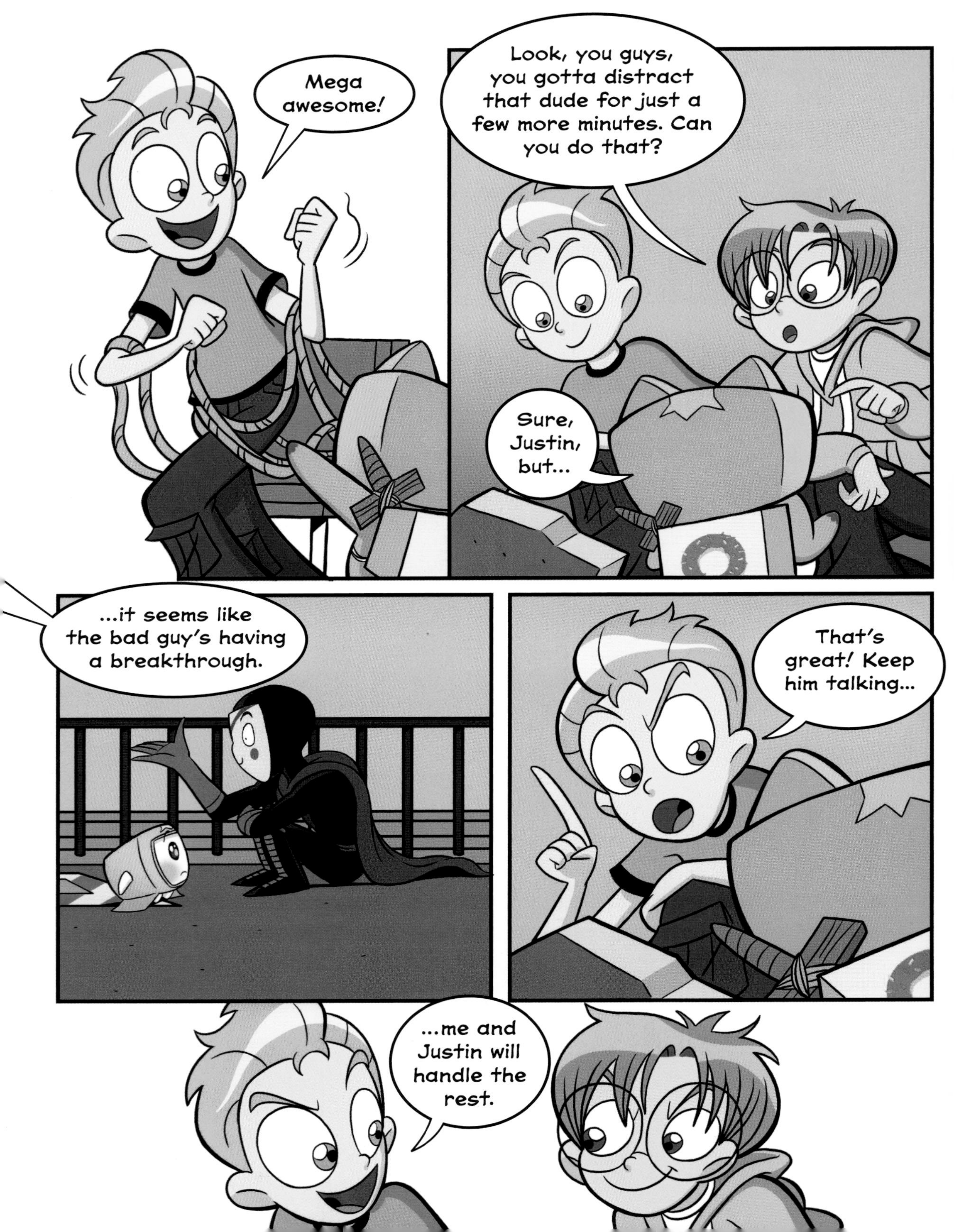
Mega awesome!
Look, you guys, you gotta distract that dude for just a few more minutes. Can you do that?
Sure, Justin, but...
...it seems like the bad guy's having a breakthrough.
That's great! Keep him talking...
...me and Justin will handle the rest.

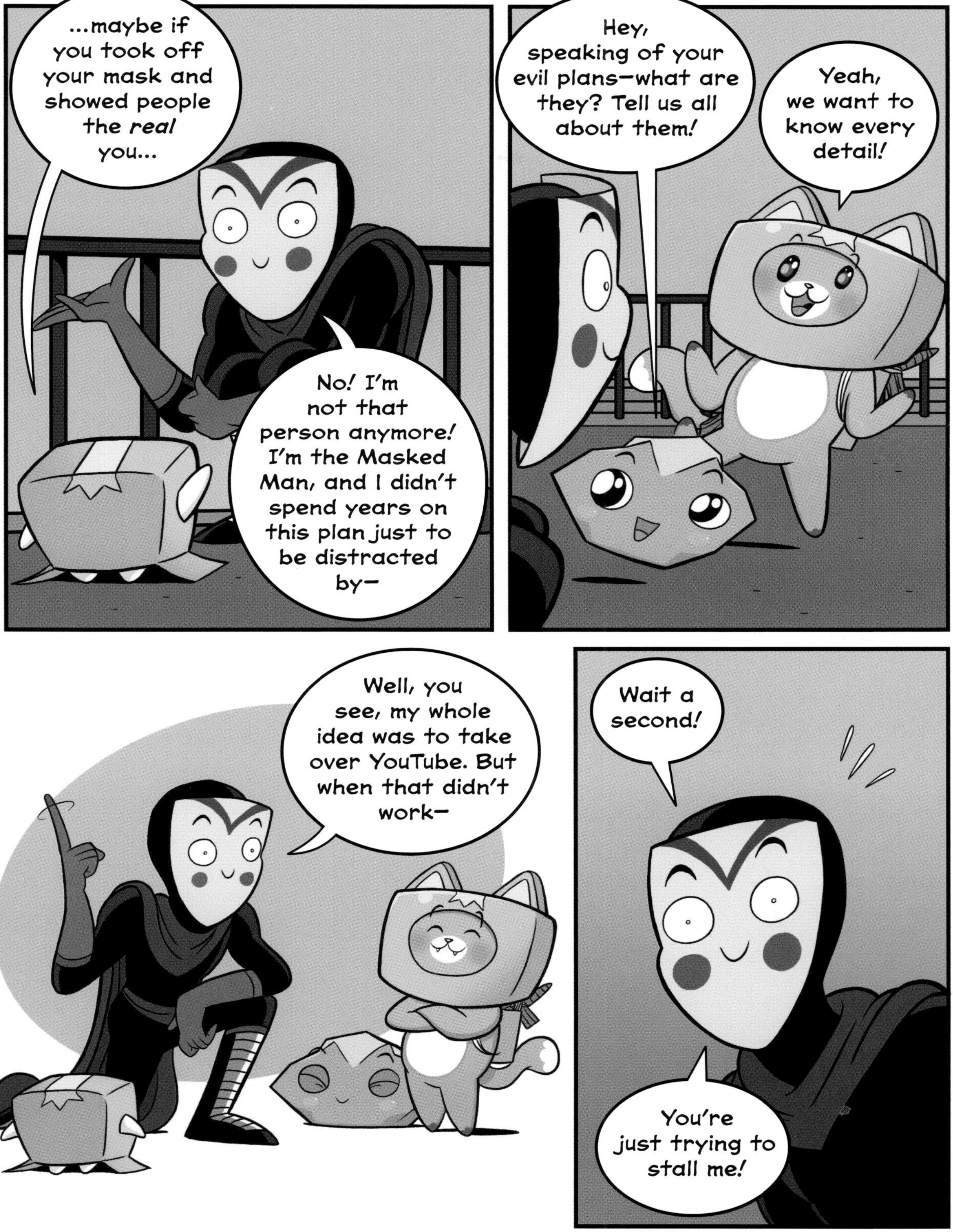
...maybe if you took off your mask and showed people the *real* you...
No! I'm not that person anymore! I'm the Masked Man, and I didn't spend years on this plan just to be distracted by—
Hey, speaking of your evil plans—what are they? Tell us all about them!
Yeah, we want to know every detail!
Well, you see, my whole idea was to take over YouTube. But when that didn't work—
Wait a second!
You're just trying to stall me!

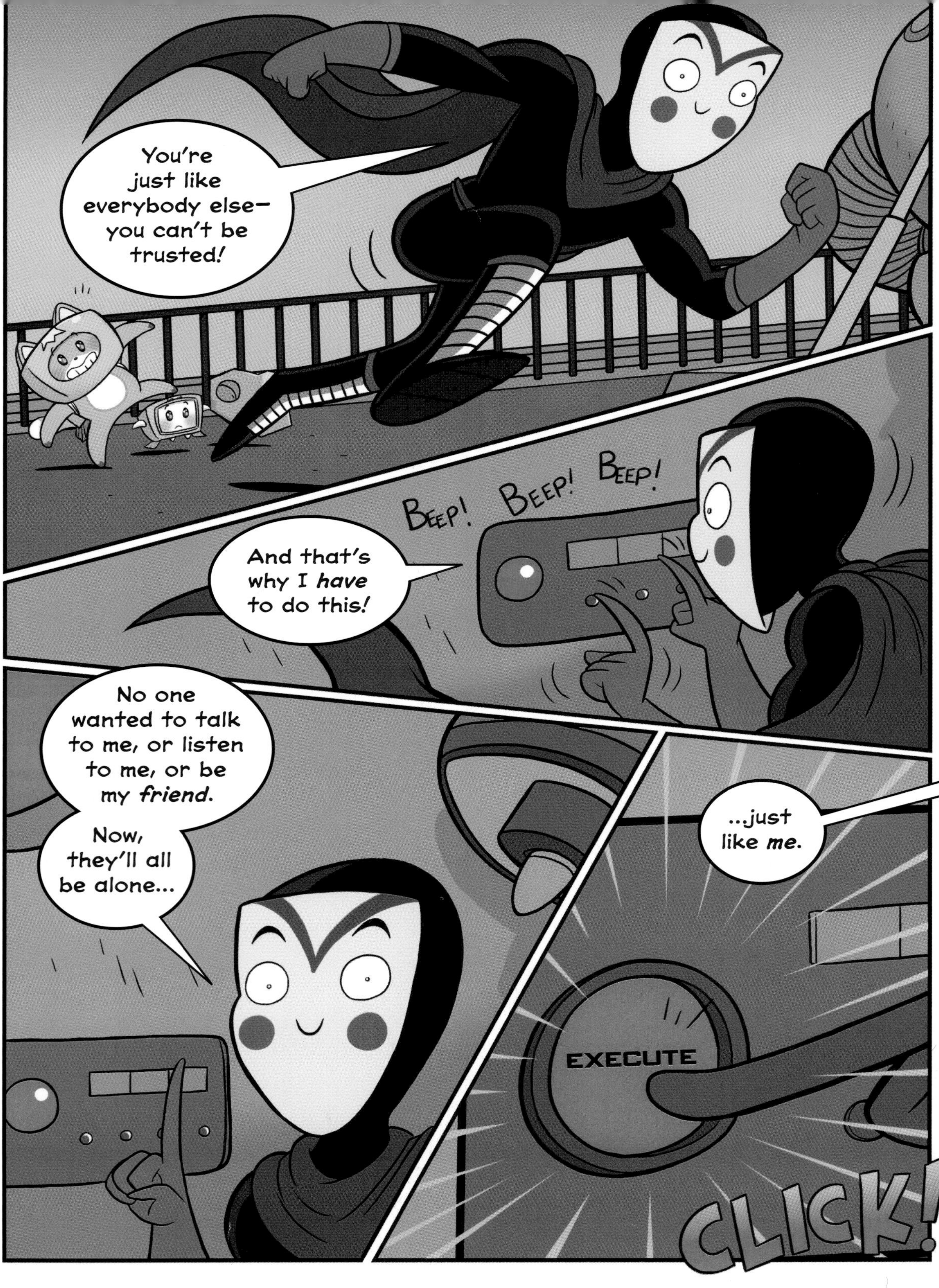
You're just like everybody else—you can't be trusted!
BEEP! BEEP! BEEP!
And that's why I *have* to do this!
No one wanted to talk to me, or listen to me, or be my *friend*.
Now, they'll all be alone...
...just like *me*.
EXECUTE
CLICK!

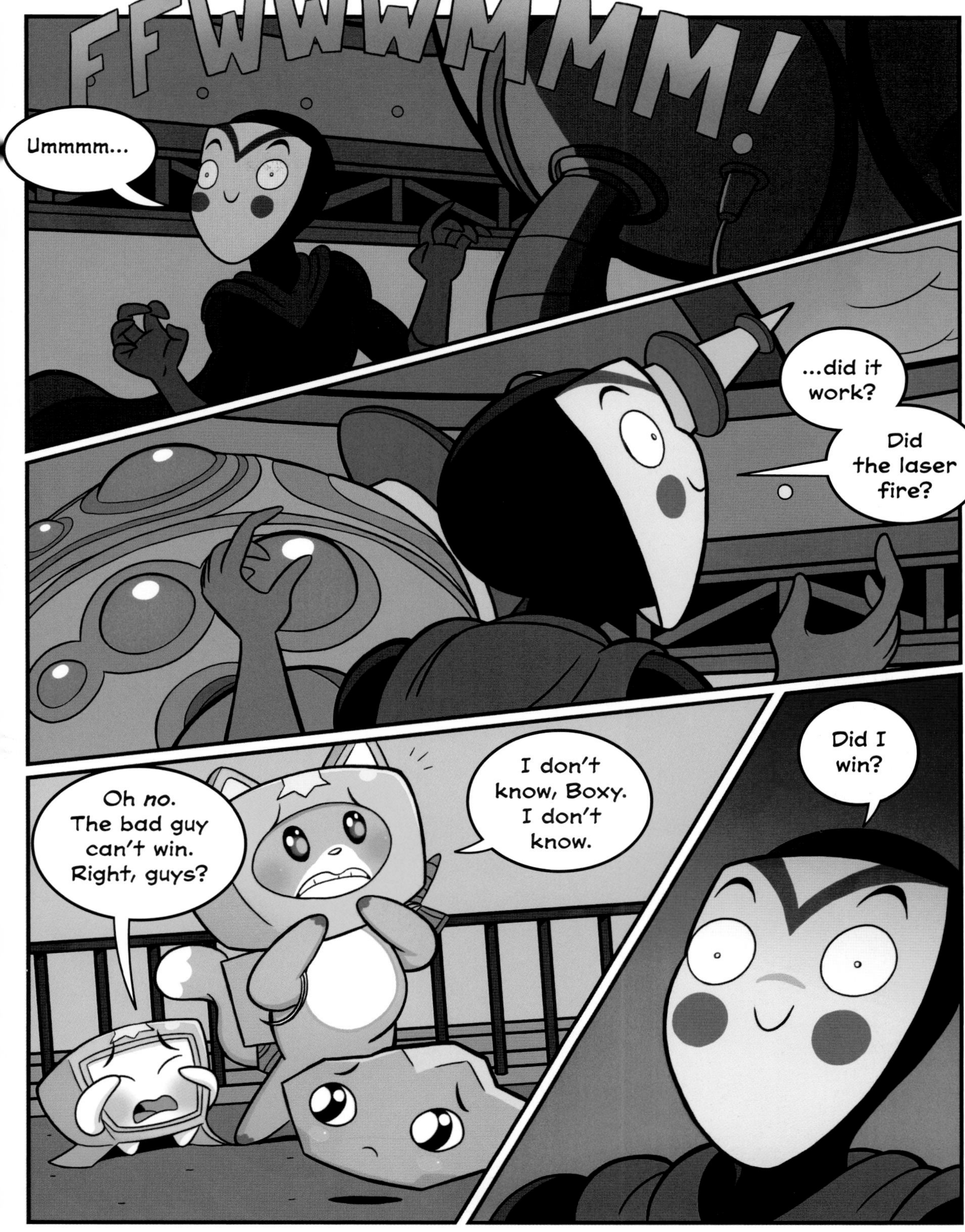
FFWWWWMMMM!
Ummmm...
...did it work?
Did the laser fire?
Did I win?
Oh *no*. The bad guy can't win. Right, guys?
I don't know, Boxy. I don't know.

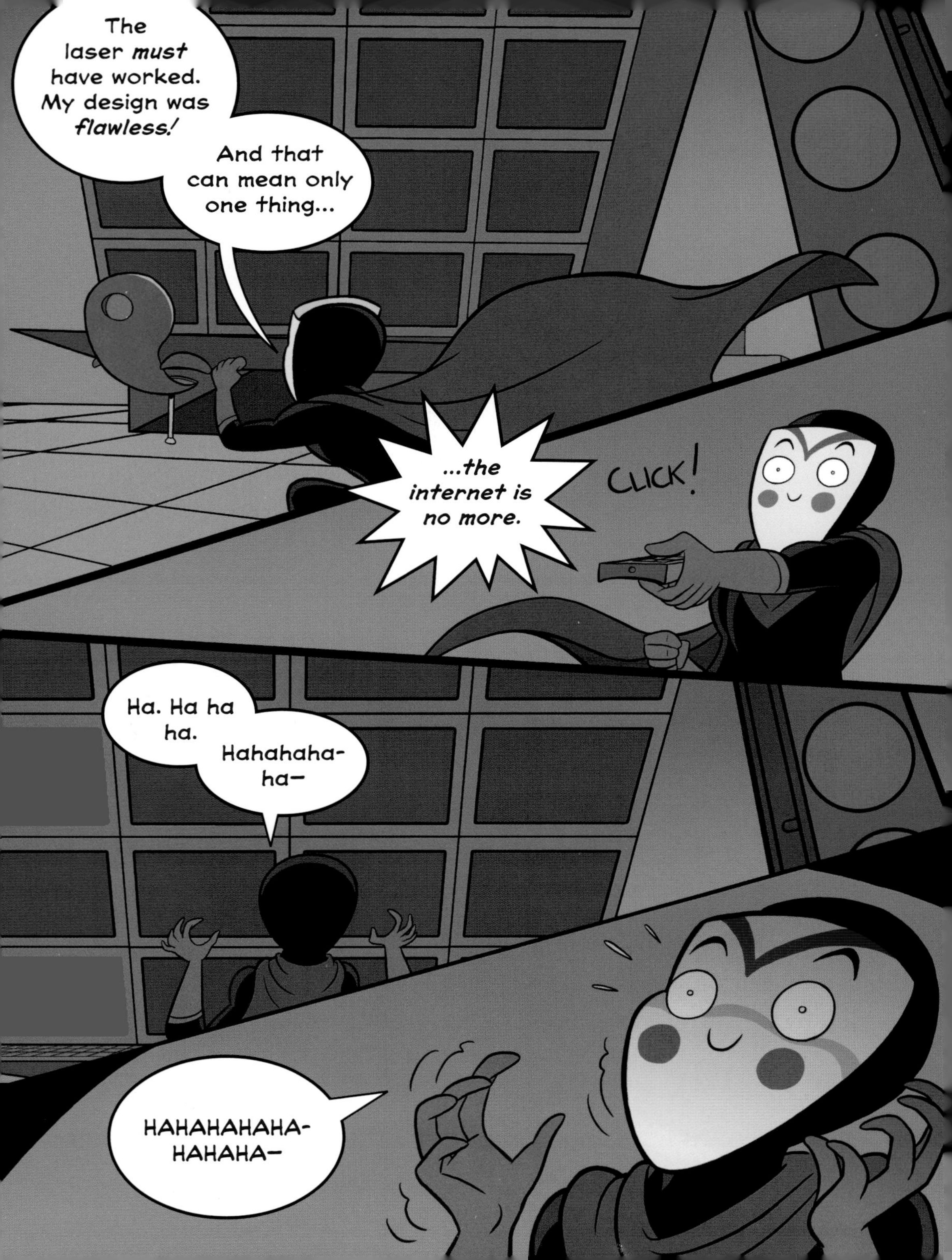
The laser *must* have worked. My design was *flawless!*
And that can mean only one thing...
...the internet is no more.
CLICK!
Ha. Ha ha ha.
Hahahaha-ha—
HAHAHAHAHA-HAHAHA—

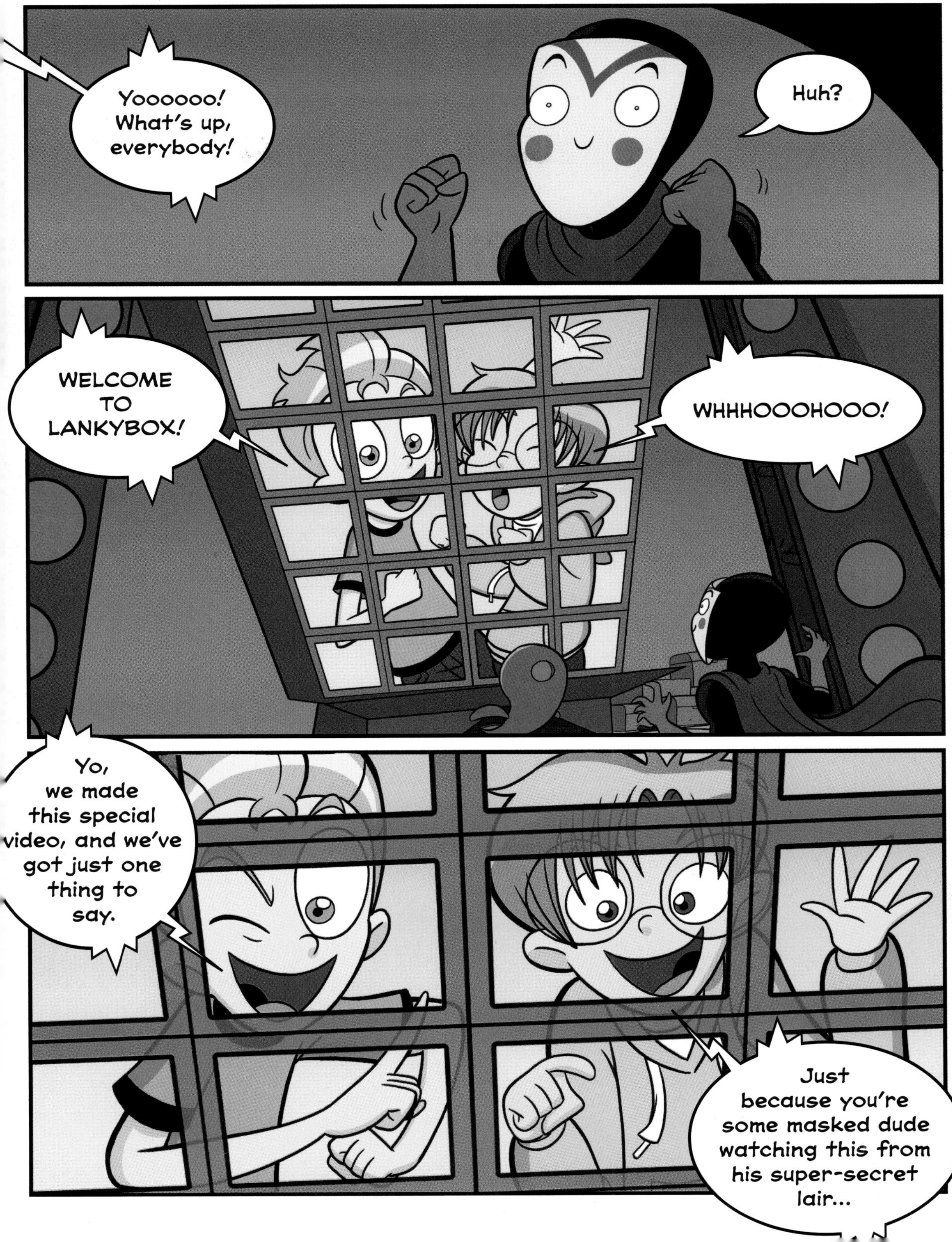
Yoooooo! What's up, everybody!
Huh?
WELCOME TO LANKYBOX!
WHHHOOOHOOO!
Yo, we made this special video, and we've got just one thing to say.
Just because you're some masked dude watching this from his super-secret lair...

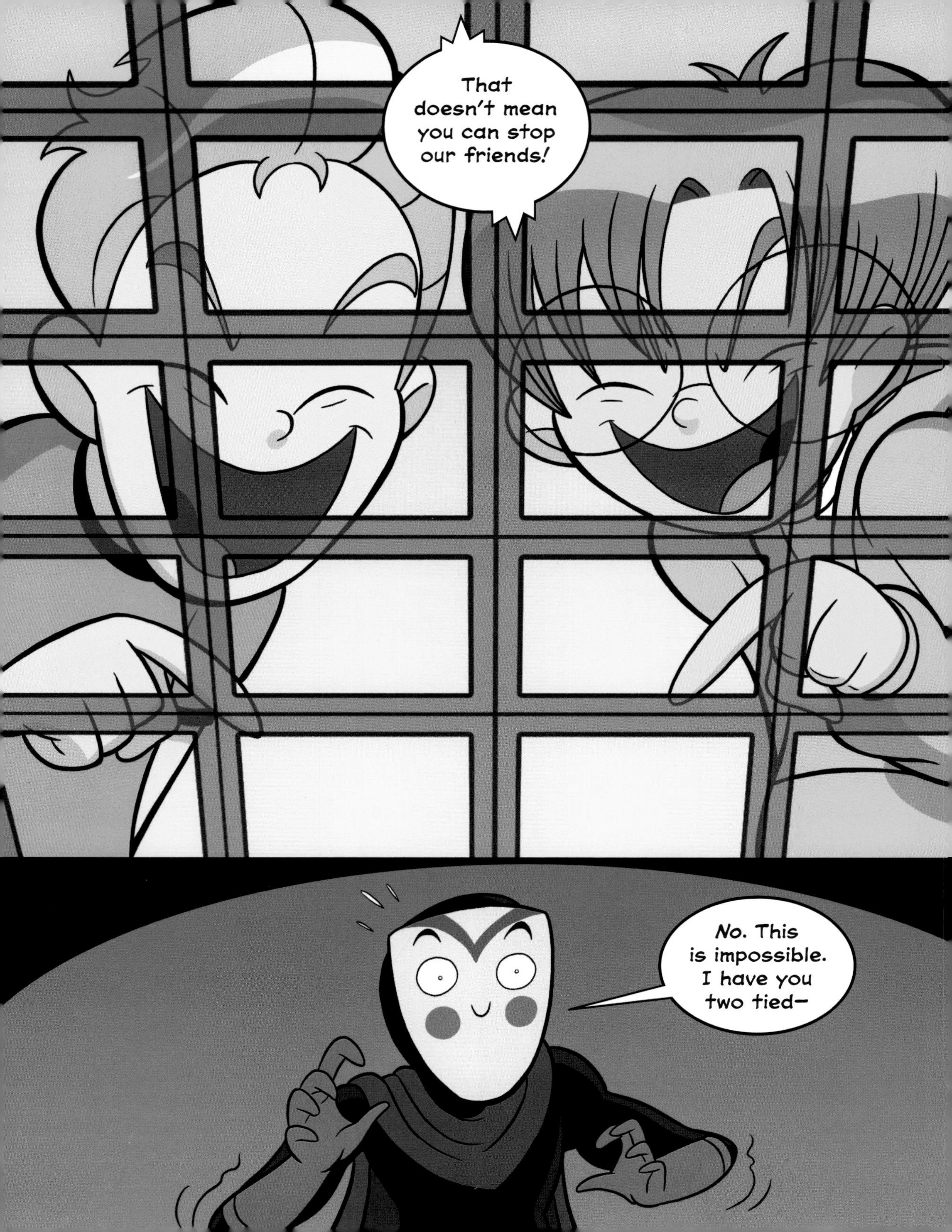
That doesn't mean you can stop our friends!
No. This is impossible. I have you two tied—

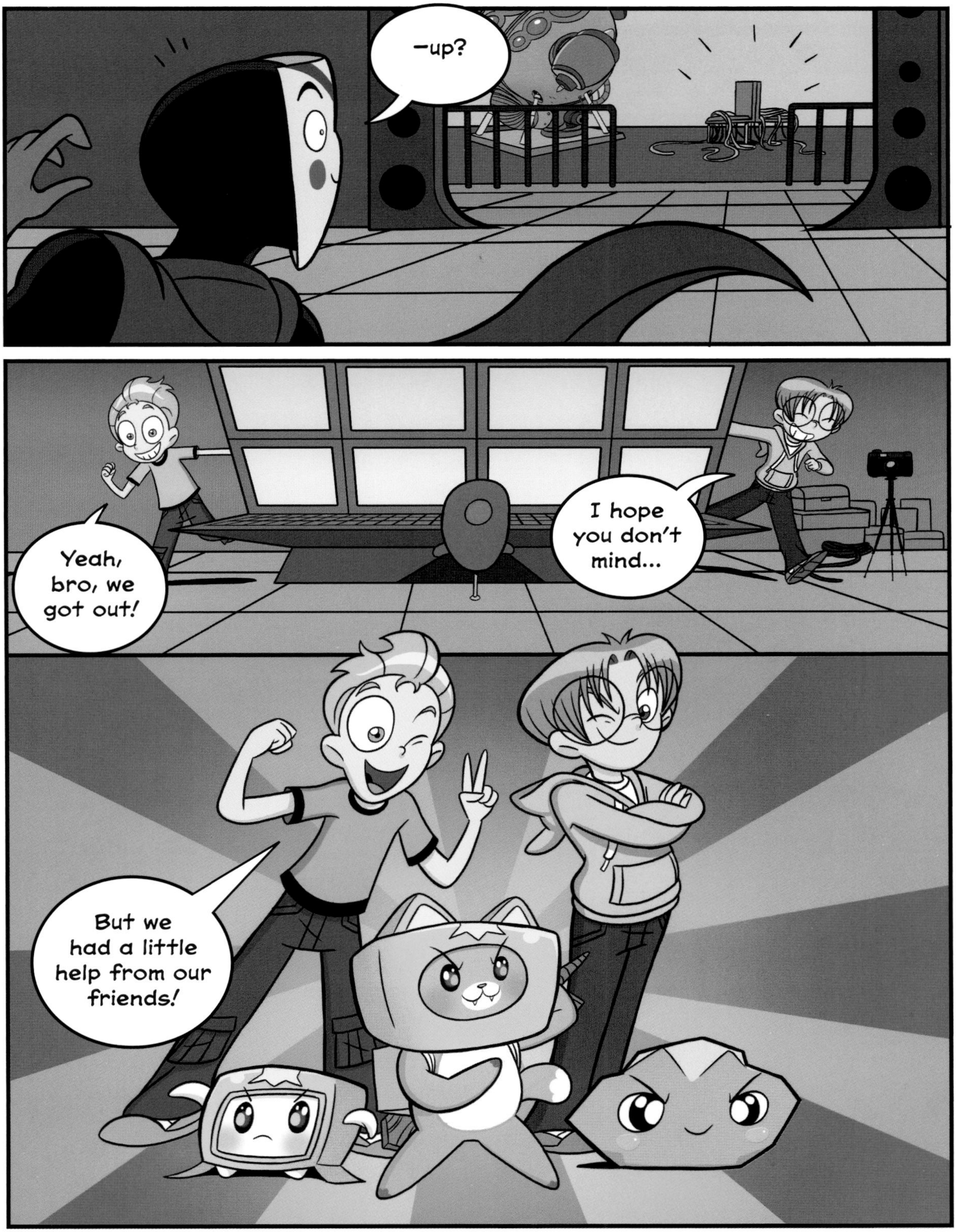
-up?
Yeah, bro, we got out!
I hope you don't mind...
But we had a little help from our friends!

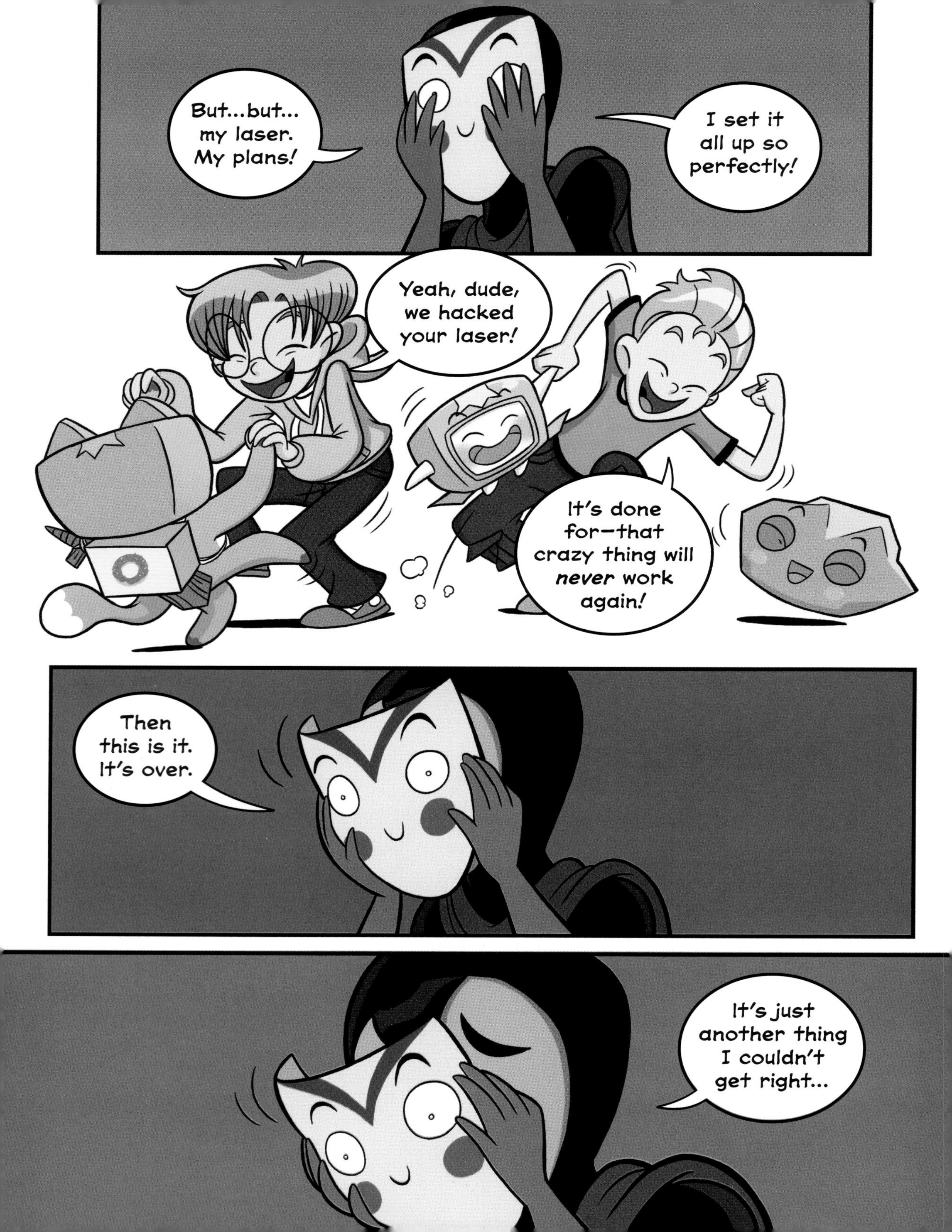
But...but...
my laser.
My plans!
I set it
all up so
perfectly!
Yeah, dude,
we hacked
your laser!
It's done
for—that
crazy thing will
never work
again!
Then
this is it.
It's over.
It's just
another thing
I couldn't
get right...

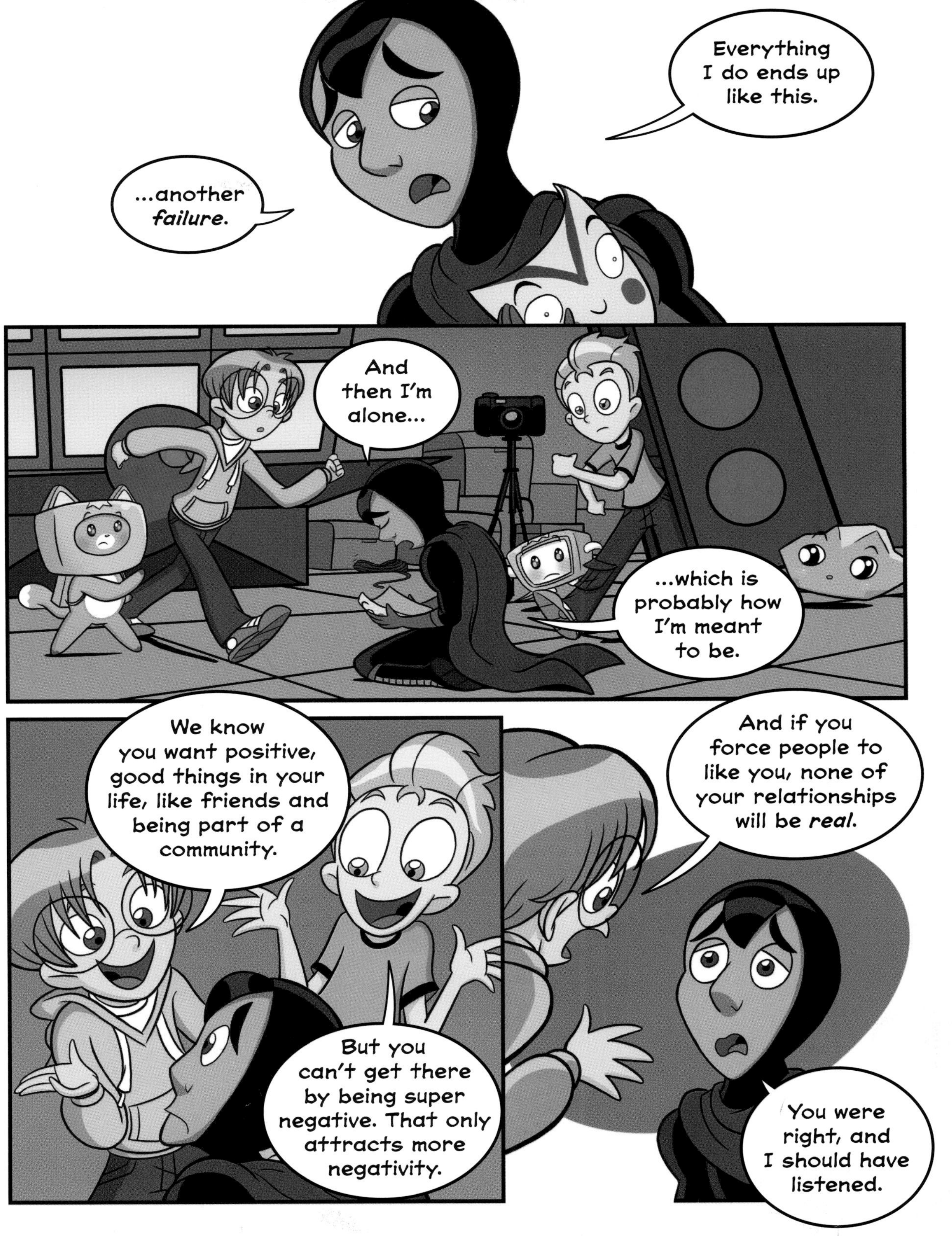

...another *failure*.
Everything I do ends up like this.
And then I'm alone...
...which is probably how I'm meant to be.
We know you want positive, good things in your life, like friends and being part of a community.
But you can't get there by being super negative. That only attracts more negativity.
And if you force people to like you, none of your relationships will be *real*.
You were right, and I should have listened.

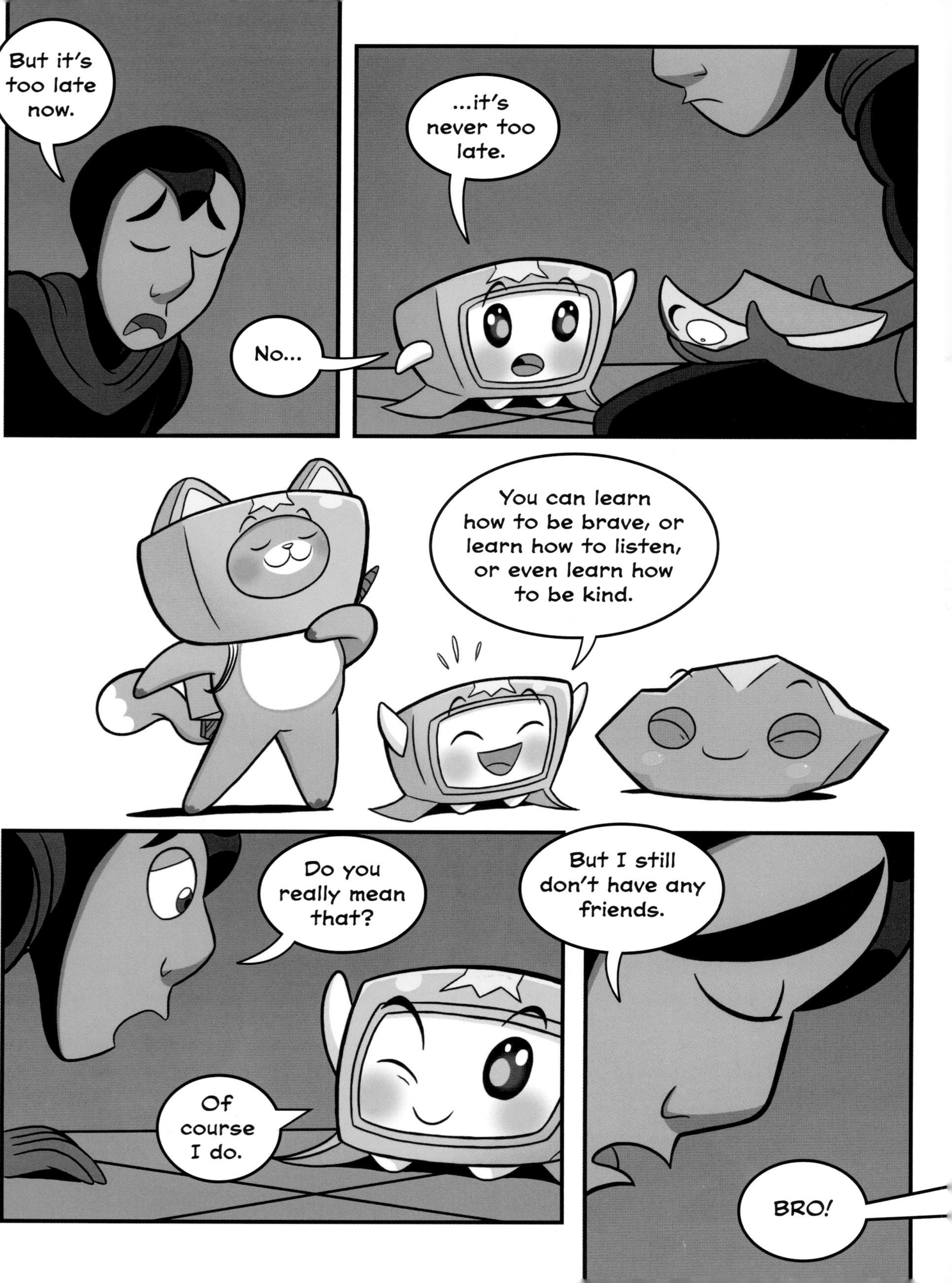
But it's too late now.
...it's never too late.
No...
You can learn how to be brave, or learn how to listen, or even learn how to be kind.
Do you really mean that?
Of course I do.
But I still don't have any friends.
BRO!

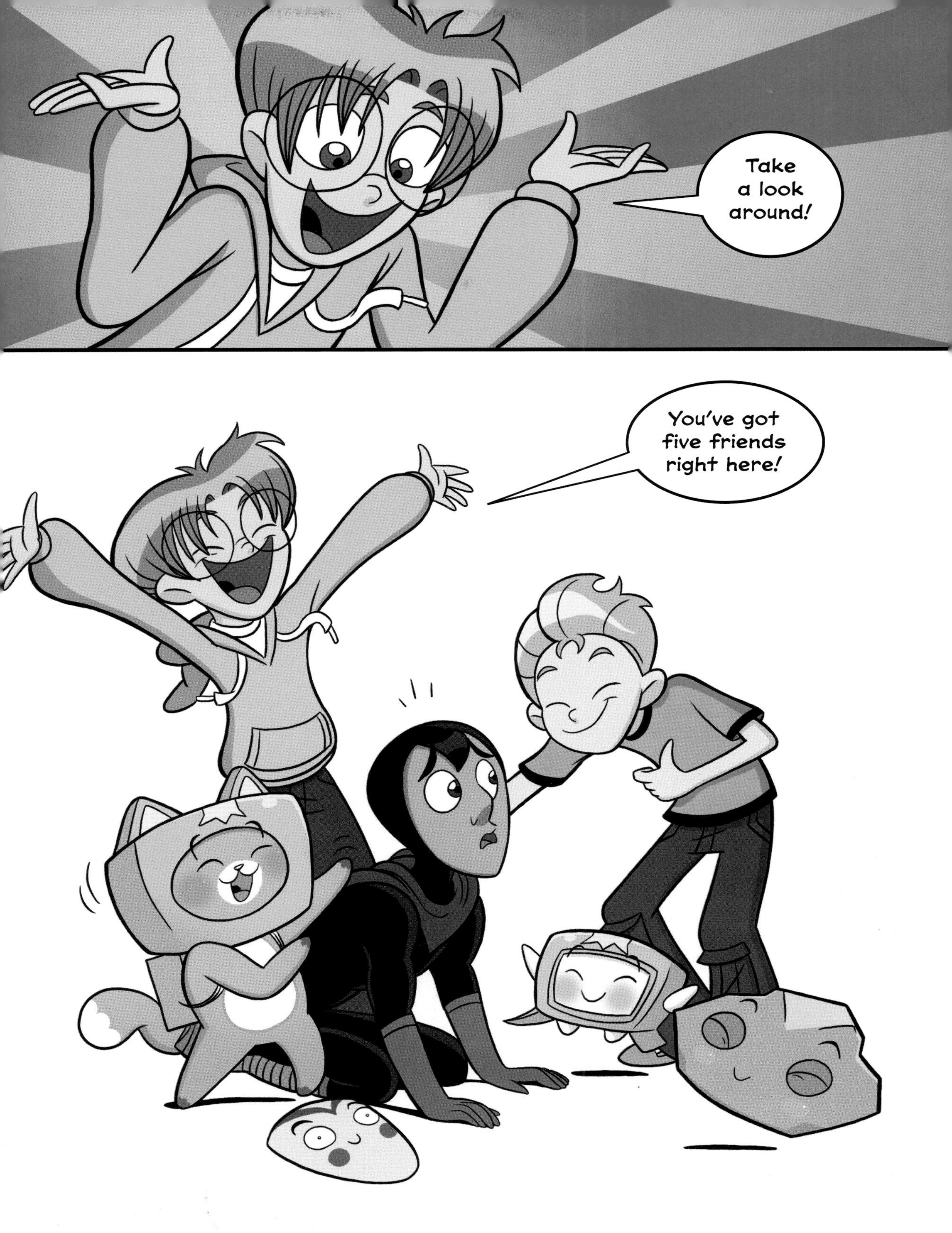
Take a look around!
You've got five friends right here!

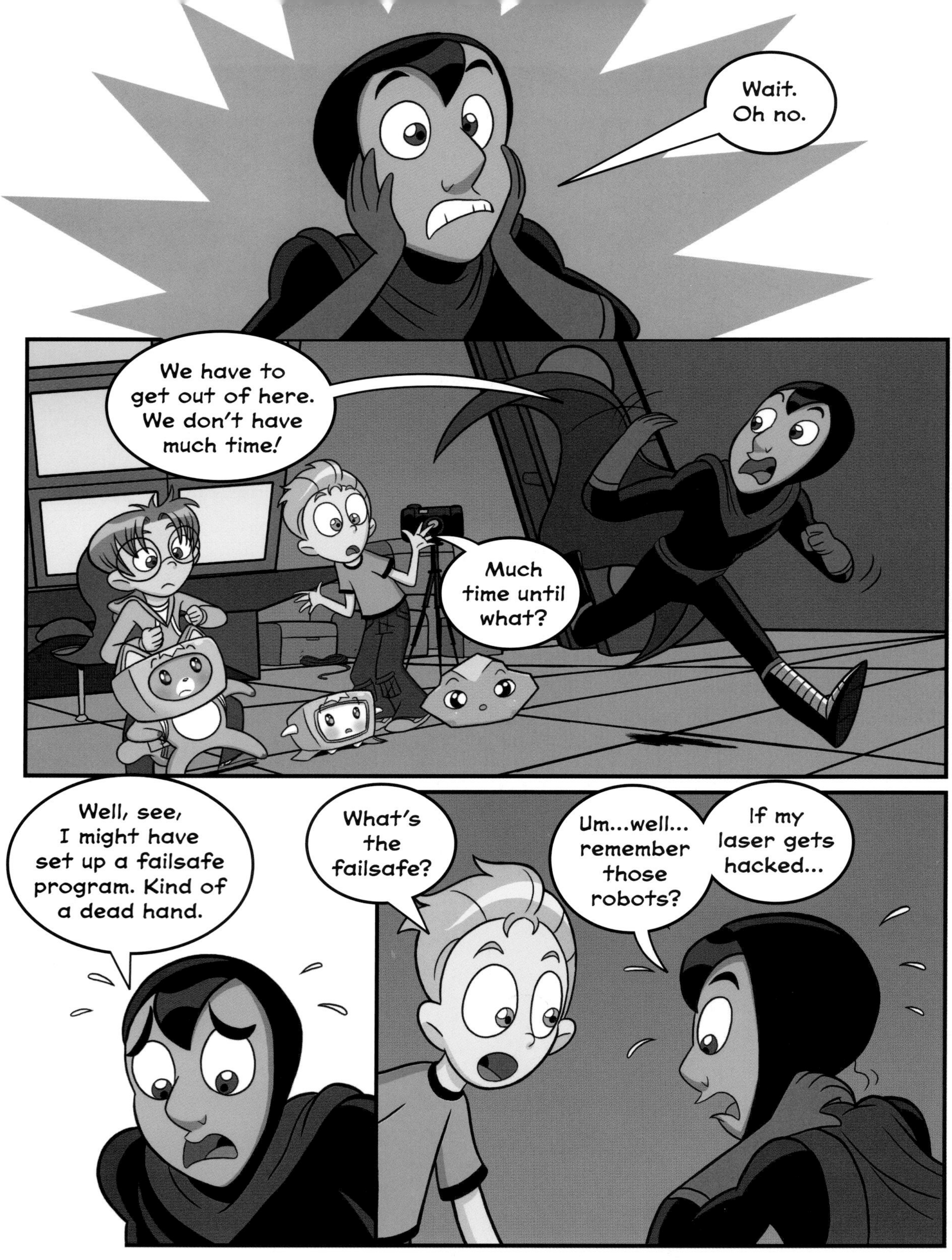
Wait. Oh no.
We have to get out of here. We don't have much time!
Much time until what?
Well, see, I might have set up a failsafe program. Kind of a dead hand.
What's the failsafe?
Um...well... remember those robots?
If my laser gets hacked...

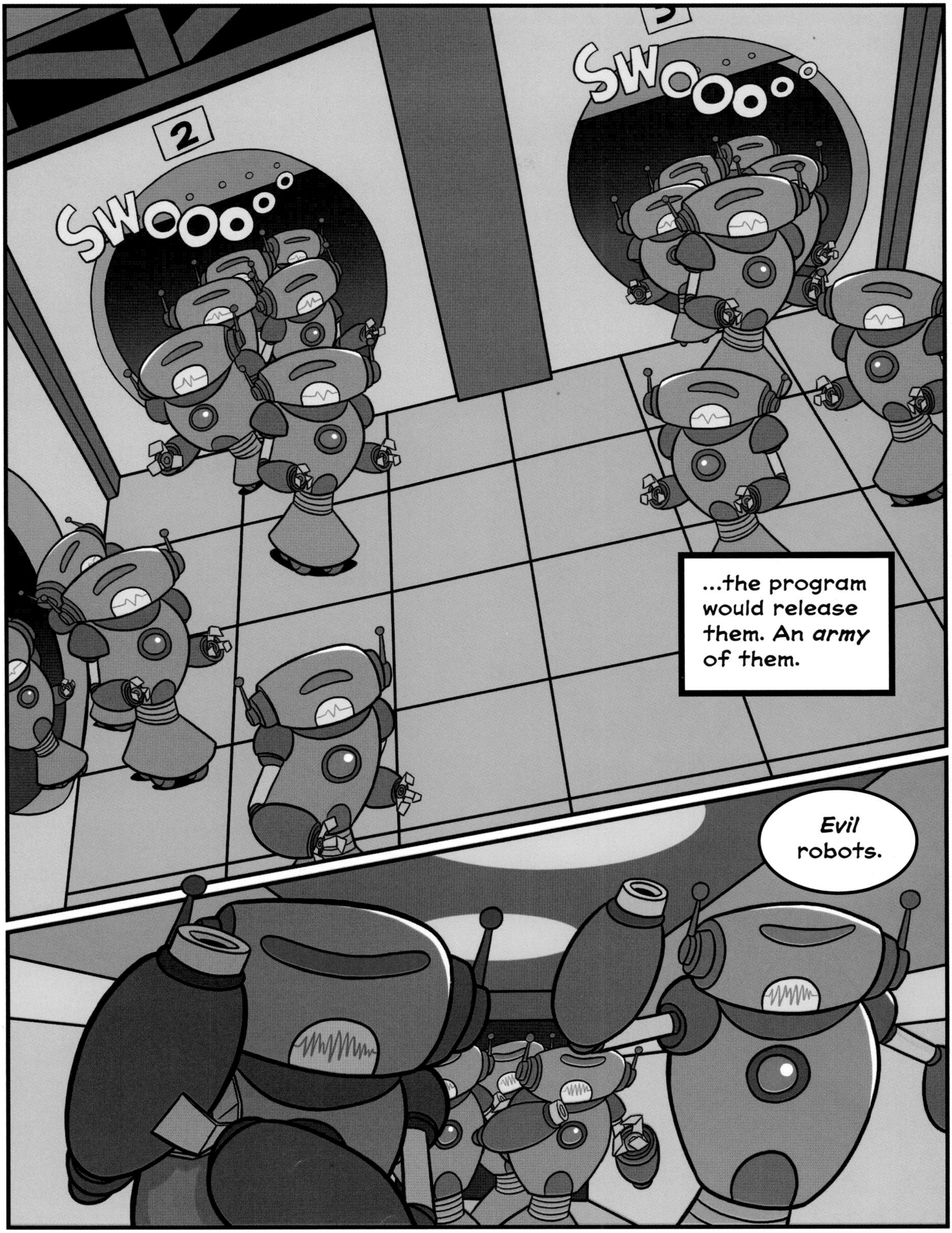
2
SWOOOº
SWOOOº
...the program would release them. An *army* of them.
Evil robots.

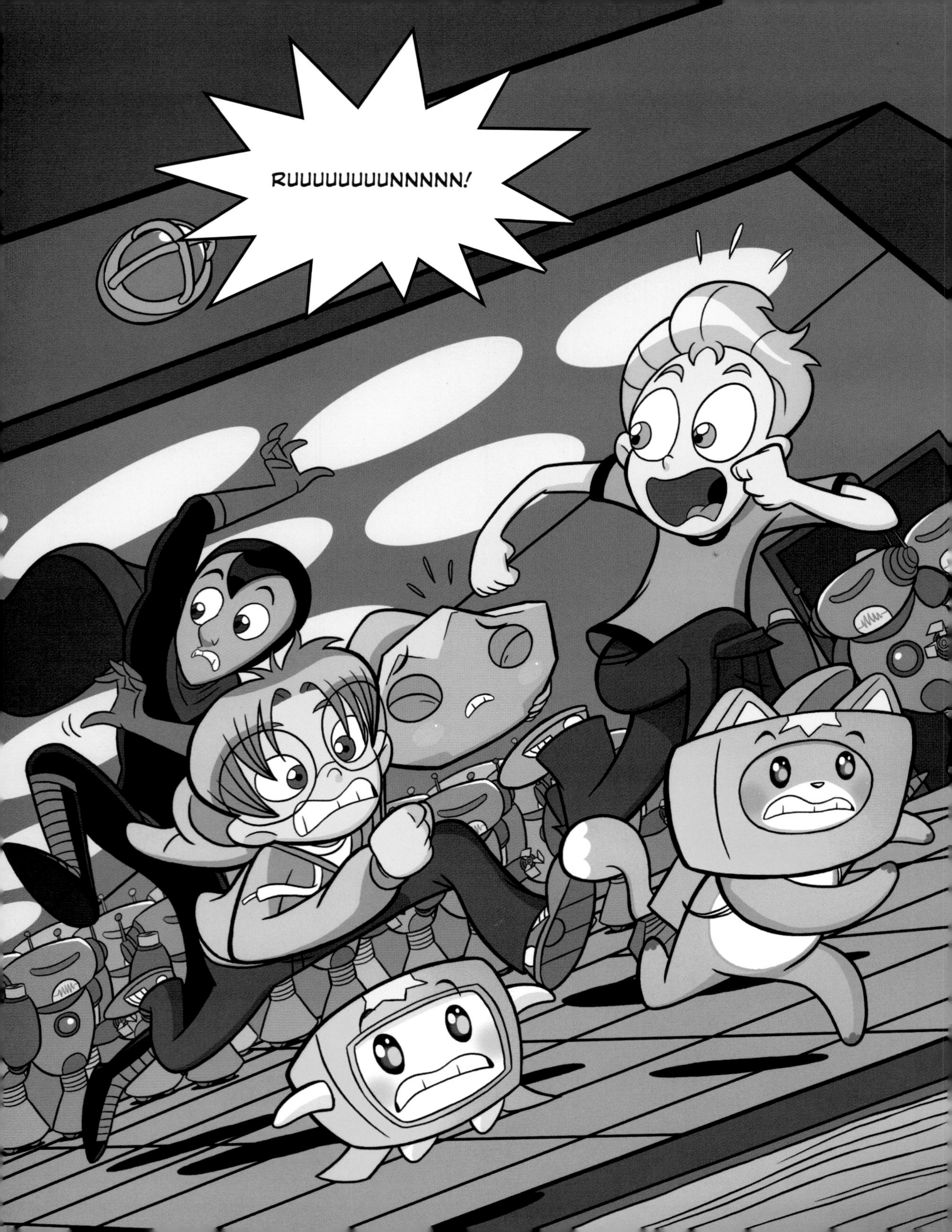
RUUUUUUUUNNNNN!

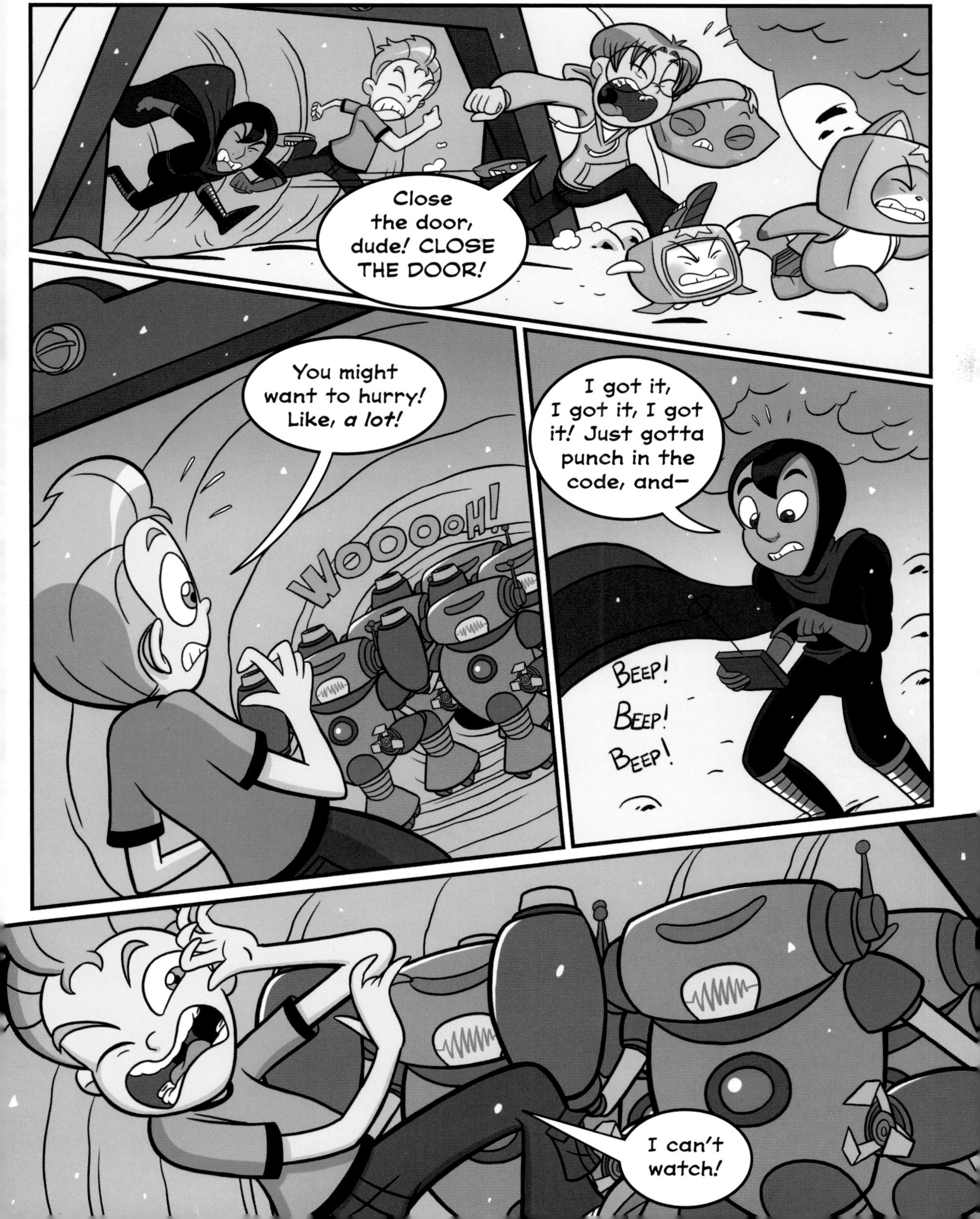
Close the door, dude! CLOSE THE DOOR!
You might want to hurry! Like, *a lot!*
WOOOOOH!
I got it, I got it, I got it! Just gotta punch in the code, and—
BEEP! BEEP! BEEP!
I can't watch!

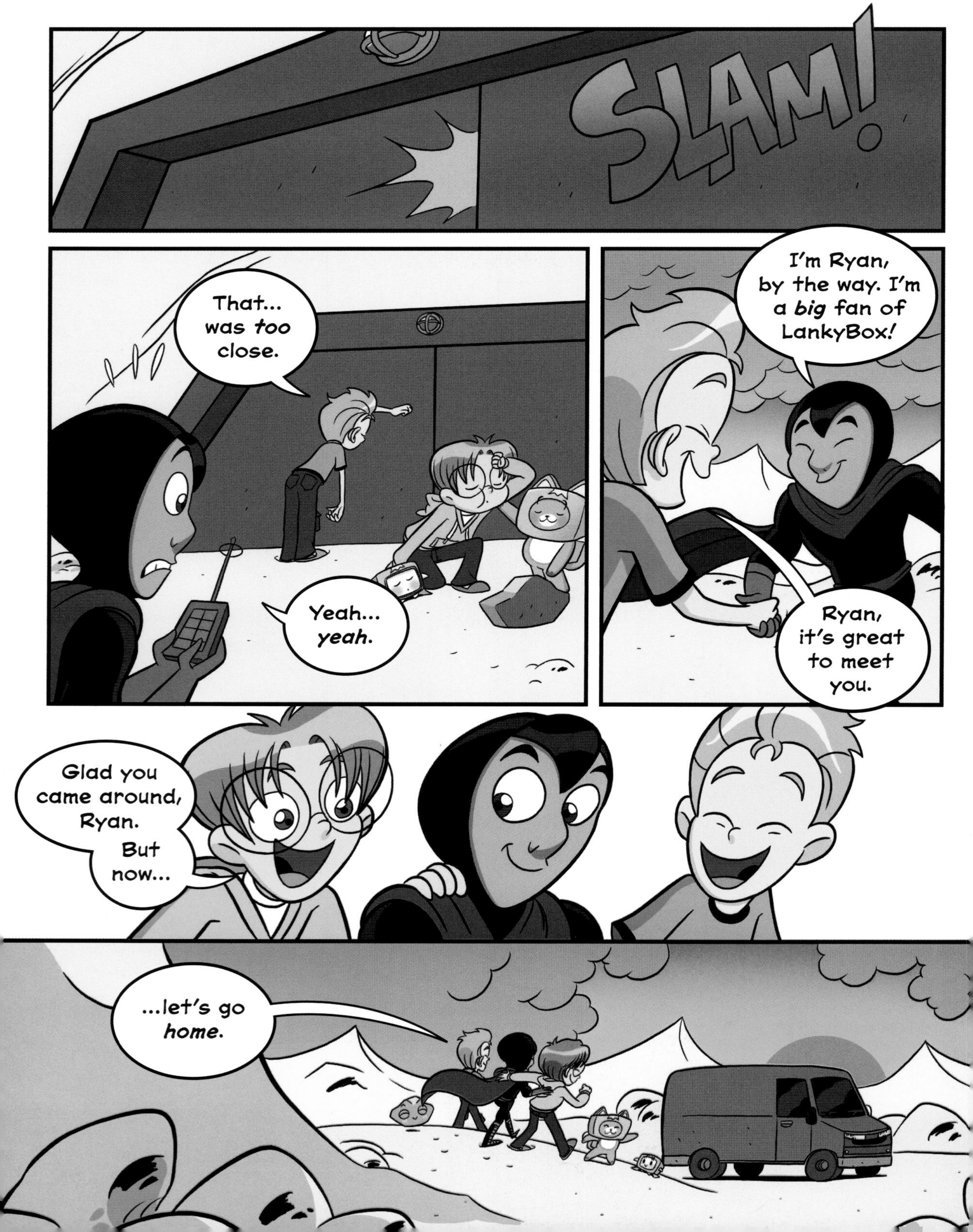
SLAM!
That... was *too* close.
Yeah... *yeah*.
I'm Ryan, by the way. I'm a *big* fan of LankyBox!
Ryan, it's great to meet you.
Glad you came around, Ryan.
But now...
...let's go *home*.

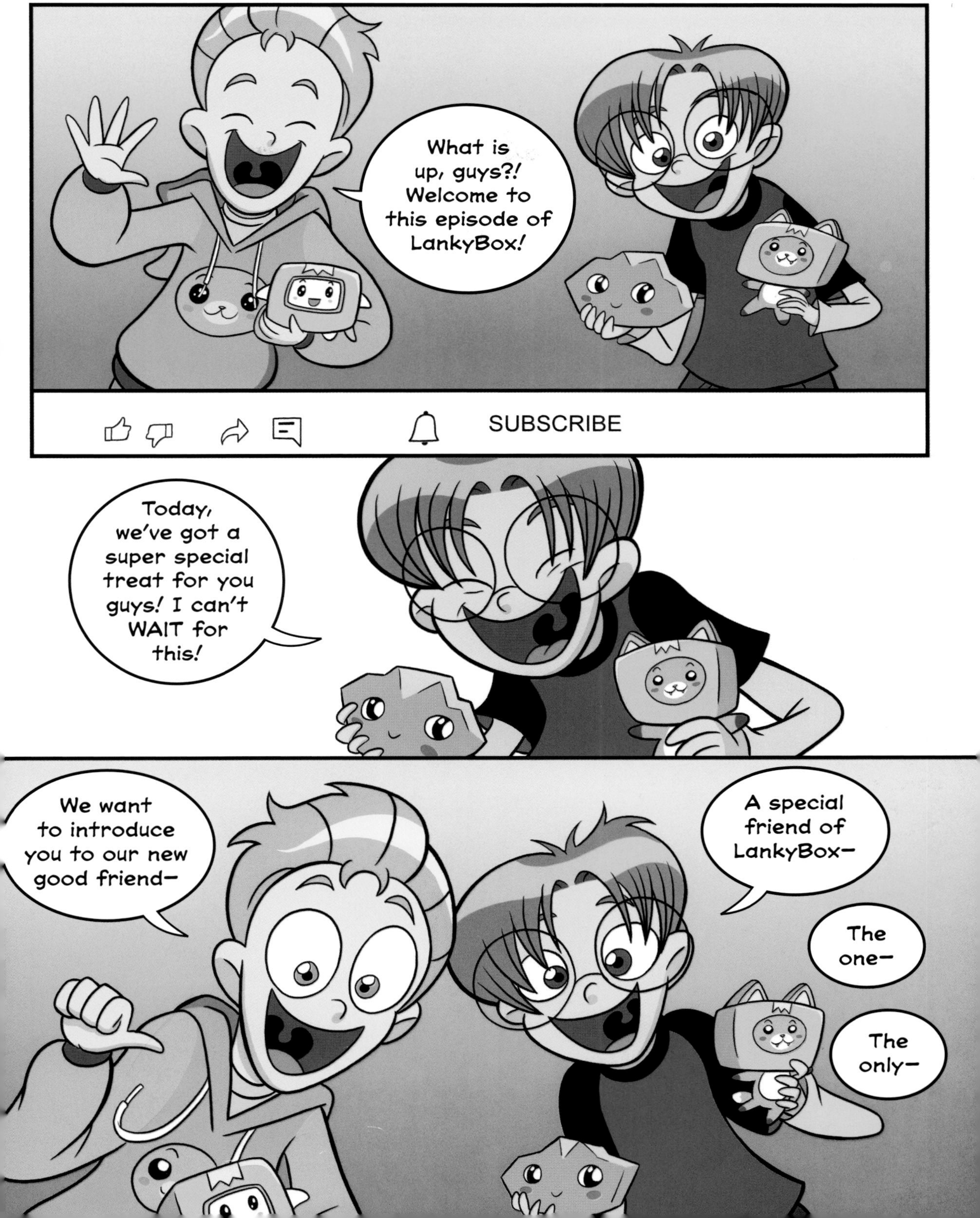

What is up, guys?! Welcome to this episode of LankyBox!
SUBSCRIBE
Today, we've got a super special treat for you guys! I can't WAIT for this!
We want to introduce you to our new good friend—
A special friend of LankyBox—
The one—
The only—

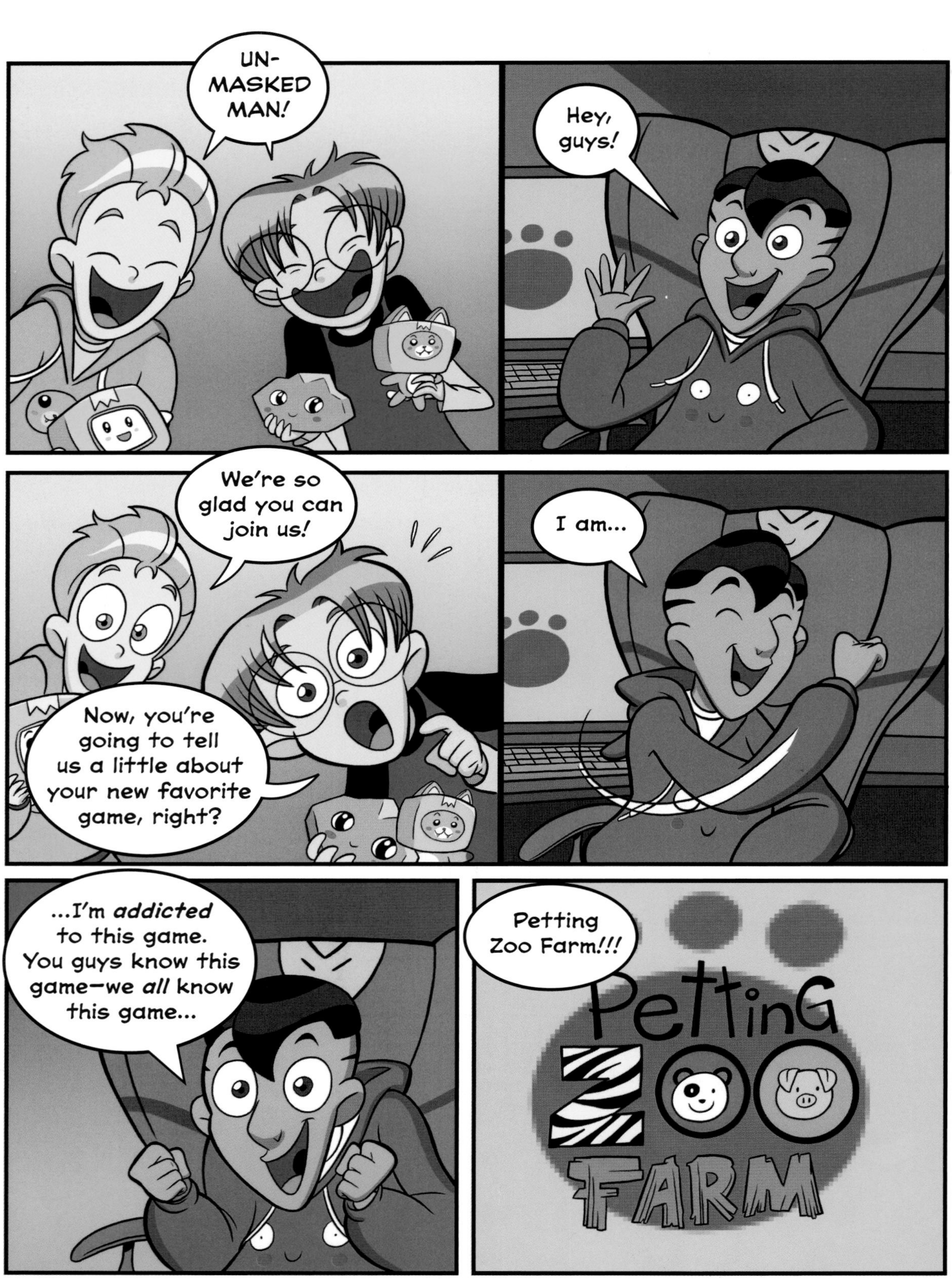
UN-MASKED MAN!
Hey, guys!
We're so glad you can join us!
Now, you're going to tell us a little about your new favorite game, right?
I am...
...I'm *addicted* to this game. You guys know this game—we *all* know this game...
Petting Zoo Farm!!!
Petting ZOO FARM

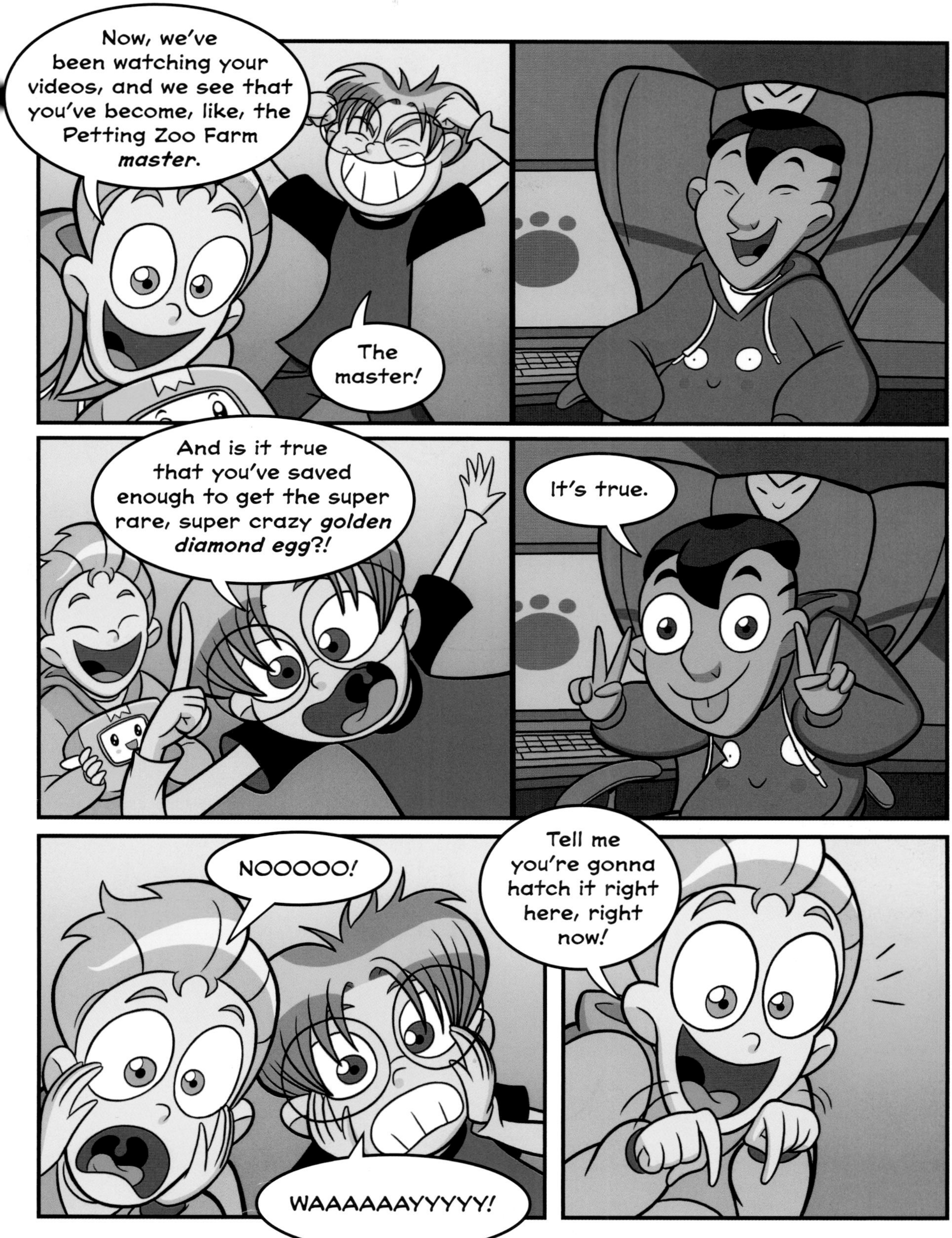
Now, we've been watching your videos, and we see that you've become, like, the Petting Zoo Farm *master*.
The master!
And is it true that you've saved enough to get the super rare, super crazy *golden diamond egg*?!
It's true.
NOOOOO!
WAAAAAAYYYYY!
Tell me you're gonna hatch it right here, right now!

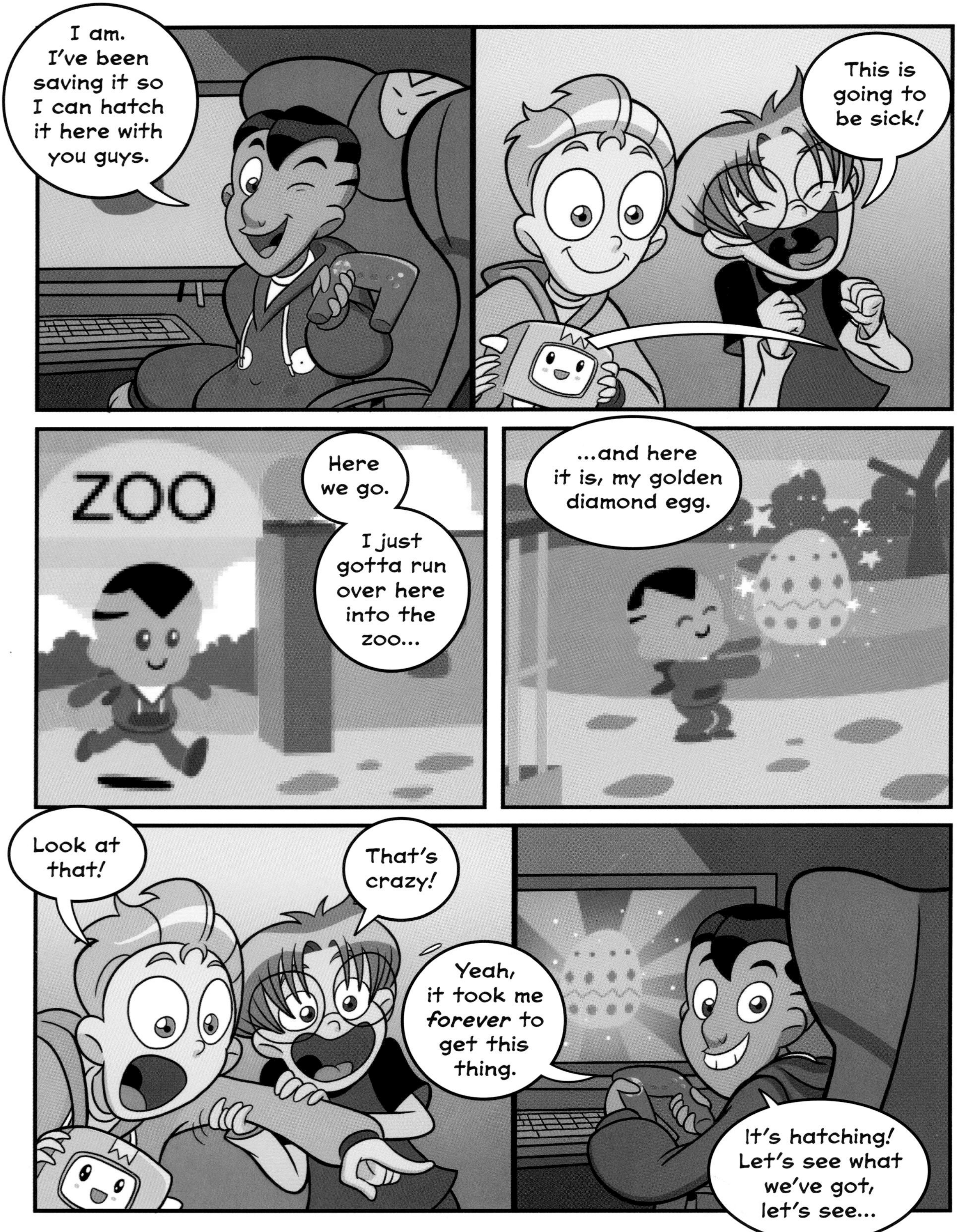
I am. I've been saving it so I can hatch it here with you guys.
This is going to be sick!
ZOO
Here we go.
I just gotta run over here into the zoo...
...and here it is, my golden diamond egg.
Look at that!
That's crazy!
Yeah, it took me *forever* to get this thing.
It's hatching! Let's see what we've got, let's see...

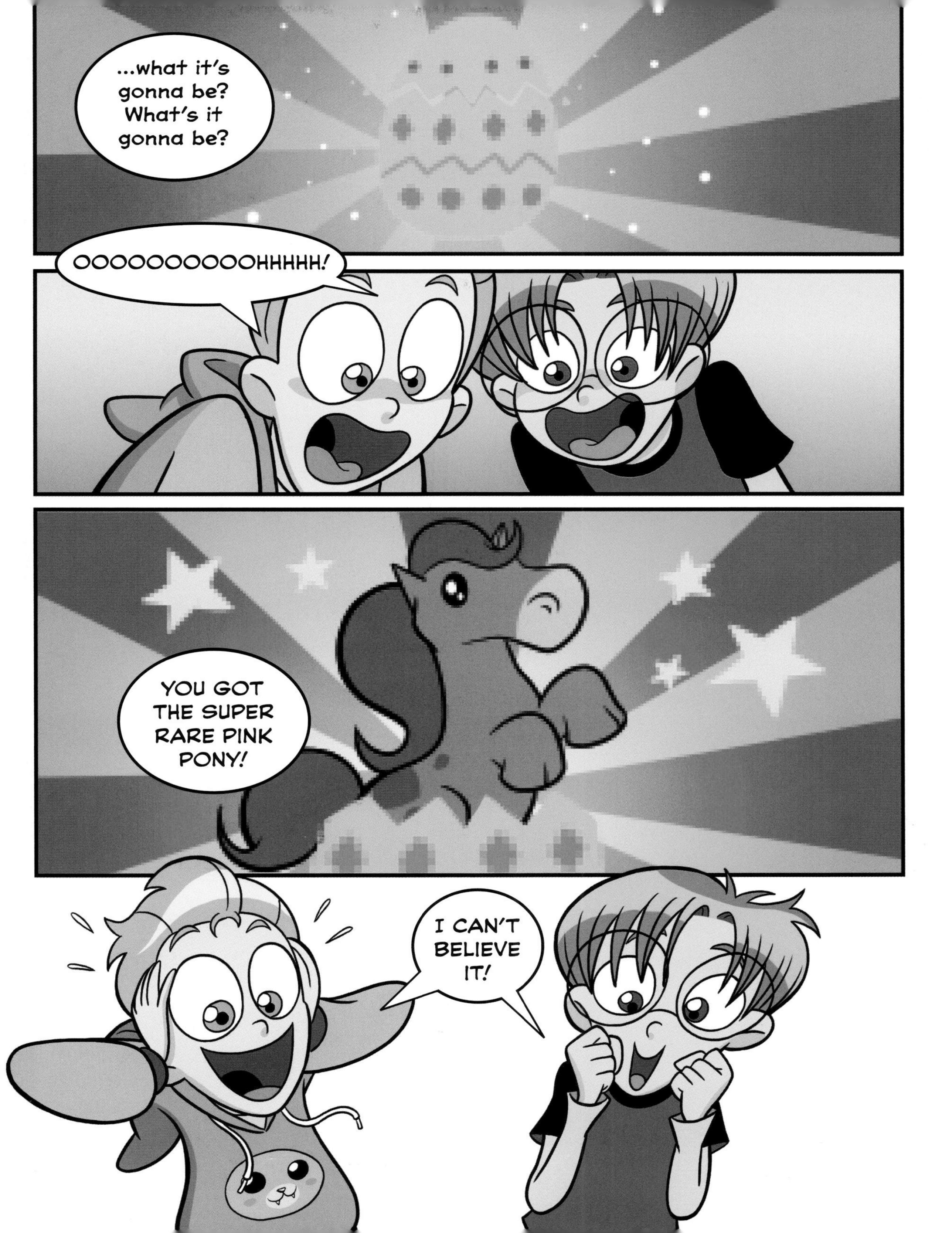
...what it's gonna be? What's it gonna be?
OOOOOOOOOOHHHHH!
YOU GOT THE SUPER RARE PINK PONY!
I CAN'T BELIEVE IT!

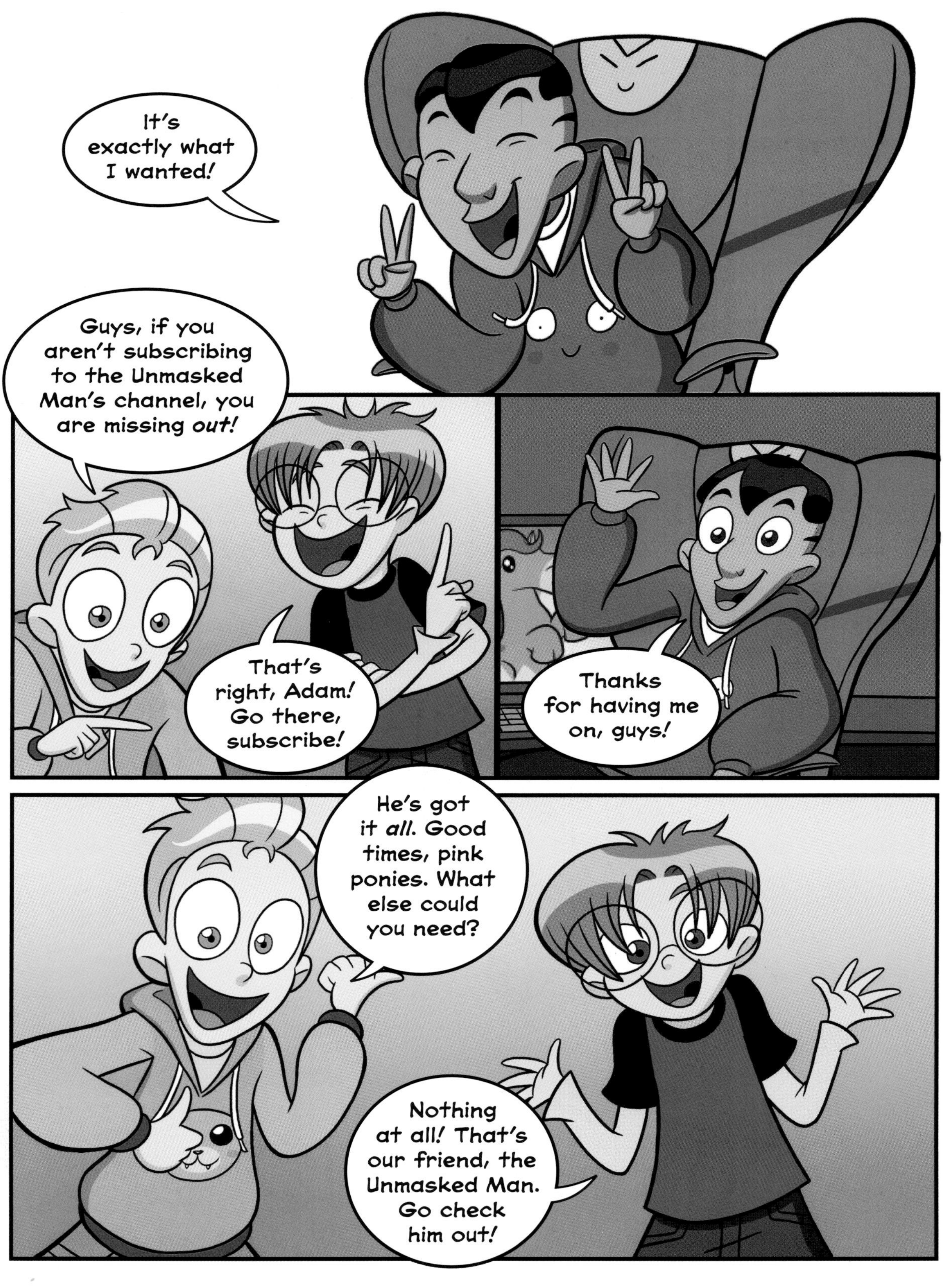
It's exactly what I wanted!
Guys, if you aren't subscribing to the Unmasked Man's channel, you are missing *out*!
That's right, Adam! Go there, subscribe!
Thanks for having me on, guys!
He's got it *all*. Good times, pink ponies. What else could you need?
Nothing at all! That's our friend, the Unmasked Man. Go check him out!

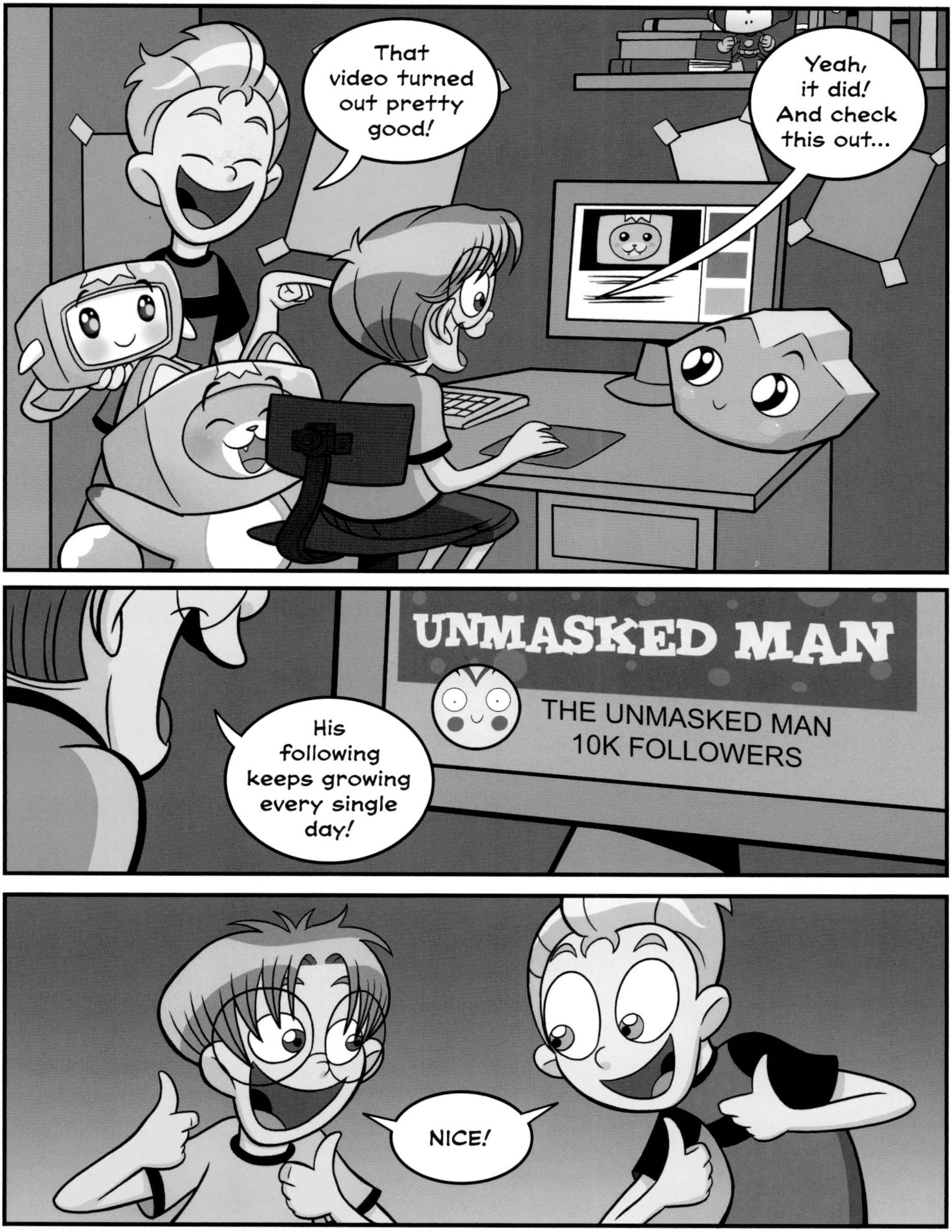
That video turned out pretty good!
Yeah, it did! And check this out...
UNMASKED MAN
THE UNMASKED MAN
10K FOLLOWERS
His following keeps growing every single day!
NICE!

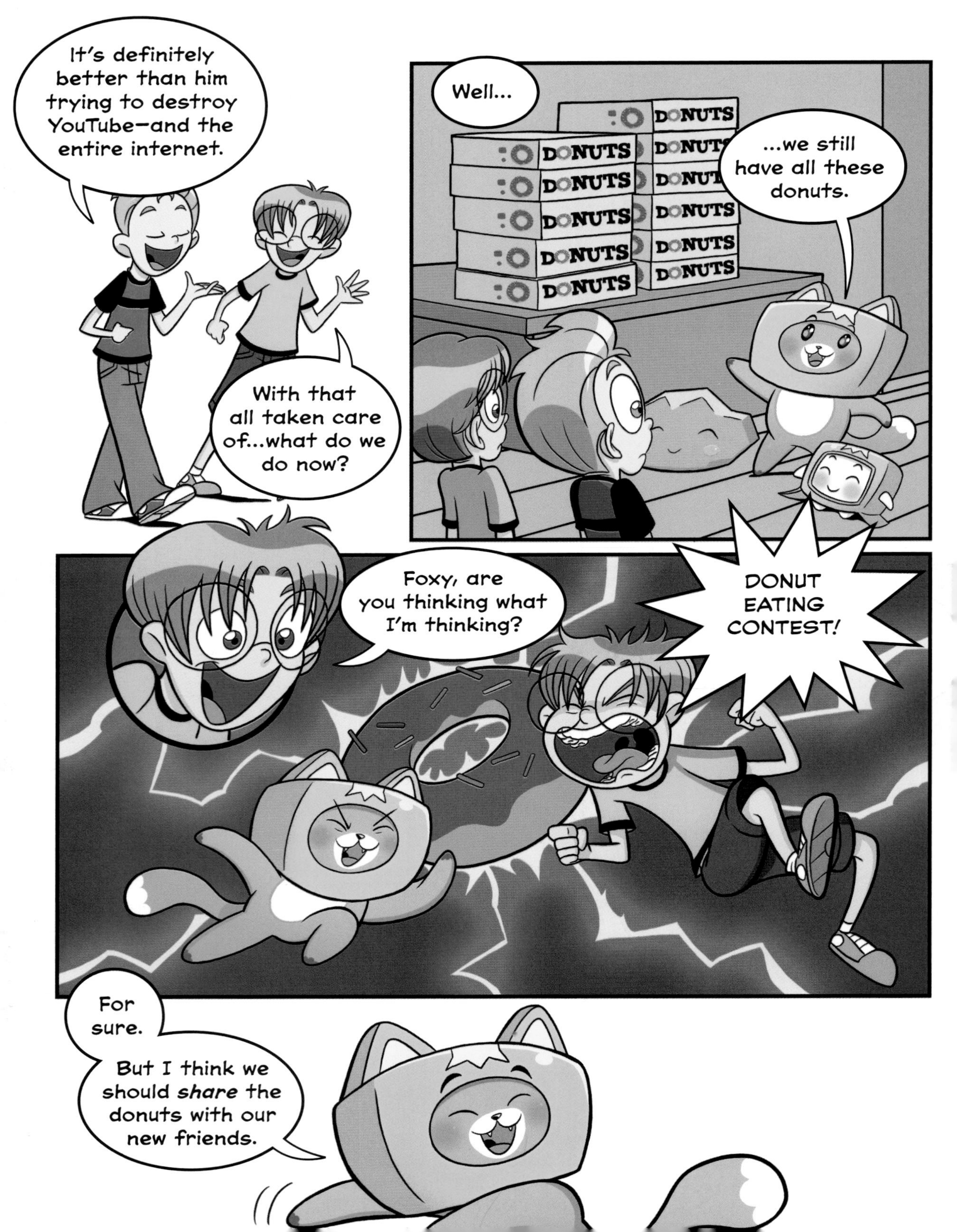
It's definitely better than him trying to destroy YouTube—and the entire internet.
With that all taken care of...what do we do now?
Well...
DONUTS
...we still have all these donuts.
Foxy, are you thinking what I'm thinking?
DONUT EATING CONTEST!
For sure.
But I think we should *share* the donuts with our new friends.

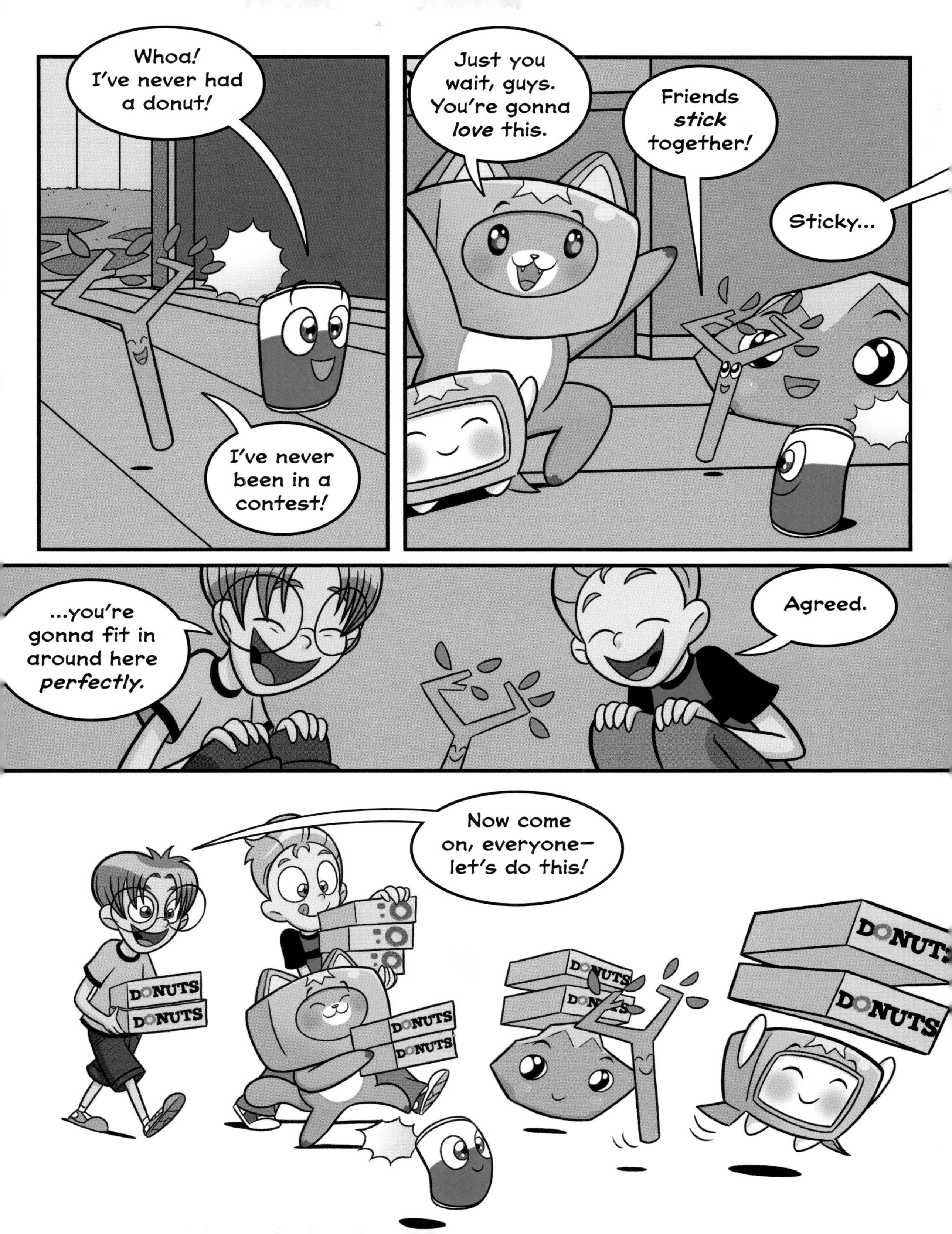
Whoa! I've never had a donut!
I've never been in a contest!
Just you wait, guys. You're gonna *love* this.
Friends *stick* together!
Sticky...
...you're gonna fit in around here *perfectly*.
Agreed.
Now come on, everyone—let's do this!
DONUTS
DONUTS
DONUTS
DONUTS
DONUTS
DONUTS
DONUTS

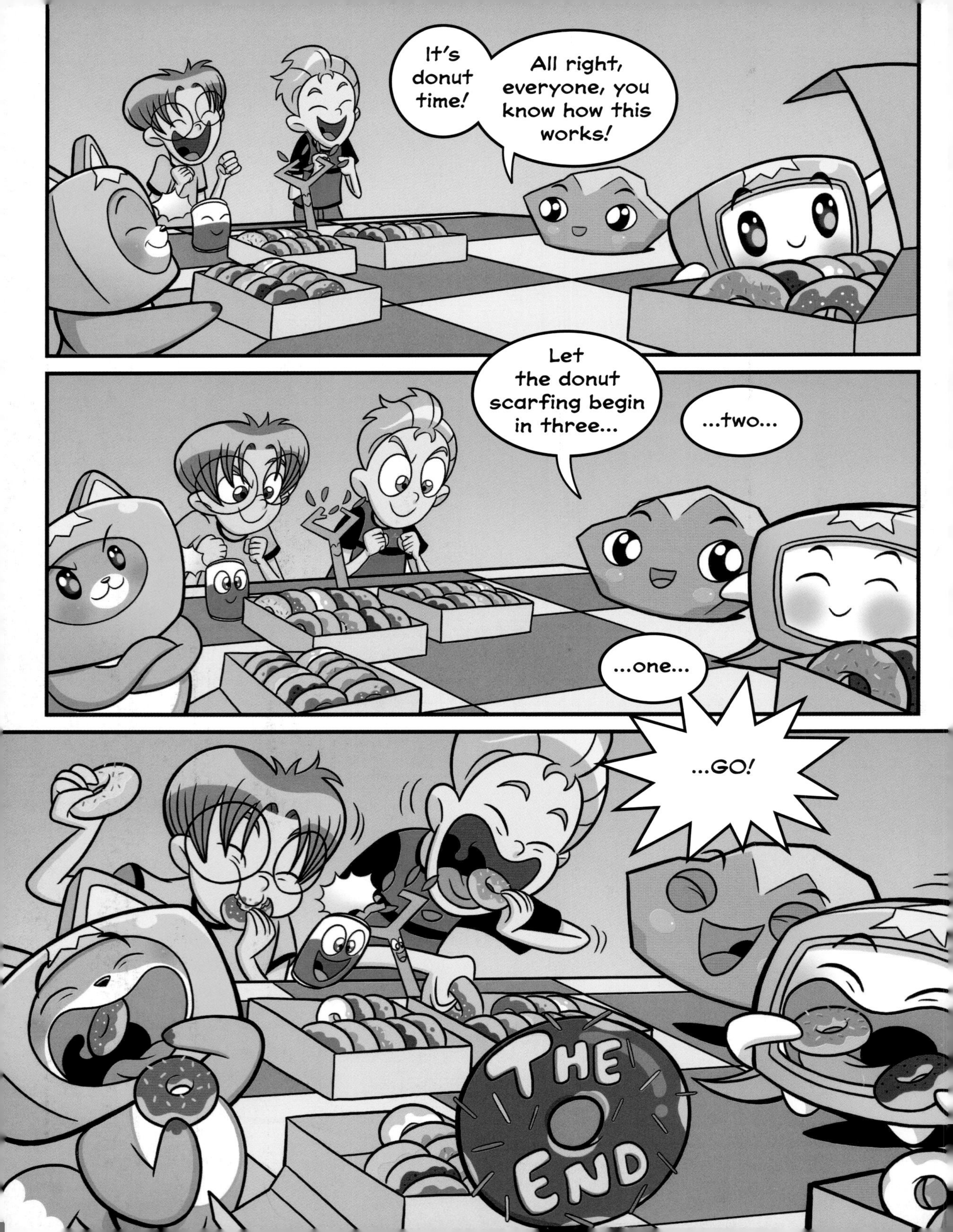

It's donut time!
All right, everyone, you know how this works!
Let the donut scarfing begin in three...
...two...
...one...
...GO!
THE END